THE UNWANTED SERIES

Full Series & Bonus Content

LIMITED EDITION COLLECTION

C. M. NEWELL

THE UNWANTED SERIES

THE UNWANTED SERIES: Full Series & Bonus Content
Limited Edition Collection

Copyright © 2023 by Cassie Newell
Publisher: Sassy Press (First published October 2023)
Cover Designer: Booklytical Designs

ISBN eBook: 978-1-956049-07-7
ISBN Print: 978-1-956049-08-4
ISBN Hardback: 978-1-956049-10-7

AuthorCMNewell.com

CONTENT WARNINGS

Attempted Assault,
Bullying Behavior, Manipulation,
Death, Murder

CONTENTS

MAGICK
THE UNWANTED SERIES, BOOK I

BONUS: HIS BLOOD VOW
THE UNWANTED SERIES, NOVELLA 1.5

REIGN
THE UNWANTED SERIES, BOOK II

SACRED
THE UNWANTED SERIES, BOOK III

MAGICK
THE UNWANTED SERIES, BOOK I

PART I

The girl calls to fate.
Fate is silent and watchful.

CHAPTER 1

My mother died when I was six years old. My father and others labeled it "the accident," but my life and his were never quite the same after. Today I'm looking into the eyes of my newest psychiatrist, retelling the same old story of the accident. Although in truth, that's not even the reason I'm stuck talking to a shrink. Not this time.

It's different talking to him instead of Dr. Bauche. She transferred me to him—something about a specialty and trying something new before the court-appointed therapy ended. His dark blue eyes are kind and thoughtful; he prefers I use his first name. Trying to be relatable to a teenager, I suppose.

"You've become disconnected in retelling your accident. Is this all your memory or what others have told you, Willow?" he asks.

"Well, it happened a long time ago. Part is from what my father and others told me, and part is what I pieced together." I gauge his reaction, which reveals nothing. Then he writes something on his notepad. I hate the writing in the notebook part; it feels judgmental.

"Have you ever undergone regressive therapy, to learn more about the accident?"

"No! Why would I want to do that?" I move further back into the chaise lounge and hug my arms tight. I guess we're going to be on the "accident" topic for the next sessions. Why do I always end up back there?

"That isn't why I have to come here," I stammer.

"I'm aware of the incident with the boy."

"You mean the potential rapist." I shiver at the thought of being pulled into that dark alley with his breath on the nape of my neck, he hands are grabbing and touching me, asking if I was scared, taunting me.

"Let's not call it rape, it was an assault. Willow, I don't fault you, but it is a mystery about how he got hurt. Did that boy simply get what was coming to him? That's not for me to decide. I'm here to address the anger issue the judge perceived you couldn't control during the trial."

The boy attacked me and pushed me to push back, and I did. Granted, I don't remember the outcome of his arm breaking and the fact he caught fire,—too damn bad his victim turned it on him, and he was injured. Serves him right! That boy's lawyer berated me, the victim, for their gain. We won the case, but it didn't feel like winning. My outburst when that boy said I wanted it and asked for it—set me off, it felt appropriate when I hit that lawyer. He got up in my face and wouldn't back down. The judge disagreed and although Daddy Dearest gave a payout in closed court proceedings, counseling for the trauma was part of the court appointed deal.

"It's been almost two years from the assault and I haven't had any issues. Anger is appropriate for a teenager," I snap.

Closing his notebook, Dr. Evan put it on the side table next to his chair. Leaning forward, he clasped his hands on his crossed leg.

"Addressing the accident where your mother died would help with your last year in high school, Willow. There are a lot of pressures. The accident is important for you to understand, in order to face your future."

A burst of air leaves my lungs in a short, sarcastic huff.

My response takes him by surprise. Apparently he hasn't met or talked to my father to know my future is mapped out. Did he read the previous notes from Dr. Bauche? A prestigious business school is awaiting me—most likely Harvard, my father being an alumnus and financial contributor. I can smell the old dusty hypocrisy waft in the air.

"Something funny?" Dr. Evan raises his eyebrow and smirks.

"I just . . . my future is an expectation." I grin without joy. "The legacy of a Warrington, you know?" It would be a tough one to live up too, with a grandfather and father who took the world financial market of acquisitions and mergers by storm.

I look around the office distractedly. Dr. Evan's bare, modern, steel-and-glass desk sits in the opposite corner, a red light blinking on the desk phone. The bookcase behind the desk is too far to focus on the books displayed. No pictures or diplomas hang on the light gray walls. The only fixture to pay attention to is Dr. Evan.

"Your father has agreed to my treatment plan and is aware of this approach," he says. "Talk with him, and let's plan on scheduling the session early next week."

Did I want to relive the accident? Ah, no thank you. Been there, done that. Before getting into that discussion, a timer signals that the session is over—saved by the bell.

Thank god.

"Goddess," he mumbles.

"Huh?"

"We'll talk about this more next session. Let's make our opportunities together count," he says as he walks me to the door of his office.

I wave goodbye to the familiar receptionist on the phone, who hits the buzzer that allows me out of the office. Security for entering, security for leaving. It is a prison, ironically.

I get into the elevator, push the button for the ground floor, and exhale. Leaving the building, I pass Dr. Bauche. She has a puzzled look on her face.

"Hello, Willow."

I respond with a polite smile.

Only a few more sessions with Dr. Evan and I'm done. Free!

I walk to my car in the empty parking garage, slip into the driver's seat, and lock the doors. My own space on my own terms. I open my Coach purse and reach for my phone; I have text messages from Daniel, my boyfriend, and Lucy, my best friend.

Lucy confirms that she is picking me up for school tomorrow, and Daniel is being typical, lovable Daniel with a simple text that says, *I love you can't wait to see you.*

I smile to myself and drive into the early evening, toward the Warrington mausoleum of home sweet home.

CHAPTER 2

K nock knock.

"I'm up. Getting dressed," I announce.

"Good. Your father wanted to make sure. Breakfast is ready when you are. Big day!" Mrs. Scott, the house manager, sounds too awake for normal, un-caffeinated people.

I sit up and stretch, wishing I could lie back down for a minute.

"Be there in a few," I reply.

I step into my walk-in closet and take my school uniform off the hanger. I'm happy this is the last year I'll have to wear that boring blue skirt. The skirt and the white button-down oxford with the prestigious Trinity Cross School logo proudly displayed on the left chest will be retired soon, along with Chepstow, Massachusetts in my rearview mirror. I slip my feet into my purple Chucks, breaking the blue-and-white uniform school rule. My personal rebellion. I open my door and Duke, my black lab, runs past me, his stomach leading the way for both of us. He paws down the back stairs of the house, turning left through the small hallway that opens right into the gourmet kitchen. The aroma of breakfast food and coffee fills the house.

Father's eyebrows are tight as he taps the screen of his smartphone. I walk around the kitchen's island to the large copper cappuccino machine and make myself a chai latté.

"Morning," he says, still looking at his phone.

"Morning." I sit at the table holding my wake-up juice, blowing across the top while warming my hands.

Overly happy, plump Mrs. Scott comes into the kitchen and retrieves a plate from the gas stove. She places it in front of me.

"You need a proper breakfast. Eat," she says in her laughably stern voice.

The plate contains scrambled eggs, bacon, and toast. More than my thin frame could eat, but my stomach betrays me at the sight of it.

"Thanks." I smile up at her, picking up the piece of toast.

"I can't believe you're almost done with school! Senior year, wow. Can you, Mr. Warrington? Growing up too fast." She touches my shoulder and turns away from the table.

"Um . . . yes, growing up," Dad says, too involved with some message on his phone. He snatches a piece of bacon from my plate.

Perfect, he's distracted.

"So, you don't mind about the back-to-school senior camping trip this Saturday? I'll be there with Lucy and Emily. A group is going. We have our tent. I'll be home the next morning."

Still looking at his phone, he nods.

Excellent. Time to get out of dodge. I'm almost out of the kitchen when he speaks up.

"Is Daniel in the group?" He raises an eyebrow, taunting.

Shit. Here we go.

"He's a senior, yes."

His lips purse and his eyes drop to half-mast. The father-daughter stare down begins.

"All incoming seniors go. It's tradition to start off the new school year." I try to sound matter-of-fact, pulling the emotion from my instinct to whine.

"Let's see how this week goes. I may have a trip to New York and I don't want you there if I'm out of town."

"That's silly; you travel all the time. What makes this different?" I hold in my pissed-off voice. "Mrs. Scott is here and—"

"I'm sure Juliette, under normal circumstances, would be fine, but I'm the parent here, Willow. This isn't a school sponsored event, despite the tradition of it. I'm working on the details of my trip and hoping I don't need to go. Give it a couple of days."

I nod and put my cup in the sink. I spy Lucy pull into our driveway at the side of the house.

"Gotta run," I announce. I'm out the door, slinging my backpack over my shoulder and getting into Lucy's silver Audi Q3.

I smile a bit too broadly.

"He said yes!" Lucy squeals.

Laughing and taking my hairband from my wrist to pull my long dirty-blonde hair into a ponytail, I say, "No, but he didn't say no. It was better timing."

She takes off down the drive from my house. "I have a great feeling about this year."

I turn the radio up and smile at her. "You said that last year."

"But just think about it: we're outta here soon and going across the country to sunny Cali."

We drive out of the posh estate neighborhood with its perfectly spaced oak trees on either side of the street. It must have rained earlier this morning—the road is wet and the green lawns showcase wealthy manicured perfection.

We turn onto Pike Road, Lucy singing to the Twenty One Pilots tune "Stressed Out" and winking at me.

Yep, she's right; last year was good. All I'm hoping for is a quick year then onward to college, out from under my father's control. I can't wait. I already have early acceptance to Harvard, Columbia, and Stanford. My father is completely unaware of my applications outside of Harvard. Lucy is unaware of my acceptance to Columbia.

Lucy and I wait in the school parking lot until Emily pulls in and gets out of her sensible Camry, a car at odds with her personality. Her hair is messy like she just woke up, and her uniform is wrinkled, further complimenting her disheveled appearance.

Smiling wide and walking toward us, she calls out, "What up, my bitches?"

I laugh while Lucy cowers with a grin, afraid to notice who might have heard Emily. Probably everyone walking through the white stone archway of Trinity Cross that leads from the parking lot to the school grounds.

"Em, not funny. Let's not get kicked out our first day, okay?" Lucy turns to walk toward the entrance.

"Okay, mom," Emily pouts. She pushes her hand through her short-cropped auburn hair. It makes the left side stand up more than before. I point, and Emily does the maneuver again. This time, her hair seems to obey. "So, where is that heavenly mocha Marco at? With your handsome boy toy, Daniel?"

I shrug. "I guess in school already."

Marco is Daniel's best friend. He's the captain of the football team and very smart. He's at Trinity Cross on scholarship and everyone likes him—he has a smile that can win over almost anyone.

Daniel is laughing down the hallway with a group of friends. His eyes seek me out like he knows I'm near, spotting me in seconds. Daniel's tall, lean frame pushes off the wall of lockers with athletic grace and he comes toward me, Lucy, and Emily.

I can't help but grin at him. He returns his dimpled smile.

"So, we all have Mr. Brandt for homeroom." His arm casually hangs over my shoulder. He smells like a meadow on a spring day.

"Aren't you the lucky one," Lucy says. Emily laughs, surprised at Lucy's uncommonly sassy comeback.

"You're rubbing off on her," Daniel says to Emily, wide-eyed.

Lucy blushes.

Mr. Brandt has us sit in order by last name, so naturally I'm in the back of the room. I like being in the back, out of the spotlight, with no eyes staring at the back of my head.

Mr. Brandt announces that as seniors, we are required to attend the morning assembly and to demonstrate the best that the school has to offer, which is code for being less goofy—especially the boys—and being quiet. We head to the auditorium and I sit next to Daniel.

Headmaster Chin starts by welcoming the freshmen and talks about the new open wing of the technology center. She reviews the academic code of the school and the rules of conduct. With few exceptions, the speech is full of all the same stuff as last year.

Walking out of the auditorium, we run into snobby, beyond-vain Coral Yang, Daniel's ex-girlfriend, as she waits with some of her cronies. She cues the fake smile and says hello to Daniel, all the while throwing visual daggers at me.

Ugh.

I don't like that Daniel is still friendly to her, but I try hard not to give Coral the satisfaction of showing it. I turn away while he continues to talk to her, still holding my hand. She laughs, which sounds more like a cackle. I could puke. Emily hooks my elbow, quickly turning me around and detaching me from Daniel.

Emily sings, "We're off to see the Wizard, the wonderful Wizard of Oz!" We skip forward. It seems perfect, since the Wicked Witch hovers behind us with Daniel. Gah, is it too much to ask that flawless Coral get a spontaneous nosebleed or trip over her own feet?

In the hallway, the bell rings to usher us all to our first period classes. I have Advanced English without my friends and walk away, spying Coral hugging Daniel. She stares right at me with a smug expression. A little nosebleed would indeed perfect her airbrush makeup. I huff and turn down the hall toward class.

Later, I have third period lunch and spy Marco at an empty round table. I plop down next to him with my tray.

"So, we've got the same lunch period," I say.

"Yeah, well, us brainiacs, ya know? Speaking of, where is Lucy? Isn't she in this lunch period?"

I look around. The cafeteria is buzzing, but no one new is entering. "She does. Maybe she ate and left already?"

Marco shrugs and takes a swig of his drink.

"How are your classes so far?" I ask, stabbing my fork through my salad.

"Good. It will be fluff all year, except for Mrs. Simpson's organic chem."

"Ugh, tell me." I roll my eyes. "I have that with you next class."

He laughs in his easy way. Marco has the charisma that most guys want, he is dialed into school, and doesn't get roused up easily. Emily started to crush on him over the summer, which has resulted in some exciting flirting.

"So, what about—"

He interrupts me. "Nope, not talking about Emily, okay? We're all casual, and I've got enough on my plate." He laughs to himself and shakes his head.

I smile and finish off my salad and iced green tea. "Want to head over? Mrs. Simpson awaits to torture us with chemical madness."

We walk out of the cafeteria and down the hall. I look around for Lucy but she's nowhere to be found. Instead, Coral's cronies are huddled around some poor underclassmen, laughing and teasing her.

Marco catches their eye and winks at them. They smile and walk toward us. The girl slips away from continued torture as the bell rings.

"Nice job," I whisper to Marco. "I'll save you a seat." I leave just in time for him to be flanked by Team Bleach Blonde.

Marco slides into class as the final bell rings, grabbing the seat I saved him at the lab top bench.

"Cutting it close, Marco," Mrs. Simpson says.

"Oh, what I do to save those in need," Marco mutters under his breath with a grin.

Mrs. Simpson takes command of the class and starts in with a baseline quiz.

"Does this woman have no heart?" Marco asks.

"It doesn't count for anything, just a baseline of what we already know," I tell him. Although, I sympathize with Marco; who gives a quiz on day one?

The bell rings and I'm off to the technology center. I walk as quickly as I can past the plaque that proclaims "Warrington Hall." It's hard to be anonymous when your name is everywhere.

At the end of sixth period, the last class of the day, I meet up with Emily and Lucy at our lockers. They act as our central hub; we've had the same lockers since freshman year. Emily is laughing, but Lucy is wringing her hands and biting her lip.

"What up?" I open my locker to put in all the new textbooks I've been lugging around.

"You're gonna love it," Emily squeals with joy . She bounces up and down.

I laugh. "Oh, goody. Something happen to Coral?"

Emily nods.

"Wait, what?" My eyes grow wide as I look from Emily to Lucy.

Lucy is quiet compared to Emily's obvious excitement; whatever it is, it must be bad.

"Whoa, calm down Em. What happened?" I ask quietly. There are a few people looking over our way.

"It was epic! So, after assembly, I had World History with her, and she had this nosebleed. Nothing big, but like, it wouldn't stop. Tissue after tissue. She was wiping away her makeup with it, blood and foundation all mixed up—so gross. It got everywhere, and Ms. Johnston—old bottle glasses—was, like, blind to it. She told Coral to get a little princess grip and deal until after class, to go to the nurse. It was hilarious; you should have seen the extravagant fit Coral was throwing. Then Lucy came in at the bell, and Coral ran into her and SPLAT! Coral, face-down, nose busted! Her skirt up over her ass." Emily giggles wide-eyed.

"Oh my god!" I breathe in disbelief.

"I think she chipped a tooth," Lucy says. "I was sent from the library during my free period to deliver a few books Ms. Johnston wanted.. I wasn't paying attention when we ran into each other. I feel horrible"

"Whatevs, you shouldn't. It was an accident. Coral is as mean as a rattlesnake. Happy to know she bleeds like the rest of us."

I can't believe it. Karma is on my side. "Did she go home?"

"Coast is clear. No more Coral sightings for the rest of the day. This is gonna be a great year, I sense it!"

"Ah, she was hurt, Em."

"I understand how awful it is that she was hurt, but the humiliation part she was due considering how she treats everyone she thinks is beneath her." Emily puts her hand on Lucy's shoulder and pats it. "I'm sure Coral will divert it all to her advantage soon anyway."

Lucy's eyes are cast down to the ground as we exit the school. My phone sounds with a text from Daniel; he has football practice and will call me later. I beam, getting into Lucy's car.

In the driveway at my house I try to reassure Lucy that Coral will be fine, but her mood stays the same. I climb out of the car, she turns up her stereo and heads back down the driveway. She must be worried about a Coral repercussion. She's famous for them. I should know—I spent most of last year experiencing them when Daniel and I started dating.

CHAPTER 3

I t's three in the afternoon and I have an hour and a half before my appointment with Dr. Evan. So, like most well-adjusted academic kids, I decide to goof off and grab a snack and watch TV. Duke and I take our usual spot in the living room. I'm sipping my Coke and noshing on kettle chips when I hear the back door. Duke perks up and then lays back down on my feet.

"Mrs. Scott?" I ask

"Just us," Mrs. Scott replies.

I get up to help and see Chef with Mrs. Scott, both carrying bags. "What's going on?"

"Special dinner tonight. Didn't I tell you that this morning?" Mrs. Scott starts putting items away in the pantry. Her hair is messy and she is looking and counting items frantically.

"No, I don't remember. Who is coming over?"

"A family dinner meeting of some sort; your father has requested you join." Mrs. Scott waves me off as she organizes items from the bags to the counter and puts some in the pantry.

"I have my doctor's appointment until 6 and was hoping to hang out with Daniel later," I whine.

Gah, let me find a way out of this.

I try to get more information out of Mrs. Scott, which

reveals nothing because she doesn't know anything more. Finally, I leave, hanging on the word "family." It's an odd thing for her to say for just me and my father. I don't have much time to ponder the thought as I get ready for my appointment.

At the office, I hit the button that announces I'm at the door. The receptionist isn't at her desk to notice me and let me in. Instead, Dr. Evan walks over and hits the button himself.

"Sorry about that. Heather is out sick today," he says. A couple walks out as I walk in, smiling and holding hands. Wow, couples counseling and they are smiling? Okay, maybe Dr. Evan isn't a quack after all.

The office is quiet and I follow him to his office at the end of the hallway. He opens the door and gestures me to the chaise lounge, then goes to his desk to retrieve a notebook and pen. I realize he has several files on his desk, and he closes one.

"So, how was the first day of senior year?" he asks.

"Good. Typical, and some returned karma."

"How so?"

I shouldn't have opened with that. Counselors and their probing questions can't just let a dog lie. "This girl, Coral. Well, she's Daniel's ex-girlfriend. She's nasty to everyone, sits on a high throne. She got knocked down a peg today with an accident. What's interesting is I was thinking about this accident, and karma delivered, so yay universe!" I pump my arm in a small gesture, then immediately feel wrong. I'm a horrible person.

He leans forward, looking more serious than before. "So, you thought of what should happen, and it happened as you pictured it?"

Ice-breaking playtime over.

"Kinda." I avoid his eyes and tuck my legs under so I'm sitting cross-legged on the chaise. "I just saw her hugging Daniel, and she was giving me this smug look, so I briefly thought, 'It would be great if she got a nosebleed.' An innocent thought, right?"

"A nosebleed?"

"Well, the way my friend described the scene, it wasn't a simple nosebleed. She ran out of class, then ran into another person and fell, possibly chipped a tooth in the process."

Why was I feeling bad about this? I didn't physically do anything here. All I did was think about a nosebleed and about her tripping over her own feet. I shake my head.

"Coral had a rough day, by the sound of it." Evan's lips curve upward.

I nod.

"Tell me, were you happy about Coral's accident? Don't you find it interesting that you thought something and it happened?"

Where is this going? "It's just a coincidence. Coral isn't just mean to me and my friends. She and her crew are nasty to everyone. Everyone who she deems beneath her. I hate that."

"So, a core value for you is battling inequality?"

"Yes, of course. In this day in age, why wouldn't it be?" I ask.

He changes the topic. "It's interesting that your coincidences are a trending theme. In Dr. Bauche's notes, you wanted to hurt the boy who attacked you. You wanted to break his arm and throw him backward. It all happened. The fire was something you envisioned as well."

"No, no, this is completely different," I stammer. "I was overwhelmed with adrenaline and I was able to break free. I can't help his arm broke. It was at a funny angle; I'm guessing the way I turned put pressure on to break it when he fell and tried to catch himself. He was taunting me saying I wanted him while he was grabbing me, asking if I was scared. And the fire wasn't me at all! There were trash cans around that were burning. He knocked them over. I was in a bad part of town and it—there were homeless around. I think someone helped me."

"Why were you in Boston, Willow?"

"I got turned around. We just moved to Chepstow, and I was there with Mrs. Scott, shopping. We were going to meet at this one store. I dunno, it was all just messed up." I hesitate.

"Do you blame Mrs. Scott?"

I untuck my legs and stand. "No! Why would you say that?" I feel the heat of my face. Mrs. Scott called the police, she took me to the hospital and she cared for me. Father came when he could—a day later—but she was there for me and held me when I cried and babbled.

"She wasn't there to help you when you needed her in that alley." Dr. Evan stands up and places his notebook on the desk, then ushers me back to the chaise. I hesitate before sitting. "I'm simply curious as to your thoughts on this. How you ended up alone. How you ended up in that alley. How you got away relatively unharmed, but your attacker was hospitalized with multiple injuries."

My thoughts? *My* thoughts?!

"I'll tell you what, that jackoff was telling the court he was trying to help me when I attacked him! He tried to turn it all around. He's the one with a record of assault, and he was blackmailing my father with his lies." I'm breathing faster. I know that if I don't retain control of my breath, the threatening tears will fall.

Breathe, Willow. Breathe.

"I don't want to argue over this. It's over. Why can't the past be the past and we just move forward?" I wrap my arms around myself and lean back into the chaise, closing my eyes.

"The 'why' is that you refuse to acknowledge the past and how it affects who you are. You block it as a self-protection mechanism, even though it is not protecting you at all."

"I don't know what you mean."

"Willow . . ." Dr. Evan pushes his hand through his hair. "Your accident with your mother. You blame yourself when, by all accounts, it was purely a car accident which you survived and your mother did not. In fact, she most likely saved you by getting you out of that car. You blame yourself for the attack in the alley and talk about how your father came to your aid with the plea deal to make it all go away. Again, not your fault. You protected yourself and got carried away at the closed proceedings that prompted this therapy." He pulls something from his pocket that catches the light and shines a moment before his hand cups it from view. "Your blame is misplaced, and you will continue to have hard situations come your way that you will need to navigate through without self-sabotage. This is why regressive therapy is a good option, but you have to be open to it."

My collar is wet. I touch my cheek; my face is wet too. Shit, I'm crying.

"You're angry, and rightly so. You need to be able to release this anger and not implode."

This is a first. Dr. Bauche wanted me to adjust the focus on the positive, the future, blah blah blah.

"What, like take martial arts or something?" I shrug.

"Sure, or something." Dr. Evan's eyes shimmer.

I avert my eyes because I don't want to acknowledge my struggle versus how casually he sits in the chair across from the chaise.

"Willow?" He smiles. "You're more capable than you know. Deep down, you have a magick inside that you've tucked away. That needs release. It's a connection to who you are and what you are capable of."

Dr. Evan is now sitting next to me.

"What, like yin and yang?"

He nods. "How about we start this session? Are you open to this?"

I scoot back so my back is flush with the chaise. "I dunno. I have to be back for a family dinner thing. Will this be longer than our scheduled time?" I spy the small clock on the side table next to his chair and see I have less than half an hour left.

Dr. Evan's face changes. He is no longer sympathetic; instead, he almost looks angry.

"What do I have to do?" I stare down at my feet.

"You need to be open-minded and I will put you under

hypnosis. Your subconscious will walk you through the past for you to understand those events better."

"Will it hurt?" I ask.

"No, not at all quite the opposite. Typically, you'll feel refreshed afterward."

"My father is aware, you said?"

He nods in confirmation. The idea of going back to my mother's accident weighs heavy in my heart. I want the ability to see and be with her again, but the cost is temporary and will surely haunt me. I miss her so much that it overrides my fear.

"Okay, then let's start."

Dr. Evan stands up and open's his hand , then pushes his chair closer to the chaise. I put my hands under my legs to steady myself. He's rocking a flower pendant in his hand and holds its chain loosely. Looking closely, I realize it isn't a flower; it's an intricate design of wrapping loops and circles. It seems oddly familiar.

"What is this design?" I ask.

"A triquetra, the balance of the mind, body, and spirit. A Celtic symbol."

I repeat "triquetra" and feel a tingle in my leg as if falling asleep. I squirm to adjust how I'm sitting. The chaise is firm but I'm able to gain some purchase of my position to snuggle in it better.

He begins swinging the pendant. It shimmers under the lights and follows the path of its curving design, where the three petal-like patterns intersect and are connected by a circle.

"I want you to listen carefully to my voice and relax, Willow. This is a place of safety."

My shoulders dip and my body sways. I follow the silver pendant swing back and forth, back and forth.

"Count with me—"

"One, two, three, four . . ."

CHAPTER 4

Back at home, I sit in the kitchen nook holding my warm cup of tea. Staring out the windows, I'm at ease, but sad for some reason. How can you be sad about something you can't remember?

I can't recount what I said during hypnosis with Dr. Evan; he said it was common. But I should feel a sense of clarity over the next day. He gave me his personal cell number should I have any questions. When I asked him what I said, he wasn't straight with me, and I knew it. He asked for patience and said we'd talk more when I could recall for myself more.

Has he worked with many teenagers? Seriously? Asking for patience when I wasn't all hip to this idea in the first place?!

The back door slams and I jump in my seat. Mrs. Scott is standing there.

"Sorry, didn't mean to scare you." Mrs. Scott hurries by me and heads for the pantry on the other side of the kitchen. "Why don't you go ahead and clean up? The company will be here shortly."

"Who is coming over?" I ask. "Come on, spill."

"Your father didn't say. I think some distant family member. I get the impression he was surprised, since we didn't have the event in our calendar." She pops a cashew in her mouth from the bowl I set on the counter.

"Is he home from the office?" I ask.

"He's on his way; he had a late afternoon meeting." She takes off her apron and hangs it on a hook inside the pantry door. "You know your father, always working."

I eat some of the trail mix from the bowl, then head up the back stairs to my room. My door is ajar, and I push it open to find Duke sleeping on my bed.

"Duke, you do realize you have your own bed, right?"

He lifts his head and starts to stretch.

My cell phone buzzes in my backpack and Duke is up and out of my room by the time I retrieve my phone.

Deserter.

I have several texts. I click on Daniel's first.

Sr camp trip? Didn't get to talk about it tday. Headin to work will call tnight.

I text him back to fill him in, then end with a kiss emoji that has me smiling as I hit send. Why do silly yellow pictures of facial expressions give so much extra meaning?

The other text is from Lucy:

Sorry about this afternoon. It was just Em, getting on my nerves. I don't like seeing anyone hurt, even if it is Coral. Gah, shoot me.

I get it. You have to admit Coral's a bitch... oops, I meant Karma.

LOL, let's hope it gives me some slack.

Stop worrying.

A moment later, the FaceTime app on my phone pops up with Lucy's grin. Lucy is sitting at her desk in the corner of her room by all her books. They're piled up from the floor like the Eiffel Tower. "Okay, I'm done sulking. What's going on?"

I tell her about the mysterious dinner that I need to get ready for.

Lucy's eyes open wide. "What are you going to wear?"

I smirk. "Are you Emily?"

Lucy belts loud laughter. Soon I'm laughing with her. Stress bounces off us both. When we finally stop and hang up, I immediately fret about what to wear wishing we had settled that question.

A closet full of clothes is daunting when you're not sure what to wear; everything seems wrong. Do I dress up for family? The safe bet, I decide, is to put on a pair of nondescript black pants and a sweater set. At my dresser, I finish up my routine. I brush my long dark blonde hair and tuck it behind my ear. The last accessory I add are my earrings, simple pearls with diamond points that were my mother's.

When I'm done, I'm out the door, heading to the beige and maroon abyss of the designer house. The decorator decided the accent color would be maroon, to represent my father's commanding place in the world. Of course, over time, I noticed her eyes lingered on my father whenever she was over. Thank god, I was able to divert her decorating eyes from my room, where I worked with Mrs. Scott to have bright colors everywhere.

I walk down the hallway, trying to hurry. When you're situated at the back of a 10,000-square foot house, it's difficult to go anywhere quickly. I round the large staircase that gets me to the front of the house. My father is there talking to a woman.

I stop in my tracks, and a vision of her crying flashes before my eyes. It's gone in an instant.

Do I recognize her?

Her long red hair waves as she turns, and she puts her hands to her mouth. I start down the stairs toward them tentatively.

My father comes to the stairs. "I would like to introduce you to your . . ."

She walks toward me, meeting me at the end of the stairs. Her eyes are glistening with tears. "I'm your grandmother. Sabine MacKinnon."

She is familiar, but she doesn't look like my mother, whose maiden name was MacKinnon. Mother was blonde and I'm more like her than Sabine with her bright red hair. She doesn't seem much older than my father, not nearly old enough to be my grandmother. I realize I'm assessing her and haven't come off the stairs yet. I step forward to shake her hand but instead get pulled into a hug. It is awkward and familiar.

"I've waited so long, and I'm so sorry," she says in a whisper.

Why is my heart beating so fast? I can't comprehend that my grandmother is hugging me. I thought she had disowned me, but the details are fuzzy. Father always clams up when I ask innocent questions about my mother's family over the years, so I dropped it. It wasn't like anyone from mother's side of the family ever reached out to me.

Sabine lets go and I move back from her awkward embrace, but she keeps her hands on my forearms. "You look just like our Nuala. Oh, Willow, I'm so happy to finally be back in your life."

I glance at my father, who is tense and standing like an oak tree in the foyer.

"Back in my life?"

Mrs. Scott appears and purses her lips as if she ate a sour grape. "Ahem, dinner is ready." My father escorts Sabine to the formal dining room. There is an extra place setting.

"Is someone else joining us?" I ask my father in a tone that is a little more accusatory than I intended.

He sits down while watching Sabine take her seat.

She lowers her eyes. "I'm sorry to say that, no, it's just me this evening." She places her hands on her lap and studies me with dark eyes full of sorrow. "Your grandfather, my husband, Harkin, recently passed away. He wanted to be here. I like to think he is, in some way, here in spirit."

Sitting next to her, I want to reach out and touch her shoulder or hand, but I don't know her. The sadness, that she wears on her face is genuine. "I'm sorry for your loss."

It was my loss too, for a grandfather I'd never known, already gone. I guess that's true for many in my family; my father's mother died when he was young too. His father passed when my father became an adult before I was born. I've never had relationships with grandparents.

"I have something for you." Sabine reaches into her flowing skirt pocket and pulls out a rectangular velvet-covered box. "It was your mother's. I wanted to make sure you had it."

My father's smile is constrained as he nods to me.

"Thank you, Sabine."

I take the small box and open it slowly. The necklace that lays within is similar to what Dr. Evan used in our session, only a little different with more loops. I've seen this necklace before.

"A triquetra," I whisper.

Sabine corrects me: "The pentacle of the Goddess."

I touch the pendant and it shimmers under my touch to various colors.

"That's a rare type of opal—"

Sabine stands up, interrupting my father, and reaches out. "Let's try it on. Your mother wore this as a teenager. It seems fitting."

I smile at her, thinking about my mother and how I miss her. My fingers lightly brush over the necklace, its smooth stone embedded in silver. When I glance at my father he seems off. He has a scowl on his face from being interrupted by Sabine.

Mrs. Scott brings the first course to the table and I take a sip of the soup. Happily, I taste a simple mushroom broth.

The silence is like a fog settling in for the long haul. I break the tension by asking, "So, has this dinner been planned for a while?" I ask my father.

He scoffs sarcastically with a sideways glance toward Sabine, "No, not really. I'm afraid that my input to this evening is as a bystander, regardless that I'm the head of this household."

"Aiden, you can't keep Willow hidden from us any longer." Her voice rises as if she holds authority over my father. It's impressive since so few do.

"I don't understand," I say to him, then look back at Sabine.

"I thought it was your decision that you didn't want me around, because of the accident that killed her." My voice shakes.

"What? No. No, that's not true at all—"

"Sabine!" my father exhales. "Willow, I have had rules about the association with your mother's family since the accident to keep you safe. It was agreed to, not only by me."

"Why? Why would you do that? Why would you only tell me now?"

The next course is brought in, and my anger at my father mounts. I had always thought that they chose not to be in my life because I was in part to blame for an accident I don't remember. One of the deep scars I carry.

A vision flashes before me—my mother and me in an upside-down car. She is hanging by the seat belt, her hair like a mop in front of her face. I move from the back seat and start to shake her. "Mommy." My voice as a little girl pleads to get her attention. Someone grabs me and pulls me out of the car and I scream and yell when my mother reaches for me.

I blink several times and the image is gone. I'm no longer in the car, I'm back at home in the formal dining room. My vision refocuses on my father. He stares back with pinched lips and waits for Mrs. Scott to exit the dining room.

"You're angry."

"Damn right," I snap. "You've been hiding things from me, lying to me!" I scoot from my chair and he rises from his.

"I need a minute." I walk to the washroom out in the hallway and shut myself inside.

Looking at myself in the mirror, I shake my head. "Okay. You've been lied to. Long lost relatives. No big deal. Control the controllable. I can learn." I shrug and wash my hands. The tingle of the water is icy and cools my hands and thoughts. When I turn off the water and leave the washroom, I can hear them talking.

"Can't you sense the change in the air? Her binding will not last long. The tide of change is here, Aiden, regardless if either of you is ready."

"We have time. This was not a good idea, you coming tonight. I'm not sure how she's going to react. There are others here to protect her. You're entitled motives do not override the fact—"

Sabine laughs sarcastically. "She can protect herself if you allow her too. You can't keep this tucked away and run off again. I can feel it. Surely you can too? Me being here is not the trigger, it's already happened."

Then they both spot me standing in the open archway to the formal dining room. "What are you talking about? And before you say 'Nothing,' " I say, pointing my finger toward my father, "neither of you are quiet speakers."

Sabine smirks while my father stares at me with a clinched jaw. He is ready to ground me for life. I never speak to him or guests disrespectfully, but tonight my tongue and brain don't seem to have any restraints.

"Willow, you are royalty," he announces.

I double over and laugh, my hands shaking and static electricity runs across my fingertips. The tingle in my arms ignites the familiar feeling from Dr. Evan's office.

I spy Sabine's wide-eyed grin, as I shake my hands free of the sensation.

"This is a joke, right? I mean, come on, there isn't real royalty anymore. I've been going to school like any normal kid."

Okay, normal wealthy kid. Let's be fair, here.

"You're descended from an ancient line of druids and Wiccans. And with Harkin's passing—your grandfather—the crown belongs to you." Sabine clasps her hands together. She's . . . hopeful?

I sit down, processing what she just said. Pause, rewind, and play again. Is this a joke?

She's serious and it looks as if she is holding her breath. I'm angry, but good grief, she doesn't know me and she just came in and dropped a bomb.

My father sits back in his chair and observes me. I hate that —the parenting tactic of sit and listen. What's the right reaction here? The long-lost grandmother is speaking of craziness, royalty, and witches. Why is everyone calm?

"Let me get this right: you're here because I'm the next in line for some crown that I never even knew of, and I'm from a line of witches?"

My eyebrow shoots up and I withhold my verbal doubt out of respect for a lady who obviously believes this deep down. I glance over at my father for some kind of interruption, but his jaw is firm, his eyes steady.

I huff at them both and wiggle my fingers in the air. "So I have some kind of magick, then?" As the words leave my lips, the electric tingle runs across my fingers again and a faint blue light appears on my skin. I shut my hand and it disappears.

What the hell?

"What do you call that then?" My grandmother gestures toward my hand, eyebrows raised. "Static electricity?"

I wave my hand accusatorially. "Static electricity does not equal whatever craziness this is!" I say, frustrated.

She grins at my father. "See? Are you going to deny her? Unbind her at once!"

My father leans forward and unleashes his deep commanding voice. "Sabine, you have no authority here. This is my daughter and you came here to trigger an event. It isn't all about you and your political power trips. Are you scared she might deny you?" He pushes back and stands from the table to continue his rant.

Mrs. Scott is walking down the hall and, upon seeing my father, turns right around.

This is ludicrous. What is she talking about, unbinding me? What's he accusing her of?

There's a flash. I shield my eyes. Then the light is gone.

I'm in the dark woods with my mother. She is touching my

small face. Her familiar dark blonde hair reaches her shoulders in waves. Her blue eyes sparkle and her smile is reassuring. Her hands are touching me, warm, soft, and loving.

"Stay here, sweetheart. It will be okay."

I nod.

I blink and my eyes are swelling with tears. I just heard my mother's voice! I haven't seen or heard her since that night. I had forgotten her voice. Air catches in my throat.

There is another flash and I'm back in the dining room no longer that little girl in front of her mother.

I fidget in my seat, then stand, overwhelmed. The uncontrollable part of me is building. I shake all over. A loud hum sounds all over my body.

"Willow." My father brings my attention back to him. "As strange as it sounds, everything you are doubting is true, from magick to royalty. After the accident, I used magick to take away your memories of that horrific event. I also removed your memory of our heritage and extended family as a safety precaution."

I listen to what my dad is saying. I'm his little girl, caught in his shadow, hoping to make him proud and awaiting his grin of approval. This time, however, all I can do is gape at him while tears escape my eyes.

My voice shakes. "Is that what Sabine is talking about—unbinding? I'm . . . bound?"

He's standing in front of me. "Yes," he replies, reaching for me.

I move away from the table and from him. "Don't! I don't want to be unbound then."

Sabine's mouth hinges open.

"I don't want what you're saying! Keep it. I don't have to accept it, do I?" I'm still shaking. I clasp my hands into fists at my sides to steady myself. My mother—I miss her. I want to listen to her voice again. None of this changes anything.

My father's eyes are wide and his forehead creases. "No, you don't. But your magick will beat on the surface and build. Your mother and I are from particular family bloodlines, and your choices will be irrelevant. Magick will come."

Irrelevant? No choice. *No choice.* The words ring over and over in my head. My father and Sabine are talking to me, moving toward me, but I can't understand them. My anger builds—the static electricity moves over my body and down my arms, filling my clutched hands with zaps of pain.

No choice.

No choice.

No choice.

I'm shaking more now, and the electricity is compounding. It shocks my arms hard. It hurts, but I bear the pain of stabbing needles into my skin. In all this chaos and confusion, the pain at least is known and something real.

Sabine is no longer moving toward me but retreating.

She should. She brought it.

Her fault.

No choice.

My vision lands on my dad, my father—the man who lied to me. Protected me. Kept me in the dark. Loved and provided for me. His hands are up and he is chanting something, his eyes fill with tears.

Crying? That's not like my dad. Oh, this is bad.

The detachment, the unbinding, it hurts—it's as if it's ripping my soul.

"Wil-low!" My mother's voice calls out, but she isn't here. I look for her but my eyes show me someone other than my mother. Someone I don't know, but yet he feels familiar. The energy is all around me, consuming and drowning. I suck in more air to breathe, then release.

My scream reverberates through the house.

The dining room bows and the windows shatter as I fall to the floor. My dad catches me.

Darkness engulfs me.

CHAPTER 5

C old, crisp, artificial air blows on my arms. I'm struggling to wake up fully when I hear, "Okay, Sleeping Beauty, time to rise and shine before the warden makes her way in here."

I open my eyes slowly and see the white walls and beige tile surroundings. Emily is sitting across from me in a twin bed, dressed in jeans and a plain white T-shirt. Her short-cropped hair is messy, as usual.

"Where are we?" I ask, sitting up. My eyes still refuse to completely work. I rub them and focus more on Emily.

She gives me a funny smirk. Before she can answer, there's a knock at the door and Dr. Bauche enters the room. She tucks her shoulder-length wavy hair behind her ear. Her composure is graceful as she stands at the end of the room in front of the window. The soft light surrounds her in an ethereal effect that has me tongue-tied.

"How are you feeling today, Willow?" she asks.

Emily announces her departure and is out the door before I can exhale. I watch her leave and want to go with my friend. What am I doing here in the first place? Why would Emily be here?

As if reading my mind, Dr. Bauche says, "Willow, we've been

through this before. You've been here before." She taps on an iPad and scrolls. "I'm more concerned about the outburst at dinner."

Dinner? I don't . . . I shuffle back toward the headboard of the bed I'm sitting in. It suddenly floods my brain—dinner.

Sabine.

Magick.

Royalty.

A vision flashes before me of Sabine crying and hugging me. She is dressed all in black and she tells me how much she loves me. We are at a funeral—my mother's funeral, I realize, because my arm is in a cast. How can I have forgotten Sabine at my mother's funeral? I'm not here though, I'm somewhere else. I shake my head to clear it and I'm back in the small white room.

Dr. Bauche's demeanor changes as she sits down on the bed next to me. The springs of the mattress squeak under the new weight.

"You had an outburst that wasn't coherent. The staff last night had to sedate you. Instead of placing you in confinement, I recommended shared quarters."

She waits for me, but all I can do is stare at my hands, remembering a blue light, thinking about my mother's funeral and meeting her mother, my grandmother. She continues, "Something about a grandmother and Wicca?"

Did she just read my mind? I survey the room, stalling. Oh, no—it's what I always dreaded. I'm at a psych treatment center. How did Emily end up here too? She wasn't there at dinner. I remember the hypnosis with Dr. Evan. It must be what's causing visions.

"Is Dr. Evan here?"

Her eyes search me over in an evaluating way that makes me uncomfortable. She must notice.

"I don't know a Dr. Evan. Is he your internist?"

I stammer my words, confused. "No, no. I started seeing him a few weeks back at your practice. He's a new doctor." I need him to help explain this—the visions that keep popping up and the regressive treatment therapy. I don't need to be in a treatment center.

"Willow, we can meet at our regular session time today. I'm not aware of any Dr. Evan." She stands. "You can go to group, but first take your meds." She hands me a small paper cup with three pills in it.

I consider the cup and then her. She nods to the sink, toward a drinking glass.

"What are these for?"

"I need you to take them, Willow, as part of your therapy regime while you're here."

I stand and walk toward the sink hesitantly, thinking about how not to take the pills. That regression therapy, last night . . . I'm not taking these pills, who knows what they will do to me. She watches me take the pills and drink the water. I have to show her my open mouth and move my tongue to show I'm not holding pills hostage.

Where's the trust?

I grip the pills in my left hand, where I slipped them next to my water glass. Score.

Dr. Bauche quietly leaves, satisfied.

I study the pills in my hand and decide to keep them. I open a door next to Emily's bed to find a full bathroom. I walk back to my side and open another door to find a closet with clothes and shoes. My clothes are recognizable, especially my favorite hoodie. I put the pills in a hidden pocket in the sleeve. Then I get refreshed and open the door to a bare white hallway. I feel like an escapee, but I'm lost. I need an exit sign.

There's laughing at my left and I walk to a room labeled "Yellow Brick Road." Several teens are lounging around on beanbags, sofa sectionals, and floor pods. I see Emily in the far corner. A counselor acknowledges me and waves me in. I sit by Emily.

"We need to talk," I whisper to her.

"This is some crazy." She is distracted, looking at a guy sitting across the room in ripped jeans and a black T-shirt with a gray hoodie. His long, messy hair falls forward on his face and his arms are folded. He appears asleep until he speaks. His voice is soothing and deep.

"I'm not going to talk today, so let's move it along," he says.

The guy running the group replies, "Theon, this is not going to move you forward on an outpatient basis. You have to put in the work."

Theon settles back in his beanbag chair, and the counselor turns his stool to me.

"So, Willow, did you find your triggering point?"

Emily is staring at Theon, smiling. Most in the room are paying attention to other things besides me, except the counselor.

"My triggering point? I don't really—"

"From yesterday's activities? I observed the trigger with your family. There is anger. A lot of anger."

The counselor mentioning my family and accusing me of anger heats up my face. I don't know who he is and how he knows anything about me or my family, despite him talking as if I do.

"Sure, I think most teens will say they're angry—it's not unique."

A few kids sitting to my left affirm my statement. Emily half-heartedly laughs.

"Yes, that is certainly true in the general sense," the counselor says. "However, none of you are here in the general sense. Actions intended to hurt either yourself or others have brought you here. Your time here is to teach you how to control those triggers and behaviors."

I take a sharp inhale. Did I hurt someone? No. No, I couldn't have—could I?

Emily leans forward. "Those actions make me, me! Are you trying to change me, Brad?" She drags out his name mockingly.

He smiles, unmoved by the outburst.

"No, not change in the sense you're assuming, but I do want you to become aware of your impact on yourself and your surroundings."

Flipping her hand dismissively at him, she says, "I'm totally aware."

Theon stands up with small grin that barely shows under all his hair. Two bumps on the top of his head are just visible beneath his hoodie.

"Theon, ready to share?"

"Uh, no, it's time to go," he says in his smooth voice.

"Ah, lunchtime," Brad confirms, looking like he's happy too.

Everyone stands up and leaves the room. I walk with Emily down the hallway.

"What is going on?" I ask.

"I'm not sure, but it's your party, so I'm just along for the ride." She claps me on the back.

"My party?"

We turn the corner and follow the line that enters a small cafeteria. Emily stops me and guides me to an open door on the left, a storage closet.

"Listen, we can continue to play psychoanalysis rehab if you want, or you can get on with it."

What the hell is she talking about? I'm in the process of asking when she holds her hand up and cuts me off.

Her eyes are staring directly into mine. "You're tougher than you think, or we wouldn't be such close friends. You need to snap out of it, Will." She snaps her fingers. "You, me—we don't belong here in your head." She lightly touches my temple.

"My head?"

"Ask yourself why you'd have me here, besides the fact that I'm awesome. I do what?" Her eyebrow raises.

I search and say the obvious response: "Tell it like it is?"

She nods.

Ding ding ding. I'll winning the fair prize if I can just complete the puzzle.

"Why would I—"

"Don't focus on the 'why,' focus on the 'get-out-of-your-way' task. You think too hard and long about stuff, and sometimes you just gotta do and move forward." She scans around real quick and adds, "Although you did do a great job bringing that demon, Theon, here. At least it was worth my time."

How did I bring or do any of this?

She's becoming translucent. I reach to touch her hand, and she chuckles at me as my hand passes through hers. I'm starting to fade along with everything else in my head.

"Bravo, Wills. See you soon," Emily whispers.

Before I can process it further, I'm gone and laying in my bed at home.

I grab my phone and text Emily.

I just had the strangest dream and you were in it.

I wait despite the late hour, hoping she might respond.

Yep, I'm so dreamable. Go back to sleep girl, you're interrupting my beauty sleep.

Chuckling at Emily, I put my phone down and close my eyes.

CHAPTER 6

"Willow, sweetheart, wake up."

The bed dips as my father sits down. I'm home. Something about that word—home—warms my insides. Home can mean different things, but for me in this moment it is stability, a constant, and, in my changing world, a necessity.

I blink at the bright light, remembering my weird dream with Emily. My father turns off the lamp on my nightstand. I must have left it on.

"Hey. You're home?" I ask, slowly sitting up.

"Of course I am. Do you remember last night?"

I sit up and see he's in casual clothes: jeans and a long-sleeved, dark green shirt.

"Yes, I do. Is Sabine still here?" I rub my eyes of sleep.

"No, just us. Mrs. Scott is out today; she'll be back this evening. Let's take the time to talk."

"What about school and—"

"I already spoke to Lucy and the school." He swallows and stares at his hands. "I want to spend time with you and answer your questions about magick, along with the whole royal succession that is expected of you—and there is an anticipation of your —coronation."

I can't help but cringe at the word "coronation." Me, a girl who trips up the stairs on a regular basis—a girl who understands nothing about how to preside or rule, or whatever the heck it is all about—Queen?

Is this something I really have to do?

I want to go back to sleep and just veg out and forget all of this. I can't though; I recognize the hum of the magick in my veins now.

Duke pushes his nose in through the open door and jumps up on my bed. His tail wags and both my father and I pet him, as if the silent moment we share will be one of the last normal things we do.

He breaks the silence in a soft, unassuming voice. "Come down when you're ready. Mrs. Scott made French toast that I'm sure even I can reheat."

He leaves and slowly closes the door.

Duke licks my face and lays his head in my lap. When I touch my face, the tears flow as if from a hose down my face. Gah. I'm not usually such a crier, but I'm a cry-baby now.

I waggle Duke's ears, wipe my face dry, and get dressed in my comfy clothes. Duke leads the way to the kitchen.

I'm greeted with almost the typical scene, except father isn't on his cell tapping or talking. He's staring out the window, holding a cup of coffee. He appears older to me. His dark brown hair is brushed back, revealing glints of silver at his temples. His square jaw is taut. I don't want to interfere his thoughts, so I stand in silence.

Duke gives us away when he barks.

"I'll feed him if you can heat up Mrs. Scott's delicious French toast," I say.

Duke bounces up and down when I pour the kibble in his bowl. His happiness changes my solemn mood.

The plates are at the table, garnished with strawberries for flair and two slices of bacon. The syrup sits in the middle of the table. My father is staring at the cappuccino machine with his forehead creased.

"Need help with that?" I ask.

"If you want your tea, absolutely! This takes high skill." He laughs.

I lift the lever into my cup to steam the milk, adding my tea to finish it off. Then we head to the table.

We eat in silence for a long while before I break the tension.

"So, you grew up and always had powers?"

I still can't believe this. Here I am asking my father about magick and powers. I pinch my leg just to make sure I'm not dreaming still.

Damn it—it hurts. This isn't a dream.

Taking his last drink of coffee, he answers, "Yes, I grew up with magick, although my powers were bound until I was older. This is the case for most families where powers are anticipated. Powers vary for Wiccans and can depend on bloodlines. For our family, specifically, you will be envied by many." He pauses, frowning. "Actually, by most, which is dangerous."

"Why is that dangerous?"

He stares out the bay window. "It's dangerous because of my bloodline—and your mother's. Nuala's bloodline is royal and is of pure white magick, whereas mine, although a noble bloodline, is full of dark magick. Our union was not sanctioned. Nuala was next in line for the crown. Her older brother, Liam, renounced himself from the family and died young. Her younger brother, well . . . he passed away when you were little. The MacKinnons' royal legacy boils down to you."

His expression is pensive. I don't want to talk about mother and death; I want to focus on something light.

"Rebel. You and mother ran away, then?"

He grins and laughs. His eyes light up at the thought of my mother. "We did. We got married and pregnant with you within a year. The best year of our lives. But Harkin, your grandfather, and the Guardians caught up with us. When we went back to face punishment because we went against your grandfather's wishes, it was more of a celebration that you were with us. Not all was forgiven, but your mother was next in line for the crown, so she committed to the duty."

"So she would have been Queen?"

He nods.

"But the accident . . . changed everything." I breathe in the weight of my words.

So much for something light and easy to talk about. That accident has been the reason for so much change in my life and our family. I can't look at him directly, so I look out the bay window and hug my knees to my chest.

When I glance back at him, his eyes are gray and sad.

"After the accident I met with Sabine and Harkin, and we made a pact to protect you. We've moved around to keep you safe. There are many in Edayri that believe there should be a sovereign government over a royal one. We didn't believe the accident was just an accident. We all knew that, in time, you would need to ascend the throne following Nuala. Your mother was the white light in my darkness, just as you are. She was brave and smart, and ready to change the times—which, unfortunately, I'm sure others didn't agree with. Harkin and the Guardians worked hard to learn all they could about the accident, but unfortunately, all I can tell you is that demons were involved."

"Demons?" My mind reels. "So, what types of magickal beings are in this place that you call a realm?" I'm not sure I really want him to answer me.

"Every kind you can imagine, and some you may never have heard of. The big five are Wiccans, demons, valkyrie, fae, and shape shifters."

"No vampires? You know, the kind that sparkle?" I giggle to myself, thinking, Go Team Edward!

This is all absolutely nutso. The smug smirk on my father's face doesn't gel with my sense of humor at that moment. Seriously though, fae and shape shifters? I don't even know what a valkyrie is, but this is just—

Watching my father, my lightness is shattered. It's all I can do to keep my chin up and stare at him—my father, a dark magick Wiccan. A man who is formal and overly organized, a man who is usually in a suit and tie in some board meeting. This man has magick at his fingertips, and now I do too.

"I'm sure there are, but I doubt they sparkle. You need to take this seriously, Willow."

I lean back in my chair and look him in the eyes. "I am taking this seriously. I didn't mean to offend, but this is a lot to take in. I don't want to be the whiny teenager throwing a fit, but my world is rocked, and a little levity now and then is okay . . . right?"

I cringe, hoping he doesn't jump down my throat. He doesn't, and that's worse.

"I do forget how young you are." He gathers his dishes and mine and goes to the sink. I follow him to his office, and we sit in the maroon wingback leather chairs that face each other in front of the fireplace. I tuck my left leg under my right leg. I'm waiting, not sure what to say, what to ask. What I can handle. I think learning everything in the full rush last night broke me somehow; I'm timid. I don't want to break—I don't want to have an episode and wake up again. Besides, it has been a while since we've sat and talked at any length about something important and meaningful.

My father opens his palm and a blue light dances around his fingertips. It's like the light I saw in and around my hands last night. My eyes follow the wave of light. I can't help but be amazed. It's like nothing I've ever seen before in real life; magicians on TV have got nothing on this. It is seductive and intimidating, and I can't help but feel cool that I have it too. This whole magick thing is unwanted, but at the same time, maybe—

My trance is interrupted when he says, "You are unique when it comes to our family's powers. You embody both the light and the dark. I like to think Nuala is more prevalent in you than I am, but the fact is that you have more dark magick. You should know it's taken me decades to learn that magick is magick, no matter where its base form comes from. Dark doesn't necessarily mean bad, just as light doesn't necessarily mean good."

"What does it mean, exactly?"

"The power derived from you is as individual as you are. I leaned full into what I needed to accomplish in order for the power to carry out what I needed it to, which some label dark magick. Your mother, on the other hand, leaned more toward what something should be, like a remedy, again, to which some would label as white magick."

He closes his palm and the dancing blue light extinguishes immediately.

Frowning, I ask, "Do others believe that dark magick is wrong?" The word "dark" worries me. Will it change me? And if my power is as individual as I am, who am I?

"Willow, there is a lot of prejudice within magickal families. I think you would use the terms 'snobby' and 'over-privileged brats.' Whether it be light, dark, or anything in-between, they will measure magick in percentages like DNA. For Wiccan culture, it's about purity above all and one with nature, the Goddess, and the spirit. It's not that different with other magickal beings."

"So, they're behind the times it sounds like. Joy."

"In many ways, yes," he replies. My sarcasm is not bothering him.

"How am I going to learn everything? I know nothing about —what's it called? Edayri? Or about who lives there. I'm an outsider. I can't imagine anyone will be thrilled with me showing up. If I don't accept the crown, what will happen?"

I really hope he answers with "No big deal" or "Democracy wins out."

"A little chaos will ensue."

Of course. I sigh and lean back in my chair.

"But the biggest impact would be to those of the previous crown. Legend has it that the family's bloodline magick can be reversed. I doubt it's true, but the belief is that once things are undone, the space-time continuum in which we live will change and revert, ripping. A rift. Who knows? The point is, no one has seen it, so we can't predict exactly what would happen. I'm sure you've heard the saying 'magick comes with a price'?"

I nod; every movie or TV show that has witches notes it as some moral aspect. I guess there may be a few Wiccans in the entertainment business. Hopefully I'm not as far behind in learning as I thought I was.

He continues. "The same goes for the royal position. There is a price for each judgment, each sentence, and each law. The idea is that this balances out the power of the position to limit the person who holds the crown, and their family."

"Okay. Interesting."

My father stands up and walks to the fireplace, where he pulls a hidden lever. I never noticed it before. The bookcase rocks backward, revealing a dark passageway. I stand in awe. He walks in and, with a wave of his hand, the entryway lights up.

I follow him, remembering to close my gaping mouth. This is wild; my house has a secret room!

The room is painted dark green. Shelves of books adorn one wall and an oversized, puffy, paisley-patterned loveseat acts as the only casual seating. There's a table like the one in my chemistry class, with a sink and burners in the corner with a cauldron. A fireplace shares the wall with my father's office. The room looks like just the place I'd want to hang out in with tea and a good book.

"What is this?" I ask.

"I guess you could call this my lair. Or you can just call it my private coven, since I'm a singular practice witch."

My father's eyes twinkle with excitement and his whole demeanor changes like he's an excited kid at Christmas. I can't help but mirror him. The father before me is so different from twenty-four hours ago. I wonder if he sees me the same way.

"What do you do here?" I gesture to the cauldron and the bookshelves that house a few glass bottles with stoppers. "Do you practice magick or make potions down here?"

"Truth?"

I roll my eyes. "Yes, truth. It should be an open book."

His smile reaches his eyes. I haven't seen that since I was a little girl. It's like I have my daddy back. I suddenly want to do anything to keep him happy.

"Speaking of books," he says, pulling a thick one from the shelf, "this book not only contains all our ancestry information, but also magick incantations, potions, and fortunes."

"Fortunes?"

His smile broadens. "Your mother really liked that toy—the magick eight ball—so she developed a spell and added it to be a part of the Book of Shadows to make it a fortune teller. Although I suspect it only tells you what you are ready to know, sometimes it's good to have the confirmation."

"That is so cool!"

My father shows me the book. Flipping through, I find that several places throughout are blank. He explains that only family can read the book, and it will only show each individual what they need to see. This book is especially unique because my father and mother incanted their separate family's books into this one. It's not that old, but it possesses centuries and centuries of information. He shows me how to get into the hidden room and how to leave it. He then leaves me alone in the room with the Book of Shadows for most of the afternoon.

I think about my most basic question. "Show me how magick was started."

I flip through the book the way my father showed me and the scrolling script appears. I learn that divinity revolves around a goddess and a horned god. I read further that the pentagram is an elegant expression of the golden ratio phi which connects to ideal beauty to express trust about hidden nature. I always thought the pentagram was an evil symbol, but now I want to see if it would show Coral's hidden nature to Daniel and the school. I laugh to myself at the thought.

I keep reading and am surprised how connected Wiccans are to nature and the flow of the spirit. There are many elements to which Wiccans ascribe physical power; however, the element of the spirit is the most coveted, as it's balanced with all the elements—air, water, earth, and fire.

As I read, I lose any sense of doubt. The pages are filled with stories and facts about my heritage and my family's history, and I no longer feel like it is just me, father, and Mrs. Scott anymore.

That evening, Mrs. Scott joins us and we eat dinner together. She's a practicing Wiccan but is limited in physical powers. Her own identity doesn't come as a surprise since I knew she helped raise my father when she was much younger.

"Oh, my Willow, your father was a mess when his binding was removed. A complete mess—it was like a poltergeist was living in the house, mind you. He went through a time where he could hardly reach for something without it flying across the room. He stunk for a week—the water wouldn't stick to him to clean him!"

Listening to Mrs. Scott tell these tales about my father makes me roar with laughter. It's nice to see he struggled too.

"Okay, okay. In my defense—ah, well, it takes some time is all."

Mrs. Scott continues to giggle and I take in the ease of my father's shoulders and manner. This is my family and I love them.

I'm happy Mrs. Scott knows about everything; it means I have someone else I can talk to. It's not like I will be able to share this with Lucy, Emily, or Daniel.

I practice my ability to control my power with my father. Mrs. Scott watches in awe and laughs and claps with joy after almost every exercise. My hands and fingers develop a white, lacy, flowing pattern, like henna, when I conjure my magick into a light-blue flame like my father's. The patterns on my hands and fingers disappear a few minutes after I let go of my magick.

I can feel the pull to do more, but it's getting late. The day has gone by so fast. I've learned so much—from calling my magick to the surface to controlling my intent and use of it. Mrs. Scott pulls me into a bear hug that makes me feel like a tiny toddler, but I love it.

"Oh sweetheart, you will be the best for the all of Edayri." She kisses me on the forehead and I turn to my father as she leaves.

"Thank you for today," I say.

"I'm here for you, Willow. I love you very much. I know you have your doubts about all this, but Mrs. Scott is right—you have the makings of a fine queen."

My father walks up the stairs and I feel proud of myself. It's the relationship I've always wanted with him—what we did today, what we used to do when I was so much younger. I don't know what happened over the years, but I'm happy now, and now is what matters.

PART II

"Darkness is coming for you," Fate taunts.
The girl defiantly walks forward.

CHAPTER 7

Cabin fever is setting in; it's been three days since I've been to school. My father felt it was safer for me and my fellow classmates, now that my magick is unbound. Thank the heavens it's Saturday. He's back to work, although staying home as much as he can. I've been catching up on schoolwork and practicing my magick. Once I can prove my control, I can go back to school and see my friends. Mrs. Scott and I have been catching up on reality television in between all the work stuff. For some reason, she is fascinated with *The Bachelor* and *Housewives*.

The senior campout is tonight. Father has been putting protection spells on the property, but somehow, someway, I need to figure out how to escape the house. I miss my friends, and it could be one of the last things I'll get to do with them. I try not to think about this too much. Besides, Daniel and I've been texting and I really want to see him. I haven't reminded my father of the senior campout; why let him say no?

I enact my plan with counter spells I learned from The Book of Shadows, placing my heat signature on Duke. I will leave only with my clothes so as not to trigger the firing squad of alarms. I work on my homework because, according to the school, I'm only on leave until further notice due to a "family event." Like a private school really cares—especially when you're funding most of their projects and buildings.

9 p.m. and the time has come. I'm committed and going to the senior campout. I put on my favorite hoodie. I have Duke happy and content on my bed, and I turn on my computer and put on a music loop. My backpack in hand, I decide that sneaking out the back door is my best option. I call to my magick and have it surround me. I walk forward slowly and repeat in my mind, acceptance to pass the boundary without harm. When I'm at the yard's perimeter, I take a deep breath and step outside the spell protection borders.

I exhale. No alarms, no smoke, no fire. All clear.

Self-satisfaction beams out my body and I take off at a run to where Emily and Lucy are waiting for me.

Operation: Free Willow is a success!

Emily is jumping up and down and Lucy waits, smiling, in the car. Emily hugs me.

"Dang Wills, good to see you. I've been having wild dreams lately."

I smile at her. "You too, huh?" I probably shouldn't have told her all about it, but she seemed to think it was just some type of symbolism of my subconscious mind.

She laughs and we settle in the car. Emily parks her Camry on the north interior side of Salem Woods in one of the few parking spaces left. Lucy and I gather our gear from the trunk and hike into the clearing, guided by music and lots of laughter. You can't say private school kids don't know how to have fun, 'cause here we are, per a tradition that started long ago. Every year, class leaders apply with the park rangers for this weekend. It's all legit, although it still feels like we are rebels.

Oh, the privileged.

"Come on! You two are so slow!" Emily trots ahead with the tent on her back, slinging a small cooler in one hand and a bag in another. She doesn't seem bothered at all by the weight she is carrying.

Lucy laughs. "She'll trip soon, I swear, and then we'll catch up."

"She's definitely over-caffeinated tonight," I respond. I rearrange my hold on the bags of food and my backpack.

"I think it has more to do with Marco. He's more flirtatious than usual," Lucy says.

"Oh really?" I laugh easily. I missed the mundane gossip, and I really missed my friends. This is my joy.

Emily makes her way toward the other edge of the clearing, where a firepit is lit up with a crowd of students. I spy Daniel coming out of a nice-sized tent with Marco. He spots me, smiles, and waves. I wave back. He is handsome in flannel. I've never seen him in flannel before.

"You're so lucky," says Lucy.

I break my stare from Daniel.

"Why do you think I'm so lucky?"

Lucy nudges me with her shoulder as we keep walking. "Uh, one of the cutest, nicest, most all-American guys is, like, totally in love with you. Nope, not lucky at all. I take it back."

"Okay, hisso." I nudge her back.

Yeah, Daniel is great. It's funny, though. I would think most girls' parents would like Daniel, but for some reason, my father doesn't. At first I figured it was because he wasn't wealthy, but that idea was put to rest when Mrs. Scott informed me that he would be this way about anyone I was dating. I remember when I dated a boy named James in 8th grade who took me to a dance and kissed me on my front porch step. Father was grumpy about that too, so I guess it's just a father thing. Part of me likes his protective nature because it reminds me that he loves me.

We walk to our spot. Emily is already unpacking the tent. We all pitch in and get it up in under ten minutes. Fire pits glow all about the clearing—a large one near the concrete pavilion in the middle and several small ones around tent groups. The music is bumping at the front of the clearing, and set up in the middle by Steve Carlin's tent is a keg. Steve is the typical jock party boy, and friends with everyone, but too friendly with most of the girls.

As soon as the tent is up, Daniel grabs me by the hand and leads me to the side of his tent.

"Hey, you," he says, holding my face.

"Hey." My breath leaves me and my body tingles at his gentle, familiar touch.

He kisses me like he's starving and I respond, so eager to see him. It's familiar and electrifying—his touch, his kiss. Daniel makes my knees weak. I wrap my hands around his neck and pull him closer, and his hands have just dropped to my waist when we're interrupted by a high whistle. We turn to see Marco sporting a big grin on his face. Emily and Lucy are just ahead of him, walking toward the center pavilion.

"We're heading over. Come join us when you're . . . um . . . yeah. Finished." Marco laughs and turns to walk away.

Daniel is looking at my lips.

"Are we finished?" I whisper.

I feel like the air is gone from my lungs when he leans down and kisses me one more time, softly and sweetly.

His smirk catches me off guard as he pulls back slowly. "For now," he whispers.

Clasping hands, we round the tent and head over to chat with Steve and some of the others while enjoying our Solo cups filled with beer. Everyone is having an excellent time, laughing and carrying on about the upcoming school year. No one asks why I haven't been there. Everything is easy and fun.

Daniel has his arms around me. I love that he is taller than me and can hold me like this. Emily is off to the side, laughing and poking at Marco, who returns the favor.

"So, I hear Marco may finally return Emily's advances? Is that right?"

Daniel kisses me just under my ear. "Maybe, I dunno, but he'd be silly not to. They flirt like crazy. Might as well just get it together. Everyone thinks they're together anyway."

"Yeah, true."

I look for Lucy and spy her talking with Coral. Coral is a fashion model on a camping trip, dolled up ridiculously. If they walk over and she is in heels, I may hurl. They turn toward us moments later. I don't see any heels. I guess I get to save my vomit for another situation, and the awful beer might just do it. I dump my cup out on the ground.

"Hello, Daniel . . . and Willow." Coral says my name like it burns her mouth. Wouldn't that be nice? I notice her teeth seem to be fine, so either she's already fixed the imperfect chip that happened on the first day or she didn't chip a tooth after all.

"Hey," Daniel responds. His arms are still around me, and he kisses my neck again.

I try not to gloat on the outside, but on the inside, I'm full of in-your-face celebration. You're his ex, Coral. Stop trying to cause issues and throwing yourself at him, he's with me.

"Hello, Coral." I immediately look toward Lucy. "Hey, Lucy, we're gonna head back to the tents. Come over later and join us."

Yeah, Coral, you're not invited. Don't come, I think to myself. She leaves and heads straight to Steve, who I'm sure will relieve her of any misgivings.

Daniel puts his arm around my shoulder and walks us back to the tents where our small fire pit is glowing. Both done with our Solo cups, Daniel tosses them into the fire where the plastic burns quickly and folds in on itself, producing gray smoke. It smells awful. The smoke curls and twists like an arm. I shake my head just as Lucy walks over with Marco and Emily, chatting away and laughing.

I scratch an itch on the back of my neck.

"The bugs, right?" Lucy says. "Don't worry, I've got a little sage stick that should solve the problem!" She dives into our tent and returns with a small bundle that she lights up. It starts to smoke white, and she whirls it around until Emily snatches it from her and starts dancing around the fire.

"Are you a witch, Lucy? Seriously, this is a witchy thing to do." Emily eyes her as she waves the smoke around. I sit up a little straighter in Daniel's lap.

"Are you okay?" Daniel asks me.

I nod. "Yeah, just adjusting." I snuggle back into Daniel, but all I can think about is the rehab dream and Emily's presence in it. I haven't talked to her about it beyond saying she was in my dream. Is it just a coincidence?

In any case, it sounds crazy to speak of a psych rehab unit and say, "Oh, by the way, you were there with me!" It's bad enough my BFFs know I go to a psychologist on a regular basis. Lucy says all the rich and famous do and that I shouldn't sweat it. I'm not the rich and famous type—or, at least, I try to reject that notion. I rub my hands up my arms and come to the secret pocket of my hoodie. It has something in it.

The pills from the dream. Shit. It was a dream, right? I pinch my arm and feel the pain. At least I know this is real.

It's well after midnight now. The music is dying down and those who aren't staying over in the camp are starting to leave. The crickets are getting quieter and the temperature is getting colder. I'm happy to have the extra blankets.

Emily and Marco shout in sync, "Ghost stories! Lucy, tell one!"

Lucy's face is flushed red. "What? Are you kidding me? I don't do ghost stories!"

Marco whines. "But you're the one who reads all the time. Come on! You've gotta tell us one."

"I've got an excellent story to tell." Emily gets very animated and lifts her arms toward the fire as if she is trying to make it rise.

"You know we are in Salem Woods. These are the very woods where several witches were burned at the stake. In their damnation, there were incantations uttered that continue to linger even to this day."

Marco laughs. "Em, seriously? We live here. All the stories we heard in elementary school and junior high are just whacked!"

She gets a serious look on her face. "I'm not kidding you. My stepbrother, Charlie, knew this girl. She was a grade older than him. She came out to these woods with a bunch of friends. They were hanging out having a good time together, not that different than tonight."

She waves her hands around and the fire seems to follow her movements as if she controls it. I tuck my arms into myself.

"Someone said a chant as a joke, and the next thing they knew this girl went comatose and started to float."

Daniel sits up and begins to tap his leg as if remembering something. "Oh yeah, my sister was just a grade under them at that time, and she remembers that story. I totally didn't believe her because she was always saying stupid stuff."

Emily continues. "Oh, it was real all right. Charlie knew her boyfriend. They were on the football team together. The boyfriend was devastated. The girl's parents blamed him and even took legal action against him and his family. She was admitted to a mental institution, and to this day she hasn't spoken or said a word."

Everyone is hanging on Emily's every word.

I wonder what would happen if I did something wrong tonight with my magick, not on purpose. I bite at a hangnail absently. Which of my friends would be pulled into my fate by accident? Father has taught me more control, but suddenly I'm filled with guilt. I'm out in the open for selfish reasons, and not only am I taking a risk, but I'm also taking a risk with my friends' wellbeing.

Damn it. I suck.

"Now, the wild part is this: last year a medium came to these woods. I remember Charlie said the family hired her to help their daughter." Em shakes her head to clear her thoughts. "The medium came to the woods and stayed here for hours, then retreated to town all upset. She said this girl, their daughter, was a payment to the debt owed."

"No," Lucy whispers, raising her hand to her mouth.

"Yes. The curse was lingering when it finally found a member of a family that it could take vengeance on. The saying goes, if you step in these woods, beware of the family toll."

Emily's voice drops. "The toll must be paid, Willow." She starts to rock back and forth with her knees tucked to her chest. She repeats "The toll must be paid" several times.

I'm stuck. I don't know what to do. Is she really possessed?

Daniel hugs me protectively. "Cut it out, Em."

Marco pushes her to the side and says, "Real funny."

I hold my breath. The air shifts, changes.

Emily breaks the silence, yelling, "Rrrahhh!" She jumps up and tags me on the shoulder.

"Gotcha!"

Everyone joins in laughing, but the air shift is still there. I smile and try to play along, but inside I'm falling apart. Emily is a joker, but what if I have a family toll too? I mean, we are Wiccans and my family has powers.

The air, the change in mood—someone is watching me. I feel that creepy, icy feeling tingling down my neck. I don't consider myself brave in the least, but I'm not going to let my friends or Daniel get hurt. My own lack of safety I can accept, but theirs? No way. I wish I could lay down some protective spells. I have no idea how to use spells yet.

"Hey, I'll be right back. I need to use the facilities," I announce.

Daniel grabs his flashlight. "I'll go with you."

"I can handle it," I say, taking the offered flashlight. "I'll be back in a few."

Daniel tries to change my mind and Lucy offers to come as well. They finally go back to the fire pit at my stubborn refusal. Out of all the tents in the clearing, only a few fire pits have teenagers around them anymore. It's gotten late and most are calling it a night.

The cold air licks at my face as I walk down the pathway and pass one of Coral's obviously tipsy cronies. A boy I don't recognize wobbles after her a minute later, reeking of beer. I tense seeing him, because he looks similar to the boy in the alley I've all but tried to forget. I shake my head to clear it and stumble as I reach the edge of the bathroom facility. The lights flicker and a vision flashes before my eyes. I reach out and the building I was near is no longer there.

I'm in the woods as a little girl in my pajamas and coat, holding my arm to my body. A deep voice calls me a little witch. It is taunting me when my father appears. He has blood all over him, but I'm not scared, only relieved. He swoops me up and we hug each other tightly. It's the accident all over again. I blink several times and the vision is gone, but my goosebumps remain.

The regressive therapy and hypnosis is making rethink my decision.

CHAPTER 8

I walk past the bathroom facility to the side of the clearing, just about twenty feet from our tents. I can somewhat make out my friends, and I wave to show I'm okay.

I'm not okay. What the hell am I doing? I wiggle my fingers to test my magick, but nothing happens. I flex my hand and try again. Still nothing. Clutching my hand to my side, I walk into the woods just beyond the trees. When I hear the earth give way to something off to my left, I ask meekly, "Who's there?" I don't recognize my own voice—I sound like a little girl.

No one responds.

"Who's there?" I say, louder this time. A rustling in the canopy of the trees is all that responds.

It could be an animal. Except if it is an animal, it's not a small one.

The sound is getting closer.

I turn back to the campsite, but all I see is the forest. I went too far. I turn left, then right—my sense of direction is gone. How did I get this far into the woods?

What the hell am I doing out here? I clench my hand and feel nothing. No light, no magick.

Pop.

Snap.

Tree branches are breaking.

I'm out of time. Someone or something is coming toward me!

I jog forward. There is a faint light on my right and I head for it. Then I hear it.

The voice is deep, full of menace. "Little witch."

I freeze.

"Little witch, come play with me. I promise not to kill you quickly. That way we can both enjoy it."

My mind is locked up but my body is moving of its own accord now, running in the opposite direction of the baritone voice. I'm clumsy and scrape against rough, unfriendly trees and bushes. I flex my hand but there's still no magick. Whoever's chasing me huffs through his nose like an animal. A breeze licks at my neck and I feel my insides go cold. I'm in that alleyway in Boston, with the boy touching me and taunting me. I can't breathe.

The glowing light on my right is getting brighter, calling to me, as if it will help me get away from the threat. It's fight-or-flight time. I won't be a victim who waits. On shaky legs, I run at full speed through a break in the trees.

There is the anguished cry of an animal behind me. I run as fast as I can without tripping on the uneven forest floor. My heart is pounding. I can't see well and my breathing is labored. I don't seem to be gaining any distance toward the light. I pump my arms harder.

He's gaining on me.

Smack.

Something hits me in my shoulder and I'm on the ground.

"Aaaahhh!" The pain sears like a hot iron.

Shit!

I know I've been stabbed with something, but if I lay here in pain, I'm dead. I know it.

No time.

No time.

Keep moving.

I scramble to my feet and turn, only to find myself facing my attacker.

Death has come for me. He's real—a dark-skinned skyscraper with massive horns that rise above his head like a bull's and long claws sharp as knives. I am terrified and mesmerized by his red glowing eyes like something straight from Hell. His powerful muscles ripple. This could be a scene from a movie, though nothing that I have ever seen.

He's real. This is freaking real.

He stops in front of me, smirking. "Little witch doesn't know how to play yet. I see."

His fangs show white against his dark skin. I notice that his belt is laden with various types of knives and other weapons. Favoring my injured left shoulder, I scoot away from him. I've got to get away.

"This isn't as satisfying as I had hoped, but your heart will taste good either way!"

He lunges for me. I roll my body and push my knee off the ground to jump into a run.

I'm dead for sure if I can't move. As I pop up, the unbelievable happens! A ball of white light passes me and hits Death's chest and throws him back against a tree. He's down.

Scrambling, I turn to run, but halt as I find myself face-to-face with a warrior. He's in dark and sleek full-body armor. Have I seen him before? He is the most gorgeous guy I have ever set eyes on, with wavy hair and assessing eyes. I go from full-on flight mode to completely stunned. I can't move.

His commanding voice is but a whisper. "Stay quiet and hide."

I nod, wince and touch my bloody, throbbing shoulder. Something is stuck in it—a knife, a branch, a freaking Mack truck, I don't know! The pain pulses all over my back and side. I try to control my breathing so that it's quiet, but I'm starting to

MAGICK

shake. I have no control. I hope this warrior is a good guy who doesn't want me equally dead or I'm in big trouble.

Death laughs.

"Ah, the Guardian Captain comes to protect his little witchy queen wannabe, does he? Finally, an opponent worth my time!" The creature huffs again and again, as if smelling the air.

The gorgeous guy vanishes from my side. I hide behind the brush next to some trees and hug my knees to be as small as possible without causing more pain in my shoulder and back. I close my eyes. I try to slow my breath to find my magick. Where the hell is it? Pain overrides everything. I tug on my hoodie's zipper; my cotton shirt is sticky with sweat. I touch my shoulder and it feels wet—blood.

Smash!

The loud crash is followed by a tree falling next to me and I nearly scream. A white ball of light illuminates the forest. Then I hear the clanging of metal. Swords? Someone falls hard.

I ready myself to run.

"You can come out now, Willow."

He knows my name?

I slowly stand, my fear abated, then bend forward just as quickly. I wobble. Blood pools down my side. My shirt is soaked. I walk over to the animal-death-creep thing and kick him in the groin.

"Asshole!" I yell. My bloody hand starts to light up with the scrolling design. Geez, finally!

In his unconsciousness, he takes it like most men and curls to the side.

The gorgeous guy smirks. "Um . . . okay then." Shaking his finger at the creature, he says, "No children, Tertium."

"Tertium? This thing has a name? You know him?" I take a small step back, holding my left arm steady.

His head tilts to the side. "Yes, by reputation only. He's not a 'thing,' he's a demon blood warrior." He says this like it's a well-known fact.

63

I shake my head, not believing what just happened.

"For simplicity, he's an assassin. Although not a very good one." He kicks at the demon's feet. Then he throws a stone to the ground, which unfolds and grows four times its size, focusing light on Tertium.

Tertium opens his eyes and stares at me. "More will come. Your father will pay too, little witch. The demons will feast on his heart for all the glorious dark—"

Suddenly he's gone. The light shrinks back to its small stone shape.

My gorgeous hero sticks out his hand. "Enough of the mysterious. I'm Rhydian. Your father sent me to watch over you."

Watch over me? Rhydian doesn't look that much older than me. Wow, that face. I clear my thoughts and gesture to where Tertium just vanished. "Thank you for that."

"Yeah. Tertium isn't much of a threat. All bark, not much bite. Whoa!" He winces at me and points to my shoulder.

"It's bad, isn't it? It freakin' hurts like nothing I've ever felt before." Although the pain is starting to fade, so is my vision and balance. I think I might pass out.

He stands behind me. He moves my hair to the side and is touching my back, looking at my wound. I can barely feel him there, just the throbbing.

"It's gonna hurt for a second, but I can heal you quickly enough. Ready?"

Hell no!

"Okay," I say in an exhale, and hold on to a tree partly to brace myself and partly to stand. A moment later my back and shoulder erupt in sharp pain and I scream, white knuckling on the tree.

Then Rhydian's hand is pushing into my wound and soothing warmth takes over, followed by tingling. The iron smell of blood is overwhelmed with the smell of antiseptic. It feels like my muscles are stitching back together. The pain is gone, as if novocain has been rubbed inside all over. I straighten and wipe my face of tears and possible snot. A few moments ago I survived my first assassination attempt; now I'm sure I look like a blubbering mess.

"You did well. It's healed," Rhydian says.

Facing him, I feel embarrassed for some reason. Surely a warrior like him sees these kinds of wounds all the time.

"Thank you."

"Of course." A push of a button on his wrist band seems to disintegrate his armor before my eyes, revealing his regular clothes. He wears dark jeans and a gray long sleeve shirt that hugs his biceps and lean frame. He looks like a college student, maybe in his early twenties. His hazel eyes have specks of yellow in them.

I feel strangely at ease with him, but I don't think I know him. I can't stop staring.

"Have we met before?" I ask.

"I know your father, Aiden—Mr. Warrington. He and my family are friends. I'm a Guardian assigned to you for your protection." His friendly smile is off-putting only because it makes him even more attractive. "I don't think we've formally met until today."

A little creepy. If only his face and those eyes weren't so damn—

Okay, focus. My father.

"Does he know I'm here?" I snap unexpectedly. Did he send this guy to drag me home since I wasn't supposed to leave the house?

"I haven't spoken to him in several days." His brow creases in concern. "I should give him a call about what just happened."

"He doesn't know I'm here!" I shout out. "Rhydian, right?" He nods to confirm that I have his name right. "You don't need to—"

I can hear the faint calling of my friends. They sound worried. "Willow, where are you? Willow?"

How the hell am I going to explain this? I look down at my

bloody shirt, then up at Rhydian and across the flattened forest. I sigh in defeat.

Tertium would have been easier to explain if he wasn't trapped inside a stone.

Emily runs through the trees in front of us, looking determined. She slides to a halt, looking directly at Rhydian with her eyes squinted.

He grabs me in a quick movement as she steps forward, standing tall, then unexpectedly waves and blows me a kiss.

What the crazy hell?

Awkward. It's like she knows something that I don't. Like that dream in the psych rehab facility . . .

For a nanosecond, Emily's in front of us, and then she's not. I feel a change of footing and I stumble backward. Rhydian is holding me from behind protectively. It feels too intimate, too close, and I try to put space between our bodies.

A whirlwind of force pushes me forward and backward, but he holds me steady. The world has gone blurry and I can't see anything solid, just whites and grays smeared together in a fog. Time is folding in on itself, in on me, and outward, the pull-push sensation of weightlessness. I lean forward and my feet are on solid ground again. I feel the immediate absence of Rhydian's arms and body.

We are no longer in the forest. Instead, I'm in a room surrounded by large men.

CHAPTER 9

W here the heck am I? The three men around Rhydian and me are intimidating, muscled, and tall. One even has bruised knuckles. I step backward, away from them, only to run into another. Are these friendlies? They look to be about Rhydian's age.

"Okay, guys, back off. Give her a little space," says Rhydian.

One of the men points to my side, where my hoodie is stained with blood. "Were you in a battle? Is she hurt?" His hair is dark and curly.

Rhydian explains what happened and that he healed me. They seem to relax, and the one with bruised knuckles turns around and sits in a La-Z-Boy chair. I realize that I'm in a living room of some kind—a cabin room judging from the log walls. A small fire in the fireplace gives off light and heat. It's the only thing comforting and familiar in the room.

I turn to Rhydian. "Where are we? Who are these guys?"

All except the one in the La-Z-Boy chair smile at me. His dark menacing glare seems concentrated directly at me.

"Guardians," Rhydian says in a low voice.

"Oh. Hello." All return the greeting except, again, the one in the La-Z-Boy. He seems to be sizing me up.

"How about we get you cleaned up," Rhydian says. He guides me just outside of the room to a staircase. I don't know why I'm blindly following him, except that if he wanted me dead, he could have killed me back in the woods. He made it sound like he was assigned by my father to watch me, and I believe that—it totally sounds like my over-protective father.

We turn right at the top of the stairs. I yawn, covering my mouth. There are closed doors on each side of the hall. He opens one and I walk in. He points to another closed door. "The bathroom is in there."

"Thank you."

"Shirts and clothes are in the dresser over there. Feel free to use this room if you want to lay down or anything. I'll be downstairs."

"Can't you just take me home?" I ask.

Rhydian glances at the floor. "No. I have instructions to keep you away."

"Instructions?" My voice hitches.

He's still avoiding my eyes.

"Why? What is going on?"

He doesn't answer right away. I go to the bathroom and splash water on my face, cooling the anger that is building up inside me. Patting my face dry, I turn toward the bedroom. Rhydian is sitting on the bed.

"We're off-grid," he says. "Your father and mine think there's a coup of some kind going on at the High Coven. As soon as the coast is clear, I'll deliver you to your father."

"He didn't tell me any of this." I pull the hair tie from my wrist and put my hair up, trying to take in everything that Rhydian said. I unzip my hoodie and take it off, looking it over. It's completely ruined. My shirt looks even worse. Pulling open the dresser drawer, I find a small stack of T-shirts. I grab the black one on top and walk to the bathroom to slip it on.

"When did you talk to my father last?" I ask from the bathroom.

"It was my father who contacted me when I was on my way to find you."

The shirt is three sizes too big. I gather it on the side and tie a knot so it fits better. Rhydian stares at me when I walk out, eyes wide and assessing.

"I need to call my friends and let them know I'm okay," I say. "I totally disappeared on them; they probably called the police." I pace the room thinking about Daniel and about Emily's strange reaction to seeing me. Oh god, how am I going to explain any of this to them?

Rhydian steps in front of me, stopping me from pacing. "Tell me how you know a valkyrie. I saw her acknowledge you."

I start to chuckle, but his eyes are serious. "You mean Emily? She's been my friend for over three years. She's just Emily. What's a valkyrie?"

"The valkyrie choose heroic slain warriors to become immortal as einherjar and fight under valkyrie command. They've been around forever, originally from the Norse plane before it was destroyed. Typically, seeing a valkyrie means death," Rhydian says, his brows raised.

I almost didn't see the La-Z-Boy Guardian in the doorway, his dark clothes and skin, blended in the dark hallway, his eyebrows also raised at me.

"What?" I challenge him.

"So, your best buddy is a valkyrie, eh?" His accent sounds Irish. "Ya know, valkyrie are a rare female warrior breed and they're the best in all of Edayri. So you might wanna recheck that friendship, 'cause if push comes to shove, she's gonna choose her blooded over the likes of a Wiccan—especially a royal." He spits the last part like it tastes bad in his mouth.

"And who are you?" I spit back. He is immediately not my favorite. Apparently this Guardian is judging me, so I might as well return the favor.

He huffs and throws his hand in the air in frustration, turning around. "Food is ready," he says as he walks away.

My stomach growls at the mention of food. I follow Rhydian back downstairs to an open kitchen and hearth.

"Let me introduce everyone to you, Willow," Rhydian says. "Cross, you've met—excellent in battle strategy and fighting, and pissing people off."

Cross shoots Rhydian a squinted stare, but he ignores him and continues.

"On your right is Quinn, our resident medic, IT wizard, and typical geek." Quinn nods distractedly at me. "And this is Tullen. He's our historian and religious conscience."

Tullen has a different appearance from the others, with strawberry blond hair pulled up in a man bun and a beard in a bright shade of red. Everyone else is clean-shaven with short hair.

Rhydian and Quinn seem to be the youngest in the group, although not by much.

There's not much pretense when Cross brings the food to the table. They all dig in quickly. I follow suite as my stomach betrays me with a loud growl.

After we eat, Tullen smiles at me. Cross still looks irritated with his pinched lips and squinting eyes. Quinn leaves the room, calling someone on his cell phone.

I break the silence. "Can you let me text my friends? I understand we can't go back but they are probably freaking out."

Rhydian shakes his head. "That isn't a good idea."

"Why? Lucy will call the police." I remember he knows nothing of my life, my friends. "She's one of my best friends. You haven't met her, but you saw Emily before you—by the way, how did we get here?"

"Transporting magick," he says matter-of-factly.

Tullen taps his wristband; it's the same one Rhydian is wearing. It occurs to me that they all have the same wristband.

Nothing good will come from me disappearing.

"It's dangerous," Rhydian says, answering my first question. "Your magick is unbound and more will be hunting for you.

Before you take the crown at the winter solstice, you're fair game."

"For what, exactly?"

"Changing of the guard—taking over the crown. It would raise a li'l chaos. All are eager to take yer blood magick." Cross's eyebrows are taut and he takes a drink of coffee.

"I don't understand what you're talking about," I reply, confused.

Tullen says, "You have to die for your magick to be released. If it goes to the void, no biggie, but if someone incorporates it into themselves, it becomes their magick."

I bite my lip, contemplating that. He means the demons are coming for me.

Tullen gets my attention. "Hey, I don't mean to scare you. Do you know much about Edayri? The realm in general?"

Cross chuckles. "Hell, no she doesn't. She's what Quinn calls a noob."

"You're what I call an asshole," I respond matter-of-factly to Cross.

He seems to relish my retort. Tullen gets up and, grinning, pats Cross on the back. Rhydian tries to hide his amusement but smiles unsuccessfully. I haven't done anything to warrant Cross's smart-ass attitude, but I'm not going to be intimidated by him. He seems to acknowledge this; his dark brown eyes crinkle at the sides with a smirk. He likes to push, and I will push back.

"Basically, you're a pure source of magick and all the crazies are gonna want a taste," Tullen says from the kitchen. "Most Wiccans and beings have limited magick and physical powers, even the noble and the High Coven."

Rhydian chimes in. "Guardians, too. We have some physical magick, but these"—he points to the wrist band—"amplify our magick among other things. "

I recall Rhydian in his dark armor in the woods. The back of my neck tingles as I think about seeing him for the first time. Right before he saved me from the blood warrior demon.

I really am a noob to this world.

Quinn comes bounding into the kitchen. "Rhy, Eoin has discovered us missing and he's on the trail. They know Willow is out and has been located."

"Shit," Cross grumbles.

"He's calling out for information on us too. He's pissed."

"Who is Eoin?" I ask.

"Eoin, is the head of the Guardians, the commander," Rhydian replies. "I guess you could say we are rogue for the moment."

I listen to them, feeling guilty. I'm the reason these guys are in trouble. Rhydian says that my physical signature would be tracked back home and to my friends. He and Cross discuss their next move to take me somewhere else.

"If they don't find me, will they hurt my friends or my father?" I ask.

"Depends on who 'they' are. A fae isn't too vicious, but depending on the demon and how upset they are at your blood, they could take out their anger on someone," Tullen responds.

I stand up, alarmed. "I gotta go."

"To where? We're rogue; our ability to help is limited. I swore an oath to protect you. Your father will be all right."

Cross chuckles sarcastically at Rhydian's comment.

Rhydian ignores him. "I'll go check the campsite if that will make you feel better."

"Can I borrow a cell and just text my friends?"

"Bad idea. Then the bad guy sees who to torture to get ya to come out," Cross says.

What the hell! This is insane!

Quinn's arms reach out to steady him; from what, I couldn't see. "Did you sense it?" he asks Rhydian and Cross.

They nod. Then a shock wave goes through my body. I must look surprised because Cross makes a comment about me feeling it too. "It's the rift," Tullen explains. "It occurs when the Edayri realm portals are split between planes."

"The British are coming," Cross says, looking around like someone might come through the wall.

There's a shock wave again, although this one makes me step back to steady myself and lasts longer.

Tullen and Quinn touch their wrist bands, which immediately turn to liquid metal to cover their bodies. It works so quickly that if I didn't see it happen, I wouldn't have believed it. Everyone is suited up in sleek dark armor.

"That was the fourth movement," Quinn says.

"Ladies, we're going to have company. We need to move!" Cross has a wide grin and his eyes sparkle, like a dog getting a treat.

The rogue Guardians leave the kitchen one by one and move downstairs. Rhydian and I follow them into an empty concrete basement.

"Have you used your magick before?" Rhydian asks.

"Yes," I say in a whisper. "I'm not well in control yet, but I'm working on it." I don't know why I need to say that to Rhydian. I feel like such an outsider with them.

Tullen asks, "Do you have it in your mind?" He gestures to the rogue Guardians.

"What?" I ask.

Rhydian nudges me and whispers, "Don't worry, I'll transport us together. We need to move to another safe house." His armor is similar to the others' but fits him differently and there's an insignia on his pectoral similar to the Goddess's symbol on my mother's necklace.

"How do I transport?"

The guys all blur out, one by one.

"Visualize where you need to go," Rhydian says. "It's like folding into yourself and folding out where you need to be."

It sounds crazy, but it's my only shot at getting back home to my friends. *I can do this*, I think, trying to build up my mental confidence.

Rhydian reaches for my hand, and I close my eyes and visualize the foyer of my home. I feel my body vibrate and allow the flowing movement to envelope me.

I hear Rhydian yell "No!" When I open my eyes he blurs away, reaching for me. As I pull away from him, my vision clears. I'm in the foyer of my house. I did it!

CHAPTER 10

It's early in the morning and the house is empty and dark. I can barely make out the grandfather clock down the hall near the formal dining room. The sconces in the entryway flicker with faux light, and I can see the table in the middle of the foyer. I open and close my eyes. Everything is black and white like a noir film.

This isn't right.

The entry light turns on and blinds me. When I refocus my eyes, nothing has changed; my vision is still without technicolor.

"Hello? Willow? Mr. Warrington?" Mrs. Scott is in her robe, her hair still messy from sleep. Her plump frame and cheery face are a welcome sight. She shuffles in her house shoes and tugs at the lapel on her robe.

"Mrs. Scott."

She looks right at me and again says, "Hello? Who's here?" She is biting her lip and shivering. She can't see me. I get right in front of her and wave my hands in front of her face, but there's no reaction.

"I know someone is in here. You'd better leave if you know what's good for you," she warns.

She must be able to feel me there but not see me. I'm just

happy to see her. I want to hug her, not only to comfort her but myself as well. I need to lean into her pillowy body with her sweet, flowery scent. I need my family—her, my father. To understand what's going on and how Rhydian fits into the mix. Is he someone I can trust?

"Something is wrong," Mrs. Scott whispers. "I feel it." She turns away from me and walks to the front door slowly.

"I'm here!" I try to get her attention but it's useless. She can't see me. I'm caught in some kind of in-between from transporting wrong. I'm not really in her presence but I can see her. Rhydian warned me and I ignored him; I have no idea how to get out of this. I try to transport again by myself, concentrating on the foyer of my house, but I don't move.

A loud noise from outside shakes the house. The furniture moves and the hanging lights wave in warning. Something else is here. I exhale to control my breath. If I get scared like before, my magick will be of no use to anyone.

Bam!

"Oh goddess," Mrs. Scott says, clutching the lapel of her robe and shuffling backward toward the foyer table.

The front double doors fly open and she's flung back to the wall near the sitting room as if pushed by an invisible force. Something flies up the stairs, leaving only a trail of gray smoke. A large, horned demon with dark red skin walks in followed by three people in cloaks.

Mrs. Scott screams and holds up her hands in surrender.

My power is pulsing on the surface of my skin, but no one can see me. Will my magick even work if I'm not truly there?

I throw a light ball at the group coming in the open door. It goes through them like it was never there.

A cloaked figure floats through me and comes to stand in front of the red-skinned demon who resembles the devil similar to the demon from the woods who stabbed me in the shoulder. He's not the same, yet I feel the phantom pain in my shoulder. The familiar hum of my magick is gone.

"Father, help! Help her!" I scan the room to see if anyone hears me, but the group in front of me seems unaware. I yell again. "Please, Daddy!" I hold myself and hold my breath.

"Neither the girl nor Aiden is here. It's strange because I sense the girl. Maybe she left recently?" The voice coming from the purple cloak is female.

The demon huffs and smells the air. In a deep timbered voice, he says, "You're right, it's strong in this room." He focuses his yellow eyes on Mrs. Scott. "Where are they?"

I can see Mrs. Scott shake and I ache for her. He stands menacingly in front of her and touches her face with a clawed finger. She turns her face to the side. He will hurt her—his intention is clear to me. All I can see is the boy in the alley, the demon from the woods, and now this red devil hurting the kindest woman in the world. The woman who raised me and is not only family but my confident, my friend, and my surrogate mother.

I run and step in front of her. My magick swirls in my hands. "I'm right here! Don't you fucking touch her!" I scream, my vision blurry.

"Will you be cooperative or suffer the consequences?" he taunts.

No! No, no, no, this can't be happening.

"You will not take the crown. It isn't yours," Mrs. Scott says with a shaky voice. He leans over her. I try to touch her but my hand goes through her shoulder. It's as if I'm a ghost in this room. My voice hitches in my throat as I say her name again like a silent prayer for help.

Does she know I'm here?

"Oh? How do you know it's not already been taken? These are all just formalities at this point. The plot is enacted; your little girl will be but a casualty." He sneers, fangs showing.

"I'm okay! Mrs. Scott, please, please run—"

Mrs. Scott moves away from the wall and speaks to the one in the cloak standing amongst the other demons, their face hidden from view. "I see you. You should be ashamed," she says. "The Goddess most certainly is. You have denounced her and this chosen royal family." Tears spill down her chubby cheeks.

"Do it," says the lady in the purple cloak before she turns and floats out the front door.

My anger is at this demon in front of me. I know what he intends to do. I throw my conjured offensive magick light balls at him with absolutely no effect. I'm screaming and yelling. My arms are lighting up in the scrolling patterns of my magick, the design expanding from my hands to my wrists, elbows, upper arms, and shoulders.

She holds her hands up and there is a small glow of light. I try to add to it, to give her my magick—

Thud.

The demon is sheathing his bloody sword with an indifferent face.

I can't move.

I can't turn around.

I just keep throwing the light balls and trying everything I can to make them count. My vision is blurry. My shoulders slump in defeat when I see the dark liquid flow across the floor as the remaining demons leave the house.

Mrs. Scott.

I turn slowly to see her on the floor.

I can't catch the air through my sobs, screams only echoing in my ears. I drop to the floor and tentatively stroke her hair from her face, but it does nothing because I'm not there.

I sit, useless. My magick's hum is now silent. My thoughts are empty.

After the longest time I stand mechanically. The sun is rising through the glass windows in the entry way. I feel as if it's been only a few minutes, but it's most likely been an hour or more. I have to do something. She can't stay like this. It's not right.

A reflective light catches my eye, and I see that Mrs. Scott is clutching something in her hand. It's the necklace Sabine gave me—my mother's necklace. I want to feel Mrs. Scott's warm hug but instead it's her voice that rings in my ear.

"Ah, my sweetheart, Willow. I don't have much in magick but have attached what I have to this to be with you. As above and so below, blessed be your path." Her voice is gone and her warmth fades.

I wipe my face of the tears that remain and reach for the necklace, the pentacle of the Goddess. It slips through my fingers. I can't hold it.

If I ever thought I would be able to escape the choice for the crown, it's resolved in this moment—my choice was made by the person in the cloak when they ordered Mrs. Scott's death. They and that devil who did it will regret it.

I need help, but I don't know what to do. If Rhydian found me in the woods, could he help me here? Trying to use my magick, I silently call to Rhydian in my head. I don't know how to get out of this in-between, this hell. Will I be stuck here forever?

His voice, a welcome retreat from my drowning thoughts: "Willow? Where are you?"

I try to explain in my mind, wondering if it will work and trying not to hold my breath. A moment later I'm shielding my eyes from a bright light at the open door. Rhydian walks through as my Guardian and savior. I run to him and hug him for dear life. He's here. I can touch him and he can touch me. I sob into his shoulder. He's found me in this black-and-white in-between.

"How did you . . . ? No one else can see or hear me. How did you? Thank you, thank you, thank you."

"I'm blooded to you; I will always find you." He pulls back from holding me and sees Mrs. Scott. "We need to go; they will find you in this split plane. The rift is helping to conceal you, but not for long."

I nod in agreement. "Rhydian, Wiccans were here with demons."

He continues to look at Mrs. Scott. I can't bear it. I know

she's gone, but I can't see it anymore. If I do, I'll be torn apart. I need to keep it together.

A bright light appears and Dr. Evan is running at us, sliding to a stop.

"Dr. Evan?"

"Get away from him! He's a Guardian sent to kill you!" Dr. Evan yells. "Theon, now!"

A boy with long hair, Theon, appears from behind Dr. Evan and shifts into battle gear like a knight, similar to the Guardians but different. He draws a sword and advances so quickly that Rhydian pushes me to the side and morphs into his sleek armor. He is dark and brooding, his face not covered like Theon's.

Clank. The swords meet and they are fighting—but for what? Me?

Evan grabs my arm and transports us. My eyesight blurs as swords hit again and lights erupt. I say a silent prayer to anyone who will listen to protect Rhydian and to get me out of this nightmare.

CHAPTER 11

W hen I open my eyes I'm in the familiar surroundings of
Dr. Evan's office. I push myself up on the chaise lounge.

"Don't you dare say it—" I start. My magick's familiar hum is
a buzz in the back of my head. He knew. He knew about the
Guardians and what's going on and what I am. He knows.

"Say what, Willow? That was really close."

I start to think that everything that has happened in the last
several days isn't real; it was all in my head.

I'm losing my mind.

What about Mrs. Scott's death? The demons and Wiccans in
my home? Rhydian fighting that demon in the woods? The
Guardians? Sabine and my father?

Magick?

I go to touch my necklace—my mother's necklace—but
remember it's with Mrs. Scott, and I look at Dr. Evan to center
myself. He's in different clothes from when I was here last.
Isn't he?

"Willow. Focus, Willow," he says. His voice is smooth,
calming.

The office is twisting and turning. It's like those fun-house mirrors at the fair. I am definitely losing it. I close my eyes and breathe deeply.

My stomach is in knots.

"What's up with her?" Theon asks, entering the room. Reality snaps back into focus. Small horns are revealed through his long, messy hair. He's part demon? Or something else entirely.

"Whoa, look at her hands." Theon is holding his helmet and puts it on the desk in the middle of the room. "By the way, the Guardian is fine. Good fighter. I think I may find him just for fun next time." Theon stretches out his shoulders and neck. "Nice to get a workout with someone of similar skills."

Evan rolls his eyes.

I peer down and see that the scrolling pattern on my hands and arms is pulsing and flowing like a river. I push my sleeve up and see the design flowing there, too, and then push it back in place. I feel a hum inside as it flows up my arms and down my shoulders. It's impressive and it comforts me, makes me feel brave.

I'm not okay with being in the presence of a demon and I don't trust Dr. Evan as a result of his being with Theon. Something is off here and I'm tired of not knowing. I grit my teeth to steady myself.

"Fancy that," Dr. Evan says, looking at my hands. He takes off his jacket and throws it on a chair in front of his desk. "Hell of a night. You know the Guardians have orders to kill you. What were you doing at your house with a Guardian? Have others come to your house?"

"So, it's fair to say you aren't a real doctor?" I spit the question at him.

He shakes his head to confirm.

"As you're condemning me for being around a Guardian, exactly who are you, and why should I trust you?" I point at him in my emboldened state. I trusted this man—my doctor— to put me under hypnosis. Evan stands in front of me but

Theon stays at the desk working on a laptop. Probably a smart move.

"I really wanted more time for us to get to know one another before Sabine came riding in on her dark horse," Evan says.

"What does that mean? And how do you know Sabine? I assume you're a Wiccan?" I stand and pace the floor.

"Yes, I am Wiccan. Sabine's a bit complicated when it comes to me. I'm the bastard child of Harkin MacKinnon."

We're family? He doesn't seem to notice my utter surprise and my hinged mouth open.

He continues, "Harkin and I had an interesting relationship, to say the least, but Sabine and I . . . well, I was the reminder she hated and ignored."

"You're my uncle." I stand still, rooted. "Did you grow up with my . . . my mother?"

His face softens at the mention of my mother.

"I lived in the house with her from birth. I grew up with Liam and Nuala in the highlands of the Ember region in Edayri. The MacKinnon manor. It wasn't an awful childhood, but I stayed in the shadows as the dirty little secret of the family. Liam and Nuala were the joy of Harkin and the noble Wiccan covens." He pauses and turns away from me. "Nuala was wonderful to me. I was her baby brother." He smiles, and it reminds me of a photo of my mother where she's holding me, laughing and her eyes sparkling. "When Liam left it hurt, but when Nuala ran away with Aiden, it broke the foundation of the family. Harkin became bitter and I became a bargaining chip to retain the royal line and royal coven positioning."

I walk over to Evan, wanting to comfort him. He's my uncle, but I'm cautious. Now that I'm looking, I see familiar features of my mother in him—dark blond hair and dark blue eyes.

"Why didn't you tell me this in the beginning? Why pose as my doctor?" I ask. "Do you get how messed up that is? Surely it's illegal."

"I hope you can forgive me for that," he says. "I needed to

ease my way in. Nuala and I used to do it when we were younger—come together in magickal riffs and alternate thought planes it's a tease on reality but those in it can talk safely, or in my case, play when I was younger without outside influences. It was a safe way for me to reach you. I knew you were bound from your magick. You see, Sabine and everyone else thinks I'm dead."

I step back. Theon, who's been quiet till now, chuckles under his breath. "Surprise."

"And who are you?" I snap.

"I'm Theon. No familial relation." He goes back to typing.

"He's a good friend," Evan says. "Come on, let's get you something warm to drink and talk more." He walks to a door and I follow.

The familiar office gives way to an apartment. It's confusing. I've been to the medical suite before, but it wasn't someone's home. Through the door there's an open floor with a spacious, sparse modern living room and kitchen. I sit at the bar while Evan prepares tea.

"Just so you know, Rhydian has gone rogue from the Guardians. He wasn't there to hurt me, only to protect me. He said he's blood bonded or something like that. I dunno."

Evan raises his eyebrows.

"What?" I ask.

"Do you know what that means?" Evan says. "To have a blooded vow, a bond?"

I shrug. I figure it's like the Secret Service, but I don't want to sound foolish, so I kept my mouth shut.

"He made a bonded blood pact, and his life and duty are yours."

"Okay . . ."

"Without his choice in the matter. Or yours, I might add." He sounds bitter. "You took his vow lightly."

"I didn't, he did this with my father."

"He will die for you, literally. Should something happen to

you, he will follow to protect you in Heaven, Valhalla, or in the Elysian Fields—whichever you're inclined to believe."

I didn't know what to think or say. Why would someone commit to something like that without knowing the other person? I don't know a lot about Rhydian, considering I just met him, but I can't understand why he'd do this without knowing me at all. I don't want to be a puppet master in someone else's life.

"Yeah, a little crazy, huh? Let me tell you: Wiccans, in general, are stubborn in their profound beliefs, one of which is the dependence on royal blood lines from the Goddess. Lucky you for being in that line of fire."

"Sure, lucky me." I feel like I may collapse I'm so tired. I see the sun through the windows, bright and high in the sky. I have no idea of the time, but it feels like I've been up for over a day.

We finish our tea and Theon comes out of the office. Out of his armor, he resembles a grunge teenager about my age. "Evan, we need to get her to the High Coven. They're meeting tomorrow. Sabine called the meeting, as you anticipated."

Evan nods, but I disagree.

"I need to go home and talk to my father."

Evan nods his head up at Theon. He shakes his head no.

"Share with the class, please. What?" I demand.

Theon turns and goes back to the office.

"Just tell me."

"Your father is missing. I've been trying to reach him. Theon is excellent at tracking and he hasn't had any luck, either."

I stand and pace. "What? Oh no. That's why Mrs. Scott—" Her name hangs on my tongue and chokes me. I wipe the immediate tear that falls. "She was looking for both of us."

"I'm sorry about Mrs. Scott. Really, I am. I think whatever form of magick she had, she imparted to you. It's why your magick is flowing; it's compounding. It takes a lot out of a person."

I don't like that he talks about Mrs. Scott in the past tense. I don't like that he knows she gave her magick to me. He may be my uncle, but something is off.

I brush the faded white designs on my hands and fingers. They come to life and glow blue. "Can one person give their magick to another?"

Evan sits down on a modern sofa that faces the windows.

"Only someone very powerful can loan magick, but this is dark magick. You can only impart magick in death or send it to the void."

I immediately think of Father. He has been teaching me about dark magick, which is his heritage. It isn't like most conventional magick, apparently.

"This place is well protected, so you can stay here as long as you'd like. However, in return, I need you to take me to the High Coven tomorrow," Evan says.

"How would I take you? I don't even know where it will be."

"It's not a problem. It's at the Hallowed Hall in Edayri by the Lunar Fields, but the invite will have a magick seal that will only allow those invited. Those in attendance will be your High Coven when you take the crown." His eyes sparkle and the hair on my neck stands on end. I try to keep myself calm.

"What does that mean? My High Coven? Is that like a council or something?"

"Kind of, they hold power over commanding the Guardians, especially in the absence of the Crown." He traces a pentagram on his palm and says, "They represent royal rule over Edayri by the elements; air, fire, earth, and water."

"What's the last element at the top?" A yawn escapes my mouth. "Sorry about that. I haven't had any sleep for over twenty-four hours."

"It's the spirit element."

"So we need to go there to get the price off my head with the other Guardians?"

"Other Guardians?"

Another yawn escapes. "Yes, the rogue Guardians are helping me."

Evan nods and leads me to a guest room with a private bathroom. His apartment isn't large but it's certainly comfortable. I decide to take a shower. Unable to hold it in any longer, I melt into my emotions. My tears and anguish for Mrs. Scott, my fear of what's happening, and my hopelessness at being able to change any of it pour out of me. The water turns cold and I lean away from the tile and turn off the water. By the time I pull myself off the floor and get out, the mirror isn't foggy.

I brush my hair and examine the scrolling design that extends from my arms and shoulders down my back like a pair of wings. It's beautiful, but it disappears and is barely visible unless I call to my magick. When I call, it lights up in a neon blue, purplish color similar to the light ball I can conjure with my hand.

I put on the pair of shorts and T-shirt that Evan has laid on the bed. They fit me and it makes me uncomfortable. Was he anticipating my stay here? I pace the room and go to the window. Looking out, I see we are several floors up in a city I don't recognize. I hear Theon and Evan talking in the living room. I'm tired, but I want to listen to what they're saying. My magick flowing, I get into bed and concentrate on self-projection. I haven't tried this before—I'm not sure it will even work—but I'm pleasantly surprised when it goes smoothly. I ghost down the hall and hang back so I can hear but not be seen.

"Evan, I know you're doing this for Meghan. You should tell her what Sabine and Harkin did."

"In time. But first, we need to stay on task. It's tough to manage as it is. She's a lot like Nuala. She'll run; I feel it. We need to keep her away from that rogue group and especially Rhydian," Evan says. "She says he's bonded to her by blooded vow. Can you reach out and tell her we have Willow? Maybe she'll back off on her primary agenda."

"Fine. If I don't come back, it's because she's killed me," Theon says.

They both laugh and Evan claps Theon on the back. Evan goes to his office and Theon opens the balcony doors. I pull myself back to the bed and my eyes flutter closed.

Where is my father?

Exhaustion overtakes me to the unease of nothingness.

I toss and turn, feeling wetness around me. I open my eyes to darkness and cold. I push myself up from a concrete floor.

What—?

The liquid in front of me is dark and thick. I stand and my eyes start to adjust until I can make out bars ahead of me. I'm in some sort of jail cell? I step over the liquid and hear a shifting noise behind me. I turn but can't make anything out. I know I'm not alone.

"Hello?" I whisper.

The voice that answers croaks and is strained: "Willow? Sweetheart?"

My father! "Dad! Where are you?"

"Don't move. I don't know how long—the connection isn't strong. I'm very weak."

I call my magick and it flows, making the square cell glows. My father is lying on a cot in the corner. His face is beaten and bloody. He seems like he's lost weight; his clothes pool around him. I want to step forward, but I'm afraid about the connection he spoke of. If I lose it, I lose him.

"Willow . . . Evan. His agenda is beyond yours. Go to the High Coven and get their support with the Guardians. Find me and Lucy."

My heartbeat thunders in my chest at Lucy's name.

"Rhydian." He coughs, blood on his lips. "Rhydian, seek him out. Call to him, he'll come to you." He coughs again. The tears flow down my cheeks and I clench my fists at my side.

"I love you, Daddy. I'll find you and Lucy." My voice shakes.

"I love you too."

The creak of a door sounds. He waves his fingers and blurs before my eyes. All I can do is scream in anguish, and I wake up in the darkness of Evan's guest room. Heavy steps are coming. This real life nightmare is getting worse and I don't have time to curl up and dissolve into nothing.

Theon opens the door. "Are you—?"

My magick is fueled by fear and anger. I command the air around me and throw him back down the hall into the opposite wall. I envision my jeans and shoes and they materialize on my body.

I walk through the door to find Theon out cold.

The satisfaction of eliciting a physical outcome on someone —wow, what a rush. I should be scared of it, but I need to leave and I refuse to contemplate it now. I step over Theon and feel my magick hum. It feels like I can't transport from inside the apartment. I go to the balcony, but it's locked.

Determined and feeling powerful beyond what I've tried before, I step back, wave my hand, and command the glass to break in the sliding door. Evan comes running out of the office. I ignore him and step outside, quickly transporting myself to a white sandy beach from my childhood.

They're gone along with the apartment. The wind blows in my face and the moon lights up the beach. I came to this beach with my dad when I was little after mother had passed away, after the accident. My resolve is stone: I'll get my dad and Lucy back, and nothing and no one is going to get in my way. In fact, it excites me that someone might try. Power and strength radiate through me with the hum of my magick. Shouldn't I be scared? I'm not. I'm in control.

I take in the smell of the ocean and silently send a message: *Rhydian, find me.*

PART III

Fate whispers to the girl,
"You cannot withstand the storm."
The girl whispers back:
"I am the storm."

CHAPTER 12

I sit in the sand mindlessly touching my mother's necklace, watching the gentle waves lap the beach in a mesmerizing rhythm. It's distracting, quieting my mind. I don't hear or see Rhydian arrive, but suddenly he's sitting next to me.

"Hey."

"Hi."

He seems comfortable watching the waves with me in silence. I'm nervous to talk to him now that I know more about things—the crown, the political coups, the blood vow. For some reason, I want him to agree with all that I need to do. I know he won't let me down with the blood vow. I wonder if he has no choice but to agree if I give him an option. The thought hangs in the back of my mind—would he follow without the blood vow?

"I need you to go with me to the High Coven in a few hours," I say.

He raises his eyebrows at me. "Which is a dangerous mission. Why?"

The word dangerous excites me. What is with my magick? It's nudging me, taunting me to flex my power. I'm no longer nervous to do something wrong. I know my thoughts and will that drive it, but I'm still not familiar with Edayri and the realm in general. I need guides.

"I need the Guardians' help to rescue my father and my friend. They have been taken and are being tortured to lure me out."

He turns to me. "You have Guardians—me and the guys. You don't need the High Coven involved in this. They'll turn it into a political move to tie you down." He thrusts his hand into his hair. "Where did they take you? Evan and Theon. I've been looking for you. All of us, I mean—Tullen, Quinn, even Cross." He smirks on the last name.

"Even Cross, you say?" I peer sideways at him.

Rhydian snickers. "Cross is pretty much grumpy about everything, but he's loyal almost to a fault. He isn't too keen on the royal caste system, though, and blames Harkin for a battle that shouldn't have taken place. But his loyalty to his father and what the Guardians generally stand for keep him with us. He likes to challenge everything and everyone." He rolls his eyes, as if reliving something that recently happened with Cross.

"Oh, good. I thought it was just me."

Rhydian and I laugh together. I'm comfortable around him. He's handsome but not overly distracting like when we first met. Still, I find it hard not to stare at him. His perfect white smile and full lips draw me in.

"Seriously though, I was shocked to see Evan. I thought he was dead," Rhydian says. "What did he want? Where did he take you and how did you get away?"

Do I reveal everything that I've learned to Rhydian? Maybe he knows more than I do. There's just something about him that makes me trust him, besides knowing that he's made a blooded vow and that my father asked me to seek him out.

I stare down at my sand-covered feet and tell him everything.

He is taking it all in when I ask, "Why are you and the others rogue to help me? Out of duty? Because I don't want that. I don't want the responsibility of anyone getting hurt because of me. I didn't ask for any of this." I especially don't want to make someone do something they don't want, like this blood vow. Why would he do that?

"When we were in school for training to be Guardians, we took oaths to protect the crown and its interests. Now the crown is absent, and the High Coven is taking on that responsibility and warping it. You are the crown, whether or not you've completely accepted that yet." His eyes search mine. "There was an idea that the crown could be divided and bring harmony before the Convergence. Many are starting to recognize the Convergence is already beginning to happen. The truly powerful are afraid—afraid that you're an outsider and that your youth will bring change that doesn't suit them. I have the feeling, along with others, that you're the one who can bring about a positive change."

"Ah. So it's not all about me then?" I tag his shoulder gently and he chuckles.

His smile and relaxed demeanor are so attractive.

"What's the Convergence?" I ask.

His lips purse. "That is tough to answer."

"Why?"

He shrugs. "Because it's mythical and no one really understands it. There are some old histories that say the Convergence happens every two thousand years or so within the various realms to bring them together. Some say it's a contest of sorts; others say it's colonization and a war of territories." He runs his hand through his hair, revealing a golden ring clipped to the top of his ear. "The thing is, as a Guardian, I've been training for this unknown threat of the Convergence for a couple of years. If you ask Tullen, he'll say it's coming in the next year or so. If you ask Quinn, he'll say the Convergence is a myth. I don't know what I believe, but I do feel a change from others like the valkyrie and demons. They seem to be preparing themselves, and since Wiccans are not always on friendly terms with other species, no one shares information. It's tragic if you ask me."

I am so out of my depth here. As Queen, I will have to address this Convergence, and yet I'm only seventeen. A few weeks ago my biggest decision was which cell phone case I wanted to buy. I stressed about the start of school and who would be in my classes, wondering if Daniel and I would see much of each other because of our different schedules.

Daniel.

Have I already forgotten my life?

My father was right—magick will come whether I want it or not. But will my friends and Daniel accept me still? Am I still me? I'm just enhanced; surely I can go back to my life once I find Father. He and I can put something in place that allows me to finish out my senior year and got to college. I hope.

Rhydian and I sit in silence. I notice that our hands are close to each other in the sand as we sit back and watch the sun peeking over the horizon. The colors in the sky are amazing, purples that combine with blue hues and give way to red and orange.

"Nice spot you've chosen."

"Yes. Yes, it is. It was simpler when I was here before." I let the memory hang on my tongue and reminisce privately about my father holding my six-year-old hand. Rhydian reaches and gently brushes his fingers on mine.

I look back at Rhydian. "It's about time. We should probably go."

We arrive in Edayri at the Lunar Fields, and it's like my soul knows where I belong. There is lushness and life in the greenery all around, from the grass to the perfectly manicured trees to the gently rolling hills. The Hallowed Hall sits ahead of us with beautiful gardens and fountains. There are people scattered throughout the space, talking and sitting together. All are dressed in cloaks of various colors and patterns. I glance down at myself and conjure a red cloak similar to those in front of me by only thinking about it. Rhydian nods at the change in my clothes. My ability to use my magick is becoming easier, even if the chatter in my head hasn't stopped.

Rhydian turns to me. He's very close. Our agreement is that I will enter the Hallowed Hall by myself and he will wait on the outskirts while the others cause some chaos elsewhere in the Lunar Fields to distract the Guardians searching for me. The Guardians are ordered to retain me if they catch me. Where it goes from there is unclear, but I have the impression from Evan that someone in the High Coven is pulling strings to be rid of me.

"It's hard for me to leave you here," Rhydian breathes.

He's too close, and I could easily be pulled away from what I need to do, from who I am. I'm with Daniel, even if that seems like a lifetime ago. I step away from him.

"Thank you for the lift. I'll ring you when I'm done." I tap my head, grin, then walk down the path to the entry of the lush gardens.

My ability to walk into the Hallowed Halls unnoticed is abated with the arrival of Sabine. She stands out in her deep purple cloak. There are many eyes on her as she sees me.

"Willow?"

My magick stirs in my hand with nervous energy. Is Sabine someone I can trust? Will she allow me to attend? Or is this over, right here and now?

I nod but keep my hood in place.

"I'm glad you're here. It's a good step to meet with your High Coven and show your intent and goodwill toward our ways," she says.

Is this a trap?

I follow Sabine through the tall wooden doors. Inside, Sabine walks through the open courtyard to another pair of similarly arched doors. She places her hand on the door and it glows before opening. I follow her inside.

The room has a circular table at its center around which sit four purple-cloaked figures, all female. Their eyes watch me as I follow Sabine to the empty seat. The woman who ordered Mrs. Scott's death wore a purple cloak. I shake my head trying to stay focused, for my father.

"And who is this?" one asks with a snicker.

Another claps her hands together and rubs them vigorously, as if excited for some major event.

Sabine stands by her chair. "You would have felt someone who didn't belong enter this room. May I introduce Willow, my granddaughter and successor to the crown." She sounds proud.

She introduces the snickering woman as Celestia and the excited one as Pansy.

I gently pull my hood back to reveal myself fully to the High Coven. They are assessing me just as I am assessing them.

Then the flurry of questions begins.

Celestia is first. "So, your intention is to come into your birthright?"

"How can you do that when you're an outsider?" the one with white hair asks.

"Have you used your magick yet?" Pansy is all smiles.

Celestia sneers. "What is your elemental magick? I bet she isn't even aware!"

Only three of the women at the table participate in the questions and discussion. The one to my right is surveying her fingernails, looking bored. She seems rather young among these women, not much older than me.

Part of me wants to run out the door. The other part of me wants to scream. I always hated having to do presentations in class and this feels no different, except that I'm less prepared on a topic I can't research.

"Stop throwing questions at her," Sabine thunders over the chatter.

I take advantage of the silence. "I've come here to ask for your approval and assistance. I need the Guardians; my father and friend have been taken."

Sabine's hand flies to her chest. "By who?"

"I imagine the same demons and Wiccans who came to my home and murdered a member of my family, Mrs. Juliette Scott."

The one who was staring at her nails is now watching me intently. Sabine introduces her as Aren.

"I understand that this High Coven has control over the Guardians," I say, "and I would like to—"

"No, no, no," Pansy says, bouncing her leg.

Sabine lays her hand on her shoulder. "Let's hear her out. Would you deny her only—"

"Sabine, we are set for you to take the crown," the white-haired one, introduced as Renata, says through tight, thin lips.

Sabine shakes her head, face flushed. So, Sabine can step in for the crown? Why didn't she say anything when we first met? I wonder why she wouldn't take the crown; it would be logical. She's from here and is far more powerful than me.

There's a shift in the room. Renata's statement is echoed by Celestia, Pansy, and Aren.

This is a lost cause. They don't want me here; they have plans to move forward without me. My magick stirs against the hypocrisy of this High Coven that claims to serve the crown—my crown.

Idiots. I don't need them. I walk back toward the door I had come through. "Thank you for your time."

"You can't accept the crown without our support," says Celestia, in a lower voice that makes the hair on my neck rise.

Are you going to stop me? I wonder to myself. That could be quite fun. Instead, staring directly into Celestia's cold, dark eyes, I say, "Actually, I only need the Goddess. Get ready to be replaced. I believe the crown decides who is in the High Coven along with all other things in Edayri. You should be ready for some changes, ladies."

Empowered by my father and from what I've read in the Book of Shadows, I slam the door behind me. A nervous breath escapes my throat and my hands shake slightly. I leave my hood down and walk through the open hall, out the front of the building, and through the gardens. Several seem to recognize me. I sense Rhydian and the others on the outskirts of the gardens.

Sorry, boys. Plans have changed!

I continue to stare straight ahead and go directly to the fountain at the center of the gardens. When I turn, Sabine and the other members of the High Coven are at the steps of the building. Guardians in armor come toward me from both sides of the building.

Do they want to detain me? They want to test what I can do and who I am? Fine! I don't need them. Rhydian is right.

My magick is eager and so am I. Without thinking much about it, I thrust my hands above my head and lightning shoots upward into the clear blue sky. I control the environment here; the clear day becomes my storm of warning. The wind picks up and the clouds move in on my command. The designs on my hands and arms glow with pulsing bright light. The people around the fountain have moved away, but not far. They seem torn between fascination and self-preservation.

All attention is on me and I relish it. I sneer at the High Coven. "Does this satisfy you?" I shout.

The people retreat further away and the Guardians become cautious in their advance. I command the wind around me and rise above the ground, peering down at them—the High Coven, Guardians, and other Wiccans—searching to see if one will challenge me. No one does. The High Coven is in shock as their cloaks whip in the wind I have conjured, mouths gaping.

Sabine's eyes are wide, her red hair flying behind her as she braces against the wind.

Rhydian, Tullen, Quinn, and Cross transport to me and take positions around me like a compass. The Guardians stop advancing.

I float down to the center of my rogue Guardians and protectors. Cross and Rhydian step aside as I walk forward to face the High Coven.

I project my voice. "I do accept my duty, the crown, and my

birthright. These are my royal guard—" I gesture toward Rhydian, Tullen, Cross, and Quinn. "They are not rogue from their duties as Guardians, but serve in a new capacity as a personal guard for the Queen."

My choice is proclaimed as my father advised. Then the tide turns and all who are present lower to one knee, bowing their heads—including the High Coven on the steps of the Hallowed Halls.

"Now, someone tell me where my father is!"

CHAPTER 13

W hen you have power, it's interesting to see how others back off when you show it, but not before. It could be so easily abused, and part of me wants to abuse it. Why don't I? Because that's not who I am. Or who I was? This new part of me is addictive. My magick is so powerful that my whims can be realities. It's a little scary.

My center—my base—is my home, and after knocking the Wiccan High Coven off their pedestal with my display of magick, I transport myself back there. They didn't know anything about my father. It felt like a waste of time.

I feel like a visitor at the front door. I hesitate to open it, knowing that the chaos from the other night will still be present. Mrs. Scott needs to be put to rest and I'm not sure how to do that, but she deserves better than to lie in the foyer. I've aged five years from the girl who met her grandmother only a few days ago. My sense of time is warped; has it really only been a few days?

I take a deep breath and open the door. I'm caught by surprise: nothing is messed up or wrecked. The floors are clean, the furniture upright, the lights back on walls and hanging from the ceiling. The large, round table is in the middle of the foyer with a bouquet of flowers. Someone has to be here. I pray it is my father, knowing full well that isn't likely. No one seems to know anything about the whereabout of him or Lucy. Maybe it was all a dream and Mrs. Scott is fine?

"Hello? Anyone here?" I raise my voice, hoping she will answer me.

There's no response and, although I expected none, my heart sinks. Someone must have cleaned the house, but who? Where is Mrs. Scott?

The back door opens and I walk toward the kitchen. It won't be Mrs. Scott, but I can't help it—I want it to be her so badly. When I see Rhydian, Cross, and Tullen enter, I try to lift my mood, but I can't put up the facade anymore. Tears stream down my face.

Tullen hugs me. "Willow, I'm sorry for everything that has happened, and all that will." I don't know what to say to that, but he saves me the trouble. "It's part of your journey. It's a tough one, but I certainly think you have the guts to face it." He goes to the fridge and grabs a water.

Cross chuckles. "That show ya put on at the Hallowed Hall certainly has got folks talkin'. All the groups are a little intimidated by yer show of power. Whoever thought the monarchy was dead didn't realize it had just changed zip codes. What's ya next move?"

I squint at him sideways.

"What? Come on, Willow, I'm not always of the opposite opinion." His smirk tells me otherwise.

Tullen throws Cross a bottle of water and they sit at the kitchen table, each grabbing an apple from the bowl in the center.

Rhydian is studying me, his hazel eyes searching. Then it hits me: they are the ones who cleaned everything up. Mrs. Scott's body must be somewhere safe. His nod at my questioning look is all I need. I hug him. "Thank you. I—" My voice chokes with emotion.

I walk to Tullen and Cross at the table and smile despite my waterworks. Cross looks away as if he doesn't want to reveal his own emotions. For a big brute, he does have a sensitive side. I think I like him more than when I first met him.

Tullen excuses himself and transports back to the Hallowed Hall, where Quinn is discussing issues with Eoin, Head of the Guardians. My display brought concerns to the surface regarding the High Coven's abuse of power since Harkin's passing.

The quiet moment of sitting ends when Rhydian looks out the bay window from the kitchen. "Willow, you have visitors. One of them is that valkyrie friend of yours."

The doorbell rings thirty seconds later. When I answer it, Emily grabs me into a hug and whispers in my ear, "I'm so happy you're okay. I told them everything so we can rescue Lucy and your dad."

"How do you know?" I ask.

"I fought them; they wanted me but took Lucy. They already had your dad." Emily wrings her hands, walking into the house.

Daniel has his hands in his pockets and is tentative about coming in. Marco gives me a quick hug, then takes a step back when Rhydian and Cross enter the foyer.

"So, let's all get to know one another. Follow me to the living room," Emily says with a smile. Emily ushers everyone except Daniel and me.

Shutting the front door behind him, Daniel takes a step toward me and hugs me tight, just holding me. I melt into the familiar comfort, the normalcy of just us that I miss. For a moment I can almost forget the nightmare.

"Wills, I've been so worried about you." He leans back to stares in my eyes, reaching a part of my heart that squeezes at his declaration. "I'm so sorry about Mrs. Scott. Emily told us. It all sounds crazy. Are you okay?"

I have a hundred things I want to say, like, No, I'm not okay, and, I could be going crazy because it's not a dream. But instead, I say, "Yes, I'm okay."

He kisses me on my forehead and hugs me tight, then releases me. As we walk toward the formal living room, he hooks his arm around my shoulders. It feels normal and comfortable, like we're at school walking down the hall. Emily's voice comes loud from around the corner.

"Did you know Marco is a shapeshifter? My boy's a shifter and my girl's a Wiccan Queen."

The word "queen" makes me shudder. I don't know how I feel about it as a descriptor of who I am, but I guess I'd better get used to it.

I focus on the news about Marco, not doubting anything anymore. I'm surrounded by magick and different beings, from Guardians to valkyrie and now shapeshifters. At this point, I may be immune to knowing who is different; the shock of magick is becoming normal.

Rhydian tenses when Daniel and I walk into the room. I spy Emily deep discussion with Cross and Marco.

Rhydian walks over and shakes Daniel's hand, introducing himself and Cross.

"We may have a plan," Emily announces. She explains that Lucy and my father must be held somewhere in the Ember region. She's aware of a scry we can use to point us in the right direction if we bring familiar objects of my father's and Lucy's. It sounds like a long shot, but it's still the best idea we have.

"Tis well and good, but ya not leading this effort, we will." Cross gestures to Rhydian and himself. "Besides, we don't know ya."

Emily strides up to him, looking him over as he does the same. "And I don't know you. But that girl, is my dearest friend, my ride or die, so if you're going to lead an effort to help bring back her father and our best friend you better have a damn good plan."

"What about a bait and switch plan instead?" Rhydian asks.

Cross nods in agreement.

Emily eyes Rhydian. "Like what?"

"Me," I say before Rhydian and Cross can answer. "Whoever plans to overtake the crown really wants me—my magick, that is. It might be Evan; I overheard him talking."

Emily shakes her head quickly. "No, Evan wouldn't hurt you, Will." She pauses and looks at Rhydian. "Did you tell her what they did to him and Meghan?"

"Who is Meghan? And how do you know Evan, my uncle? Do you know Theon?"

Before she can answer, Rhydian does. "His wife, Meghan." He paces in front of Cross and continues. "Harkin arranged a marriage for Evan to a Noble Coven Wiccan, but Evan didn't want to have anything to do with it. He was an outcast because he was a bastard. His bloodline was in question, including where his power came from.

"It wasn't long after your mother passed away that Evan ran away with Meghan, who is of fae and demon descent. They married in secret. When they were found by the Guardians and put in front of the High Coven, Harkin was embarrassed and angry. He felt betrayed by Evan and tried to take his blooded heritage from him, which in turn would remove any familial physical Wiccan powers that descended from him to Evan, and condemned him to live outside of Edayri. This caused Evan's demon side to become evident. Harkin's infidelity became clear to the world, and out of anger and embarrassment at his exposed secret, he . . . he executed Meghan.

"Because Evan is not full Wiccan but also part demon, the effort to remove his magick blood only empowered him. He's been rallying with demons and fae to take down the royal caste system entirely."

Why didn't my father tell me any of this? I can't imagine the hurt Evan carries. Daniel hugs me closer to him in comfort.

"They killed her? Why didn't the High Coven, or Sabine for that matter, do the same with my father or me?" I feel sick to my stomach.

"Your father's family is high in the noble caste system; they were part of the High Coven at one time. You're pure Wiccan and your mother was next in line for the throne. Sabine, really can't take the crown for her own, but I'm sure she would want the family royal legacy to remain. It's certainly not an even playing field for Evan. Everyone thought he was dead, so it's not clear to me," Rhydian replies.

"What is Theon? He's always with Evan," I ask Emily.

"I believe one of Evan's cousins on his mother's side. Theon is also part Wiccan and demon, like Evan."

How does she know this, and why would she not have said anything before? Then I remember that the last time I saw Emily, Rhydian was saving me from a blood warrior demon. I move away from everyone and walk toward the window. Silence haunts me for the death Evan has endured. We have too much in common now, when I think about Mrs. Scott.

When I turn around, Cross is leaning on the living room entryway post. "I say our best hope is to dangle Willow to capture Evan and Theon. They must have your father and your friend. They're the only ones who would get a payoff for yer cooperation."

Rhydian agrees, but Daniel objects. "You can't use her as bait. You don't know who or what will come to her, so how can you control the scene?"

"You don't know what you're talking about. Willow is quite capable," Rhydian snaps.

I get between them and put my hand on Daniel's chest before he goes any further with Rhydian. "I'm all right," I say to Daniel. "It's a good plan and we have limited options." Daniel has no idea how I can handle myself now, or about the magick that is part of me.

"Okay," he says, "then I want to be there."

Rhydian laughs mockingly. "You are a casualty waiting to happen. You don't belong in Edayri."

Daniel gets up close to Rhydian. "You don't belong here. Wherever Willow goes, I'm going. Got it?"

"Your funeral," Rhydian says, closing what little gap they had.

Marco and I separate the two of them and I walk Rhydian across the hallway to the formal dining room.

"What are you doing? Daniel is my boyfriend," I hiss.

"He's going to get you hurt or killed. He's got no skills and he's all territorial about what you can and can't do. Why would you put up with that?" Rhydian's voice keeps rising as he speaks. "Your world here is ending and you can't take him with you."

"You can't make that choice for me!"

"Which choice is that? Abandon your duties and play house with him? I can sense your thoughts and feelings for him." He sneers at Daniel as he speaks. Daniel sneers back.

I tug Rhydian's arm and move us so the others can't see. "What do you care, Rhydian?" I lower my voice.

He closes his eyes. "I don't. I'm sorry; it isn't my place to advise you on such matters." He turns to walk away, but I stop him.

"You're not saying something. Tell me."

I search his face, a face that only a few minutes ago that was so full of compassion but is now turned to stone. He looks down at me, his hazel eyes no longer depth of colors I can get lost in but cold and distant. His strong jaw is set, muscle ticking at the strain. He steps back from me, exhales, and messes his hair with one quick stroke of his hand. His full bottom lip is out as if he's pouting. I'm not sure what I want to hear, but something is off. I'm hurting him, but I'm not sure how it is possible when I've known him only for a few days.

He turns away from me and, as he walks out the entryway, says over his shoulder, "It's not important. You need to focus on other things."

I stand in the dining room alone.

CHAPTER 14

B ang. Bang.
    "Open up! Police."
I walk into the foyer. Everyone seems preoccupied except for Daniel, who goes to the door.

It all happens in slow motion.

Daniel reaches for the door and is blown back with a giant ball of light, flying past me to the foot of the staircase. His head smacks down and blood spits out his mouth.

Cross, the closest to me, leaps and pushes me back into the dining room. Marco shifts into a tiger and charges the door. Raised voices are quickly drowned by a roar and growls from Marco. Rhydian is in full warrior mode, sword raised on three large demons who are entering the house.

Emily turns toward Daniel, then back around in brass armor with filigree gold designs. Her body is covered in key areas and open in others. Her helmet is the most ornate I've ever seen, like a war eagle with raised metal feathers back and down her head and a face structure that covers her forehead down to her nose.

She screams and throws her hands in the air, bringing them down with such force that the house shakes and lightning cracks outside. Cross rolls to the side of me and morphs into full warrior mode himself. His eyes are wide, watching her, and his crooked grin shows a dimple in his cheek.

Time catches up to my brain and everything speeds up.

Cross helps me up. "Ready? Let's get these fuckers."

I don't hesitate. This is my house! My hands are glowing and swirling with the design of my power. I follow him outside. Everyone is fighting all around the house, the double doors off their hinges.

Cross charges and I'm about to follow when I hear Daniel gurgle, struggling to breathe.

Daniel!

I am next to him in a split second. His body is lying oddly on the stairs and I'm afraid to move him. I kneel down and brush his hair from his eyes. "Daniel, can you hear me?"

His eyes move and he stares at me with utter pain. In all my power, I'm stunned. I can defend myself, but I have no idea what to do to help Daniel. I'm shaking as I listen to the fighting outside.

"Help me!" I scream at the open door. Daniel starts choking. "Rhydian, help me!"

Rhydian and Emily are at my side. Emily is covered in blood. "As a valkyrie I might be able to bring him back as a warrior," she says. "You wouldn't have to be separated, but he won't be the same. Your choice." I look from Daniel to Emily to Rhydian. Cross and Marco are still fighting the demons on the front lawn.

My mouth dry, I swallow in brief contemplation of Em's offer. "No, no, no. I can't make that choice."

He's dying in front of me. "Rhydian, please heal him. Do everything you can. I don't have a clue what to do. Please! Oh my god, this can't be happening."

My hands glow and I try to touch him, but it burns me. Emily grabs me and pulls me away.

"This can't be happening!" I scream.

Rhydian calmly lays his hands on Daniel. His body lifts off the stairs and hovers as Rhydian guides him to the floor. His brows furrow and I feel his concentration. I am jealous that he knows exactly what to do, but I'm also so thankful for it.

I hear the fighting stop and time slows for me. Marco lies at my feet in tiger form while Cross stands next to us.

"It's going to take him if he's not careful. We need Quinn," Cross says under his breath.

"Can you go—"

Daniel gasps and bows his chest unnaturally. Rhydian leans further over him, like he's about to collapse with his shaking and straining hands hovering over Daniel. I break free from Emily and slide across the floor to the two of them.

Rhydian's face is strained, deep wrinkles on his forehead. What have I asked for? What did I force Rhydian to do? Am I losing Rhydian? I will myself to loan part of my magick to him, laying my hand on his and removing it from Daniel's body. When I do, Rhydian collapses. Cross is there in a flash to catch him.

"This house is not safe. We need to leave," Cross says.

"We can't. Not while they're in this condition. I can hold the house," Emily says. She produces a staff out of thin air and hits the floor with it. A blanket of sheer light radiates from the staff along the floors, coating the walls, stairs, and spreading out from the front door over the entire house and grounds.

"Damn, that's hot," Cross says.

Emily winks at Cross.

Marco starts to roll on the floor. One minute he's covered in fur and the next his naked cappuccino skin is showing, back in his human form. I turn away to give him privacy and follow Cross to the formal living room, where he lays Rhydian on the sofa.

"Will Rhydian be all right . . . and Daniel?" I hesitate to add Daniel to my question. Rhydian was right when we argued earlier, but I had hoped I had more time with Daniel.

"Yeah, he'll be okay. Just needs to recharge. I think yer man needed it, though. Musta' been on the cusp. Rhydian's not a halfway guy. Guessing he wanted to make sure all the healing was right, but it puts him at risk. Glad you intervened. What did ya do?"

"I tried to give him part of my magick to use."

"Tis not possible."

"From my dark magick." I respond.

Cross's breath hitches in his throat. "Watch over him. I need to check on Daniel." Cross lifts his chin to me and I see Tullen transport in, battle-ready. He goes to Cross and Rhydian.

Marco stands next to Daniel, who lies on the dining room table. His chest rises and falls with each breath. He's going to be all right.

Rhydian is right: I can't be with him. He's in this situation because of me. My father's voice in my mind, repeats the words; inevitable—no choice.

I go to join the rest. I touch Daniel's hand and look at Marco. "I'm sorry. I would never put Daniel in danger." My voice cracks at his name.

"I understand that, Willow. I'm here for him though, not you." He says it matter-of-factly, but there is something hidden in his eyes. Gah. I hate me too right now.

I leave the dining room and come to stand in the foyer. Emily is there with her staff, protecting the house and everyone in it.

"Do you blame me for Lucy?" I ask her.

"No. Why would you ask that?" Her eyebrows draw together and her lips quirk to the side.

"I do." I sit on the stairs avoiding bloodstains, the living room on my right and the dining room on my left. I'm right in the middle, between Daniel and Rhydian. My familiar life and my new life.

CHAPTER 15

Like a siren's call, a sharp noise bellows through the house. I yell and cover my ears, but everyone else just seems puzzled. I stand with my hands over my ears, yelling, "Can't you hear it?"

They all shake their heads no.

I follow the noise, rounding the back of the stairs to my father's office. The secret door is cracked open and a glow beckons me in. The sound pulses are lower and lower as I near. I'm nervous to walk into the hidden room, both afraid and hopeful about what I'll discover. Is it possible that my father and Lucy are there? I go into the chamber like a hopeful child but am disappointed when I see no one. The passageway door shuts behind me, enclosing me in the empty room.

The family Book of Shadows is not on the bookshelf where I placed it last; instead, it's open on the coffee table. An eerie, soft, white light glows from the pages, and the noise is gone.

The book summoned me.

I head to the overstuffed chair and touch the book. I snap my fingers back from the pages, feeling an electrical charge. The book comes to life and pages flip of their own accord. It stops on a blank page. I move the book closer to me and ink begins to appear.

It shows me what I desperately want to figure out: how to locate my father and Lucy.

The ability to find blooded family resides in a potion for transporting. The book lists out ingredients I'm not familiar with, but the most important is something from the blooded family member you're looking to find—including shared blood.

In my excitement, I pick up the book and walk from the hidden room, ready to show everyone our golden ticket. I stumble when I find everyone already in the office, including now-conscious Rhydian and Daniel.

They sit in opposite chairs, and I stop myself from heading directly to Daniel.

"Oh, thank god, you're okay! Both of you," I say.

Daniel adjusts himself slowly in the chair. "Thanks to Rhydian and you."

Rhydian nods to me. "Is that your family Book of Shadows?"

"Yes. How did you all realize I was in there?"

Marco pipes up. "I watched you go in and Tullen suggested it might be a Wiccan solitary circle space, so we stayed out here to wait on you. Plus, with Rhydian awake, he'd sense if you were in trouble."

I look at Rhydian, but he's avoiding my eyes.

Daniel cocks his head sideways at Rhydian.

"Thanks. I found a way of locating my father with a transporting potion. I think that if we locate him, Lucy should be nearby and we can rescue them both."

Emily looks at the book. "Great, but it's a blank page, Will."

"No, it was, but not anymore—can't you see?" It dawns on me then: they're not my family, of course they can't read it. "Don't worry, it's there—I'll read it aloud and we can work on it."

Cross shifts his legs and says, "Yes, and make enough so that several of us can go cause there's no way he's not heavily guarded what with his powerful magick. Whoever has yer father is most likely counting on ya to show up hot-headed and ready to do something stupid, and then they'll have ya both."

I smirk at Cross. "Hot-headed? I thought that was your title."

"Only when required." His dimple appears, and I swear Emily grins.

Tullen writes down what I read and then he, Cross, and Rhydian start gathering items from the hidden room. I go upstairs and pull a piece of my father's hair from his hairbrush. Upstairs, Duke is whining.

"Oh my god, Duke!" I open a closet door and my dog bounds out, jumps on me, and begins licking my face. I hug him, thankful he's okay in all this chaos. He follows me down the stairs and begins to growl deep in his throat. The hair on his back is ruffled. He's staring at Marco.

"Easy, Duke," Marco laughs. "I'm guessing he doesn't like cats?"

I laugh. "Easy, Duke."

Duke follows me into the room and lets Emily pet him, but he huffs and growls at Marco. When Cross and Rhydian walk in, Duke bounds over to them with his tail in full wag mode.

"Funny, a witch who likes dogs over cats. I think I like this about you," Rhydian says. Duke has made a new best friend, deserting me.

"We're ready. Quinn is on the way," Tullen says.

Daniel sits near the empty fireplace alone, looking out of place. Emily nods her head toward him and murmurs, "He can't go. It's too dangerous. Marco's going to take him home. Once I know where we're transporting, I'll come back for Marco if we need him."

I nod. I don't want to put anyone else in danger. I'm overwhelmed that Emily and Marco want to help me not just for Lucy but for my father too. Daniel would be in the middle of it as well, but he's not like us. Rhydian's right, it's inevitable there is no choice. My mind is set and it squeezes my heart.

The sun is starting to set and time seems to be getting away from us. Marco helps Daniel stand and I walk with them to the front door, past Emily's glowing staff that protects the house.

"Daniel, I'm really sorry you were—"

His finger is on my lips and he moves closer to me. "Let's not, okay?" He knows, that I would keep him safe in the only way I can. He won't let me say it.

He almost died. My friends are being used against me, and he doesn't belong in this craziness. Plus, it's all my fault that he's here at all. All I can do is nod.

"Be safe, Willow, and when you're back, let's talk. Good luck." Daniel wipes a stray tear from my face and kisses me, gentle and soft.

I don't want him to go with so much left unsaid. But it's not safe for him to be associated with me and I know this. I conjure my magick and command it to change his memory of the camping trip so that he thinks we were together all night, that I never left. When he wakes in the morning, an amicable and simple breakup. Our relationship ran its course. He'll be a happy Daniel with no regrets. I kiss him goodbye and he holds me to him. The memory I have conjured is released from me to him as I pull away.

"I love you."

"I love you, too." He releases me and is gone.

I should have taken note of that more. I touch my lips to feel his warmth leave me. I turn back to the house just in time to see Rhydian walking away.

"Rhydian, wait!"

He turns in the hallway to face me, rubbing the back of his neck and staring.

"Rhydian, Daniel's my . . . why are you . . . are you mad?"

"This is dangerous, is all. I'm not mad, but I don't need to be an audience member for your private moments." He nods to the front door.

"I don't understand why you're acting this way."

"There isn't anything to tell you that I haven't already said." He huffs as if he's been holding his breath. "We have about an hour or so. Go get some rest. You're barely standing as it is."

Instead of following him into the office where everyone is gathered, I turn toward the stairs, where Emily is watching and holding her staff.

"I noticed what you did, Will."

I stop and hold the rail. It steadies me so I don't break into tears. "I had to, Em. He . . . I can't have him hurt because of any of this."

"I know," she says simply.

I walk upstairs to my room. I shower and change clothes, then lay on my bed with my eyes closed. I sink into my mattress, allowing the peacefulness of the dark to claim my mind quickly.

CHAPTER 16

T he elevator is familiar, blankets tacked to its inside walls due to construction activities. I'm alone when I enter and hit the button for the sixth floor. Arriving, I turn to the right as I've done millions of times in the past and walk through the glass doors into an office.

The familiar blonde receptionist smiles and says that Dr. Bauche will be with me shortly. I pick up the two-month-old *People* magazine and flip through the pages. I've already read this magazine several times, but I keep flipping the pages to keep myself occupied. As I set the magazine down, Dr. Bauche appears in the hallway and calls my name.

Familiar and friendly as always, her hair is perfectly styled and she wears a dark pencil skirt, silk shirt, and black high heels. I follow her back to her office like I've done for so many sessions in the past.

"Willow, I'm actually surprised to see you. What brings you in today?" Her voice is soothing.

"A lot of changes in both my family and personal life," I say.

I tell her about everything, and I mean *everything*. Her response to the information is accepting. I tell her all the lies about where I come from, about meeting my long-lost grandmother and uncle, about discovering that I come from Wiccan royalty and I'm next in line for the throne. I tell her about the lure of the magick within myself, but how I also want what was my normal life. About Mrs. Scott and the threats on my life. I even tell her that a few of my friends are from the Edayri realm, and about the rogue, now royal, Guardians and how I don't want to disappoint them; I want to be a positive change in Edayri. I tell her how Daniel got hurt and almost died. I tell her about Rhydian's connection to me and his blooded vow. About how I am indebted to him, and the fact that I'm attracted to him even while I love Daniel. About how I let Daniel go to keep him safe. About how fatally broken my heart is at the loss of Mrs. Scott and Daniel.

I needed to release. I exhale heavy, yet my chest feels lighter.

"I'm sorry for the heartbreak, but that's a part of life that allows us to grow in companionship and in ourselves," she says. "Not what you wanted to hear?"

I shake my head and stare at my hands.

"How do I manage this? I'm going to burst. I'm scared this is all for nothing and that I'll fail at something, and I'm worried about who that will affect. This crown, the anticipation of it, is overwhelming on top of my own selfish desires to stay the normal teenager I am."

"Those who accept and manage personal change well are those who are clear about what they want. They are also good at taking the necessary steps toward change and taking control of those elements that they can." She stands and circles to the front of her desk to sit on the corner. "Willow, I get the impression that you have decided how you feel about a few of the situations you've described to me. About the others, it's okay to take some time. Nothing is permanent."

She's right. I've been trying to speed my way through everything because I really haven't had a moment to pause. I've been running a marathon ever since Sabine came to dinner, since I walked into the Salem Woods.

"I want you to try some relaxation breathing techniques. They will help you to slow down as you face some of these challenges, when you note anxiety coming on. They help to center yourself and your thoughts, to clear out the noise so that you can focus on directive intention.

"Inhale and draw your breath in from your core. Pause and hold, but not uncomfortably, then release in a slow and steady stream of air. Count to yourself as you do both. Ten, twelve, fifteen seconds is typically good, though you can do longer if you have the time."

Dr. Bauche leads me in a routine to breathe in deeply and exhale deeply, first for twelve seconds, then increasing the time with my next breaths. It really does help, and I'm better and more focused on the immediate tasks I need to deal with.

"Look at compartmentalizing issues, especially when faced with compounding issues and tasks. This will allow you to judge what to spend time on now versus later. It's a way to manage your time. The key is not to push off an issue and never address it. When you do that, it comes back to haunt you." She pats me on the hand and tells me time is up.

I follow her to the door. I don't really want to leave, but I know I should.

"Thank you for seeing me on such short notice," I say. "It was helpful . . . your guidance."

"Anytime, Willow. I'm here anytime you need me."

Her eyes are like mine, dark blue. Her chin and pert nose are just like mine. She opens the door and the office hallway morphs into my bedroom.

Awake, I rub my eyes and feel the wetness of my tears. Evan had said this is how he and my mother would communicate sometimes. Having access to my mother brings me comfort. Whether this is in my head or real doesn't matter. It doesn't even matter if she's really Dr. Bauche or Mom. I picture her as both, and maybe she is both. I cup my face and smile through my tears. Before I know it, I'm laughing and crying together. I have my mom with me and the idea of it is joyous.

A bump on my door tells me that Duke needs something and is on the other side waiting. I open the door and pet him on the head, then follow him down the back stairs to the kitchen. I put food in his bowl before I find Cross, Emily, Tullen, and Rhydian at the table, just waiting in silence. All eyes turn to me.

"Ready?" I ask.

PART IV

The girl throws her fist to the sky
"My destiny is my own!",
Fate is satisfied, for now . . .

CHAPTER 17

The potion that we've made is finished and ready. Quinn and Tullen are moving the foyer table into the formal living room. I have chalk in my hand, ready to draw the pentagram required to transport us wherever my father is being held.

"Start here in the north, where the stairs are." Rhydian points.

I nod and draw the pentagram star, then complete the circle. It feels strange to draw it, yet somehow familiar. I'm not much of an artist, but I think I do a decent job considering I have them all watching my every move.

"Okay, just so we all understand how this is going down," Cross says, "the plan is that Rhydian, Emily, and Willow will transport first. They'll scope out the area and, if able, Rhydian and Emily will return to us. If they can't both come, just Emily will return so that Rhydian can help protect Willow." Cross looks at Tullen and Quinn, who nod their heads in agreement.

Emily rolls her eyes. "Whatever. You know I'm the best regarding protection, and you've seen what she can do on her own. Your little hang-up that Willow needs *your* protection is cute though."

I love the confidence she has in me. I can't help but smile. The fact is, my magick is stronger now and I'm in control. Not everyone has real magick like mine in the Wiccan community. Plus, I think I scared the shit out of most of them at the Hallowed Hall. If whoever took my father and my best friend didn't see that display, hopefully they've heard about it by now.

"Let's go."

Rhydian is all business, pure focus. I envy him. I'm a mix of nerves, fear, and anger. Rhydian pours the potion into the bowl in the center of the pentagram. He, Emily, and I stand in the center of the circle. He nods to me, and I prick my finger and squeeze a drop of blood into the potion, add the last ingredient —my father's hair—then quickly grasp Rhydian and Emily's hands. Transportation is becoming easier for me, but this time the pull in various directions makes my stomach drop. The force of wind pushes us and I get thrown backward. My hand slips from Emily's and, in an instant, we fall into darkness onto a hard dirt floor.

I land on Emily and Rhydian touches my ankle. We all made it.

"Where the hell are we?" Emily whispers. "I can barely see anything."

"In some type of dungeon," Rhydian answers. He's already suited up in his sleek armor.

"Can you give us some of that glow magick, Wills?" Emily asks.

I light up my hand in a dull blue glow and the designs on my arm appear, the glow of magick flowing through them.

We're in some type of cell but the door is open. It is moist and damp, the air is stale with rust and mold. Outside the cell is a tunnel of aged stone and dirt floors. Lanterns spaced along the walls give some light to the left, but on the right the spacing is further apart, leaving everything dark.

"Which way do we go?" I ask.

"We need to split up," Rhydian replies.

I don't like that idea, but our options are limited. We take a step out of the cell and the barred door slams shut. The tunnel lights up entirely and an alarm sounds.

"Shit!" yells Rhydian.

"Bring it!" yells Emily.

I have a feeling we need to go left. I start running. "Come on, guys. This way!"

When I round the corner, I skid to a stop, less stunned by the gruesome torture tools in the middle of the room than by the sign my eyes are drawn to. It hangs over a door with stairs leading out of the dungeon, proclaiming its ownership simply.

"MacKinnon Manor."

"No," I whisper in shock.

"No time!" Rhydian yells above the alarm.

"Aiden! Lucy! Aiden! Lucy!" Rhydian and Emily yell in chorus.

Lucy yells back and I can breathe again. We take the stairs out of the dungeon, following her voice to the floor above. This newer part of the building has tiled floors and proper walls. The recessed lights are lit by bulbs, not fire. The doors are square with peek-a-boo windows and openings at the bottoms for trays.

The alarm stops blaring. Rhydian runs down and knocks on all the doors, shouting my father's name.

"Lucy, move away from the door!" I use my magick to blast the door off its hinges.

Lucy uncovers her face. Tears are streaming down her cheeks.

"I can't walk," she says, pointing to her leg. It's splinted on each side. My magick lights up my skin and hums loud in ears. They hurt her!

"I've got her." Emily swoops in and picks Lucy up like she's a doll. Lucy pushes her face against Emily's shoulder and says "Thank you" over and over again.

Rhydian yells, "He's here, he's here!" He kicks down a door the old-fashioned way. There is movement sounding from outside the building and above us.

"I've got Lucy. I'm taking her back now," Emily says. She tries to transport, but nothing happens. "It must have a protection spell against transporting."

"Go back to the cell."

Emily takes off with Lucy, running in the direction we came from. Lucy's eyes are wide and she's shaking. "Don't stay, Willow! They want you!"

Emily is fast and even Lucy's weight doesn't slow her down.

I'm at the end of the hall where Rhydian has found my father. He's lying on a cot at the back of a small, square jail cell. He turns slowly so we can assess his injuries, and my magick flares at the sight of the bruises on his face. His right hand is discolored, swollen and puffy; surely the bones are broken. He coughs up blood before speaking.

"My smart girl." He reaches with his feeble good hand to touch my face.

"We've got to go," Rhydian says. "Is there another way out of here? We can't transport. Something is blocking us."

My father sits up slowly and cringes. "Maybe back through the older part. There should be a way outside to the grounds."

Rhydian is all business as he helps my father up and walks him out to the hall. The steps above us are louder now.

We start down the stairs when I hear Sabine's voice calling: "Wait, wait!"

I have no interest in speaking to her after what she's done. I thrust my hand upward to break the ceiling, and it crumbles down in grand fashion, complete with smoke and rock to block her path. A pipe bursts and water showers down. I don't bother to stick around, leaping down the stairs behind Rhydian and my father.

I use my hand to light the way in the old tunnel. There is no light beside my magick and I am beginning to wonder if we are heading in the right direction when the tunnel turns and starts to slope upward. Outside light comes in through slats of wood in the door ahead. We start moving quicker and my father moans as he hangs on to Rhydian.

I throw a light ball at the door, busting it apart, and we run outside. We're at the edge of a forest. When I turn, I see the castle: MacKinnon Manor.

"Rhy! Wills!" Cross yells, running down the tunnel toward us in full armor with Quinn and Tullen. We're all outside now. It's damp and foggy.

"We transported as soon as Emily let us. She had to get Lucy home." Cross pats me on the back. "I'm so sorry, Wills. To think Sabine would do something like this to yer family—*her* family . . ." His face says it all.

My father struggles to breathe and Rhydian sets him down.

Father coughs. "I'm not sure it was her . . . not completely, anyway." He blinks several times. "It's all off. Something doesn't make sense. She was never present . . . the torturing . . . but the High Coven . . ."

I cringe at the word *torture*. Looking over my father, I can't help but think of what I saw in that dungeon. Lucy with a leg splint. My father spitting up blood, his body weak and broken. I gnash my teeth together and shake my head.

"Where's the guard of her estate?" Quinn asks.

In the same breath, we look up to see Sabine and a team of five walking across the acreage toward us. Her hair is flowing down her back, red like fire, and there's a look of concern in her eyes.

"It's a trick."

Rhydian puts a hand in front of me to keep me from walking to them. "She's part of the High Coven," he reasons. "Wait a minute and let's listen to what she says."

I can't believe his calm demeanor, but I take the advice. I

take a deep, even breath, and it calms me—sort of. Someone needs to answer for taking my father and Lucy, not to mention the horrible condition in which we found them. My inner rage is building and I'm ready to go crazy, but, thanks to Mom, I decide to put it on tap until I need it.

CHAPTER 18

The grounds of the MacKinnon Manor are immaculate, several acres of lush green grass surrounded by forest. The manor itself is a modern-mansion-meets-castle. A black Lincoln Town Car comes down the drive.

We stand tense in the front yard—the royal Guardians, my father, and me. We're all waiting for Sabine's explanation of the fact that I just found my father and Lucy on her property, abused, tortured, and locked in an old dungeon. Sabine has several security guards with her, and neither of our groups seem like we want to talk.

"Who's coming down the drive?" Tullen asks. The way he's staring at the car, you'd think he could see right through it, but the blacked-out windows reveal nothing.

Sabine doesn't answer Tullen's question. "There must be a huge mistake," she says. "I didn't know. I truly did not know that part of the grounds was being used. My security is only set up in detail for the main house. That part of the property and the underground have been closed for years and only kept for their historical significance. The property is registered with the historical society. We only have alarms on the second floor in case of intruders or vandals." Sabine's face doesn't give much away.

I quirk my eyebrow at her.

Does she really think that I can believe this? That there could have been two prisoners held captive below her home without her knowledge? I look at my father to see him struggling. His stomach is bleeding and Quinn is bent over him, bandaging him up and using magick at the same time. I need to get him medical treatment. I could just transport us away and get him to safety.

Bam!

A light flashes at the back edge of the back of the property, radiating wide and strobing a couple of times. I blink to clear my eyes and focus, but I hear it first—a loud, slow clap coming from the woods.

"Excellent. Now the game is afoot. Here is my highly regarded evil Stepmother, trying to talk her way out of something devilish, I'm sure," Evan says, his voice mocking. "And my niece, naïve enough to believe that her grandmother would care about her." Evan approaches us, an army of demons and other magickal creatures close behind.

Sabine's hands cover her mouth. "But you're . . . you're—"

"Dead? I'm sure you'll continue to wish that was the case, especially with Willow here."

Evan is about twenty feet away. Cross, Rhydian, and Tullen make a barrier with their bodies between me and Evan. Quinn is checking my father's vitals and pulling things out of a bag next to him.

"Can you use magick to heal him?" Rhydian asks.

"No, I tried. They used curses!" Quinn replies. My father's face is tormented, his eyes dark.

"Evan, I don't understand. Did *you* do this?" I don't really want him to answer, afraid of the outcome.

"Being the bastard son of Harkin has some privileges—like blood." He spits the word as if it tastes rotten. "Sabine is the cause of many deaths. She's the orchestrator of many events, such as the accident that separated you from your mother." He points a finger between us. "The problem was, she was hoping to steal you away, but instead Nuala fought back and ended up dying. Good thing Daddy Dearest came along because he saved you from a similar fate."

Sabine's eyes are full of tears. "Don't talk about her! You have no right!" she yells.

Evan's voice echoes across the field. "Of course not. There are no rights for those who are not fully Wiccan. You'll always see to that, won't you, Stepmother?" He sweeps his arms out dramatically. "Welcome to the new world."

Evan waves his hand and the army waiting behind him yells, "Ooh-rah!"

The army is ominous—all broad muscles and horns. Their skin is dark and varies in color, armor covering their thick bodies. The snarls on their faces and tensed shoulders show they're ready for a fight.

Evan smirks at Sabine. "I have every right because Harkin's contract was in place for me to be the next in line with a betrothal of marriage to one of the Noble Covens." He waves his hand in the air. "It didn't matter anymore that I was a bastard, a little different. But you saw it. You knew I wasn't full Wiccan!"

Sabine keeps looking from him to me.

"You had every intention of killing me, to be rid of the next in line. When that didn't work, you were responsible for the death sentence given to my Meghan." Evan's voice grows louder and his face tortured. "You had information that we married in secret. The question is, did you know about the baby!"

Sabine hangs her head. "I didn't affect his decisions like that. I tried at first, I admit, but all my children were gone. Liam left. Nuala and Aiden had taken Willow away from Edayri. You were our last child—" Her voice hitches.

"But not *your* child. Let's never forget that. You don't like anyone different. Meghan being anything but Wiccan made her less, made her life unworthy—kind of like me. You gave her a death sentence so you and Harkin could save the image of the crown and its royal traditions. That was a mistake. Holding power that shouldn't be restricted is not what the Horned God and Goddess would want, Sabine. Killing innocents? Tsk-tsk." He waves his finger back and forth.

Horned God? I haven't heard about him since I first looked at the Book of Shadows.

The demons rush the open lawn and yell, holding fists and swords aloft. There is a change in the air. I gravitate up from the grass and my magick comes to life, lightning and power licking all over my body. It feels like controlled static electricity, the tingling and hum becoming intense. I point to the front line of the army and they sail back in one motion, knocking over the next advancing group.

Sabine turns to me. "Willow, run! Take your father. This isn't your fight. I'm so sorry." Her hair picks up with the wind and she throws light balls at the advancing demons. Her security detail has some type of shockwave guns which they fire at the advancing army. I look back to witness my royal Guardians in full battle gear, swords drawn. They form a semicircle protecting my father.

A few of the demons are on the ground and Evan floats over them. He has powerful magick. I'm not surprised. He drops to the ground, and so do I. We're only about ten feet from each other. His eyes are changing color; horns peek through his hairline; his skin darkens; his canine teeth grow. "This reign needs to end, Willow. It's a secular monarchy that boasts nothing but destruction. You can't accept the crown—this family must destroy it! And if you stand in my way, well . . ."

Well, what? He will kill me? I can't believe that; he could have done that long before now. This is a vendetta against Sabine.

"Evan, look." I point to my father. "You are doing just what you want to rage against."

"No." He shakes his head. "Don't follow Sabine. That gives me only one choice."

"My mother will never forgive you." I hope it will give him pause.

Rhydian is beside me. "So, we're all just collateral damage, then? Destruction for destruction's sake? There has to be a better way."

Evan glances behind him. "Nuala is no longer here to judge me. I can't let this divisive reign continue."

Evan morphs into armor similar to that of the demons all around him, flexing it with his movements. His sword is thin like a samurai's. He advances toward Rhydian. I throw my hand out and hit Evan with a light ball, moving him back.

His menacing laugh echoes across the lawn. "Ah, are you protecting Rhydian now? You're saddling up to the vow and accepting it all?"

"Shut up, Evan, and let's fight!" Rhydian yells.

"All you Guardians are the same," Evan sneers. "You're all about the short game and forget the long game."

"No! You hurt my friend and my father! Is that your long game? This isn't a game!" I yell. "This is my fight!"

My anger swells my magick. My grief for Mrs. Scott; for leaving Daniel. My anger at this life and the manipulation of it all.

I'm done!

I conjure every bit of the emotion inside me—disabling pain, hope, frustration, anger, love, sadness, regret—and I throw it straight at Evan in the form of a light ball. It hits and covers his body. Evan screams. His arms drop to his sides as he falls to the ground.

He will not be getting up.

The fighting around me continues. The demons are advancing to conceal Evan's downed body. Rhydian hits his wrist band and calls for reinforcements from the Guardians. They transport directly in front him and engage quickly with the demons and Sabine's security.

Lightning shoots across the sky, but not by my will. Emily, along with several warriors and another valkyrie, are suddenly in front of me, ready for battle. Emily winks at me before they charge the demons standing between me and the castle.

The roar of a large cat echoes from the edge of the forest. Marco must have brought support as well. A glowing light pulses as more demons enter in droves.

Quinn shouts at me, "Transport us to the hospital! He's dying. I can't help him. Someone has control near us and is making it worse."

"Put me down," my father coughs. I'm at his side on the ground and he touches my face. "Willow, my sweet girl. I release my magick—" I hug him in my arms and we're on the ground together. This can't be happening. This can't. He's broken, bleeding. His eyes plead with me.

"No! Don't do this. I can't lose you. I can get you . . ." Tears puddle in my eyes. I'm shaking. He's leaving me.

"Another did this . . . don't trust High Coven . . . Sabine . . . Evan . . . Evan is hurting. I'm sorry for . . ." His hand drops from my cheek. He takes a shallow breath and says, "I freely invoke my magick to my daughter, Willow Sola Warrington . . . in the Goddess's name. So mote it be."

And then his breathing stops.

"No!"

My screams echo and move everything around me in shockwaves.

I don't care.

I wail to the sky and curse it all.

I couldn't save Mrs. Scott; I couldn't save my father. The rain is tumultuous and mirrors my tears, my utter agony. I see nothing but us. My father in my lap, dead in my arms. My power is useless; I can't bring him back.

My family is gone. I'm alone.

A black magickal smoke surrounds us as it departs from my father and licks at me. I jerk away from the pain; it scorches my skin. His magick surrounds me and pulses at my skin. I scream in agony, my flesh burning, as I'm lifted into the storming sky. I don't want any of this, I want my father back!

The pain and hurt are never-ending. I embrace it. The smoke twists my body and turns me. I want to go with him—with my dad and my mom. My vision flashes a new scene, the car flips and flips; we land hard. I'm upside down. Someone pulls me out and throws me to the ground. She's out and reaching for me. A huge beast with wings is before me. A sword slices through the air; she grabs her neck. Red. Lots of red. A light. My father yells her name: "Nuala!" The beast yanks me to my feet. My father's face is stone-cold; his hands wave light from my mother to me. I fall and the beast explodes apart; I cover my small child face, before the vision changes where I am now. Throwing my arms wide, I open my mouth and swallow the black smoke to the sound of screams—echoes that are not my own.

The smoke clears and the rain stops. The fighting halts, all eyes on me.

Ants. That is what they are. To be stepped on.

The ground thunders when I drop to the ground. My vision is blurred, but I make out Quinn standing near my father. He is wide-eyed and holding his hands up. The darkness—it speaks to me, in my thoughts but not in recognizable voices, as if I'm split into two very strange and very powerful parts.

Make them pay. Make them feel the hurt, the pain.

Rhydian appears in front of me. "Willow?" He moves slowly, cautious, his hazel eyes worried, brows dipping with a question. I smell him, his scent like the ocean breeze. The beach . . . sand . . .

His lips are moving. He touches my arms and radiates warmth. My arms are no longer burnt but wisps of smoke hover around me. His pure magick, his voice, his comforting tenor speak only to me.

Willow, don't fight it. Accept it. Accept who you are becoming. Don't leave me, Willow. We are all broken. This is how the light shines through.

I breathe his name into my mind to shut out the other voice.

Rhydian.

I close my eyes and accept my father's immense, dark magick.

CHAPTER 19

The wind sings in my ears. I open my eyes to see an ethereal woman in a gossamer gown that clings to her perfect form. She is the Goddess. Waves of air and shifting spaces in my peripheral vision tell me that some of the fighters in the field are transporting away. Where Evan was is empty. Those who remain are on bent knee, including Sabine.

"I'm ready to take my place," I say.

The Goddess assesses me with her eyes. I'm sure I appear awful with dried tears and mud caked to my face, but I am more than my appearance. I am my mother, Mrs. Scott, and my father. There is no turning back.

She waves her hand and I'm wrapped in a light that is not my own. It turns and twists me in shades of white, pink, yellow, and blue. I gasp as I bend backward and forward. My hair flies in all directions. My arms lift from my sides and I'm covered in the sleek Guardian armor, then morph back into my clothes, then into a purple cloak, and finally into my clothes again. I'm being weighed and measured for service by the Goddess. I feel judgment pass on the unwanted magick, but it is now accepted and owned. Dark and light have become one in me.

A female voice in my head speaks with authority.

You are the most powerful among them—the prophesied spirit element. Inexperienced in the realm of magick though you may be, they fear and respect you. Unite with all. The Convergence is coming.

Her face appears in the mist around me. She's beautiful. Her hair waves like the ocean, her face is like that of a Venetian angel sculpture, and her voice echoes so that all can hear.

"Willow Sola Warrington serves as Queen to the Edayri realm of magick royalty, in my name."

All below me answer in unison, "Blessed be."

I speak to the Goddess in my mind. *Thank you.*

Nothing lasts forever. Be of care, Willow.

I float down and land on the grass in bare feet. My clothing has changed to a gossamer gown and flowing purple cloak that dances behind and around me with the wind. My hair is waved. I've been presented in likeness to the Goddess, an honor not lost on me. I survey everyone around me on bended knee, heads bowed—Wiccan, demon, valkyrie, shapeshifter.

What do I say?

After a minute, Rhydian peeks up at me and winks. This moment is historical and epic, but I can't help it. In the gravity of the moment, I do exactly what I shouldn't: I giggle. A weight is lifted. Will I or won't I accept my predestined fate? It's all answered. It's done.

Those nearest look up at me and my cheeks heat. Eoin, the commander of the Guardians, shakes his head with a smile. I smirk at Rhydian. Time to honor the Goddess.

"You." I point to a demon who strikes me as someone in charge, a leader. I see it all over him—the confidence and bravado. He's taller than most, broad and muscled, dressed in armor that strains over his body to cover only his legs, arms, and back. His large horns sweep back and away with his long dark hair. He's adorned with markings on his chest and wears several long necklaces.

He comes forward, head held high and chest thrust forward. He represents a new magick I can invoke at my will. I sense his anxiety; it licks off him in waves that are almost delicious. I try to change my thoughts. The dark side is inviting and intrusive, so with a quick shake of my head, I steel my resolve.

"Do you challenge me without knowing me?" I ask.

He thinks about this, then replies, "Do you judge me and my kind without knowing us?"

The circle of waged hatred without knowledge or understanding hovers on the horizon, on the cusp of a tipping point.

"No, I don't. I'm an outsider to Edayri and the prejudices of the past are lost on me, as they should be lost going forward. Don't you agree?"

The demon, his stature proud, smiles. Although it could appear evil, it's a genuine smile, and the emotions I feel running through him are clearly of acceptance. The magick is guiding me and I'm letting it.

"I do, Your Majesty."

He bows his head and the other demons follow his lead.

"The vendetta of vengeance is over. Take your wounded home. You and I shall meet again."

Rhydian tries to interrupt me, his brows creased. The demon in front of me pays him no attention.

"You're not afraid of—"

"Should I be?" I ask, flexing my hand and showing my magick. A guiding voice in my head says, Mark him.

He continues to smile, his fangs more evident as they peek through. "No, I don't think so."

"Your name?"

"Ax. Formally Thaxam."

"May I, Ax?"

He nods and I touch his hand. My mark appears, a royal brand in a scrolling design that burns his skin. He makes no noise of discomfort and doesn't let on if there's any pain, although I appreciate pain differently now and don't deny him the experience. The mark will allow me to call him to me, he will be part of the royal Guardians. It's not a two-way street, but this doesn't seem to bother him.

Rhydian's jaw is tight and his lips thin. He stares ahead over the other demons.

The demons follow Thaxam into the forest in silence and transport away. The Guardians are tending to the wounded and leaving as well. I scan for Emily and see her smiling, talking to warriors and Cross. I turn and see Tullen and Quinn smiling and talking.

This battle is over.

"Willow?" Sabine says my name tentatively.

I turn to her. She is grasping at her hands, her knuckles white, sweat on her brow. I should want to comfort her, go to her, but my disdain and hurt for what she's done to Evan, my mother, and me keep me where I am.

"I . . . I did not take your friend or your father and do this."

"I know." She was too busy fighting to continue to wield a curse that killed him.

Her shoulders relax. Sabine's security roughly brings forward the dark-haired High Coven member. "This is Celestia. She admitted to orchestrating the capture of your friend and father. She was working with Evan."

I don't think Evan would agree. Dad said he was hurting and he had plenty of opportunities to hurt or kill me, until today he took careful steps to show me magick. Celestia however, took whatever agenda she had beyond Evan.

Celestia pulls at the security guards holding her. "Get off me! I don't have to answer—"

Her voice! Now I can place where I've heard it before. My inhale is sharp.

"You, don't know the half of it! You're not fit to rule. Even the trigger from two years ago, didn't work." She pulls her arm from one of the security guards.

She orchestrated my assault at the age of fourteen. She was at my house. She's who Mrs. Scott was talking to—the woman in the cloak. She's the one who ordered her killed. The recognition is immediate.

Judge her.

"For me, Mrs. Scott, and my father," I say, devoid of emotion. Celestia's mouth falls open and she gasps as I let my magick warn her.

I lift my hand and quickly twist my fingers in command.

Her neck snaps. Celestia is no more.

The security guards drop her limp body. Her magick is released—all mine if I want it, but I don't. It is tainted with the memory of hurt and death. I direct it to the sky to empty it into the void.

Sabine looks like a deer in headlights. It is all I can do to swallow my tears back in anguish over the deeds of Celestia—the assault in the alley, the killing of Mrs. Scott and the torture that led to the death of my father. I feel justified in my actions . . . almost. I rub my hands on my clothes, wondering if it will clean me of my actions.

Rhydian's voice comes from behind me. "She killed Mrs. Scott, didn't she?" I nod. Sabine stands stunned and I turn from her to Rhydian. "She also tortured and cursed my father and caused his death."

Rhydian says something to Eoin, then comes to my side. I ask him to take me home. I'm drained of any more thoughts and actions. I don't care to behave in a way that is perceived acceptable. I hug him, my head on his shoulder, and I cry. I barely register him transporting us back to my home in Chepstow.

CHAPTER 20

I stand in the entrance of my house in Chepstow, Massachusetts, still hugging Rhydian. I lean my head away from his shoulder, but otherwise we don't move. I focus on the pentagram drawn on the foyer floor and the magickal staff leaning on the wall to the side. Although the blood from earlier was cleaned, the house is stained.

Welcome to your new life.

I'm numb at being the only one to come home. Mrs. Scott and my father will never walk down the stairs, never be in the kitchen or anywhere else in this house again.

"Can a blooded vow decipher my emotions?"

The look in Rhydian's eyes and a slight quirk of his lips tell me all I need to know.

He waves his hand and whispers words to put everything back as it should be. The round table is centered under the hanging chandelier with a vase full of flowers. The chalk is removed from the floor, replaced by an oriental rug under the table. The dirt and marks on the walls vanish.

Duke bounds in from the office, wagging his tail. I can't help but smile and waggle his ears. His dark fur is warm and soft as I hug him around his neck. He licks my face and I laugh through my almost dried tears. In the kitchen, I feed Duke and catch a glimpse of my reflection in the stainless steel refrigerator. My hair is brown. I pull it forward on my shoulder and examine the ends.

"It changed when you accepted his magick," Rhydian says. He's clean and back in street clothes now, jeans and a gray long-sleeve shirt.

"What else changed?" I ask, looking down at my body. I'm still wearing the white gown and purple cloak.

"Come."

Rhydian grins and takes my hand, leading me to the half bathroom down the hall. He places me in front of the mirror.

I look the same except for my hair, once dark blonde but now a chestnut brown resembling my father's. I touch it and think about him briefly. I lean forward and see that my eyes are still ocean blue like my mother's.

"Conjure your magick, Willow," Rhydian says.

I stare down at my fingertips and the design lights up and swirls around my fingers, hands, and arms. Rhydian gently tilts my chin up toward the mirror.

"Oh!" I gulp.

A design on my forehead pulses with the familiar blue glow: an interwoven band that resembles a crown. I tentatively touch my forehead; the crown doesn't waver. I angle my palm and light shines into it. Rhydian is watching me in the mirror.

"Is this common?"

Rhydian grins. "No, but Willow Sola Warrington, nothing about you is common. You are very special. The Goddess crowned you directly today, and that hasn't been done since the beginning, to my knowledge."

As I let go of my magick, the hum and the blue designs fade from my body, including my crown. The moment feels intimate with Rhydian behind me in the closeness of the bathroom. I'm afraid to turn around with his assessing eyes watching me in the mirror.

A voice calls out: "Wills?"

Rhydian closes his eyes and backs out of the bathroom, making room for me to leave. It's Emily and Cross. They walk into the kitchen and Emily is hugging me before I even see her.

"Wills, I'm sorry about your father."

I hug her back. Cross speaks in a hushed voice with Rhydian.

"Willow, Sabine and the remaining members of the High Coven have been sequestered in Hallowed Hall and are under Guardian watch. Edayri is buzzing about the Goddess crowning you, your magick, and that you marked a demon general to your royal council. You have all the realm on your side. Everyone is waiting for you!" Her smile is infectious, reaching her eyes. She shakes my shoulders. "Wills, did you hear me?" She hugs me again. "I knew it!"

I pull back from her. "Lucy?"

Her voice drops in enthusiasm. "She'll be okay. She's home. I had her leg healed before I took her home."

"She isn't part of this world, is she?" I bite the inside of my cheek, waiting for Emily to respond.

Her bright eyes darken. "She doesn't know who she is, Willow. She's—"

Cross interrupts. "Another valkyrie?"

"And human. A dangerous combination. I've been with her for most of her life, protecting and watching her grow."

"You can't keep this from her," I say.

"I know," Emily answers. "But she could stay human too. I'm not sure if she will become more, but with your triggering, she could."

Rhydian's head moves to the side as if he's listening to something I can't hear. Cross does the same. I shrug my shoulders when Emily tilts her head at them.

"Cross?" Emily asks.

"Evan. The Guardians are reporting that he and others crossed into the rift here."

"Here? In Chepstow?" I wring my hands.

Rhydian shakes his head no.

"Where?"

"He's here on this plane, Willow. They say he was hurt in a bad way by whatever magick you pushed at him. They must be looking for a healer. Tullen thinks Cross and I might be able to track him."

"Don't." The mood of the room changes. "This is enough, Rhydian. If he comes for me, he comes."

Rhydian takes a step toward me. "That's not acceptable."

"He's my family, my uncle. Rhydian, he had plenty of chances to hurt me before now."

"You're not invincible, Willow. He could—"

I hold my hand up. "Stop. It's enough for now."

Rhydian tenses his jaw. The muscle ticks and he turns away from me. Cross doesn't reveal much, but his eyes glint toward me in approval before he speaks.

"Eoin, wants to meet with ya soon, but until then, he's ordered that we put protective magick around yer home and stay here on watch. Tullen and Quinn will relieve us and we'll take shifts."

Looking at Emily I ask, "Will you stay here too?"

"Duh. But to not protect you, you've got that shit in spades. I'm here to whip up my famous tacos and hang."

I laugh and hug her.

CHAPTER 21

Five months later

Lucy pulls her car into my driveway. I run out into the snow flurries, bundled in my coat and school uniform.

"Hey. Looking a bit gloomy today," she says. "Need some pep up music?"

I shake my head. "Depends on the tunes. If I have to listen to Lukas Graham's '7 Years' one more time, I might blast this car apart."

She laughs. "Don't hurt my car. You know she doesn't control the tuneage."

We park in the school lot and Emily slides up next to us in her Camry. Getting out of Lucy's car, I pull my scarf around my neck a little tighter, breathing in the crisp, clean air. Spring will be here soon. Of course, that doesn't mean the snow stops in Chepstow.

"So, Lucy," Emily says, "did you tell her?"

"Tell me what?"

Lucy bites her bottom lip and keeps walking toward the school entrance. Emily smiles and fluffs her unruly short hair into a new mess. At our lockers, I stand next to Lucy tapping my foot, hands on hips.

"I got a scholarship."

"What?" I'm not surprised, but I pretend for Lucy. "What kind, exactly?"

Her grin stretches from ear to ear. "Stanford, full ride!"

I hug her and jump up and down with joy. Emily shakes her booty with us. Lucy is all smiles.

Coral and her cronies pass by as we celebrate. "Oh, look, the village idiots," she says.

Being snubbed by Coral just makes me more joyous, especially when she trips over her own feet. She recovers quickly.

Lucy pushes me. "Wills, don't."

Emily laughs. "Oh, come on. You can't prove it." Winking at me, she hooks her arm through mine and we walk down the familiar hall toward homeroom.

I told Lucy about my Wiccan heritage after the funerals for my father and Mrs. Scott. She took it in stride. I still haven't revealed the other part, though—the part about being crowned Queen. I made a pact with Rhydian and the Guardians to finish high school in as normal a way as possible. Having Eoin, the commander of the Guardians, move into my home isn't really normal, though. It does help to pass him off as my legal guardian, some long-lost uncle, so that I can stay put in an effort to be normal until I have to go back to Edayri.

In homeroom, Daniel is seated at his desk. He grins at me and leans over to say something just as Mr. Brandt shuts the door and announces an assembly. We all shuffle down the hallways to the auditorium. Daniel sits next to me. Headmaster Chin starts with the spring semester schedule changes and announces the date and theme for prom, then dismisses us with good wishes for spring break.

Student enthusiasm for the next class is non-existent as they linger in the auditorium and hallways. I follow Lucy out of the auditorium. Daniel taps me on the shoulder to get my attention and I turn around just as Coral is walking by.

"So, I know we aren't together, but would you want to do the prom thing with me?" he asks.

Coral purses her lips together in a tight smile and stares me down as she passes.

"I'm guessing Coral was hoping for that invite," I say, pointing at her with my thumb. Daniel keeps his hopeful eyes on me.

His hand brushes his wavy hair back from his face. "Yeah, maybe. Just . . . most days I can't remember exactly why we broke up."

That hits me right in the heart. "Well, with going in different directions for college, I think it's best. You should ask Coral."

"Really?"

"What?" I hug my books to my chest.

"Who are you? You can't stand Coral, but you're pushing me off on her?" Daniel rolls his eyes, confused, then smiles his easy way. "Will you be around at all for spring break?"

"No, I'll be with my grandmother in Europe," I say. "I leave in two days."

He nods as Marco strides over.

"Hey, Daniel! Stuart is getting a pickup game together. What do you say?"

They walk off together and I feel his disappointment. I'm upset with myself too. I'm pathetic; I should do something or act awful so that he hates me, so that I can keep him safe. I still care about him and trying to put distance between us when we're around each other is hard, especially when we share friends.

I head to Advanced English, which drags on forever. Like all the students, I'm waiting for the half-day bell that will free us for a week. Usually spring break is equated with warmth, but living up north, we're happy just for the sun to shine on our frozen faces. The news has been projecting snow for tonight.

I've been visiting with Sabine at the manor in the Ember

region of Edayri and have learned that she experiences similar weather, as her location isn't that different from living in Ireland, where our Celtic heritage comes from.

My visits with Sabine have been good. We're trying to build a relationship. Our last conversation still rings in my mind: "The more entanglements you have there, the harder it will be for you here." I can't help but think of Daniel. I had planned to go to homecoming, prom—all of it. It's all wishful thinking now.

The half-day bell sounds after what feels like hours. I walk with Emily and Lucy to the parking lot.

"So, we're still on for girls' night?" Emily smiles.

I beam. "Yes! I've got a movie lineup and all kinds of junk food for us."

"As long as Ryan Reynolds is in one of those movies, I'm a happy girl," Emily says. "See you in a few!"

Lucy and I climb into her car and make the trip to my house. She parks in my driveway and says, "Will, would you be okay with . . . oh, never mind." She turns off the car. She looks nervous.

"What? Just ask."

"Daniel asked me to prom. I kinda said yes. Are you okay with that?" Her face is scrunched up. She's prepared for me to be angry. But I have no right to Daniel. All I can do is shake my head affirmatively. I hug her. She's my best friend and she deserves happiness, including someone as great as Daniel.

"It's fine, Lucy," I say, sounding more confident than I feel. I get out of the car, happy she'll be back later. It's just a dance. It doesn't mean they're together.

Duke greets me excitedly at the door. I waggle his ears, but then I smell something strange coming from the kitchen— smoke. I drop my backpack and run to the kitchen to find a fire.

"Eoin!" I yell. Duke barks in the background.

The fire grows from the stove. I wave the smoke away and call my magick, thrusting my hands forward just as someone behind me pulls me backward. The fire extinguishes. A black bag comes down over my head and I'm dragged, screaming, back by my armpits. Bracelets are clamped to each of my wrists. My magick stops. I can't do anything, can't even find the ever-present hum.

I kick and yell, mentally reaching out for Rhydian, then Ax. Duke is barking. There's more than one person in the kitchen with us. I connect my foot with someone in front of me and they cuss. I'm being transported. I hear Rhydian's voice in an echo, calling my name. I'm pushed and pulled and twisted in the transport. My stomach drops as I hit the ground.

I try to push myself up, but the heel of a boot pushes me back onto hard dirt.

"Stay down," a young female voice says.

"She's not going to help us. She hates him," a male voice says. "They'll locate her."

"I've got this," another young woman says, and a sharp pain shoots through my head.

Lights out.

BONUS: HIS BLOOD VOW

THE UNWANTED SERIES, NOVELLA 1.5

CHAPTER 1

The training floor mat has a familiar spring under my feet as I shuffle to the side. Sweat drips into my eye—it stings, but I refuse to flinch. My sight is on my sparring partner, the behemoth, Cross. Light on my feet, I drift in the opposite direction, avoiding his fist to my face. Speed is on my side as I rotate around him, and finally he throws his gloved fists up into the air.

"Come on! Rhy, are yer here to train or dance?" he says in his lilt accent.

I smirk and mockingly taunt the bear with a wave.

"Ah yes!" Cross taps his padded hands and his muscles bulk even higher on his shoulders and neck.

His approach is methodical and not straight on. My left side smarts from his jab and a right hook connects to my body. I take advantage of the opening and land my right hook. He stumbles back from the momentum and I'm moved off to the side. My ribs barb in pain from the twist.

"Goddess, Cross, I'm gonna feel that for a week," I say.

I move before he can track me. I land another hit and then attempt to sweep his leg. Instead, he catches my foot and twists me down to the mat. Next, I know, comes the ground-and-pound, so I roll before Cross can land on top of me. I twist behind him, which allows me to get my arms under his with a choke hold, and then I lock him up tight with my legs. He laughs and taps out.

Clap. Clap. Clap.

It's Quinn in the corner, smiling as Tullen hands him money.

"What the blasted shite? Did I lose a wager I knew nothing about?" Cross asks.

"Oh, don't be a poor sport. There was no way Rhydian was gonna let you get the best of him in a five-minute speed round. He's too quick," Quinn says.

I clap the back of Cross's sweaty shoulder. "It's not as if you don't bet, Cross."

"Aye." He laughs and claps me even harder on my shoulder in return. "Private bets, just not as fun, ya know?"

"No doubt." I laugh as well, wiping my face with a towel and chugging water from my bottle.

I've trained with Cross since we were kids, prior to joining the Guardians—before either of us had any muscles, smarts, or size to us. It's in our nature to be competitive. A rematch will come soon.

"So what are ye interlopers doing here?" Cross asks.

"Actually, Rhy, your scores came in and Commander Eoin wants to speak with you," Tullen responds.

My testing scores for Captain rank. I've passed all the physical pieces, and this is the last assessment to determine if I can move up in rank and lead my own command. I've been working toward this goal since joining the Guardians. It's an elite position, one that would elevate my career as a Guardian and my family's standing. I swallow my water and try to be calm, but my gut rumbles and drops. This is it.

"Rhy, yer pale like a ghost. Man, ya did just fine." Cross pushes my shoulder before throwing me a new hand towel.

"I'll shower and go see the Commander. Was there and ETA?"

Tullen nods. "Yes, he's expecting you in ten, so clean up fast."

Back to the locker room, I move swiftly. This opportunity is hard won—not everyone gets a shot at promotion and increasing their family's station. This year there are four other candidates besides me, all much older and more experienced. My unit will change, and I most likely won't be with my buddies, my brothers-in-arms.

I transport to the hallway in front of Commander Eoin's office suite. The two recruits who manage the office do not look up from their desks. Instead, one of them points to the opposite door and says, "He's expecting you. Go in."

A door. A simple thing that provides privacy in a room. But then again, for me it's a gateway to my future. I knock with one knuckle then open the door and step across the threshold to see what future waits on the other side.

"Have a seat, Rhydian."

The deep baritone of the Commander's voice is unsettling. His face is stone, and I promptly take the seat in front of his desk.

"Your Captain has good things to say about you. I've been pulling all your records and scores."

He shuts the folder in front of him and looks me straight in the eyes. Nothing is readable on his face. I let the silence continue as he studies me. It's a test of patience. He rests his hands on the desk.

"Rhydian, you're young, but certainly promising for the Guardians in a leadership role. You earn respect quickly and are decisive. But"—Eoin stands— "your father is interfering by speaking with the Wiccan King, and I don't appreciate the interference in Guardian affairs—especially command decisions."

Shit, what has my father done now? I keep myself steady on the outside and watch my Commander walk around to the corner of the room to look out a window.

"What are you thinking?" Eoin asks.

"I'm not my father, sir. I should be judged on my merit, not on his."

"Fair enough." Eoin returns and sits back in his chair and I'm trying to maintain my stature. "So, let's get to it. Your Captain is appointing you and the final decision lies with me. I'd prefer to choose a more experienced candidate, such as Rory or Collins."

Breathe, Rhy, breathe.

"But your scores in tactical strategy blew them away. Go ahead, smile and relax, Rhydian."

The brief smirk from Commander Eoin allows me to exhale.

"I'm glad to hear the scores were satisfactory," I say.

"Modesty. I like it." Eoin signs his name to something and looks back at me. "Rhydian, I'm promoting you to Captain. You will relieve your current Captain of his position and resume command over your current assigned unit. It won't be easy, but your buddies will need to fall in line and it's your job to make it happen. You think you can handle that?"

"Absolutely, sir."

"Good." Eoin pauses and stands. I stand with him. He extends his hand and I shake it. "You must get outfitted. See Billows at the desk outside. Also, keep your father out of Guardian affairs to the best of your ability from this point on. All missions and intel are not for civilians, regardless of their Wiccan rank."

"Understood, sir. Ah, thank you, sir."

"No need for thanks, Rhydian. You worked hard and earned it, quicker than anyone. You, son, are a natural. But don't rest on your laurels. You must work hard and put your unit and the Guardians first from now on."

"As above and so below, sir."

I can't help but smile wider as I leave Commander Eoin's office. Despite my father's meddling, despite my ruined family name and ranking, I did it. I'm the youngest Captain in the history of the Guardians.

CHAPTER 2

Before my keys hit the kitchen table, I grab the bottled ale out of the refrigerator, pop the top, and swig two large gulps. It's been a rough week since my promotion. The Captain rank comes with extra drills and strategy training that exhausts me at the end of each day.

"I hear we have a celebration in order."

Pfft.

Ale dribbles from my lips, and I wipe it with the back of my hand.

"Father? What are you doing here?"

"Apparently catching you by surprise," he says. He leans against the frame of my small hallway from the living room.

I need to change my locks and enchant them to only my signature. I sit at my small bench table and gesture for my father to sit.

"Yes, well," I say, "considering this is my home, and I wasn't expecting anyone . . ."

My father pulls out the chair at the end of the table and sits. Interlacing his fingers together, he sets them on the table. I want to relax and celebrate with my father, but I catch myself sitting with my back straight. He could have hurt my career with his meddling with the Wiccan King. I've learned if I confront him, he will be defensive and dismissive. Right now I don't need to spend the energy.

Thank Goddess that the Commander didn't let my father's political exploits interfere with me and my standing within the Guardians. He is up to something per usual, but for now I push it out of my mind. I swallow the last of my ale and smile. The pride in his eyes stops me from arguing.

"Son, I couldn't wait to see you. You've done so well for yourself and now"—he leans back and straightens his tweed jacket—"you're the youngest Captain in the Guardians. With your rise in rank, you can apply for other prestigious positions after your commission is over."

I laugh. "Father, how about one step at a time? I'll be facing more training and constant reviews of performance for the next two years."

"Did they tell you the unit you'll be over?"

I don't wish to tell him, nor receive the lecture of how to handle and manage my brothers-in-arms. My friends.

"I'm sure that will come soon. Is there another reason for the visit?" I ask.

He takes my empty bottle of ale and throws it in the trash under my sink. He washes his hands at my sink and looks over at me. I'm a teenager again, under his roof instead of my own.

"Do you have plans this evening?" he asks.

I do, but his wide eyes and raised eyebrows indicate that I should change them.

"Why?" I ask.

"I'd like you to join me for dinner and meet an old friend of mine, Aiden Warrington."

"Wait, Aiden Warrington? Warrington, as in the royal Wiccan family? Father to the princess? The princess who has been missing for over a decade?" I ask.

My father doesn't speak, but pinches his lips together and nods.

Goddess, what is my father dragging me into?

CHAPTER 3

As I walk into my childhood home, dread washes over me as if I expect the disappointment in my father's voice—a well-rehearsed speech about arriving late, my lower-class friends, or my informal casual attire. None of that is going to occur tonight, but it sits on my shoulders, the disapprovals of the past, regardless that I haven't lived here in over four years. I joined the Guardians right after my higher education in order to escape the noble education Father wanted for me. My personal rebellion was to retreat into service. Old habits remain, however: I check my tucked shirt and belt, then brush aside any potential wrinkles on my pant legs before I open the back door.

The housekeeper Beatrice is wiping her hands on a rag as she rounds the corner.

"Rhydian, is that you?"

"Good evening, Beatrice," I reply.

She is the reason this stuffy house is a home.

"Boy, don't stand there! You come here and give me a proper hug."

I do as she says and smile with relief that she harbors no ill feelings that I haven't called her in a while. Her small arms envelop me as if I'm still a small boy. The only difference now is her gray short hair. She has been with my father since I was young, and Abigail went abroad to a private school.

"I hear we are celebrating the Guardians' youngest Captain!"

She beams when she releases my shoulders that are two times broader than she is. She smiles, pride shining in her eyes, and I'm humbled in her celebration.

I smile back at her. "So Father already relayed the good news then?"

"As if that man says anything!" She snaps the towel like a whip. "Of course he did, because I hounded him! Come help ol' Bea out and let's set the table."

I follow her down the entryway into the galley kitchen. When she opens the door, the smells conjure memories and I'm salivating to the picture of roast beef, carrots, and other comfort foods. I spy her homemade bread with a cheese spread on the wooden pallet and go to sample it.

"Don't you dare! You can take the appetizer to the sitting room."

Laughing, I pick it up and do as I'm told. Returning, I find my father sweeping in and looking over the food.

"I thought I told you it would require a more elegant and leaner meal."

"Mr. Boward, this is what we had on hand. If you're unsatisfied, I suppose I could magick it into something else, but I cannot guarantee the outcome of its taste and stability."

My father's face almost pouts at her even response. Beatrice is the one person who will not cower to my father, and he never pushes or tries to manage her as he does everyone else.

"Father, I'm sure this is more than fine."

"It'd help if he told me who he was hosting tonight," Beatrice says.

He taps Bea on the shoulder. "Your food is always delicious. Thank you for this fine meal tonight." He turns and says, "Tonight we are hosting one of my oldest friends, who I haven't seen in nearly a decade."

"Mr. Boward, that is just lovely. I will make sure it's perfect! The dessert is just finishing up."

The doorbell rings.

The man is tall like my father, and they meet each other's shoulders and hug briefly in greeting.

"Aiden."

"Esmund. It's been far too long."

I stand for a beat as I wait to be presented by my father, but he's interrupted by his guest first, who looks at me and says, "Rhydian?"

"Yes, sir." I extend my hand, and it's met with both of his in a warm clasp.

"You were just a young toddler last I saw you. Now you're a man! How time flies. Is your sister here as well?"

My father escorts us to the sitting room and explains that Abigail couldn't make the dinner tonight. My father fills glasses with an amber alcohol elixir next to the wooden palette of bread and cheese. We all take chairs around the smaller table. I wait them to drink first as custom before I take a sip of mine. I don't remember this man at all from my youth. He isn't like Frank, who came over when our mother left and checked in on us.

My father doesn't have many he would call friends, and when Frank passed, Abigail and I wondered exactly what Father would do. It was clear he would throw himself into his work, and he did.

"So where is your lovely daughter this evening?" my father asks.

Oh Goddess, if this is a setup I will—

"She's at home in the terra realm. I judged it best if we met alone. She is unaware of Edayri and her Wiccan heritage."

This can't be.

"How can she be unaware? Sir, aren't you linked to the royal family?" I ask.

"Yes, by marriage."

Bea is eavesdropping, pretending to accidentally drop something as the kitchen galley door swings on the hinge. My father purses his lips but doesn't look back at the door as I excuse myself in order to check and help Bea. I find her bent over a broken plate, picking up shattered pieces.

"Let me do that."

"Thank you, child. I need to get another plate and get moving. I did not know we'd have someone from the royal family here. Oh, bless the Goddess. I need to clean up, I need to go back and—"

I stop her before she gets too carried away. "It's okay, everything is fine. You heard Father: they are old friends, and it stands to reason Mr. Warrington wanted little pomp and circumstance, or else they would have had their evening meal at MacKinnon Manor."

Wiping her brow and again taking a deep breath, Bea clutches her apron. "True, certainly true."

She ushers me out of the kitchen once we clean the mess. I return to find my father and Mr. Warrington in deep hushed discussions, but that doesn't stop my father from waving me into the room.

"Rhydian, come and have a seat."

"Is something wrong?" I ask.

Mr. Warrington's face is solemn, and his eyes seem to search the room.

"It's my daughter, Willow."

I wait, but he doesn't divulge any more. I'm not sure what to say. I look to my father, who avoids me.

Mr. Warrington's hand waves and iridescent magick surrounds the room like a cocoon.

"This is confidential. So, pardon the magicked enclosure, but it's quite necessary so that we can speak freely."

"About your daughter, sir?"

"And the Wiccan King," my father responds.

My father's statement makes my stomach sink. He is plotting something that entangles me in some family scheme in order to test his standing among the high covens. As a Guardian, I'm duty bound to the Wiccan King and his interest, I am duty-bound to my superiors. If I don't, it's not only a decrease in rank, but larger punishments, like being discharged altogether from the Guardians. Does he ever consider what might happen to me?

"Before we go any further," I say, "I'm a Guardian Captain and anything said here—"

"I don't plan to speak ill will of the Wiccan King, Rhydian," Mr. Warrington cuts in. "However, the passing of his reign is tied to my daughter."

I'm not sure where this is going, but Father is too quiet, and that alone fuels my disappointment. He should have at least prepared me versus leading me to dinner as a social matter, when he has games afoot.

"Father, you seem more aware. Have you both already spoken on this matter?" I ask.

"Yes." The answer weighs heavily on my shoulders. My father, the orchestrator of yet something else. Why can't he just leave me out of his plans?

Bea rings the dinner bell, and my father stands.

"Let us discuss more over dinner."

Eating is the last thing I want right now. I follow my father and Mr. Warrington into the formal dining room. I should walk right out of this house. What is my father thinking involving me? This may be his undoing of status because of my service, my oath. But he knows better, he knows I would help him, serve him—because although my oath is to be above family, it's never above him and his approval of me.

CHAPTER 4

The dining room is set with the finest dishes my father owns. In the center is food that Beatrice prepared, and she added a magickal flare of décor that shines glitter and light.

"Well, Esmund and Mrs. Beatrice, you flatter me. Thank you," Mr. Warrington says, sitting at the table.

I knew that although Bea was not in the dining room, she was listening and most likely grinning ear to ear in satisfaction at her name being mentioned. I take a seat at the table next to my father, who sits at the head of the table.

Before we eat, my father, in a bit of dramatic fashion, says, "Before we consume our lovely meal let's give thanks to our Goddess who graces us this evening." I nod my agreement and hold on to Mr. Warrington's hand, his over mine, and my father's, mine under his. "Aiden, would you mind giving the graces?"

This request is interesting. As a matter of status and as head of the household, my father always gives the graces in this house. His request to Mr. Warrington is one that honors the status that is above my father's in his own home. I've never seen my father move to the side for another. Come to think of it, he seems so relaxed and at ease with Mr. Warrington—not something I see too often from him. They must truly be friends. He usually only has acquaintances and connections. I see his need of approval from this man, and I steady my emotions, surprised at seeing this side of my father. The facade of a formal Wiccan man shed for a man I do not know of outside of what I've read or heard from others.

"Blessed be," they both say in unison. I follow and come out of my reverie.

"So, tell us about your daughter, Willow," my father says.

Mr. Warrington smiles and says, "Esmund, she looks so much like Nuala. It would take your breath away. It's almost like staring at the past."

"You must share a photograph with me."

"After evening meal, yes." He pauses. "The issue at hand, as you may have surmised from our brief phone conversation, is that she is unaware of her Wiccan heritage and of her magickal power."

I'm shocked at his admission. How can she be unaware of the power she holds, especially as a royal family member? Royal family members have an abundance of magick. It would be hard to bind her for so long in her life that she wouldn't notice.

"Mr. Warrington, how could your daughter be unaware? Isn't she close to my age?" I ask.

"Rhydian, please call me Aiden. Yes, but it's becoming clear the bind is breaking. I placed it on Willow following the accident that killed her mother. I did this by myself, but with the royal family's blessing. There was speculation that Willow was a target as well, so—"

"You hid her," I interrupt.

He nods.

"It's only in the last couple of years that we've settled into one location. I felt it was important for her socialization and schooling. The royal family has reached out and been in touch with me, wanting to see Willow, because, well, the rumor you may have heard . . ."

My father finishes in a hushed tone for Aiden: "The curse."

I shouldn't be here. I can't hear this information without reporting back to the Guardians Commander. My oath and loyalty to the crown. Hell, I'm an officer now and it's even more significant because of my station.

"Father." I say the word as a warning. His eyes look from me to Aiden as if he understands the weight of this conversation. "You know my position. If this is anything against the Wiccan crown, I'm duty-bound to report it." I push my linen napkin next to my plate, where the food has barely been touched.

"This isn't against the Wiccan crown, Rhydian. It's *saving* it," Aiden responds before my father.

"That may be, but you're speaking about the Princess. The long-lost Princess."

"That is true." My father nods. "But son, I think there is a way for your loyalty and oath to be sustained without punishment of non-report, because I fear my daughter's life is in more danger now than ever before," Aiden says.

He has a plan. My father, of course, would have a plan. All I can do is sit back. Looking at these two men, it's clear they have been discussing this topic without my attendance, because it's clearly orchestrated specifically for whatever this dinner is.

"Lay it out for me," I say.

Aiden's hands light up, and when he separates them, a dim light encompasses the dining room just as it did before.

"For the safety of us all. It's a protection spell, so our conversation is ours alone."

This is the first thing that makes sense to me—finally, some sort of protection around this discussion. I shift in my seat before grabbing the wine and taking a drink of courage.

"The curse is taking its toll on the Wiccan King, and it's expected he will not last the next month."

"That is not what is being communicated to the Guardians."

My father interrupts and says, "Nor with the high or noble covens. This information is only guessed at, but the Wiccan King sent a message to Aiden."

This is secretive information. I'm not some high-ranking commander or high coven member, and neither is my father. Although I bet he is salivating at the opportunity to know more than those who are above him.

"What was the message?"

"He confirmed his expected passing. He wants his grand-daughter, my daughter, to fulfill the calling to her royal place as Wiccan Queen. Harkin is concerned that when word is more public, his demise may come soon, and he'd like her established ahead of his death to ensure her safety with the Guardians," Aiden says.

"But . . . wait, she knows nothing about this? Why don't you talk to her now?"

"It's a good question, Rhydian, but it's more sensitive. I know my daughter. And I also realize that she is a target for others now. Those tempted to harm or kill her for her magick before she learns how to defend herself. We need more time. I require someone as her bodyguard. Her security and someone who can—"

"Because she's an outsider. You need to keep her safe during her transition, to mold her into her royal duty," I say.

I realize what they are asking: they want me to infiltrate her world and get to know her. This is irresponsible. If they just brought her here to Edayri and allowed her to transition within the actual system, that would be definitely smoother and less suspicious, instead of this cloak-and-dagger shit.

"Will she?" I ask.

"Will she what?" my father asks.

I can tell by Aiden's cast-down eyes he has doubts. He knows that I'm asking if she will even accept who she is and take on the duty. If he's hidden her away, she has a choice. She can stay out of this. Which leaves the royal rule to the high coven and most likely Lady Sabine, Harkin's wife.

"You don't seem certain, sir."

"Willow . . . she doesn't know this world, doesn't know her potential power or abilities. Some would love this, but she is one who would rather not be in the limelight. She would rather be with her close friends and just experience life."

Who can fault someone wanting to live their own life on their own terms? I haven't met her, but I already may like this girl. She most likely won't be the power-hungry royal everyone has been so used to for decades. She could be a fresh perspective, even a new beginning.

"Do you think she would choose a different path?" my father asks.

Aiden laughs, sitting back in his chair. "Oh, she will rebel, but I sense her integrity will push her to what's right and what's fair. She is a lot like her mother that way."

My father's shoulders tense. His eyes stare off. He is calculating something.

"The point is, she won't have a choice. Her bound magick will release, could happen upon Harkin's passing, I'm not sure. Once her magick is free, she'll be a beacon to anyone who would want her dead in order to take her magick and birthright."

"She could still—" my father interjects.

"I know her, she won't."

"So what is my role in this? Her bodyguard from afar?" I ask.

Aiden looks to my father, who nods before he continues. "We've been discussing a pact, a conscious effort for you to—"

This is where my father's influence is. Go big or do nothing. He wants our families tied together, and this is the opportunity. I know exactly what it is when Aiden says the word *pact*.

"A blood vow? To the future Wiccan Queen?" My heart is thundering in my chest and my ears don't seem to work when he says yes. "Why would she accept a blood vow from me? I'm honored, but you haven't even told her who—"

"The vow would be a conduit, through me for my daughter."

"Won't she be offended?"

He nods. "It's quite possible."

CHAPTER 5

The discussions of the evening have me in a zombie state when I enter my small-unit home. I unlock the door from my touch. The sound of my footsteps barely registers on the tile floor, but the familiar hum of my icebox signals to me like a beacon. I pop the top off of the ale and make my way through the short hallway to the living room and set my second ale at the side table before I fall into the usual place on the couch.

To accept a blood vow is an extreme honor, notably in my position, but it's also a lifetime responsibility. A lifetime commitment to the crown, to the sovereign of Edayri. What will happen to my unit? I would continue in my military path, but now, surely, it would be a royal one. I appreciate what my father wishes me to do. The status and changes wouldn't just be mine—they would be his as well. He doesn't appreciate living in the shadows of what his former family was within the noble covens. This would make him pleased. I can see him talking with the noble covens and bragging that my achievements are his: one of the youngest captains and tied to the royal throne, the Wiccan Queen.

I grab the second ale and drink almost half of it in one gulp.

The liquid is a rush and a fire in my throat. It does nothing to answer what they have asked of me. How do I make this decision? Is it even mine to make? Am I duty-bound as a Guardian? It's an honor of the worthy, and isn't this why I became a Guardian, to protect the crown? I can't go to the Commander to talk about this, because if I do that puts this young woman's life in danger. If I can't trust the Commander and the oath of being a Guardian, that makes me a deserter, a washout. They have lost her for so long, so many years, and this would undo that in one report. The political aspect of Edayri could maneuver to put her in more danger, since she isn't ready nor has support of the covens or High Council yet. I can't do that, she needs time. The urge to protect her is already present. Does that mean I've already decided?

Even in my zombie state, I call my sister to come over. She's the only one I can talk to without harm. She knows all the family secrets and this will be a big one.

Knock, knock.

"Front door's open, Abby. Come on in," I say.

She walks straight past me toward my small galley kitchen; I hear her opening the fridge as she's talking, retrieving an ale for herself.

"Hey, baby brother, what's going on? This fancy dinner at Father's house—he said I was invited but was busy, which is complete and utter bullshit. He didn't want me there, that is for sure." She sits down right in front of me, taking a drink of the bottled ale, and leans forward. "What could he have possibly wanted? Seriously, to get you calling me in the middle of the night, my curiosity is thoroughly piqued."

Her eyes are searching my face. I hesitate and she stays silent. I can't find the words, don't know where to start.

"What is it, Rhydian? Goddess, I thought it was just something to do with your promotion. By the way, congratulations! But now I'm completely worried."

Taking a swig of the last of my ale, I set it on the end table next to the first one. Tapping my wrist cuff, I execute a silence beacon so that if I am being spied on in any capacity, this conversation is as private as the one at my father's house. The beacon bounces through the room, removing any possibility of someone listening in.

The wrinkles increase on Abby's forehead; her mouth opens. "It's that serious?"

I tell her everything, and I feel lighter. She won't say anything to anyone, but I tell her three times that this is not something she can speak about to anyone and she nods in compliance each time. When I'm done, she is finishing her ale and sits back into the couch. And speaks for the first time.

"I missed some kind of dinner. Rhydian, I don't know what to say. What do you expect you will do? You're going to be hell-bent on honor and loyalty, but this is also for someone you know nothing about. Can you at least meet her first? Gain some kind of perspective?"

These are not unreasonable questions. Hell, I've asked them myself a hundred times since I've gotten home. I shake my head in silence.

"Goddess, I feel for that girl," Abby says. "Can you imagine most of your life being hidden from you? Your capabilities, who you are at your core, just aching to be out? I mean, you haven't lived as a teenage girl, but damn . . . this will not be easy."

I can't help but laugh. "No, I have not lived as a teenage girl, thank Goddess."

I picture Abby and her teenage years with my father. The shouting matches, the slammed doors, her stage of purple and blue hair. Lots of head-butting, but now Abby speaks her mind in a more concerted way with my father and has accepted her role in his life. She can separate the differences, something I've yet to master and acknowledge that I never will.

I continue, "And she's not that young. Her father said she's seventeen. Almost eighteen."

"Not much younger than you, even. I'd like to say you should focus on the situation of commitment, but I know you're debating father's role in this. I am as well."

Her nose wrinkles before shaking her head, standing dramatically with a sweep of her arm. "I get that they've been friends, but father's goal remains to elevate the family's status within the coven hierarchy to its former glory." She laughs before falling back into the chair. Under her breath she says, "So ridiculous."

She's right. She's not saying anything I haven't already thought about. The difference between me and my sister is she gave up a long time ago at trying to appease and make Father proud of her. I'm stuck—I seek his approval, I want his approval, I *need* his approval. Being his son, has a certain pressure that I can't escape.

"Abigail, I feel like I need to do this. Something within me is tugging me in this direction. I'm not positive of Father's role, but it's suspicious. He craves a royal position or . . . Could he want it for me?"

My heart lifts. Father might want something, yes, but something just for me, for my positions in this world to be elevated for my own success.

"Well, whatever you do, do it for you, not for him," Abby replies.

She's right—he doesn't need to be in this equation. I have Mr. Warrington's number. I'll reach out to him and leave my father out of it as much as I can.

"You're right. I needed to hear that."

"Baby brother, I'm happy I could help you. I'm here for you anytime, anywhere. I'm so proud of you and all that you've accomplished on your own. But could you help a sister out too?"

Her smile reaches her eyes, and I imagine, since Father always said she looked like Mother, that she would be proud of me too and would look back at me in the same way. Someday I will search and find her, our mother, who left us in Edayri.

"Thank you. Now, what do you want?" I laugh and tease her.

She scratches her chin as if to think about something very hard on her "want" list.

"Maybe an introduction to that buddy of yours, what's his name, Tullen? The one with the red hair," Abby says.

I laugh at her. "Are you serious? Do you really have interest there? I don't think it's a good idea, one of my closest friends dating my sister."

It wouldn't be a problem on my end, but I know Tullen has taken a vow not to date, and he is devoted to the service of the spiritual Goddess. No reason for me to deliver his truth to her right now.

A blush covers her cheeks ever so slightly, but it's there. "Whatever," Abby says. She rolls her eyes and leans back in her chair.

I tap my wrist cuff and the beacon returns home on my wrist. We chat for another half hour, about nothing and everything, and I love it. My mind is quiet. I haven't talked with her like this in a while. I go to bed after she leaves, realizing I'll be at work in three hours.

Today has been a long day.

CHAPTER 6

It's a new day and I am dragging my ass. I'm pacing my physical exertion so that I don't fall flat on my face in front of everyone. I'm in the middle of the unit run and all I can focus on is the end. Cross must see it in my eyes, because instead of being in front of me relishing the fact he's keeping pace with me, along with Tullen, he's quiet and not boasting. Quinn is up in front keeping pace with Marlowe. This is the end of the exercise course, the long running stretch, and if I can get through this, I'm that much closer to being done. Meaning shower, debrief, home, and straight to bed.

"What did you say?" Tullen asks.

Did I say something out loud? I don't even have the energy to respond and, breathing heavily, I shake my head.

"It's the last kilometer! Shall we push it, little girls?" Cross says.

Normally that would get my engine revving, Cross taunting me, but not today. I shake my head in a quick motion. Cross's brow furrows. I shrug as I pump my arms in pace with my feet. My breathing is all I can concentrate on so that I'm not dead last when usually I'm somewhere at the head of the line, usually leading it. I stare straight ahead, knowing they are exchanging looks.

Just a little farther, just a little farther.

That's the mantra I keep saying to myself so that I'm not constantly thinking about Willow Warrington and the brief dream I had last night.

The debrief is over. Thank Goddess.

I check my comm in my ear before turning it off and relieving my duty to another Guardian.

I make my way for the doorway as quickly as I can, but I have no chance of escape before they flank me: Quinn, Tullen, and Cross. The look on Quinn's face is quizzical—Cross and Tullen have probably filled his head with whatever concerns they have about me. It doesn't look like I'll be heading home soon.

"Yeah, I think the pub is where yer headin'," says Cross.

"Actually, I'm heading home. I got little sleep last night. I'm swamped in my new commission."

The clap on my back is Cross's subtle way of saying, *I don't give it shit.* He steers me toward the exit of the building and to the left toward Wolfbane's Pub.

"Well, Rhydian, ale has the finest ability of relaxing one's mind for a deeper, more restful sleep—if one doesn't overindulge," says Tullen. The brief smile on his face also confirms that I'm not going home soon.

I sigh and say, "One pint. But then I must go. Agreed?"

"Aye, that's the spirit. Plus, we need to celebrate, Captain." Cross punches my arm lightly, his smile wide.

"Oh, because we didn't celebrate already?"

Scratching the side of his temple as if he's forgotten, he says, "Do ya really want to debate this? I mean a proper celebration, not one where you run off to a dinner with your father."

These guys are my chosen brothers, my family, and I love them. How the heck am I going to tell them what I'm about to do? What I decide impacts them as well. There is no way I can make this happen without their knowledge, so it might be best to tell them now.

Quinn is silent as we walk to the pub. Wolfbane's Pub is a short walk from the operations building on the Hallowed Hall grounds. I could go to the officers' club, but the pub is for everyone and I can't quite see myself in my personal time going to an officers' club without my brothers. This is all changing so fast—soon my role is advancing and my brothers will be in a different unit.

The laughter pours out of the door as we enter Wolfbane's Pub. The tables are full and the bar is two lines deep of people standing and yelling to the bartender for their drink order. More people dwell on the stairs leading to the second floor, which is mostly for Guardians and other Wiccan officials in various capacities. Tullen nods as he makes a path toward the upper level of the bar. I follow with Quinn behind me. As we round the corner of the staircase, the noise is more of a dull roar than downstairs. The crowd is half of what it is downstairs, but still lively. Tullen is marching over to the familiar corner of an empty table, and he claims it for the night as we all sit and grab chairs to join him.

Cross is the first to break the silence of our group as we sit around the table.

"All right, ladies, let's get to the business at hand. What the heck is going on, Rhydian? It's apparent when you show up late to drill, even if it's a few seconds, when you are always early. And then of course you can't seem to keep up with the group when you're usually leading it. I mean, am I right?"

Quinn interjects, "Perhaps you're having an off day? I mean, a lot is going on. You were just promoted and—"

"Exactly, freakin' promoted, like, how are you not leading us, I mean what kind of example are you setting? I mean, Jesus, anybody can be Captain if that's the case," Cross says.

Tullen pats my shoulder and says, "What's going on,

Rhydian? Lay it on us. Get it off your chest, your back, or wherever it is."

I can't tell them. Not right now. I have to tell them, but definitely not in this bar. It's not safe. I wonder if I can do this a different way.

"So I'm getting the impression ya can't verbally tell us," Cross says.

Everyone nods—including me.

"Well, fuck, let's head over to your house then."

I shake my head.

"Guys, trust me, and understand that all is okay. I'll update you later. How about we celebrate with one drink?" I reply.

Everyone nods.

The server comes over and takes our order. Cross flirts with her shamelessly and we are off to our celebration—minus my much-needed sleep.

CHAPTER 7

The smartphone in my hand feels heavy. It's laden with secrets. I've communicated with Mr. Warrington over the last few days, who I still have trouble calling Aiden, although he keeps correcting me. We are meeting in Boston at an office building where he has space for his company.

"Do you have the credentials to go up to the Warrington suite?" the security lady asks at the desk.

I watch as others enter through a turnstile using cards with barcodes to get through.

I hold up the picture of the code Mr. Warrington provided me. "Is this it?"

She nods with a fake smile, as if she is disappointed and I have wasted her time.

"Yes. Scan prior to walking through. Take the elevators to the seventh-floor reception and they will escort you to where you need to be."

At the seventh floor, there are three different receptionists, but they all look similar to each other in their twinset sweater attire and long pulled-back hair. One greets me and then has another escort me to the fifteenth floor, where Mr. Warrington's office is. I walk out of the elevator and am greeted at the door by another receptionist, who leads me a short distance to a door and knocks before opening it.

"Mr. Warrington, your appointment is here."

The office space is immense with a large conference table, three different sitting areas, and an enormous desk off to the side. The large windows stare out at other high-rises and a bustling city below.

A door opens and Mr. Warrington is rubbing his hands on a towel. "Thank you, Jacqueline. I won't need any further assistance this evening."

My escort leaves and closes the door.

"Please have a seat, Rhydian. Thank you for making the trip here," Mr. Warrington says.

I walk toward the two-chair seating arrangement that is closer to the window, where there is a spread of drinks and food. My stomach twists at the sight. I have eaten little over the last few days contemplating this commitment to the royal family and what it will mean for me as a Guardian.

"Rhydian, please, have anything you would like."

I sit straight.

"Mr. Warrington, I—"

"Aiden, please, Rhydian."

"Sorry, yes. Aiden. I want you to know I am honored by your request to accept a blood vow to your daughter, the future Wiccan Queen—"

"But?" he interjects. "Listen, Rhydian. I know it's a large ask and one most would request of her directly, not through her father. It's unusual, and I suspect you're doubting your father's intentions, but please do not doubt my own."

The words stick in my throat. My shoulders relax. He understands my father without me having to sound like an ungrateful son.

"Sir. I will inform my Commander, because I cannot take this vow unless he is aware of my intentions. As well for the sake of my unit and brothers-in-arms."

"I would have done the same in your shoes, so I took the liberty of reaching out to the Commander myself."

My hands heat with sweat before I rub them on my pants. "You spoke to Commander Eoin?" I choke out.

"Yes, but not about you, directly. I told him I would need to request Guardian support for my daughter and that we'd be returning to Edayri soon," Aiden says. "However, he's under rule of the High Council, because of Harkin's—um, the Wiccan King's—health. Special requests and orders are no longer under the Commander's control without their review and approval. Meaning that leadership is unstable, and Eoin most likely has his hands tied. He's aware the blood vow will protect my daughter, he suspects what I'm after to secure her safety. If you inform him, in his position he'll have no recourse but to report to the High Council. As the Commander, told me, it would be better to ask for forgiveness at this point."

I rub my wrist cuff, which is magicked to hold my Guardian armor and other warrior tools. I'm so used to it that it's part of who I am, my identity.

"Then I cannot speak with Commander Eoin. He's duty-bound and it will put him in a unfavorable position," I say.

"So you will accept the blood vow to my daughter?" Aiden asks. His lifting eyebrows wait for me.

I nod, and with my grin he relaxes back into his seat.

"I don't know how I will ever repay you, Rhydian."

That he would even humble himself to acknowledge his part in this agreement says more to me about him and his daughter than he knows. It's not an expectation—he's freely allowed me to refuse.

"Aiden, the honor is mine alone. My intention is to keep the Princess safe and usher in a new era. There is no need for repayment, even to my father or family name, should it be requested. My life is to the Guardians and the royal throne."

Aiden turns toward a sideboard that has three bowls, and he picks up two and places them on the table in front of me.

"You're prepared?" I ask.

Is this happening too quickly? Maybe this is better—no regrets, no further forethought.

"I was hopeful, considering you came here. You could have said no over the phone." Aiden takes the third bowl and sets it down next to the other two.

I guess there is no time like the present. These ceremonial bowls look old with the cracked paint of the clay on the outside.

"How is this going to work without the Princess here?"

He laughs a deep chuckle before tapping each bowl with a wooden mallet. "I appreciate the formality, but she will smack you for calling her a *princess*. You'll have to get used to calling her Willow."

I close my eyes and shake my head. "Sorry. It's a tough habit to break until I meet her and get to know her better."

"I understand," Aiden replies.

He mixes a liquid from one bowl into the middle bowl and then mumbles a spell I can't quite make out. His hands light up and a silverlike string leaves his fingertips. His concentration never leaves the bowls and the contents of the third bowl as he says, "Dea est suscipere sanguinem votum in nomine tuo," and pours that liquid in into the middle bowl.

I stand next to him and repeat in English, "Goddess, accept this blood vow in your name."

The contents of the bowl look like a thin gel of silver with purple iridescent hues.

Aiden picks up the center bowl and says, "Drink."

I can't help but look from him to the bowl and back again. This is it—there is no going back. If I don't die, considering this is an unusual way for a blood vow to be accepted for someone who is unaware and not here. I swallow a gulp of air as I bring the bowl to my lips.

"Down the hatch," I say, and swallow the contents in one gulp with the tilt of my head.

The liquid moves in a rush like cool water down my throat,

and it warms my belly like a strong whiskey. I feel my extremities ignite with a levity and lightness that tingles as if the liquid is reaching all four corners of my body. The magickal power that I have feels as if it's doubling, and I step back as if I'm off balance. I drop the bowl and double over.

A voice whispers my name like an echo in my head.

Rhydian Jameson Boward.

The picture in front of me is no longer of Aiden, but a female form covered in a light. I shield my eyes and squint. It's the Goddess. I drop to my knees and bow my head.

Your vow is unto me for protection of the future Wiccan Queen.

This is not a question, but a statement. I nod and do not look up from the white-marbled floor. I have little time to think about the change in my surroundings.

Rise, young Guardian. Your service is a lifetime, your role an imprint on whatever she needs to succeed. Your duty is unto me and to her, for if you fail I will punish you with long lasting pain. Do you understand?

I breathe deep the crisp air and dare to look at her. She is draped in a Greek white gown that hugs her form and flows with a movement that is devoid of wind. Her hair is auburn and its curls frame her face. A face that is familiar from the Hallowed Hall painting and yet, here she outshines this likeness.

"Yes, I do."

Her smile is gentle, and she waves a hand in front of me that bathes me in light.

Your vow, Rhydian Jameson Boward, is accepted. Protect Edayri's future and my legacy.

I blink in rapid succession when I find myself in the middle of my home. The smartphone in my back pocket buzzes. There is a text from Aiden asking if I'm okay.

I respond: *I accepted the vow, and I will be in touch soon to meet Willow.*

First, I need to deal with Cross, who is in my living room, staring at me from my couch.

CHAPTER 8

"What the fuck is going on?" Cross asks. His eyes are burrowing a void into my face. "I've known you forever, and you're acting off."

"Really?" I laugh. "Don't you also say I'm always a little off?" I shrug then ask, "why are you in my house?"

"Screw this. We've all noticed it, and your father . . . Did you know the Wiccan King just passed this evening? We were all called, and Eoin noted that you were on a particular assignment, lips sealed . . ."

What? The King died? Cross is talking, but I'm not focused on him, because a wave of vertigo rushes through me and I fall into my recliner.

I hear . . . a voice? No, it's not a voice; a feeling, a smell, in a wave of pictures that are fluttering through my mind but not blinding me, transparent almost. A girl in her car, driving, lightness in her mind, singing loud. The smile of happiness, the laughter of missed words. The bass thrums and the hair on my skin rises, the smell of a greenway, of fresh-cut grass right after a light rain on a cool day, invades my nose.

I see her and breathe her name. "Willow."

This is my connection to her. The blood vow.

"What? Are ya even listening?" Cross asks.

"No. Sorry. No, I'm not."

I pull on the tether that connects me to her emotion. Although it's not clear anymore, her feelings influence my own.

"Why are yer smiling like a loon? Fuck, Rhydian, what is going on?" Cross asks.

I shake my head and laugh.

"I, uh—" How do I tell him? I rip off the band-aid. "I'm in service to the future Wiccan Queen."

He laughs, then becomes intense when I don't return the laugh and only nod.

"Yer sincere? How? Yer speaking of the missing Princess?" His hand rubs at his jaw. "So, there will be council to replace the Wiccan King, and the lawful heir lives? When is this happening? Rhy, he just freaking passed. How did this transpire?"

What to answer first? I start from the beginning and tell him everything. Cross doesn't respond. The twist of his mouth and the squint of his eyes tell me enough. He has no love for the caste system and coven bias.

"You can stay within the unit; you need change nothing. My decision is for the service of the crown."

He stands and I follow him to my front door.

"Say something," I say.

He spins. "So this is how it is now? You commit to yer unit and then leave us for some Royal who will be the same crap we've always had? That family is a curse."

"Cross, she's an outsider and her father is nothing like the—"

"Yeah, I'll believe it when I see it. By the way, yer not gettin' rid of us. We're brothers till the end, so . . . yeah." Cross reaches for the doorknob. "You will tell Tullen and Quinn in the next day, or I will."

The ultimatum is one I know he will deliver on no matter what I say.

"Hey." I get his attention before he walks through the door. "It's another adventure, my brother."

He nods and flashes a disappointed smirk before transporting away.

My stomach drops and my shoulders tense. I close my eyes and reach for the tether of happiness. The singing off-key.

Willow Sola Warrington.

CHAPTER 9

My eyes blink slowly at the paper I'm reading. I've read the same line twice on a report about a young soldier in training. The time of day is elusive until I look up and see it's well into the evening. I reach for my smartphone and find two texts from Aiden.

Willow is going to learn about her heritage tonight.
Sabine is pushing it.

These texts were sent hours ago. I leave quickly for my house to change. I change my shirt twice before I pick up my jacket. I'm flooded with emotion that isn't my own. It's like a limb that tingles as if asleep but awakened abruptly.

Something is wrong.

I transport to her house; she is in distress, her magick is expanding, the binding from her youth is breaking. The house is intimidating, rising high in the sky despite its white color and inviting entryway. Do I walk up the grand steps and knock on the door?

The windows along the east side of the house shatter in front of me and she screams. The distress, the smell of earth, the anger and rage, the colors flash dark and maroon. I transport to the fear, the smells, the colors, all guiding me to her. Aiden grasps her before she hits her head on the floor. She briefly sees me before her eyes roll back and she's out.

"Aiden, is she—?"

He holds a hand up.

"Sabine, your visit is over," he says.

I lower my eyes when Lady Sabine Mackinnon stares at me, her mouth pinched closed. My focus is on Willow. Her long, dark-blonde hair waves like silk to the floor. Her lean body and delicate hands. Being in front of her like this, my whole being is aware, but the emotions of her are no longer coming to me.

"Aiden, her binds are broken."

"And you triggered this, Sabine. I had no time to prepare her."

A portly lady with a kind, older face comes from the side.

"Mr. Warrington, let me take her to her room." She looks at me and smiles. "This strapping fella can help."

"Yes. Please, Rhydian, follow Mrs. Scott."

Aiden takes a moment to move before I can get to her and cradle her in my arms before standing. Her head lolls into my chest and my heart thunders. Standing, my muscles engage and I feel the burn as I follow Mrs. Scott up the stairs. A black dog meets me at the stairs, tail low, before Mrs. Scott pats his head. I smile, and the dog runs ahead of Mrs. Scott, leading us to a door. When Mrs. Scott opens the door, my senses are invaded by the smells of vanilla and lavender and the bright colors of turquoise, purple, gray, and pink. It's opposite of the house's neutral colors and bare walls I had seen.

The dog jumps on the bed and Mrs. Scott shoos him before pulling back the gray puffy blanket. I gently lay her down. Her head sinks into the middle of a pillow and she turns her head to the side. Her mouth opens just slightly. The sound of an ocean is at the back of my thoughts—her peace. I'm sensing her peace. I pull the puffy blanket over her, and Mrs. Scott turns on a small lamp next to the bed.

"Thank you," Mrs. Scott says.

The dog jumps back on the bed and lays next to Willow's feet.

"He's quite protective of her," I say to Mrs. Scott.

"Yeah, two peas in a pod. Come, let's give her time to rest."

I follow Mrs. Scott down the bare hall toward the grand staircase we just climbed. The foyer of whites and creams is empty except for a round table that holds an enormous bouquet. Aiden appears from an open entryway leading to a sitting room as we near the bottom of the stairs. He tosses back an amber liquid.

"I'm guessing the timeline is moved up then?" I ask.

"Yes. Evan, my brother-in-law, has been near her."

"Oh my Goddess," Mrs. Scott says, eyes wide.

I'm quickly trying to piece together what he's just said, but it makes no sense. Evan MacKinnon is dead.

"Sir, how is that possible?" I ask.

He shakes his head, saying he's not sure either, but that he felt Evan's magickal signature before Willow's magick broke from her binding. "She is in danger, and her magickal signature will be a beacon to others who want to challenge her for the crown. You need to stay nearby from now on, Rhydian. Sabine will inform the Commander and the High Council because of the way you came in. Your aura and behavior is of the blood vow to Willow," Aiden says.

"I have a family cabin here in Terra," I say. "I'll be there. No one will know. I can transport."

His shoulders rise and fall. His hand is out before mine, and then he pulls me to him in a quick hug. "Thank you, Rhydian."

It should feel awkward, but it's the hug I would have wanted from my father when I was younger.

Walking out the front door, I transport to three different locations, to be safe I wasn't followed, before arriving at the cabin.

CHAPTER 10

The forest is dense around the camping site. There are a lot of people here. My senses flare with the knowledge of magickal beings—and not just Willow. She may be in danger already. Her unrest is a taste at the back of my mouth, like a sore throat. I walk toward the large concrete pavilion in the middle of the scattered tents and groups of teenagers. The smell of ale saturates the soil. A few people look at me and smile big, affected by the ale. I wave and walk through so that I'm not stopped.

Reaching the edge of the forest, I use my blood vow to hone in my tether to her. She's here somewhere, and she is in danger. Her father alerted me and sent the code. She is no longer safe.

Her heart is pounding as if my own mirrors her heart. I scan the camp all the huddles of people, but she not here. She is running, the stillness here doesn't match—

A scream. Hers.

I run into the forest, my feet leading the way through cord of our connection. There is no time. I run faster, closing the distance. Almost there. Her fear is the urgency pushing me forward. I tap my wrist cuff as my armor extends with my strides.

There is a massive red figure in front of me. It's a Blood Warrior Demon. His shoulders obscure her tiny frame entirely.

"This isn't as satisfying as I had hoped, but your heart will taste good either way!" the demon says in its deep, thundering voice.

I join them just as he jumps, and she rolls away.

Summoning my magick, I throw it from my palms and hit him square in the chest. It drives back him into a tree hard enough the tree cracks. His heavy, muscled weight hits the earth hard.

I'm in front of her when she turns. She wavers on her feet. Will she run? My hands are up in submission. Her eyes, wild, blink. The shaking of her body eases.

I point toward the brush by a large tree.

"Stay silent and hide," I say.

She acknowledges me and her erratic breathing is slowing. I attempt to guide her judgments to trust me through the tether of the blood vow.

Moving toward the demon, I recognize Tertium, a pay-for-hire demon enforcer always making trouble. He's standing up, scanning the area, looking for her, before his eyes land on me.

"Ah, the Guardian Captain comes to protect his little witchy-queen wannabe, does he? Finally, an opponent worth my time!" He huffs again and again, as if smelling the air.

"Sorry, the feeling isn't mutual, Tertium."

If I wasn't used to seeing him in the holding cells after a drunken bender, the flare of his nostrils might have me reassessing this head-on approach. However, I've overheard him snore and I've seen him fight—he's clunky with his massive frame.

The demon pushes hard at the ground as if to collide into me like a ram. I sidestep his attack and kick his back to push his momentum forward into a tree.

Smash!

The tree buckles under the weight of the demon. He turns

and holds a dagger as he charges again. I unsheathe my sword, awaiting our clash.

"Boy, I'll wipe that grin—"

I meet him blow by blow and change my defense to offense. I change direction to get closer to his body and drop my sword in order to punch him with a right hook, then an uppercut. My fist lands perfectly on his chin and it's lights out for him, with a gaping mouth like a surprised fish out of water.

"Still grinning." I chuckle under my breath at his taunt. "You can come out now, Willow," I announce.

She slowly stands, hugging herself. Her eyes widen and her lips thin at seeing Tertium prone on the ground. He looks like an overgrown dog at this point, with his tongue out. Willow's face morphs from fear to pure anger. She strides toward me, and I step to the side as she rears her booted foot and kicks Tertium in the crotch.

I hold my shocked laugh and feel a touch of pity for the demon. For someone so small, she knows how to hurt a male; she is no victim.

"Asshole!" she yells.

The demon's response is like most males: even in his unconsciousness he curls to the side, groaning in pain.

She turns, and her assessment of me is brief. I don't want her to see me as a threat. I hold my hands up and my nervous laughter rises. "Um. Okay then." Shaking my finger at the creature, I say, "No children, Tertium."

"Tertium? This thing has a name? You know him?" Her eyes wide, she takes a small step back, holding her arm.

Is she injured? This is more serious; she is wavering. Her lips are almost devoid of color—she has lost blood. How did I not sense this? Taking a few steps closer to her, I say, "Yes, by reputation only. He's not a 'thing,' he's a Blood Warrior Demon," I say.

She shakes her head, her eyes closed.

"For simplicity, he's an assassin. Although not a very good one." I toss a retrieval stone to the ground with the command for Tertium's capture. It unfolds and grows four times its size, focusing light on the Blood Warrior Demon.

Tertium opens his eyes and stares at Willow and with a snarl he says, "More will come. Your father will pay too, little witch. The demons will feast on his heart for all the glorious dark—"

The retrieval stone does its job and cuts his threat off. He's captured, and the stone retracts. It will transport him directly into the Guardian holding cell. It won't take long for the Commander to trace it back to this spot and report to the high coven, so we need to go.

I extend my hand to her. "Enough of the mysterious. I'm Rhydian."

She stares at my hand. She's slow to trust—probably a good thing.

"Your father sent me to watch over you."

Did she just roll her eyes at me, at the mention of her father? Her emotions are all over the place and I can't follow them and sever the tether, the blood vow, before her exhale.

"Thank you for that," she says. Her voice hitches in a wince.

"Yeah. Tertium isn't much of a threat. All bark, not much bite." She turns, and I see a branch stake protruding from her back. "Whoa!" I point to her shoulder.

"It's bad, isn't it? It freaking hurts like nothing I've ever known before."

She wavers on her feet again and I gently move behind her to examine it. Her hair is obscuring the entry of the stake. It must be removed, and this is going to cause her great pain. Will I feel it as keenly as she will?

"It's gonna hurt for a second, but I can heal you quickly enough. Ready?"

"Okay," she says, her voice partly a whimper. She turns her head into her shoulder and holds onto the tree to brace herself.

I grip the branch with both hands, careful not to jostle her, and with my breath I pull it back straight. It barely moves and she screams. I put one of my hands on her to steady and yank again while pushing her forward. Finally, it comes free. I throw the wood as if it's the demon who hurt her. I cover the wound with my hands and push healing magick into her from my palms. I try to take her pain, but I don't notice anything and only taste the ash of fire that is her suffering. She is brave and barely moving, just a whimper as her muscle knits itself back together.

I'm awkward standing there with my hand on the small of her back. "You did well. It's healed," I say.

"Thank you."

She moves from me and she turns. My hand, wet from her blood and immediately cold, is no longer touching her. I close my fist to magick away the wetness before responding. "Of course."

I push the symbol on my wrist cuff that retracts my guardian armor so she sees me instead of a Guardian. My attempt at being less intimidating.

The twilight shines on her. She is stunning. Her long hair hugs her arms and waves around her with her small movements. Her pert nose and assessing eyes look me over.

"Have we met before?" she asks.

I'm standing there, mesmerized by her low voice. She is not a meek female by any means.

"I know your father, Aiden—Mr. Warrington. He and my family are friends. I'm a Guardian assigned to you for your protection." I smile when her mouth opens slightly. "I don't think we've formally met until today."

"Does he know I'm here?" she snaps, sounding irritated.

"I haven't spoken to him in several days. I will report what just happened."

"He knows I'm here!" she shouts, her eyes wild and wide. "Rhydian, right?"

My name drips from her lips and sounds as if it belongs there.

"You don't need to—"

I'm cut off by others shouting. "Willow, where are you? Willow?"

Some friends, just now searching for her after being gone how long? Maybe they heard her scream? There is a female—, a magickal female, is getting closer. Willow smiles at her, but I see her for what she is.

Willow knows a Valkyrie?

This is not good. She could harm her and take her powers for her own. I put myself between her and Willow. Willow says her name, I don't know who else is here, maybe others like this powerful Valkyrie?

The Valkyrie stands tall, then unexpectedly waves and blows a kiss.

There is no time as others approach. I reach for Willow and pull her into my body. She turns into me easily and I magickly transport us back to my family's cabin. The magick forces us together and I hold her steady as we are pushed and pulled with her panic. Recognizing she may have never transported before, I pull her back into me more tightly before I release her as our feet connect to the cabin floor. She holds my hand for a moment and although the connection is brief, I know without a doubt she trusts me.

I won't fail her.

REIGN

THE UNWANTED SERIES, BOOK II

PART I

By knot of one, the spell's begun
By knot of two, it cometh true
By knot of three, so mote it be

CHAPTER 1

M y thoughts surface from the depths of a dark pool of nothingness. The first things I notice are the scent of rich earth and the feel of grass and dirt on the ground beneath me. These hold me steady. I smell smoke and hear the crackling of a campfire. I work to piece together my memory, a rush of blurry moments.

Barking. Duke is barking.

Smoke. A fire in the kitchen.

I'm yelling for Eoin, then being grabbed. My magick fails.

I'm being taken from my home. I fight, but there are more of them, and I'm in darkness; I can't see. I'm pushed, pulled—and then there's nothing left. My memories stop there.

I steady my breathing to avoid drawing attention. My first thought is of Rhydian, my royal Guardian, and blood-vowed protector. Should I reach out to him? That could make things worse, not knowing where I am. Rhydian would come armored with the rest of the royal armada, ready to kick butt. I shouldn't put any of them at risk until I know more. Heck, maybe I can escape on my own and get home.

Careful not to move my body, I squint my eyes to view my

surroundings without alerting anyone that I'm awake. I don't hear anyone close to me. It's dark, but I can make out a campsite with a fire about ten meters away. The surrounding trees are tall and thick, more ominous than anything else, and possibly the best place to make a run for it. I make out some people—no, demons, with colorful skin and large horns that sweep back from their heads. There is no way for me to confirm where I am. It's possible that I'm still in Chepstow, Massachusetts, but I'm more likely in the magickal realm of Edayri. I open my eyes fully and confirm I am alone.

My body is stiff; my shoulder muscles scream because of the angle of my arms. Something weighs on my wrists behind my back. I'm still in my school uniform, the skirt twisted, but I can move my legs. I push against the heels of my purple chucks to sit up. The group near the campfire doesn't notice. A coldness comes over me. I've got to transport from here.

Holding my hands open behind my back, I mentally call my magick. I feel the familiar hum within me, but it won't rise beyond the surface. I twist to look over my shoulder and see the magick's familiar glow that should be flowing in patterns on my skin, instead contained in the glowing bracelets around my wrists.

I pull at the cuffs. My breathing is short and fast, and my eyes water as I attempt to shove the cuffs off. They don't move but instead pinch and twist on my skin. I yelp in pain. Someone at the fire turns my way.

I summon my magick again, then again.

Damn it, I need you!

I yank harder on the blasted bracelets and call to Rhydian in my mind. "Help me! Find me, please. They are coming!"

A jolt of pain travels up my arms in a snap. The connected cuffs release, and I can move my arms. The weight of each bracelet pulls my hands to my side as if each arm weighs ten pounds. My wrists glow like purple nightsticks. I could run, I think, or swing these heavy weighted bracelets at their heads. My magick shows itself on the surface of my skin more, but it's visibly muted and dull to my control; the patterns flow, ebb, pulse, and try to connect, but instead, the magick flows to these wicked bracelets!

Four young demons surround me; the opportunity to run into the trees is gone. These demons are dressed like anyone from my school, except they have colorful skin and small horns coming out of their heads. They keep a distance from me, observing the glowing bracelets.

A dark red female with short, black, spiky hair, wide dark eyes, and a taunting smirk gets closer to me. She's not so intimidating in her jeans, goth boots, and black anime hoodie.

"Your Royal Highness. You aren't much without it, are you?" She gestures to the glowing bracelets.

"Wanna test that?" I spit back, holding up the bracelets.

"Oh! So, you aren't helpless without your magick after all? How cute!" She claps her hands together, bats her eyes, and grins to reveal small fangs.

Cute? I'll show her cute when I use these heavy monstrosities on the side of her head!

The other three teenage demons move off to the side. A shorter male demon dressed in a dark tracksuit, which I hadn't noticed earlier, moves closer in my periphery. I turn on him, and he jumps back a step.

"What do you guys want with me?"

The girl demon seems to be the only one talking. "To correct what you fucked up!"

"What I—?"

A deep rumble of a voice interrupts and captures our attention. A dark figure emerges from what appears to be a tent on the other side of the campfire. The horns are more substantial, not some teenagers. My heart pounds faster, and the chill of the air makes me shiver. The figure becomes familiar as it gets

closer.
Theon.

CHAPTER 2

Theon is tall and lean, a cross between a grunge twenty-something and a samurai. He's a skilled fighter and usually near my uncle. Like my uncle, he is half Wiccan and half-demon.

His long hair is messy and obscures most of his face, but I can tell that his jaw drops at the sight of me. Marching in big strides, he focuses his attention on the feisty demon in front of me. "What the hell have you done, Sikkori?"

"We did what needs to be done. She's right here." Sikkori gestures to me with painted neon pink claws.

"No, you've complicated it more! The Guardians and the whole royal wiccan armada will be looking for her! Do you ever use your brain?" Theon pushes his hand through his hair and over his horns in visible frustration. He grabs Sikkori's arm and pulls her away. He points at the shorter demon to the side of me, who nods in some unspoken agreement.

"Please come with me and get warm by the fire," the shorter demon says in a small voice matched by a half-hearted smile. I follow him, watching Theon hover over Sikkori's tensed body.

I'm guided to sit on a large, fallen tree trunk. The childlike demon seems satisfied and gently touches my shoulder, almost bowing his head before he leaves.

He knows who I am and at least doesn't harbor the same irritation Sikkori seems to.

Theon raises his voice. "This camp location is in jeopardy now. It's not simple to just drop her off!"

Sikkori looks like a teen girl being scolded by a teacher. She rolls her eyes before pushing back. "So, she stays then!"

"And this is why. You asked. This is why you don't have more responsibility!"

Looking around, I see more tents scattered through the trees. I don't have a clear path to run. I give up on calling my magick; I can't use it because of the bracelets, and I can't seem to connect to Rhydian. I'm stuck.

I'm staring ahead, trying to formulate a plan when someone sits next to me. He's quiet and goes unnoticed by the few nearby because everyone is watching Theon and Sikkori. I know exactly who he is before I turn my head. This was the intel the Guardians had; this was why Sikkori brought me here.

Evan, my uncle, was presumably complete with the mental madness I caused by hitting him with magick during the battle at MacKinnon Manor.

He stares straight ahead like I'm not right next to him. I can't move. My uncle is . . . different. He's unkempt and messy, his eyes unfocused, nothing at all like himself.

I tentatively whisper his name. "Evan?"

The corner of his lip pulls up in recognition of his name. Without looking at me, he nods toward the arguing Theon and Sikkori. He waits until Theon throws his hands up in frustration, then speaks.

"Why is my niece here?"

Silence.

Theon walks in smooth strides to stand in front of Evan.

"Why is she here? No one said anything about this being the next step in our freedom, although plans do change."

Freedom?

"They just wanted to help you. The magick—" Evan holds his

finger up, and Theon stutters before continuing: "Um . . . gift. The gift Willow gave you. They just want you . . . whole."

Sikkori hugs her body, looking younger. How old is she? I realize she must be younger than me at seventeen, although I feel like I've aged five years in several months since starting my senior year.

Evan doesn't respond. I break the uncomfortable silence. "Gift? What gift?"

"At the battle on the MacKinnon grounds, you sent uncontrolled magick that hit Evan. It was charged by your emotions, and it injured—ah, changed Evan."

Evan stands and sweeps his arms in a wide circle, spinning like a little child. "Freedom."

Everyone stares at Evan in the silence.

"The gift of seeing—understanding. The gift of redemption within myself and of knowledge. I hate, I love, I have anger and compassion, all rolled into one." Evan drops to one knee in front of me, and I scoot back, scraping the backs of my legs. I look everywhere but directly at his waiting face until he touches my knee. "It's freedom, I do not control it. It is only glimpses of the future. A wonderful gift from my niece."

I don't like this. How can I undo something I didn't know I was doing in the first place? What will they do to me if I make it worse?

"Ah, to be so young. Don't be burdened by the battle of doubt in your head," Evan says with a laugh. "No worries, Willow. I will keep my gift of sight, regardless of what the younger Emissaries' good intentions are."

"Emissaries?"

"Yes. That's us." Evan gestures in a big sweeping motion with his arms. Theon is assessing me with his scrupulous eyes.

I'm not sure what I should be more frightened of—the abduction to help Evan or the fact he doesn't want it. Either way, I'm limited with these bracelets.

Evan snaps his fingers, and the spellbinding bracelets break.

Did he just read my mind?

Evan offers his hand; I take it and stand. Theon rushes toward us, yelling for us to stop, and in a blur, he is gone. Evan is magickly transporting us. I gently pull my hand away, but I can't budge his steady grip. My feet land on solid ground and my stomach immediately turns with the abrupt guidance of the transport.

"Don't leave quite yet," Evan says, almost asking and hopeful.

Cold air sweeps around and chills me; the temperature is freezing. Cars sound in the distance. Though it is still dark, I can make out a colorful jungle gym among the dry winter grass. There are gravel walkways lined by leafless trees. Before I open my mouth, Evan waves his fingers and chants, covering me in warmth with new clothes—a thick puffed jacket, wool hat, and gloves. He has dressed for the cooler climate in a long, formal, black wool jacket and leather gloves. His horns, still visible, blend into his wavy hair.

"Why should I stay? Last time I saw you, Evan, I was collateral damage. Remember?"

"I wouldn't have."

I believe him, but it doesn't change the fact that the Guardians and Sabine don't believe that.

"Where are we, Evan? When can I leave?"

He squints and looks all around us, then stops and points over my shoulder. "Ah, there it is. Look."

The tip of the Eiffel Tower is a distant silhouette against the evening sky. So that's where we are. I have a sense of déjà vu that I can't connect.

"You were not born yet, when your parents took a stand against dear old dad. Later, I believe your father brought you here a few times." His smile turns from joy to sadness. "I needed to bring you away from the Emissaries. I must protect them; the Horned God would want that. You also need to see and understand this place because of its ties to my sister. The history is important for you and your future, and for the Emissaries."

I have so many questions. I settle on the most immediate one. "Who are the Emissaries?"

"They are equality seekers."

"Who is the Horned God?"

"Quite simply, me." Evan laughs, and his horns glow just a little.

Okay . . .

"So, my Wiccan Queen and niece, what shall we do? Oh, yes —first, the warnings. Never run with scissors or knives unless your intention is to harm yourself and those around you."

He wobbles on his feet, and I back away with one big step. This is becoming even more strange than it already was.

"Evan? Are you okay? You seem . . ."

I can't bring myself to say it. Even's eyes, his face, look happy and carefree. He's different, but I'm different too. So much has happened since we first met under his guise of a therapist. He helped me connect to my magick and learn about my heritage. I look at him, and I long for my mother, my father, and the life that was normal—or more normal than this, anyway.

"So, do you recognize this place? Is it a place that calls to you, like a raven in another life?" He takes a deep breath and closes his eyes as if savoring the memory of something.

"Evan, why did you bring me here? It may be familiar, but I don't understand."

What's his intention? Is he going to let me go?

"We are tied together. Not physically, but the Goddess and the Horned God—we are their embodiment."

"How is that?" I breathe into my gloved hands and watch the chilled air turn white.

He laughs. "We are evolving and new." Evan waves his gloved fingers as if they are wings and his body moves by flutters in and out of my vision. "The caterpillar experiences the most evolution but its end result, the butterfly, has a lifespan that isn't very long."

What do I say? This is so weird.

"Remember this place, Willow. Ask Sabine about it. Consider what noble covens want and why. Don't be the status quo. Be a different Queen."

My mouth is dry. I don't know what to say to him. I want to be the right kind of Queen, but I can't be something I'm not. It strikes me that those teenage demons were worried about Evan. He's important enough they came for me and risked their lives. I could easily take the Guardians to them and have them all arrested or worse, but I won't do that. I can't do that.

"Call to Rhydian through your blood vow."

I need more from him besides my freedom. "Wait. Tell me more about this place before I leave. Why bring me here? How is it connected to my mother?"

He closes his eyes briefly. "This is where your father and mother took a stand against the Wiccan crown and the rule of betrothal. The place where we all flee toward a beacon of light." Evan points to the Eiffel tower in the distance and pulls his scarf closer to his neck. "The High Coven is not one to trust, but—" He laughs before continuing, his canines showing. "You already recognize that. Good girl. Don't let Sabine's perfect exterior fool you into thinking it mirrors an authentic interior. Chaos follows her—a type that is not only harmful but deadly."

I see it as soon as he says the word "deadly" his grief in a conjured vision of my mother and another lady I imagine was Meghan, his wife. She was killed by order of my grandfather, the Wiccan King, Evan's father. If it wasn't so cold and the light was better, I believe I would see tears gathering in his eyes.

"I'm sorry, Evan." I mourn as he does, for my mother, Mrs. Scott, and my father.

"You cannot have a funeral for someone without having a funeral for yourself." He shrugs, then says, "I'm sorry for all the losses we experience. Life is death, and death is life."

His eyes are haunted as they look everywhere but at me. Evan's weird riddles and words are true. I buried part of myself in the loss of my father, his death coming just as we were connecting, and he was sharing magick with me.

"Back into the mouth of the monster you go. Slay the dragon. If not, our time together may be brief."

His riddles sound like a threat and a warning at the same time. The sincerity of his worry is something I don't doubt.

Who is the dragon I must slay?

Evan transports himself, his presence is gone too soon. Despite wanting to get home, I turn toward the jungle gym. He said so much that I don't completely understand, but the fact that this place is significant because of my parents gives me a reason to look around. I walk to a stone bench on the small greenway facing the jungle gym, pulling the collar of the coat closer to my neck. The cold wind whips my long hair and surrounds me in the quiet of the night.

A bronzed memorial plaque on the bench catches my eye. Summoning my magick to my fingers, I use the light to better see the inscription.

In memory of Nuala Warrington.

I remember so little of her. I take off my gloves and touch my mother's name as if that will bring me closer. I sit on the stone bench and tuck my hands into the warm pockets of the coat. I could easily transport myself home, but instead, I silent my mind and call to Rhydian as Evan directed me. I reach through space for the bond that connects us and comprehend his immediate connection and anguish.

The breeze on my face is instant. New warmth radiates from three royal Guardians who surround me in full armor and defensive stances.

Rhydian turns and I stumble to speak. "No one is here . . . um . . . besides me."

Cross's face drops from a scowl to a frown.

Tullen speaks first. "Willow, where have you been? It's been almost two days."

"I was taken by Emissaries and released by Evan, who took me here," I say with a shaky voice pointing to the plaque. Tullen reads it and touches my shoulder gently.

Rhydian hasn't moved. He's watching me as if he can't believe I'm in front of him. Finally, he speaks. "Cross, Tullen, search the park to see if there are any signs of magickal transport signatures."

"We arrived over there." I point to the spot where Evan brought us. "I don't think you'll be able to track him. Can we talk at my house? I just—want to go."

There is no verbal agreement, only Rhydian's outreached arms. The enveloping hug comforts me and releases the pit in my stomach. My tears fall without notice, and all I can do is breathe steadily in relief as Rhydian transports us to my front door in Chepstow, Massachusetts.

I don't release him, burying my wet face in his armored chest. Rhydian lifts my face gently to his and lays the sweetest kiss on my forehead. The moment is too brief. His forehead rests on mine in a physical and emotional connection that doesn't feel like a forced blood vow.

"I was so worried, Will. I couldn't sense you, and it was Evan all along. This could've been so much worse." Rhydian's statement is heavy on the cold night air.

"It was other Emissaries who grabbed me. Evan is—different." How do I describe him without sounding crazy myself? I'm not even sure who to trust from his warnings.

"Why would you trust Evan? I don't care how different he seems; you agree he's partly responsible for Mrs. Scott and your father. Why are you wavering?"

The deaths of Mrs. Scott and my father are what Rhydian really wants to say—that Evan had a direct hand in what happened to my family. The twisted part is that Evan is my family. He's my uncle. Evan didn't kill anyone, Celestia did. She was responsible for Mrs. Scott's death and the torture and, ultimately, the death of my father. But I'm the killer that enacting justice on her. Deep down, when someone points out Evan's dark nature, I see that it mirrors my own—the dark voice I hear luring me from time to time.

"I don't believe Evan is a threat."

But do I really believe that?

CHAPTER 3

For a moment, I think Rhydian will leave me in the cold on the other side of the door. He purses his lips, his frustration palpable. Ever the gentleman—or maybe just adhering to his blood vow—he holds the door open and waits for me to walk in.

The foyer is unexpectedly crowded. Sabine, my long-lost grandmother, runs forward and hugs me hard. I stiffen and return the hug awkwardly.

Have we ever hugged before?

Evan's voice bounces in my mind, telling me to ask her about Paris, but I don't want the others around for that conversation. I keep it to myself.

The commander of the Guardians, Eoin, smiles and keeps his distance while watching Sabine continue to hold on to me.

"What happened?" Sabine asks. "Who did this? Are you okay?"

"Yes, I'm fine. It's okay."

"It most certainly is not okay for someone to enter your home and forcefully take you from it. You, my dear, are Queen; this is not acceptable. I've spoken to Eoin. You will have more security here as long as you are to remain. We are putting up warded magick around the grounds of this house. No transporting in or out without warning." Her wide eyes are searching me, as if she is waiting for me to offer some accolade for her worry.

A tall, lean man enters the foyer from the stairs near the kitchen. He has a familiarity about him, but I don't recognize him. He strides forward gracefully, looking out of place in a formal navy pinstripe suit.

Sabine's attention gravities toward him, and she releases me. I'm grateful for the reprieve.

"Willow, allow me to introduce Mr. Esmund Boward. He represents the noble covens and is—"

"Your Majesty." He gives a bow so gracious it feels out of place for my home in Chepstow and my casual outfit. "I am also Rhydian's proud father and was a dear friend to your parents." He holds his hand out to me, palms up, waiting.

"Nice to meet you, Mr. Boward." I put my hand in his, and he holds it gently for a moment before releasing it. It's awkward.

"So, is the mystery of who abducted you solved?"

Before I can respond, Rhydian answers. "It was Evan."

The gasp from Sabine is audible, almost comedic. Is she putting on a show in front of Mr. Boward? Eoin is no longer leaning on the wall but at attention.

Clearing my throat, I look from Eoin to Sabine. "Before you get carried away, it wasn't Evan directly. A group of demon teenagers abducted me."

"Demon teenagers," Sabine repeats, as if the idea is foreign.

"They are part of a group called the Emissaries? Their intention was for me to heal Evan. He was completely unaware of their plan. He—"

"Unlikely." Rhydian is quick to interrupt me. His expression is set in a challenge as if he wants me to change my mind just because he disagrees and the others side with him. Shaking my head, I stare hard at him. He is unmoving.

"Yes, quite." Mr. Boward agrees.

"Why would they want you to heal Evan? What is wrong

with him?" Eoin asks, moving in to join the group that surrounds me.

Well, according to Evan, it's a gift. How do I describe that? I go for the most accessible explanation, knowing that I can tell Eoin more later. I have a feeling Rhydian will get to Eoin before me, per some official report to his commander, but Eoin lives with me in this house. Besides that, I trust him. I think he will be more objective than Rhydian and Sabine.

"He's very disheveled. His words don't always make sense—kind of like riddles, or that he has so many thoughts in his head he gets them confused as he speaks." My voice almost pitches to a question as I finish. This is not how I wanted to describe Evan. Everyone is waiting for me to explain more. "I don't know, he's just not what I'm used to seeing. They said I must have conjured an emotional magick into him when I fought him at MacKinnon Manor. I essentially caused this."

Cross smacks his large hands together in a loud clap. "All right then! Evan is incapacitated."

"No, he's not," I snap. Why am I defending him?

"Did you get a good look at the demons so that you can describe them?" Sabine asks.

"Not really."

The stare from Sabine is one of complete disbelief, but I continue, "I really don't think we should be going after a bunch of young teenage demons. Evan and Theon were not happy about it either. Anyway, I'm fine."

That did it, the roar of voices by saying Evan and Theon's names.

Thaxam, the demon general who I've added to the royal Guardians, shuffles his feet. Despite Ax's towering height and large red body, I didn't realize he was here until now. Eoin approaches Ax while Rhydian, Sabine, Cross, and Tullen talk over each other.

They are so engrossed in their arguments that no one notices me go to the stairs and take a seat near Ax and Eoin, except maybe Rhydian.

Mr. Boward's voice booms over the commotion. "It is unacceptable that someone came into this home, protected as it was, and removed the Queen against her will. This will not be viewed favorably by the noble covens. Her Majesty's ability to reign will be under question if it is not already. She should make her permanent home in Edayri at her ancestral estate of Mackinnon Manor. There is no reason to stay here."

Why is he trying to manage me? I'm tired, and nothing is going to happen tonight—or is it almost morning? Eoin begins to argue. I stand and interrupt.

"Thank you for your concern, but this is my and Sabine's decision. The agreement is to maintain my home and schooling here in Chepstow until the summer. This arrangement is supported by the Guardians. Eoin continues residency for the short term of this assignment."

Sabine is at my side. Her arm around my shoulders, awkward again, as if to show a united front. "Esmund, it has been a long day. We can discuss this later. For now, a report should be made that the Wiccan Queen is safe and sound in her family home."

As if a game is afoot, Mr. Boward's sly grin creeps across his face. "I'm glad that if the Queen is staying here, the Guardian's agreement on Rhydian's presence at her scholastic institution will be enacted. This will be important for her safety as well as that of the others who attend—" his voice hitches before he finishes "—like mortals."

"What?" My eyes snap to Eoin. I feel heat flush my face. Arrangements about my safety are being discussed without my knowledge. Rhydian didn't even say anything to me. Was this done ahead of my disappearance?

Eoin turns from me to place himself in front of Mr. Boward. He's the same height as Mr. Boward, and his presence alone is substantial. Eoin's tone is direct and low. "Mr. Boward, the Queen's security, is not a political or gossip tidbit for you to discuss. If you cannot maintain royal confidentialities, I will see that you are removed from consultation as the noble coven representative."

Eoin turns to me before continuing. "Rhydian has enrolled at Trinity Cross High and will be in several of your classes." Rhydian does not look at me, but he doesn't have to. I can sense his agreement on this arrangement.

"Are you serious?" They can't really think this is a good idea. As if I can't be alone at school? This is so ridiculous.

"Willow, Rhydian isn't but a couple of years older than you. He can pass as a student at your school. No one will question it," Sabine says, confirming her agreement with Eoin. Before my temper ignites, she quickly adds, "This doesn't change that you will split your time between here and Edayri. You will have a set schedule for training—you did agree to this, after all. This is the most normal we can give you while ensuring your safety and that of others."

This is far beyond ordinary, but I'm not ready to give up this little slice of my life. I say my goodnight and slowly climb the stairs as the rumble of discussions continue without me.

CHAPTER 4

Staring down the school hallway, I watch my best friend and ex-boyfriend, Lucy and Daniel, like a voyeur. I recognize their new-couple dance—the shoulder touch, the lean in, the smiles and laughter. Realizing how creepy I am watching them, I give it up to walk to homeroom. They are moving toward a future that I don't get to belong to. I'm happy for them and comforted that Daniel isn't caught up in my royal mess of a life. It wasn't long ago that he was on death's door at my house. I don't regret breaking up with him; his life is on the path it should be on.

Homeroom is faster than my reverie of internal thoughts. The bell rings and lifts my mental fog, dismissing us to first period. We spill into the hallway, the class breaking up to go their separate ways. Coral and her cronies pass, giggling. They are gossiping and fanning themselves in dramatic teen girl fashion. Emily rolls her eyes as we walk toward them.

"What the heck is Coral all excited about? A new Tiffany color or something?" Emily asks.

A girl nearby overhears. "Ah, the new transfer. I mean, whoa!"

Emily, ever the flirt, turns to look for the student who is causing the girls to overheat, but I already know.

She spots him. "Oh, it's just—"

"Rhydian," I finish without looking.

"Yeah. Although I've got to say, he does brighten up the school a bit with his GQ quality looks." I grimace, but Em continues without a beat. "If you're into that sort of thing." Her smile is infectious, and she nudges me in my side.

"This is different and you know it," I say in a whisper.

Walking in, I go to my seat in the back near the window. He walks in seconds later. I guess I can't put this off any longer. It's happening—Rhydian is attending my school and my classes. "Hey," I say, waving.

Everyone is watching, most notably Coral with squinted eyes.

"Hey, Willow. I knew you went here. How fortunate we're in class together."

"I know, shocking." I try not to sound overly sarcastic and work to keep from rolling my eyes, but it's bubbling on the surface. I've never been a good actor.

The bell rings and class begins. I am trying my hardest only to watch Mrs. Gunter, but every time Coral turns her head to spy Rhydian, I can't help but look her direction.

This is all we need—a triangle conflict between me, Coral, and Rhydian. Haven't we traveled this road before? Coral, Daniel, and me? Rhydian is not just any guy. I don't like the idea of her flirting and pursuing him. Her gossipy nature will not keep anything under wraps where I'm concerned.

After class, Rhydian is slow to leave, waiting for me.

"Are you in my next class as well?" I try not to snap.

"Can we not be seen together?"

I roll my eyes at him.

"That hurts Willow. And yes, of course, we are in all the same classes except two."

We leave together. Coral is waiting just outside the door to pounce on Rhydian. She clears her throat. "Welcome to Trinity Cross and Chepstow." Did her voice just raise two octaves? She's shifting her weight back and forth.

"Yea, thanks. You're Coral, right?"

Why did she giggle at her own name?

"Yes. I was curious if you'd like to get to know some of your fellow students—"

"Hey guys!" Emily interrupts, bouncing in and hanging her arm over Rhydian's shoulder. "Plans today, right, Rhy? Plus, you know our little tribe."

Coral stares hard at Emily before focusing back on Rhydian, her smile plastered. "Maybe another time then."

Saved by the bell, but not before she touches Rhydian's arm in a too-comfortable gesture.

Laughing, he catches up to me. "Boy, she really gets under your skin, huh?"

Oh, he has no idea. It's not just me. Or is it? I shrug. Whatever.

It doesn't take me long to realize that the only classes Rhydian's not in are the ones I share with Marco or Emily. Smooth, Eoin. Very smooth. The air I breathe at school is weighed, measured, and totally secured. It's suffocating if I think about it too hard.

At the end of the school day, when I can finally breathe in my own car, Rhydian surprises me by jumping in the passenger seat. He slings his dark backpack onto the back seat. He fits well in school. In the school uniform, he seems younger than the Guardian warrior he really is.

"So, are my friends, my keepers, as well? Emily and Marco? This is so wrong! I don't need a babysitter."

"I'm not your babysitter. I'm your protector and royal Guardian. Very different." His smile disarms me, but I focus on driving out of the school parking lot and toward home. "I don't get this. It isn't as if I don't have magick at my fingertips. It's insulting that Sabine and Eoin are interfering at school. And this was decided without even talking to me! What's with that!"

I realize I'm speeding and being aggressive in traffic. Rhydian grabs the overhead handle on the door.

"What? Don't like my driving, either?" I smirk. "I'm sure you'll have to be my chauffeur before too long."

He laughs, relaxed. "Maybe because your driving skills are equivalent to those of the elderly."

"Are you kidding me right now?"

He lifts an eyebrow and his mouth quirks. I push my car's speed and turn the wheel hard on the street, heading west toward the house. The two-lane road is smooth and empty, the black tar glistening in the afternoon sun. I floor it.

My BMW grabs the road like the premiere car it is. My smile widens, and I weave, testing the grip of my tires—Rhydian rocks in his seat with a wide grin. The tall trees speed by us in a blur of green.

"Okay, okay. What do they say here—speed kills?"

Laughing with him, I pull into the driveway. I exhale the air from my lungs and turn to Rhydian. "I'm sorry."

"You'll resent me if you think I'm your captor from freedom. Can you look at this as us getting to spend more time together instead?"

I nod. He's right. I shouldn't lash out at him; he's doing his job. Wow. What a jumbled web of "have to," "ordered to," and "want to."

"Sorry," I say, "but if you say Coral is pretty or nice, I will blow up!"

"So, you're jealous?"

I return his playful grin but don't respond. Instead, I tease him before going into the house. My control in any part of this situation is my ability to make the most of it.

Light from the windows bathes the foyer when I wander downstairs later. In my father's office, I find Tullen and Quinn on security detail. They are seated at the curved game table by the window playing a high-stakes game of chess. Father once told me that he would sit with his father at the game table every Sunday and play various strategy games. I should have done this more with my father.

"Hi, Willow. What's the plan this evening?" Quinn asks, moving his knight.

"Just relaxing. A 'welcome back' day, as far as I understand. Although Tullen, maybe you have something else planned?"

Tullen scratches his red beard, studying the chessboard. He finally settles on moving a rook that takes one of Quinn's. "How about you play the winner? I'm finding this game to be quite a challenge."

"I've never learned to play."

They both look at me, stunned.

"What? It wasn't something I had an interest in before."

Quinn, without studying the board, moves a piece that captures a pawn. "Check."

Tullen laughs in a jovial way that shakes his top knot bun. "Well, it looks like we could both use a lesson in this game of strategy. Quinn, would you indulge me in another round?"

Quinn smiles and sets up the board. "Sure. You're getting better, and what's another game?"

"I'll leave you to it."

I wander into my father's secret coven room behind the office bookcase. Entering the room, I inhale the familiar scent of him—spices mixed with lush forest. The room illuminates with candles and lamps at my presence; the green paisley print, over-stuffed chair calls to me from the last time I was here. The bookcase and its cabinets hold books about magick and history alongside various spices, roots, and other liquids with hand-written labels from my father and mother. The table against the wall displays only a small metal bowl and a stone pestle and grinder.

I think about my father's words about dark and light magick.

I am a combination of both—my father's very dark magick and my mother's light magick—although I realize I'm more connected to my father since accepting his magick at his passing. He had said magick is simply magick, but at times I wonder if it's influencing. I find more temptation in my thoughts to do something cruel. I did take vengeance on Celestia without much thought. Was I justified in doing so, since it was her order to kill Mrs. Scott and my father? These thoughts can overwhelm me, although I try not to dwell on them. But seeing Evan . . . I did that to him. Maybe what I did was a gift, but the fact is, I did it without much thought. I was hurting and wanted him to hurt just as bad.

I sink into the overstuffed chair and pull my family's Book of Shadows into my lap.

Flipping through the Book of Shadows, I ask, "How strong is my father's magick's heritage?"

On a blank page, a family tree that starts with a noble coven member, William Warrington Senior, begins to appear. The lines and squares connect, and toward the bottom of the page, my father's name is written in a scripted font. Aiden Warrington. The ink continues and sketches portraits of each person. My father's portrait is of him as an older teen. I touch the familiar face with my fingertip as if to really touch him. A welling tear escapes, and I wipe it away quickly with the back of my hand.

Taking a shaky breath, I ask the book, "Am I fit to be Queen?"

The answer appears within seconds on the page.

Cannot predict now.

I chuckle at the response, remembering the day my father told me about my mother and the gift our family Book of Shadows has with magic eight ball responses. As my mother drifts into mind, so does Evan and Paris.

If I dive into the question, do I really want the answer? I've lost everything for a crown that was inherited. I can't help the nagging feeling that knowing will pull me further from my normal life—my life before the start of the school year, one where there was no magick or royal crown, even if "normal" was secretive and flawed.

I square my shoulders and ask, holding two fingers to the empty page. "Paris. Is it important to my family? Or to who I am?"

The ink on the page swirls around my fingertips at first, then grows in big loops that suddenly dissolve into the thickness of the paper. Lifting my fingers, I exhale and lay my head back into the chair, staring blankly ahead.

A movement on the page brings my attention back, and I stare at the response.

As I see it, yes.

So, I'm not playing into some bigger plot at Evan's hands?

My sources say no.

I didn't ask another question while touching the page, did I? I trace the unmoving words. "Why?"

Better not tell you now.

"Well, you have to now," I say, as if I'm confronting a friend who evasively answers questions with non-answers.

Outlook not so good.

The Book of Shadows is sassy. Great, just what I need.

The words begin to morph again without me touching the page.

Without a doubt.

I'm not sure which thought this response actually answers. I suppose the book is much better than an actual magic eight ball, and I should be relieved I am getting some type of answer.

"Will you always be available to me to answer questions?"

Ask again later.

As I touch the page, the words sink into the paper and disappear. I don't have any other questions besides major ones that need more than a three-word reply. Those I'll save for Sabine.

This is going to be difficult, but at least the Book of Shadows is not judging me.

As I see it, yes.

Great.

CHAPTER 5

It's Friday, but I'm not at Trinity Cross High School. Instead, I'm in Edayri for a different type of education: physical training, royal business, and etiquette.

The joy of being me.

I think I would rather be in Mrs. Simpson's Organic Chemistry class, which is saying something. Sabine and Mr. Boward insisted that I spend Fridays in Edayri because my weekends are not enough for me to assimilate my royal duties. Like I have any time to myself anymore. How am I supposed to have a normal life if I'm not home on the weekends?

Wiping the sweat from my brow, I try to stay in the present by funneling my frustration into magickal sparring. Eoin is shouting commands and instructs me while I face off with Rhydian in the Guardian private gym. Usually, Cross is my opponent.

"Are you intimated? Come on. Attack," Rhydian says, wiggling his brows and bouncing around the mat like a boxer. He's moving like we haven't been here for over a half-hour.

"No. I'm not intimated." I'm appreciative of his muscled frame. And yes, I'm a little intimated.

"Okay then, attack."

Cross would have already taunted and yelled at me to get under my skin and invoke a response. In his absence, I think about Sabine and how my freedoms are slowly slipping from me.

Magick flows like liquid across my skin. I pull it from my arms and lift my hands to ignite a flame mid-air. Rhydian is moving his hands in a shielding pattern as he takes a defensive stance. I guide the fire forward at Rhydian, but he catches me off guard by ducking and rolling toward me. I jump back, and the flame disappears along with my footing. As I fall, I sweep Eoin's legs even though he's only observing. He goes down with me.

Eoin doesn't stop training me from the floor. "As your power builds within your body, your goal is to control your thoughts, so they become actions with the outcome you desire," Eoin says. He has said this to me almost weekly since I've known him. It drives me nuts. As if I could forget with him always harping on about it. "Are you rolling your eyes at me? That's not very royal of you."

"I controlled my graceful fall into complete action. Your ass is down just like mine."

"Funny," Eoin responds dully, but the smirk on his face says something else. He's not just the commander of the Guardians; he's also my parental Guardian and the reason I can stay at school in Chepstow. For that, I am so grateful. He's like an adopted father figure in my life.

I laugh and lay back into the mat, one sweaty mess. Rhydian chuckles under his breath before giving me his hand to help me up.

"Apologies. Now should I conjure a light ball to throw at your head?" I ask playfully.

Eoin holds up his finger and taps his earpiece. "Yes? I understand. Be there in five."

Eoin stands to leave. When Rhydian and I stare at him waiting for directions, he says, "Go ahead and wrap it up. You've got twenty minutes before etiquette training. Your instructor will meet you at MacKinnon Manor in the royal sitting room by the gardens."

I nod, feeling grateful as Eoin leaves the room. A break. Finally.

Sweat trickles down my back, sticking to my shirt.

"Want to shower?"

My jaw drops open. I close my mouth, open it to respond, close it again, and try not to look like a fish.

"By the blush on your face, I can tell you thought I meant together. I didn't mean that initially, but if you would like, I'm happy to please the Queen in whatever way I can." A smirk highlights the deep dimple in Rhydian's cheek.

Damn, he's so handsome and appealing even sweaty. "Yes, I do need that shower, although I may take a rain check on the other." Did I just say that out loud? Where is this confidence coming from? Goddess, I want to hide under a rock.

"Rain check?"

"It's a saying for another time. Besides, I don't think Eoin or Sabine would approve." I'm an idiot. Switching subjects, I go for the question that's been weighing me down lately. "Can you tell me more about the blood vow?"

Rhydian comes forward and takes my hands in his. My heart beats loudly in my ears; my skin tingles touching him. It feels natural and straightforward, and simultaneously it is anything but. I like the way my hands fit in his, despite that they are slick with sweat.

"The blood vow that I made to your father was one of protection and duty. Part of that vow provides an instinctual magick that allows me to be what and where you need. It's not something any Guardian takes lightly, as the vow connects you for life. The only exceptions are if I break the vow by causing physical harm to you or if the recipient releases you, although I hear that if you are released, it can be painful beyond measure for both in the vow. That's not a common thing. Usually, the vow is beneficial to both parties."

I think my world is rocked. How can he make a vow like this without knowing me? A one-sided vow. The desire to kiss him nags at me, and I push it to the side. "But you have control over what you do, right?"

"A vow didn't tell me to hold your hand."

My hands slip from his, and I'm aware of the instant loss, the connection of his touch. He reaches back for them.

"See?"

"Not really. You felt a need to hold my hand?"

"You needed me to comfort you. You wanted a physical— how do I describe it? A physical connection, but you're not committed, so I held your hand."

I pull back my hands and step away from our closeness. I'm completely embarrassed that he can sense my attraction to him. How is that possible, besides my beet-red face? Is he forced to do anything to comfort me? "So, what you're saying is you're compelled then? Is that it?"

"Exactly." He smiles.

I'm now something to be obeyed? He doesn't seem upset by this at all. Is he brainwashed? Am I? I want him. Oh crap. This is wrong! He should be moved by himself, not by me. This is one-sided. I want to scream at him, but he's a grinning like a happy puppy dog.

"Unbelievable!" I snap. I grab my bag, slinging it behind my back.

"What? Why are you—angry?"

"Are you serious?" I turn on him and catch him off guard. In my head, shout, "Kneel before me now!"

He smiles and begins to take a knee.

I point to his action before he reaches the floor. "That is why!"

"You just told me to—"

"Argh!" I turn away from him. "I'll see you later, Rhydian."

Realizing I have one-sided power over him, that even when I command him in my head, he obeys, I scream in frustration in the hallway. He can sense my emotions, wants, and needs, and this vow is a command. I can literally command him in my mind!

Some rational part of my mind reminds me that, as Queen, I can command anyone.

Are his feelings toward me even real? Or am I transferring my feelings in a way that commands him?

CHAPTER 6

I'm late, but no one is in the office suite. I take a seat at the window that overlooks the well-manicured grounds of MacKinnon Manor. My eyelids are heavy, and my mind is quiet for the first time. My eyes are almost shut when a male voice grabs my attention.

"I'm sorry to disturb your reprise. I was detained with noble coven matters." Mr. Boward walks with long strides and places his leather-bound notebook and fancy pen on the table in front of me.

"Are you my teacher? I wasn't sure who to expect for this lesson."

He looks very similar to his son in height and coloring, but not in facial features. His nose is rather large and screams aristocrat.

"Yes. I will be your guide through all things royal, per etiquette, and other miscellaneous expectations as it were. I hope I can be of assistance to you as you adjust."

"I thought Sabine would be showing me the royal ways," I say, using air quotes around the word royal.

"Lady MacKinnon continues other royal work in your

absence by reviewing and signing various decrees as your proxy."
He straightens his suit lapels before sitting in front of me. "I
would surmise that she wants to be more of your grandmother in
her free time than anything else."

That's kind of him to say, but the fact that he isn't looking at
me gives me the feeling there is something more to his statement. There is something about him, an air of superiority that is
off-putting.

"Well, let us start, shall we?"

He starts to open the notebook, then closes it. "Maybe we
should start by getting acquainted with one another. You may
not be aware, but I was close friends with your mother and
father. We all grew up together."

My father never mentioned him, but he did go to him and
Rhydian for this blood vow. I can't believe my father did that—
tie me to someone I didn't know without talking to me. Then
again, when it comes to my protection, it seems like something
he'd do. I also have a hard time seeing my father being good
friends with Mr. Boward. Then again, it wasn't as if I met any
close friends of his before. Everyone I ever met was a colleague
or some finance titan. I want to like Rhydian's father, but he
reminds me of the elite who look down on everyone and only do
things to support their agendas. The judgment in his eyes is a
reminder that I'm not like him. I'm sure others like him would
probably prefer a more refined elite sitting at the Wiccan
throne.

"I wasn't really aware that you knew my parents. How long
had you been friends with my father? When did he go to you
regarding the blood vow?"

"It does seem like a long time ago, even though it's only been
a few months. I think your father had some suspicions last
summer; he reached out to me and we discussed various options.
I proposed the blood vow to your father. With Rhydian's captain
ranking in the Guardians, it was a good choice."

How easily he would offer up his son for a blood vow that links him for life. Did Rhydian not even have a choice in the matter? "What other options were up for discussion? Was this all about my safety?"

Mr. Boward shifts in his chair and leans closer to me. The look of sympathy in his eyes is off-putting. "Willow, you are your father's greatest treasure. He would do anything to protect you. Having a Guardian in the position that Rhydian is in puts you in the safest hands possible. The crown is heavily sought after, especially unclaimed. The realization that keeping you from Edayri put you at a disadvantage meant that you needed protection by someone who grew up here. From there, it became apparent that there was only one choice."

I mutter something about the word "choice" under my breath.

"And trust me, Rhydian had a choice. He chose duty and sacrifice. It is an honor for him and our family to serve a royal." I'm stuck on the word sacrifice. I elicit sacrifice from people for my wellbeing? I never thought of it that way. It's a lot to absorb. "Our ways may seem antiquated and different, but they are traditional and at the root of Wiccan laws. They will take some time to understand, and I am happy to provide guidance on your journey. Sabine has been kind enough to appoint me to the position of Scepter to you and crown interests."

Why do I get the feeling that handling me is his new position? What is Sabine doing? I don't need extra handling, I have enough of that.

"Mr. Boward—"

"Please, call me Esmund. May I, in turn, call you Willow?" His smile is strained.

"Oh absolutely, please call me Willow or Will." The look on his face suggests I've gone a little too far with the informal response and nickname. "Okay, Willow, it is. Thank you, Mr.—sorry, Esmund, for the time to get more acquainted with you."

"My pleasure, dear. Our family is here for your service. It is a great honor."

Esmund stands and touches my shoulder, which sends chills straight to my spine. Sabine's voice echoes into the room from the hall outside. She sweeps in full of grand style in a skirt that fans out with her steps and her hair streaming behind her in long red waves.

"Oh, Esmund, wonderful to see you as always. I hope today's lesson went well. However, I must cut the time short. Willow has crown business to work through this evening with me. It's come to my attention that dinner will be ready soon, and somehow the day has passed too quickly."

Thankful for Sabine's timing, Esmund says his goodbyes and quickly leaves. Sabine and I enter the formal dining room where only two places are set.

"I hope you don't mind the change of scenery, but I do love this room and the open stone fireplace. I find it relaxing, and I need to get away from the various office suites in this Manor. Some days my home does not feel like my home at all; it is more like a company office space."

"I totally understand," I reply. The dining room is welcoming with its dark wood table and high back chairs. The room is rich in maroons and purples, the low light coming from the fire warm.

There is no time wasted as we eat dinner. Sabine talks me through the procession of decisions that have already been made regarding arrests and incarcerations of other creatures. I'm not really clear on all the particulars, but it certainly seems that Edayri is experiencing unrest with various crimes. The crown role of delivering any type of sentence to anyone is uncomfortable. At the same time, I have no idea how to push back with Sabine.

"Are all of the crimes being committed confirmed? Are there trials?"

Sabine chuckles as she takes a sip of her wine. "Willow, trials are something that would've been a part of the High Coven that you disbanded, but only for high crimes against the crown. These misdemeanors and the lower-level creatures who perform them are under your jurisdiction for judgment."

"That is completely unfair. How am I supposed to pass judgment on someone else? I don't know what the laws are and how to go about that. Isn't there something in place for this type of thing?"

"Which is why I do this, as a proxy until you are comfortable and trained on all your royal duties. You may read over each plea and change the order as you wish; however, I have taken it upon myself to stay within the current Wiccan tradition in all judgments. I highly encourage you to remain consistent in these ways."

I feel the heat rise all around me. Embarrassment at not knowing the laws and frustration of expectation makes a heady mix. I sorely don't like being told what to do. I want to respect this tradition, but I'm turned off by thinking that the laws are only beneficial to Wiccans.

"Also, we might as well extend your stay for the week. A lot is going on regarding these crimes that I feel may be a threat to you directly. It's not just Evan or the Emissaries, it seems. We need to show unity and strength."

"Sabine, we can show unity and strength, but our agreement is our agreement. I will be going to high school during the week."

"You do realize how superfluous this is—high school nonsense in the Terra realm. Your job will be here. Your family, your responsibility, your duty is here in Edayri."

"You do realize that my life is in Chepstow, Massachusetts. That is my home, the Terra realm. It isn't something I'm giving up."

"If you would only consider—"

"You have Rhydian attending school with me. Isn't that enough for now? I'm here until the end of the weekend."

Sabine huffs in resignation. She finally nods and takes a long drink of her wine. Of course, I will continue next week at my high school.

I doubt many of my friends would have argued so heavily to stay at school. I have lost my mind.

CHAPTER 7

It's my third day in my MacKinnon Manor room, which is more like an apartment than an actual bedroom. The decor is neutral with light browns and creams. The dark wood of the furniture matches that throughout the rest of the manor. The only patterned items are the rug and cream curtains. It's as if I'm a guest in a penthouse hotel. I even have a sitting room with a large fireplace and couches, and a closet the size of my room back home. It's overwhelming. Too big, too much.

When I'm in Edayri, the one thing I'm connected to is my cell phone. It has been enchanted so that I can text my friends in Chepstow. It was the one thing Eoin did for me, despite turning the enchantment into a lesson. Needless to say, I'm grateful for the connection.

I'm using that connection now as I lay on my four-poster bed, texting Emily. I tell her that Rhydian is showing me around Edayri tonight. Strictly speaking, it wasn't part of my training schedule coordinated by Sabine, though she did put it in my calendar later.

So, it's a date!

I hesitate. Rhydian's idea and he didn't attach any work formality to it, but . . .

I don't know if I can call it a date.

And why not? An outing planned by the two consenting parties is a date bonehead. Emily responds.

My stomach churns. Leave it to Emily, call things the way they are.

I guess so. Now I'm nervous.

Her response is immediate. *Oh yeah, it's a date.*

This is complicated, he's a royal Guardian, there's this whole blood vow thing, and this is a date?

Girl, you like him, just go with it and get out of your head.

She's right. I should just go with it; there are too many things weighing down on me anyway. This could be what I need to escape—just being a normal teen girl with a crush. Damn it, I'm so stupid—of course, this is a date, regardless of Sabine recording it in a calendar like a task.

Emily proceeds to tell me exactly what to wear. I completely ignore her. I have no idea where we are going or what we are doing, but I know it will be here in Edayri, and I don't want to be the crown. My goal is to be myself, just Willow, with no title or motive. Therefore, no dresses or skirts. I smile as I pick out an outfit—shiny black jeggings, a dark gray V-neck sweater with a purple tank underneath, my mother's necklace tucked into my shirt and black flats. I check myself in my full-length mirror. I pull my hair out of its twist ponytail and shake it out, catching a whiff of my lavender shampoo as the long waves cascading past my shoulders. I swipe on some lip gloss and mascara and smile, feeling my heart swell with happiness.

I'm going on a date with Rhydian.

Yara, a familiar house staff member, knocks on my door and announces that Captain Rhydian Boward is waiting for me in the formal foyer downstairs. I thank her and grab my black coat. I take the stairs two at a time and try not to run down the small hall that leads to the foyer. The thought replays through my mind over and over: I'm going on a date with Rhydian.

Like a regular date, Rhydian is waiting in the foyer without

Guardian armor on. He's dressed in dark jeans and a navy peacoat. His wavy dark hair is tamed tonight, and he's cleaned up the smooth undercut around his ears and neck. His hazel eyes sparkle as he smiles. My heart races when he reaches for my hand, and my stomach does a little jump when I close my fingers around his.

"Ready to discover the homeland?" he asks.

"Yes. Am I dressed okay for where we are going?"

"I think so. Sorry, I should've been clearer about what we are doing tonight. I think being a little inconspicuous might be nice for you to observe Edayri as it is rather than as people would like the crown to imagine it."

"Perfect."

Walking out of MacKinnon Manor, I breathe in the crisp twilight air, and my anxiety melts away. Emily is right; I need to get out of my head and be in the present. That is my entire goal for tonight.

Rhydian escorts me to a car, the likes of which I have never seen before. It's some type of convertible sports car that sits low to the ground, dark with an iridescent blue and purple sheen that shimmers in the light of the manor's gas lamps.

Rhydian opens the door opens for me. I sit and look for a seat belt that isn't there.

"There are a few differences in our vehicles. Don't worry, it's safe. Besides, we have nowhere near the amount of traffic you do."

I laugh. "That is definitely something I wish we had." I wait until he takes his seat before asking, "So, where are we going?"

"I thought it would be nice to drive to the Lunar Falls. This way, you can appreciate the landscape and see where magickal water flows to Edayri."

The lush green forest that expands well beyond MacKinnon Manor is impressive. The thick trees and twilight sky inter-mingle in hues of blue and green. I love the winding road and

REIGN

constantly changing view. Everything is perfect and breathtaking.

Rhydian breaks me away from my daydreaming. "Tell me what you're thinking."

I start. "Wait, you don't know? Can't you read my mind or something?"

"No, I only sense emotions that come through, and I'm still getting to understand yours. I can't read your mind, Willow." He grins. I smile back.

"Nothing. Taking in the scenery. It's beautiful."

Looking at me intently, he grins. "Yes, it is."

The words to flirtatiously respond are lost in my throat; my confidence is suddenly hidden. Instead, I smile back, meeting his eyes only for a moment before shyly turning back to watch the trees pass us by in thick green lines.

We come upon the biggest tree I have ever seen, the trunk is split and straddles the road as if it was made that way, and we drive through it. The moon shines brighter on the other side of the tree. The moon is on the right side of us, and it looks like an unreal, a liquified reflection in various shades of white that extend unnaturally on the ground as if it's part of the water off to the side of the road. Is the moon feeding the water? I almost feel as if I could touch the stars. Rhydian pulls the car off the road onto unpacked gravel.

"From here, we walk." He opens my door before I can figure it out myself and takes my hand. When I stand, I'm close to him. The space between us is electric. My magick hums lightly, and I hold it in so that it doesn't show on my skin. He leads me toward a dirt path I hadn't seen before.

"Rhydian, tell me something about you."

"Like what?"

"Whatever you'd like to share. I dunno. I guess I'd like to know you better outside of work."

"Aw, Willow, happy to talk about anything inside or outside of work. Let's be clear—tonight is definitely not work."

My heart and magick rise together in a beat. Tonight is not work. I am not a task.

We arrive at the edge of a tree-lined path that leads toward a slope. I assume that this will guide us to the body of water we came to see. "So, tell me about your family then. Your dad—he seems to be fairly close with Sabine and quite important with the noble covens."

Rhydian's eyes grow a little somber at the mention of his father. "He's an ambitious man for sure, and strictly one for tradition. He's quite prideful. He raised me and my older sister, Abigail. My mother left when I was younger."

"I'm sorry about your mother."

His smile is quick, but the sorrow behind his eyes shows. We come over a ridge, and the lake comes into sight. He leads me to a spot in the grass near the water, and we sit. "We have quite a bit in common," he says, "with regard to mothers. Although yours didn't choose to leave."

My heart aches for him. I'm not sure what to say, so I just sit next to him at the edge of the lake and lay my head on his shoulder.

"You'd like Abby. She's spunky like you. It drives my father crazy."

"Is that your nice way of telling me that I drive your father crazy?"

"I would never reveal such a thing," he says, then laughs, giving away the truth.

"Do you ever see your mother?"

"No. Actually, she's in the Terra realm like you. I remember visiting her when I was about seven years old. It isn't something I've ever pursued. Hard for me to pursue her when she left is us so easily."

There is no anger in his voice, but I feel something from him —a hint of sadness. I hold his hand and squeeze it gently. He responds in kind.

"Do you hear that?" he asks after a moment.

I listened intently, but I don't hear anything except the wind sweeping through the tall grass and reeds at the water's edge. Then, almost buried by the wind, I hear something like a whistle. The faint sound draws my attention.

"Maybe? What am I listening for?"

Rhydian stands, still holding my hand, and pulls me to my feet. He puts his finger to his lips, and we inch behind the very tall reeds. Rhydian points to where the moon reflects on the water. He smiles. I follow his eyes, not sure where to focus.

"Fairies," he whispers.

I look closer, knowing that fairies reveal themselves in various ways. Being the small creatures they are, they mostly shield themselves; that's what I remembered from a book Tullen gave me. I find them at last, shimmering like the moonlight. There are about a dozen of them playing in the light on the water. If I listen carefully to the whistles and rings, I recognize a sort of music. Their wings flutter and pause in a way that makes it look like they were dancing. They interlock their arms and kick their legs in unison. I stare, amazed. I've never seen anything like this before.

Rhydian moves one of the tall reeds for us to get a better view, but this alerts the fairies, and they disappear by extinguishing their lights. Only a few continue to glimmer, curious. One bold male dressed in suspenders moves closer toward us, heedless of the squeaks of warning behind him.

"Hello," I say in a very small whisper, hoping not to scare him. "I'm sorry if I interrupted. I was curious when I heard your song and saw your dance."

Rhydian stays still behind the reeds, but the fairy does not miss a beat. He points at Rhydian. I smile and shrug my shoulders. "He's with me."

The fairy seems unimpressed with my apology but continues to point at Rhydian. "Rhydian?" I ask.

"I'm afraid he is aware that I'm a Guardian. I believe we've met before."

When I look back at the fairy, he is on one knee bowing to me. The fairies who were behind him are now unshielded and also bowing. They recognize who I am, but I don't want a scene, and I don't want them to treat me differently.

"I'm sorry I've interrupted you. May I join your party?" I circle my finger and draw a light circle in the air, similar to what they were doing on the water.

The fairy smiles and the other fairies come to life. Lights twinkle all around like fireflies.

"Thank you." I turn to Rhydian with a questioning look. Why did they change their manners so quickly?

"The fact that you apologized and asked was beyond their expectations of you as Queen. You honored them, and fairies take this highly. Besides, most of them look like they are a bit drunk from the party."

I laugh, seeing a few stumble into the water.

The music gets louder, and the fairies begin dancing and laughing and kicking up water all around in tiny splashes. Amidst all the fun, I spy my reflection, the crown on my forehead ebbing and flowing with my magick. The fairies don't seem to care as they continue with their party. Rhydian claps his hands together, and a magick comes from them that amplifies the fairy music in lovely cello tones. The fairies project a magick that controls the colors reflected on the moving water.

"May I?" Rhydian holds his hand out to me.

"What? Dance?"

"Sure. Why let them have all the fun?"

I'm not much of a dancer, but the twinkle in his eye is challenging. "Ah . . . I make no promises—"

"About what? Dancing technique or something?"

I laugh, and so does he. I put my hand in his, and he leads me around the edge of the water in what might be a waltz. His smile lights up. The entire perimeter of the lake glows as fairies join in, contributing their magnificent colors and music. Rhydian turns me out, and I leave his hand and swing wide before I return to him. He swings me into his body.

"You're so beautiful."

My breath escapes in a shudder at being so close to him, and I find myself staring at his lips.

"May I kiss you?"

I don't answer. Instead, I pop up on my toes and connect our lips in a quick peck. He places his hand behind my neck and leans into me. His kiss is careful, teasing, and soft. A welcome sensation of electricity travels through my body straight to my toes. I kiss him back with an urgency that's returned. Wind surrounds us as if to push us closer together, and I'm lost in the moment.

Cheering pulls me from his lips. It's the fairies, and all I can do is laugh with Rhydian. "Voyeurs." Rhydian whispers.

"Apparently."

We leave the fairies, and Rhydian holds my hand the entire ride back to the manor. As the entrance gets closer, I know I'm not ready for this night to end. Still, it does. When Rhydian escorts me to the top of the manor stairs, I turn to him. "Thank you for tonight."

"Anytime. I like being with you," he laughs, and with a sly grin adds, "outside of work, that is."

"Funny."

He reaches out and tucks a strand of hair behind my ear. His hand moves slowly down my neck. I catch myself watching and stepping closer to him before he pulls me in.

"I should probably walk you in; it's late. But—"

I capture his lips with mine on the unspoken word. Our kiss deepens and our tongues tangle and explore. I'm all sensation and desire; with one hand at his neck and one on his arm, I feel like I'm spinning carefree.

Back in my room, I flop on my bed and touch my lips, reminiscing about the entire night. My magick still hums under my skin. There is no way I'm going to sleep.

My phone buzzes. A text from Rhydian.

I can't sleep. I keep thinking about kissing you.

I smile. *I was thinking the same thing.*

I know, can't get it out of my mind either.

My good mood is instantly invaded by thoughts of his blood vow, and a pit forms in my stomach. He knows my emotions. He can feel them. Heat rises to my face. I huff at the one-sided aspect of the blood vow. Nothing I feel will be unknown to him.

Willow, are you okay?

I stare at his text for a minute, my mind reeling with thoughts. Did he kiss me because he wanted to, or was he satisfying an emotional need from me? Do I want to know the real answer to that? Ugh!

Willow? Should I come over?

I hesitate. *Tired, talk to you at school tomorrow?*

Okay.

Goodnight, Rhydian.

I wait to see if he'll say anything more. He doesn't, and I immediately feel like a bitch.

Did I ruin the perfect date?

PART II

By knot of four, this power I store
By knot of five, the spell's alive

CHAPTER 8

M ondays at Trinity High School are always full of
weekend buzz—new gossip about hookups, breakups,
and sport scores. I navigate the hallway to my locker on
autopilot and spy Emily and Marco laughing. They look good
next to each other, his mocha skin and white oxford shirt in
complementary contrast to Emily's paleness. I wave to them and
open my locker, hang my coat, and grab my books. I shove them
in my backpack. I sense Rhydian's presence but don't seek him
out. I can tell he's keeping his distance because of our text
conversation, which has me swimming in a pool of regret.

"So, how was the date?"

"Shhh. Don't be so loud," I say to Emily.

"What's this about?" Marco asks with a smirk.

Emily fills Marco in on the date that I had with Rhydian last
night.

Marco grunts. "Ah dating Rhydian, so he's around you like all
the time right even here at school?"

"I guess so, why?"

"Since he's here at school now and you're a magickal royal
badass, why am I being ordered by Guardians to watch over you
at school?"

"What? That is not my doing, Marco, and you don't have to do it. I can certainly take care of myself," I huff.

"If only it was that easy, Willow. Did you realize I would be breaking the law if I went against Guardian orders? I mean, sure, how would they find out? We only have a couple of classes together. But if something goes down and I'm anywhere near you and don't engage, it could cost me my head or other vital parts."

Emily smacks her gum and dramatically rolls her eyes at Marco. He responds with an indignant, "What?"

"Could you be more bitchy? You're a freakin' shapeshifter, not a little puss—kitty." She winks before continuing, "Come on, tiger man, grow a pair."

"Always challenging the fighter in me. Why not the lover?"

"Gotta earn it."

"Get a room," I tease. I'm never so bold, especially in public places, to say the things they do. Heck, I'm still grappling with the fact that Rhydian can sense my emotions.

The bell rings for homeroom just in time. I can't focus on the announcements. Instead, I think about the predicament of Marco being given orders. He's ordered to do something because he goes to my school and is part of Edayri. That doesn't seem right. It isn't as if he volunteered. Sure, I'm a little hurt that he seems put off by the idea of helping me if something happens, but in all reality, he's only my friend because I was dating Daniel. He's always been friendly to me, and he certainly flirts with Emily all the time, but we're not directly friends by ourselves.

The bell rings for first period, pulling me from my thoughts. When I arrive, Rhydian is already in his seat. He's flanked by Team Bleach Blonde with Coral at the front. He's smiling and talking with them, but his eyes are on me the moment I walk in.

"Hey, Willow."

That puts the pin in Coral, her mouth open and her perfectly manicured eyebrows creased. I smile weakly in their direction and take my seat.

During class, Rhydian looks back at me twice and catches

me staring at him. He projects warmth and happiness to me through our connection. It feels intimate even though I'm surrounded by fellow students. As much as I look like I'm listening to the lecture, I'm really not. The sense that I should be in Edayri learning my duties instead of here has me doubting myself and my goals. Rhydian projects the cheering of the fairies following our kiss. I giggle and try to hide it from everyone around me. Coral notices anyway and looks from me to Rhydian.

Rhydian waits for me after class, and we leave together.

"Still need some space?" He doesn't seem angry, but his eyes are wide, waiting for my response. Goddess, I'm a brat. What am I doing? Most girls would love a guy who has an inside track on their emotions and who is sensitive to that. Here I am pouting about it like an idiot.

"No," I say. "I'm sorry. Call it a momentary overthinking brain hiccup."

Coral approaches and I turn to Emily. Her eyes wide and mocking.

I mouth a dramatic, what? When I see Coral reach out a hand to touch Rhydian's shoulder then step into his space.

"Hey guys!" Emily interrupts, bouncing into the crowded space and hanging her arm over my shoulder. "And the sharks circle," she whispers in my ear.

"Funny," I reply.

Without a missing a beat, Coral continues. "I was curious if you'd like to get to know some of your other fellow students this weekend at my house. I'm having a little party—"

Rhydian looks at us. "Wanna go to Coral's party?" Coral's mouth drops open and I choke down a laugh as Emily announces that we will all be there.

"Oh, that's just great." Coral stares hard at Emily before focusing back on Rhydian, her smile plastered. "I'll see you then." She walks away hips swinging.

"Thanks, Coral, for the invite." Rhydian says as I elbow him.

Rhydian laughs, fidgeting with a knotted rope in his hand. "What's with the rope?"

"Oh, knot magick?" He holds it up for me to see. I raise my eyebrows. "It's almost like when girls sing that song and pull petals from a flower. It's a spell-like rhyme that we learn when we are young. 'By knot of one, the spell's begun. By knot of two, it cometh true.' You work through the knots to the end."

"So, you're wishing for something?"

"Maybe." He shrugs, watching my face, then steps closer to me.

I know how it looks to everyone around us: that we are a couple. We haven't even talked about it though. Are we dating? Sabine and Eoin mentioned Rhydian needing a cover to be with me at all times in Chepstow. Whether or not we are a couple, that would make a good cover.

Coral corners me before my organic chemistry class to ask the question I can tell she's dying to ask. "Are you and Rhydian dating?"

"I'm not sure that is any of your business, Coral."

"Cut the shit, Willow. Because if you aren't, I'm making a move."

"Yes, I think you were making a move anyway. Why does it matter what I say?"

"I'm not that person."

That's news to me, because I could have sworn that's all she ever did when I was dating Daniel. I'm tempted to search for her thoughts, which is not only wrong but also a type of magick I've never tried before. I wouldn't want to mess something up, like whatever I did to Evan. I shake my head of the idea.

Yes, you should.

"Okay, yes, we've gone out on dates and are getting to know each other. I don't think I can define it beyond that right now."

He's mine.

Coral doesn't respond; she just turns dramatically, swinging her long black hair, and walks away. Whatever. The tardy bell rings, so I step into my classroom—then freeze.

Evan is at the front of the room, horns and all for everyone to see.

"Please, have a seat. I'm your sub today. You're blocking the doorway; it's a fire hazard. Come in now please."

Marco, also apparently late, pushes me, and we enter with several other students. Marco gives me an irritated look but doesn't seem to recognize Evan. He knows Evan! Why is he acting so causal?

I look all around the classroom waiting for the cavalry, but nothing happens. Evan is talking and smiling, and on closer observation I notice a wavering of light around his body. He's projecting a different image to everyone; why can I see him as he is? I slow my breathing. If I don't control my emotions, I'll be inviting Rhydian to come into the class for sure.

The sharp elbow in my side from Marco shocks me. Evan is looking directly at me, smirking as if this is some game. "Ms. Warrington, let me ask you again: Can you advise on where you are in the chapter work?"

"Didn't Mrs. Simpson leave a lesson plan?"

"She is out unexpectedly. If you don't know, can someone else advise?"

Before anyone responds, I say, "We're on complex bonds and dissolution of materials."

"Very well, then. If everyone can go to that chapter and read for a moment, I will try to find the handout for today's sample experiment."

Marco is still staring at me, trying to figure out why I'm acting so odd. "What the hell?" he mouths. But Evan is next to our table with the missing handout that has somehow appeared.

"Are we going to have a problem, Ms. Warrington? I thought from Mrs. Simpson's note that you are her star student in this class. She said you would be willing to assist, though it seems she may be wrong."

The laughter from behind me makes the hair on my neck stand. He's trying to get a rouse from me, and at school!

"She's not wrong," I reply, staring at him hard in warning.

Marco kicks my leg. I continue to shake him off; he clearly can't see that the substitute teacher is Evan.

"We'll see. Stars are just gaseous energy that eventually combusts under changing circumstances—then, poof."

"Clearly, that's not right; that's how stars are formed under immense pressure. Is this a test?" I am trying hard not to combust myself. My classmates mirror Marco's open mouth and wide-eyed expressions. "I'm sorry, I shouldn't have—"

"Well, at least you're not tempted to be in the herd of followers." Evan waves his hand and time stops. The lights dim. "That's better."

"What the hell, Evan! Why are you here?"

"I don't have much time. We need a way to communicate; as you say, shit is going down. Give me your hand." He rolls up his sleeve and reaches for me.

I pull from him. "No. Tell me what's going on. Here?"

He pulls my arm forward, wrapping his hand near my elbow. Reluctantly, I follow his lead so that our forearms are touching. He whispers a spell that lights up our arms, and it's as if our magick merges and flows. The lights flicker in the room.

Evan releases my arm. The real substitute teacher is standing next to me, looking confused before moving off to take his seat at Mrs. Simpson's desk.

What did I just allow Evan to do? Will Rhydian know? Marco kicks my leg. "What was that?"

"Nothing." I shake my head and pretend to read the instructions on the handout.

CHAPTER 9

O n the drive home, Rhydian is behind me in one of my father's flashy sports cars. He comes up on my car's tail, egging me into a chase. I grin and push the accelerator. My BMW has an engine built for speed and his comment from last week about my elderly driving fuels me. The suburban roads are not empty and they don't provide much of a challenge to getting a good lead. My car radio is blaring the bass of the radio music, which radiates through my body and charges me further. I pull into my posh neighborhood and whip into the drive that leads to the house.

The chase doesn't end there. I make my way into the house and run up the stairs to my room. Duke is at full attention when I shut my door and giggle. His entire backside shakes happily with his tail. I waggle his black ears and put my forehead to his and kiss it. The wind rushes around me as Rhydian transports into my room. Duke barks and jumps off the bed to get more head rubs from Rhydian.

"You're not supposed to transport into my room," I smirk. That was a specific order from Eoin, which means he knows Rhydian transported in the house.

"You win," he grins. "See you tonight?"

"Okay."

He reaches for my hand. Still on a high from the chase, I step up to him and lightly kiss him on the lips before stepping away with a smirk.

"Duke, wanna go outside?"

The response is a half bark and bounce. Rhydian transports out of my room. I quickly change into leggings and a T-shirt before running down the stairs with Duke at my heels. It's a race to the back door, where Duke passes me in one big jump through the doggy door and out the garage. I run pass Quinn.

"Hey, Quinn!" I yell, grabbing a frisbee out of a bin to play with Duke.

Quinn is behind me and talking to someone on his earpiece, but I have no care in the world except to play with my dog. It's been forever since we've played like this and the weather is beautiful. April in Chepstow is volatile—one minute there's snow, then the next it's sunny, warm, and cloud free like today. I wouldn't miss this opportunity for the world.

Before Duke gets too far, I shout his name. He turns to watch the frisbee fly from my hand and takes off in a big leap to catch it midair. He trots over for my praise and lets me take the frisbee back.

"One more time?" I ask as Duke waits impatiently. I throw the frisbee in a high gentle arch. I run with him a few feet, then stand and watch him catch it again. I laugh and clap as he brings the frisbee to me. Petting his furry head, I sense a bit of vertigo, like a wave that hits and moves down my body.

I'm caught off guard as my vision wavers and changes. The dried dead grass of my yard is replaced by a bright green lawn with a technicolor effect. I shake my head but the scene in front of me stays. My legs feel like jelly and I take a moment to sit down. A man with white hair and a commanding presence appears right in front of me.

"Evan, you get back in this house right now and you apologize."

My jaw drops. It's Harkin, my grandfather; I recognize him from portraits at the manor and at the Hallowed Hall. His distinguished face and stature are the picture of legendary royalty.

A reply comes from behind me. "No. I am not apologizing to the step-monster." I turn and recognize in the small boy behind me the hair and features of my uncle. This is a young Evan.

"Don't call her that. Sabine and this family are all you have. You need to step up and take responsibility for who you are in this family."

Evan looks to be around the age of ten. He is so small and yet does not seem discouraged from talking back to Harkin, a man who towers over him and who certainly intimidates me. Evan's hands are buried deep in the pockets of his plaid shorts. He looks up at Harken. "She says I don't belong here, so how am I supposed to be part of the family? Only Nuala talks to me and cares."

Harkin ruffles Evan's wavy hair. "Come on, my boy, let's go back in the house. But you will apologize."

I watch father and son walk back toward the familiar gray stone of MacKinnon Manor. The image starts to waiver and change again, and my stomach feels it.

A voice in my head, the distinct sound of the little boy now an adult, says, "Who you are in this family? Sometimes family has the best intentions, but not ours. The legacy is poison. It seeps into the ground and affects more than us."

I respond with my thoughts to Evan. "Why show me this?"

"All the right questions; she is smart. Smart, smart, smart."

"Thank you, I guess?"

"No guessing; know it. Feel it. Observe it." Evan responds so loudly that I cover my ears. It does nothing to help.

"Geez, Evan, there is no need to yell. You realize I can hear you just fine in my head, right?"

"In your head, in my head, two heads together and two heads apart."

The rattling of Evan's thoughts in my head is starting to give me a headache. I'm not sure what he's trying to say; it's just garbled nonsense, as usual. "Esmund, Rhydian—the interlinks of the Boward lineage to the MacKinnon royalty ties. Oh, he likes your interest in Rhydian."

The view in front of me changes again, this time from the back of my house to the patio at MacKinnon Manor. I'm looking down at feet that aren't mine. My head turns toward a female voice, one I recognize. It grows more urgent. A stern sounding male voice causes me to hide behind a large group of potted plants. I pcak around them toward the voices.

Esmund stands near my mother. He's reaching toward her, and she keeps backing away.

"It's over. Don't make this hard and more complicated," my mother says.

"We are betrothed, Nuala. This doesn't only affect you, it affects me and our families. This lineage was promised."

She hugs herself and takes a step forward toward Esmund. "I'm tired of being the political pawn for a royal rule that shouldn't even exist. You may want all of this power, and you may believe in its old tradition, but I'm done with it. It has made my family bitter and separated us. I want love in my life, and that's with Aiden. You may not like it, Esmund, but you need to accept it. And all I wish for you is to experience this type of love also."

I watch in awe of my mother—the boldness, the calm she possesses. Esmund's eyes look wild and he towers over her, looking like he might blow up or even hurt her. After a brief moment, his shoulders slump in total resignation.

"Nuala, I have always loved you. You minimize my experience and that wounds me."

"Esmund, you will always be a dear friend to both myself and Aiden, but trust me when I say that you love the idea of me, not really me."

"You will regret this. Your father and mother will never accept this. My vow to you—"

"I reject your offered service of a blood vow that connects you to me."

"No!" Esmund bends forward and drops to his knee in agony.

I gasp. My mother waves her hand, and a bright white light shines from her palm like a spotlight directly on my face.

But it's not my face—it's Evan's. He was there.

There's a car in the drive, headlights fixed on my face. Duke is lying next to me. The warmth of his sun-heated fur has almost gone cold. The sky tells me that it's dusk.

"Willow? What are you doing out in the middle of the lawn? It's getting cold. You ready to come in, maybe get a bite to eat?" asks Rhydian.

I pet Duke's head and wave. "That sounds great," I shout back. I stand to walk across the lawn.

"So, there's the boy wonder. The highlight of Esmund's family. And how close you were to being siblings."

"Evan," I warn him. "How do I turn this off? You can't be in my head like this."

"Just flip the switch."

"And exactly where is the switch?"

"Oh—private time for boyfriend, eh?"

"Evan!"

"Turning the switch off, but be careful. Those blood vows, they play havoc when they are not equal or wanted. Esmund understands this, but so far his gamble is paying off."

"I'm not something to be gambled with, Evan." I purse my lips together in an effort not to scream.

"Preach."

"Evan, you are too weird."

CHAPTER 10

Tullen is droning on about the history of Wicca in Edayri. My mind wanders to Rhydian. We're getting closer and spending a lot of time together. I'm completely attracted to him and enjoy being around him, and when he's not around I'm thinking about him. Still, the idea of the vow sits in the back of my mind.

"Earth to Willow. Earth to Will—no, wait, Edayri to Willow. Check in." I laugh and blush. "Seriously, Willow. I've been talking for over ten minutes and you're in some sort of daze. What's going on with you? Anything you say is between the two of us. Unleash it."

I cave. "Okay, here goes. What is the deal with blood vows? Because I—I really like Rhydian, but is his affection a result of his vow or by his choice?" A grin pulls at Tullen's lips, and I continue with what I'm sure is a red face. "I ask him, but he avoids the topic, and I just can't let it go. Am I stupid?"

"I see. No one doubts the connection you both have, but I see where you'd be concerned." Yes, for once some real talk. Thank you, Tullen! "Let me tie this into the history of the Goddess, the Horned God, and the beginning of Wicca."

"What? A history lesson, really?"

"The crown should be exhibiting just a little patience here, because history may help you with your current concerns."

"But I thought the Horned God was related to the birth of the demons, not Wicca. Doesn't Wicca belong with the Goddess?"

"Ah, so you are listening to me." Tullen scratches his short red scruffy beard. "Yes, it belongs to them both. The Horned God and the Goddess are responsible for Edayri. Our kind was birthed out of Edayri." Tullen pauses to make sure I'm paying attention, then continues. "The Goddess and the Horned God were connected not only by the same family but by requited love, but the Goddess also fell in love with her creations. She felt that she had built a better creation than the Almighty with doses of magick and other special abilities. The Horned God was jealous because he loved the Goddess and wanted her attention, so he gifted her with his own creation. He made a mirror of himself—you know them as demons. The Goddess took this as an insult and was outraged that he would add another creation to her beautiful, perfect world. The Horned God was offended because they are of the same family, but his difference was seen by the Goddess as a weakness and imperfect. The bond between the Goddess and Horned God was strained. It was said the Horned God left her and the Goddess cried for weeks on end. A Wiccan by the name of Brekaen made a vow to the Goddess to honor her in a way that the Horned God could not, per his loyalty he offered to tie his soul to hers, if she would accept this he could be anything she needed. Since Brekaen was a Wiccan and part of the creation she loved, she accepted his vow, and this is where the blood vow was born. Others wanted her attention, but they were not as well-intended as Brekaen. As a result, the blood vow became one of service per serious commitment and honor, paid in blood and life. If you broke your vow, the Goddess owned your soul and the physical pain of your deceit would always be present."

"This is interesting, but what strikes me most is that you're telling me that both Wiccans and demons are from the same family? If this is true, how can Wiccans deny it?" I ask.

Tullen, ever thoughtful, pauses and scratches the side of his face where his beard and hairline meet. "It's complicated. We are full of pride, if you will, and with the love of the Goddess. Because of this, we are her perfect creations."

"We are far from perfect."

"Depends on how you define perfect. Needless to say, the Horned God felt he was giving the Goddess a gift. When she rejected it, she essentially rejected him. The result was a war between the Goddess and the Horned God and their creations, a war that has never ended. The Horned God, broken-hearted that she would choose Wiccan vows over his—a god's—turned them into enemies. Eventually the Horned God's presence faded, he no longer wanted the Goddess's acceptance."

This is the most ridiculous thing I've ever heard. Heck, in high school this is a daily occurrence—saying one thing and meaning it differently, and someone else taking offense to it. The intention behind whatever is said is not usually malicious. This is something you witness every freaking day!

I interrupt him. "Doesn't anyone get how ridiculous this is?"

"The previous ruler would not abide by that discussion, but there's certainly hope with the new ruler. An outsider." Tullen smiles.

When Rhydian first introduced me to Tullen as the historian and their moral conscience, I didn't understand, but today it is quite clear. He challenges the status quo and coveted traditions. We are alike in that regard, although I am rarely emboldened enough to act or speak. Does that make me complicit or just scared and young?

"Tullen, I am pulled in so many different directions that any type of voice I want to have is lost. I want to invoke change, but Sabine, Esmund, and others hold tradition in their fist and almost beat me with it. As you said, I'm an outsider, and I'm certainly being treated like one. I want to be here, but I don't fit, and that makes me not want to be here. I fit in Chepstow—or I guess I used to. My life is at a fork in the road, literally." I put my face in my hands and breathe.

Tullen is leaning forward, his elbows on his knees, hands clasped, listening. "I can't imagine. I would think that part of you is screaming to get out. Willow, don't let that part take a backseat, because at some point it will consume you and you might do something you regret. Just because something has always been one way doesn't mean it is the right or the only way." He watches me carefully. "Form your own opinions. Be aware of them. I love my Wiccan heritage and who I am, but because of the system we live in, I have had a very different upbringing and outlook than others who live here. Take Thaxam, for instance. He's a demon who certainly has a different take on Edayri."

"Tullen, are the Emissaries just a group opposing Wiccan dominance and rule? Are there any Wiccans who are part of it?"

"The Wiccans may not show it, but most lower covens are part of the Emissaries, or at minimum agree that all beings should be equal. You come from a world that has fought for equality across the Terra realm. Here, no one challenges the Wiccan royal rule with any great success. But like I said, there's hope."

I sag in my seat, and Tullen stands and claps my knee.

"I'm here to talk anytime you need, Willow. I believe Cross is waiting for you; it might be the perfect time to reflect. Training is always a good way to take out the frustrations and bothersome questions that plague your brain."

I change clothes in the training room and stop in front of the mirror. My hair is dark brown now, like my fathers, and my facial features are like my mothers, yet I am uniquely me. Judgment seems to stare back at me. What can I do? I'm quite small and I'm not fearless.

Yet you are powerful.

My magick flows on my skin instantly. I didn't call it, but it flows, and the crown appears on my forehead and lifts high like a hologram.

So, I'm powerful. Sure. What do I do with it?

Anything.

And that's what scares me.

"Hey, ya ready?" Cross is bouncing around on the mat, sweat starting to bead on his forehead. I nod back at him. "Let's get started then." He has me run on the treadmill for five minutes, then he has me limber up before we get into physical rounds of offense and defense training.

"Not that I'm complaining, but damn, yer quiet. Are ya not talkin' because ya want to quiet the mind, or is this mind to loud for ya?"

"Right, you complaining? No, never." I say, then blink dramatically.

"All right then." He puts on a padded vest that fits his blocky muscular build snuggly. "Let's see which it is. Attack, and no magick. Show me!"

"No magick?" I bring it up on my forearms and watch the swirls extend to my fingers. "Why not? Afraid?"

"Hells, I should be, but nah. If ya got none, then what? Stop testing my good nature and come at me!"

Part of me wants to knock his smug face across the room with a light blast from my hands. The other part—the competitive part—wins. I run up with my sparring gloves and move through the drill attack combo—left, right, left, high knee to round kick. He's blocking me and meeting me at every turn. I hit harder and faster, landing a few good ones that Cross shrugs off easily. The physical combat is becoming second nature. I focus on the movements.

"AHH!" I yell, my movements a blur.

Cross is no longer in defense but attacking me, and I easily maneuver around him. I'm in control. The scared girl from the attack in the alley all that time ago, the same girl who ran through the woods after meeting her first demon, is gone.

There is a loud, slow clap from the side of the gym.

We stop fighting. Cross smiles and waves someone in. It is Tullen. I try to catch my breath.

"She's still holding back," Cross says, and that shocks me. My magick flares at him. "Come on, ya are. Yer speed and efforts are not from the middle."

"Boy, I can't wait to witness you knock Cross on his ass." Tullen smiles and grabs a bo staff from the wall. "I was quite sure that today might have been that day."

"Aye, so tis to quiet yer head then." Cross tosses me a towel and I wipe the sweat from my face and neck.

"Yeh, I guess," I respond.

"She's struggling with the history and duty of royal rule," Tullen announces as he tosses a staff to Cross. They circle each other, and Tullen twirls his side to side in big sweeps, approaching Cross.

Cross's twirl overhead is less theatrical, and before I know it, they are smacking staffs and sweeping each other in a fight. They both anticipate each other's moves. They smile, taunting each other. It's a ballet I like to watch.

Tullen is flat on his back with Cross's staff on his chest before he taps the mat.

"There, the answer is no—again," Cross says, exasperated.

I wonder what the question was, but Tullen seems content.

"Willow, ya need to show them who wears the crown. The crown doesn't wear ya." Cross points to me before hanging the bo staff up on the wall. "Ya do that, and ya give hope to the masses as ya did in disbanding the high council."

This is the reason Cross tolerates me. Change.

"How is that?" I ask.

"Cause when battles are unjust to the innocent, they also tear the fabric of those who serve." Cross stares at me while he speaks. "My parents died serving the royal crown, but because we are from a lower coven, it isn't considered a significant loss."

"I'm sorry, Cross. I would never—"

"I get that."

This whole cast and the royal system is messed up, and now I am the head of it.

CHAPTER 11

After my shower, I stretch my neck, close my eyes, and breathe slowly. My muscles are sore from the workout with Cross. I lay down on the small sofa next to Duke in our sitting room. Then, out of nowhere, the vertigo. My vision flickers. I blink and observe that I'm no longer on the sofa; I'm sitting on a small cot in a medical tent. Blurs of people and demons walk by, attending to the injured.

A laugh bursts through my lips, catching me off guard because it isn't my voice. The hands I hold out in front of me are strong and thick, black, blue, and stained with blood.

Why are you happy?

A woman comes into view—no one I recognize. She has kind, dark eyes that seemed oddly familiar. "Oh, Evan, what happened?"

"I'm ready. I miss her so much. It would not be a bad thing to join her." The woman is moving things at the head of the cot. She takes a stethoscope and listens to my chest—Evan's chest.

"Who do you miss, Evan?"

The name lifts off my lips in a breathy declaration. "Meghan." My eyes shut and I see her—the full face and wide eyes, the dark chocolate, thick hair that curls at her waist. She is curvy and short, and her smile melts my heart. For me and only me. Her unconditional love, her quick wit, her brazen attitude.

My eyes—our eyes—are shocked by the penlight the woman shines. We focus and hoarsely call out, "Meghan?" We reach for her wrist, but her touch on our face is not Meghan's small hand. Her eyes are not the wide, deep purple we love.

"Can you tell me where you are?"

We don't want to. Our voice catches in our throat; we shut our eyes. The pain pounds in our head. Tears cloud our eyes.

"The Emissaries camp. MacKinnon Manor—"

"Evan, you're going to be just fine." The woman says some type of enchantment over us and our legs straighten, our arms relax, and we drift to lay down prone on the cot. "You've got more work to do. It is not your time, Evan."

We remember the venom of our words. "I did a bad thing. Willow—I couldn't save Aiden. Abby, she hurts—it won't be mended. It will be worse. She's not ready."

The woman, Abby, yells something behind her, and a young boy brings her a glass tube with a glowing amber liquid.

She gently pulls our chin down, and we comply. The liquid is warm and slides down our throat. "This will take away the physical curse, but the mental one, I'm afraid, is one we'll have to examine later."

We look at our hands; the black and blue starts to fade and return to their natural skin color. "She's going into the lion's den."

"Well, according to my brother, she's quite the lion herself. She'll need that spunk against my father. Drift, Evan, into a healing sleep." Abby's words echo in our ears.

"They will break her—"

"Shhh. Drift, Evan. Remember, the lioness is the bravest of the pride. She is a lot like Nuala and her father. She will recognize the hypocrisy."

"Compulsions, vows, the loss of free will. They will steal it from her, may even kill it out of her. I did a bad thing, an awful thing." Our chest feels heavier with each word and a fog comes over us, pushing us into the cot.

Abby caresses our face, her touch comforting.

My eyes—our eyes—are heavy. The image flutters, my heart picks up, joy replaces my guilt. My soul returns to my body.

I suck in air abruptly, pushing myself up to stand. I'm back in my suite at MacKinnon Manor.

"Oh, Goddess." I massage my throat and feel the ache of my bones. I wish there was some sort of warning before I experienced Evan's memories. I can't breathe. I walk around the sitting area and open the doors to the outside. The cooling wind greets me and takes away the weight of Evan's sadness and heartache.

"He tried to help," I say to the stars above.

Knock.

"Yes?"

"Lady MacKinnon would like your company for the evening meal in the dining hall in a half hour."

Entering the dining hall, I find my seat at the end of the table where two place settings are stationed. The white and gold plates shine from the light of the crystal chandelier overhead. Sabine sweeps into the room. I stand before she quickly waves me to sit.

"Although we do a lot of crown business here, this is your family home too. Let's relax tonight."

We engage in small discussions, and things are pleasant. Then I ask her about my grandfather, the Wiccan King.

Sabine's eyes light up and crinkle at the corners. "Harkin was a difficult man, very stubborn at times, but so easy on the eyes." I smile. "I knew him in my younger years but never paid him much attention because our family lines and covens were not intertwined. We were betrothed, per custom. I could love and hate that man all in one breath. But I think that's how most marriages go. I do miss him, though."

This is a side of Sabine I never anticipated. Her relaxed demeanor and personal engagement with me while discussing her husband are something new.

"You sound fortunate to have fallen in love."

"It's certainly something we need to discuss for you as well."

"What, discuss me falling in love?" I stammer.

"Discuss the traditions of royal betrothals and linages of noble covens."

"I don't want that." I look away before I continue. "I'm having a hard enough time understanding blood vows and why Rhydian seems so happy about it. I don't want to get married unless I'm in a relationship with someone I love, and even then, only if it is the next step for us in our lives. Besides, I'm too young."

Sabine sits back in her chair and lifts wine to her mouth. "Yes, it's time some things change. I don't disagree."

My shoulders relax. Evan holds grudges against Sabine from when he was a little boy. Sabine's protectiveness and support of me show me something else entirely from Evan's experience. I wonder if I can share this with him the way he shares his experiences with me.

"But, darling, some things need to remain in tradition too, or they get lost to future generations. I see so much of Nuala and Aiden in you. You know, Nuala and Aiden were a perfect match, balancing light and dark so perfectly. If things had been different in their matching . . . well, it would have been a different life for all."

I'm surprised by her comment that they were a perfect match. Knowing the answer, I ask a question that will test my theory.

"Were they betrothed?"

Her eyes come back to me from wherever her thoughts had taken her. "No, they were not. She was promised in betrothal to

Esmund, actually. They all grew up together and were in the same friend groups. It was hard on Esmund when she chose Aiden and they married, but over time the friendships repaired and remained."

I lean back in my chair and feel more at ease. Did I think she would lie to me? No. She seems more flexible than what Evan tells me.

"The bond your parents held was so strong. Stronger than any vow. It was you, Willow. You brought so much to them without even being born yet, only conceived. The promise of you gave them freedom, a linage."

It's a lovely moment of closeness that I have never felt before with Sabine. Feeling like I'm in a safe space, I jump in the deep end.

"Do you support change? I mean, Wiccan and Edayri change?"

I wait as she takes another drink of her wine.

"Willow, times are changing, but you have to measure how that change will affect everyone. I am one for tradition, but I also know those of us left are older and it is time for a new regime."

"But if the majority of Edayri want this change, then why stay stuck? There is more to Edayri, and I've only seen a small fraction of it."

The relaxed aspect of the room changes; there's a shift in the air. I sense someone in the doorway behind me. Sabine's face becomes hard, her lips pushed together. "Don't disappoint your parent's legacy or this family, Willow. Your every action and reaction is measured." She stands, redirecting her attention with a charming smile. "Hello, Esmund. Won't you come in?"

I turn to watch Mr. Boward enter.

"Pardon the intrusion, but you wanted the report. I'm happy to advise that I have been appointed in the official capacity of bridge to the Wiccan communities with the support of the noble coven, in addition to my current role as royal Scepter to you, of course."

"You've done well for yourself, Esmund." Sabine smiles but it doesn't reach her eyes. She is putting on her political face for him.

I stand and walk to the doorway near Mr. Boward. "I'm going to my room. Thank you, Sabine, for dinner and our talk."

"Anytime. Let us continue our discussion soon, Willow."

We will, I'm sure of it.

"Good evening, Willow." Mr. Boward squints his eyes and looks down his nose at me. "I understand you will not be here through the weekend. Going back to the Chepstow so soon?"

"Well, I'm returning for tonight. Can you request a royal Guardian as an escort? Will that make it better?"

Mr. Boward's sly grin reminds me of the devil. I want to smack the demur grin off Esmund's face. He has planned no less for me and Rhydian. I wonder if Rhydian is even aware of what his father's plans are. I'm not fond of the matchmaker grins across his and Sabine's faces.

They aren't wrong, granted—I'm totally falling for Rhydian—but this is frustrating beyond belief.

CHAPTER 12

Rhydian and I transport into the foyer of my home holding each other's hands. Finally, away from duty, I lean in and gaze up into his eyes. Someone clears their throat from the side of the staircase. Rhydian is the first to release his hand. I turn to find Eoin with a sandwich in hand, dressed in jeans and a sweater. His eyes look tired.

"Returning early? I thought you were due back tomorrow?" There is slamming in the kitchen. "Quinn is cleaning up."

Rhydian stands tall in front of Eoin, his commander, and says, "We've been invited to attend a party tonight that a school friend is hosting. Would it be acceptable, and beneficial to our cover at school, for us to attend this party?"

A lot of students will be at Coral's party, including all my friends.

Eoin is looking at me, eyebrow high. I shrug, trying to look like I care just enough but not too much. "It could be a good thing to go to some of my normal activities outside of school. It would be suspicious if I didn't. And," I throw in, "I would love to just hang with my friends for a night."

Eoin takes a bite of his sandwich, chews, and swallows before he speaks, watching both of us closely. "Both of you together, the entire time within eyesight." Why am I blushing? He meant for security only. "Do you both understand?"

We both answer quickly with a yes, Rhydian's more formal by adding a "sir." Eoin proceeds up the stairs and leaves us in the foyer. I spy Quinn at the top of the stairs. Didn't Eoin say he was in the kitchen? Strange. He quickly waves to me before rounding the corner out of sight.

"Should we leave now? The party is well underway."

Surveying myself, I realize I don't need to change—my chucks, dark jeans, and sweater are exactly what I would wear to Coral's anyway. "Yes, just let me grab my coat. Will we transport or drive over?"

"We'd be less conspicuous if we drove."

Silly of me to think differently; of course, we will drive to Coral's house together. I'm getting used to transporting magickly. With my coat in hand, I pet Duke goodbye and meet Rhydian in the garage. I get behind the wheel of my BMW. He has a wide grin on his face.

"What is so entertaining?" I ask, backing out of the garage.

"Nothing. I'm just happy to leave the confines of the walls that keep you hidden, not unlike the night at the lake with the fairies."

He's right—it's freedom on another level, and another date night. This is more public though. My classmates will see us together, and somehow that makes me nervous. It's been just us and our private moments, although I guess the fairies at the lake make it not so private.

"Are you ready for us to be public?" he asks.

I'm surprised at his question. Is he insecure about us?

Be bold.

"Rhydian, are we more than . . . tied in vows? Are we dating?"

The choke of air startles me. He lays his hand on mine, covering the gear shift. The Guardian wrist cuff is cold to the touch. "I don't think dating is more than tied in vows. Simply, I like you, Willow, and I would like more romantic opportunities. If that is dating, then yes. I don't want you with anyone else."

He sounds so formal and yet natural at the same time. I'm awkward. Heat rises on my face and I keep my eyes on the road.

"Are my intentions not clear to you?" he asks.

I turn into Coral's neighborhood and enter the gate code to gain entry. Her neighborhood is a high-end cluster of houses with manicured lawns, carefully placed trees, and intentional landscaping. I turn and see Rhydian staring at me with a smile. I fumble with my car and drive forward through the gate. "Yes, I just—I feel like I have more choice than you, and I don't want to influence your feelings or—I just—okay, I'm embarrassed for even asking now."

"Don't be. I—how do I say this without scaring you off the road?"

The hair on the back of my neck tingles, and I shift in my seat. I breathe steadily, waiting for a full minute before he says, "The vow is one of duty, but my heart is another matter, and it is mine, Willow."

He says my name like a lyric, and my chest pounds in my ears. I pull over behind a line of cars parked in front of Coral's long drive and turn to him, turning off the car. His are eyes watching my every move, traveling to my lips and settling on my eyes. How can I doubt the way he feels?

"Um—

"I know, we'll take this slow, but you want to explore this too."

Boy, I do. Why does it scare me?

"Talk to me, Willow."

Is he nervous? His eyes wander around my face as if he's mapping it to recall later. His mouth opens slightly, and he takes a shallow breath. He's waiting and wanting. I lean across the console that divides us and kiss him.

I touch his smooth face with my hand and my lips tentatively move his. I open my eyes and start to pull back, but his eyes are closed, and he's kissing me back. The warmth and excitement urge us on, and we open to each other, our tongues entangled in a slow, sweet dance. I pull back from him, grinning.

"We are dating then," Rhydian says, grinning in a cocky manner.

"Yes, we are," I respond.

We both leave the car and arrive hand in hand at Coral's party.

A weight is lifted off my shoulders, and I lean into Rhydian, not caring to hide my smile. I'm with Rhydian and my friends, and everything is normal.

Everyone is in the backyard. Emily spots us and immediately makes a scene by pointing to our hands. "So—?"

"Yeah," I say.

Emily hands us both cups with drinks. "Adorable blushing. It's time to celebrate!"

Lucy and Daniel approach us smiling. Lucy mouths the word "nice" when she sees Rhydian and I hand in hand. She leans into Daniel and kisses him on the cheek. I smile easily. We are all moving forward.

The party is a full-on rage. I let down my hair and have fun with Emily and our friends. We dance on top of the pool's hard cover. I feel the buzz of the drinks and swing my hips and long hair to the music. Emily and Marco are breakdancing, of all things, to head-banging music. We're all laughing and smiling. As the music changes, Marco turns me in a twirl, his dance style the opposite of what everyone else is doing.

Rhydian is laughing and talking to the football team. He watches me, smiling. He is so good looking, almost unreal, and he's dating me. His eyes travel over my body, and I slow my sway and crook my finger to lure him toward me. He strides toward me and puts his hands on my waist, then leans down into my neck, where he kisses me just below the ear. Everyone is fading around us—the music, the laughter—

A sudden burst of wind bellows through the party, carrying a dark shadowy figure and a shriek that rings in my ears. Lucy comes running, screaming, into the group. She is heading straight for me.

Instinct and training kick in before I can think, and I duck and throw a light ball at the shadowy figure. The figure dodges it, undisturbed by the action. I stumble on my feet before Rhydian taps his wrist cuff and is in full armor. He puts himself between us. The air around me crackles like a storm has been summoned, lightning gathering and popping across the sky. I can't track the action but see Rhydian's arm swing down with his blade. Lucy screams as if she were injured. The shadowy figure disappears from sight. My eyes find Emily, who watches Lucy fall but doesn't move from holding her staff to the ground. I realize that the students are stunned in place, frozen to their spots by Emily. Marco hollers and walks a limping Daniel toward the group.

"Shit, what was that?" Daniel says, looking around in horror at the students frozen in place. His eyes grow wider, his mouth parting, when he spots Emily radiating magick from her staff freezing who she can lay her eyes on. "What is going on?" Lucy runs into his arms, hugging him and quietly sobbing.

"It's a valkyrie phantom, but I don't know how it would have entered the Terra realm," Emily says.

"Are you sure?" Rhydian asks, his brows knit together. "I've never seen one. I thought that once the Norse realm collapsed—"

Emily purses her lips and stares down Rhydian. The silence is deafening.

"Damn." Marco says, breaking the silence. "Valkyrie?"

Daniel is stone-like, expressionless, just watching us. Watching me. He is eerily calm as he stares and pulls Lucy in closer. She seems oblivious. Before I can say anything, Rhydian is in front of me.

"It's gone, but—um, your crown is high and bright, Willow."

Shit. My magick is flowing all over me.

"It's all lies, isn't it?" Lucy sobs.

"Lucy . . ." Emily warns, but she keeps going.

"Wiccan. Is that it, Willow? Looks a bit more than some religion. How could you not say anything to me? We're best friends!"

"I didn't say anything for your protection—for both you and Daniel." Her eyes are haunted and sad. I brush my hand through my hair and turn to Emily. "When did you tell her?"

"Don't speak as if I'm not here! And it was a week ago," Lucy snaps. She's pulled back from Daniel and is hugging herself.

"Willow, I've got to call this in," Rhydian says.

Daniel's face is suddenly open, and his eyes are searching my face. "I knew this, didn't I?"

I nod to Daniel, realizing that the magick that locked his memory is breaking. He's going to remember the attack at my house. Removing that memory will have been for nothing now. My heart breaks at the turn of his head, as if he's reading my mind.

Eoin transports in next to Rhydian and me. He's looking me over and directing the three Guardians who came with him. Emily, still holding the staff, begins to shake.

"Hey guys, this is starting to get a bit tough—holding time in place for all these people. How about you all transport out and Marco and I will cause a distraction to confuse everyone into what they think they saw."

Eoin agrees and directs everyone but Marco and Emily transport. Lucy and Daniel are transported by Quinn and Tullen to my house. Rhydian and I join hands and wait to transport since everyone saw us in this spot. Eoin and the other Guardians are at posts to ensure everything goes smoothly.

So much for the buzz I was sporting earlier. Rhydian studies me carefully. I almost miss Emily releasing her staff. Marco, covered in a black sheet, rushes through the crowd of students yelling. Everyone seems confused until he tackles Emily to the ground, laughing, rolling around, and kissing. Everyone seems to buy it, but I spy Coral in the window of her room looking out. She knows something is up. Rhydian and I make our way to leave the party, and he hands the keys to a Guardian to drive the car home.

We slip into a dark shadow.

"I'm sorry about—"

His finger is on my lips. "Don't be sorry. Some things are out of our control." Before I can respond, he gently kisses me, and we are transporting. It's a wild sensation the closeness of us, how we meld together. The push and pull I expect is barely noticeable with the force of our bodies together. Maybe I'm still feeling the effects of the alcohol? As the world fades around us, I wonder, can we stay like this and not return to my house? The reality is, I don't want to stop kissing him. We move in the flow of magick; it's peaceful and wraps us together like a warm blanket. My feet don't touch the ground.

Only when we pull from our kiss do we hear the loud yelling.

CHAPTER 13

Tullen and Quinn, standing to the side, shrug when they see Rhydian and me. Lucy and Daniel stop yelling and go in different directions in my house, Daniel into the sitting room and Lucy back toward the kitchen.

I feel a pang of guilt. "I need to talk with Daniel." Rhydian's face is unreadable. "Are you okay?"

Rhydian's hand drops to my waist to pull me closer. "Yea. I'm trying not to be the jealous type."

"There is no reason to be. Daniel and I are friends. We have history, and I need to explain."

"I get it. I'm going to check in with Eoin and get an update on status. I'll be back in the office." He leans down and kisses me one last time.

Tullen follows Rhydian while Quinn nods and goes back toward the kitchen. Daniel is pacing in the sitting room, chewing the side of his cheek.

"Daniel?"

He doesn't stop pacing. "When? This was before your Dad, wasn't it?"

I step in front of him. "Yes. You got hurt and I couldn't see any way for us to be together, so we broke up."

"No, we didn't. You lied to me by changing my memory. Willow, why?" He turns away from me, his voice getting louder. "Don't answer that. I know—you were trying to protect me!" Throwing up his hands, he sits in a chair. I take the one across from him.

"I'm sorry, Daniel, I really am. I did have the best intentions. I thought it would be best, considering you were hurt right here at my house. And when I say hurt, Daniel, you almost died. Right there." I point down the hallway toward the staircase.

His eyes land on the staircase, and he stares for a moment. "You chose someone else, too."

"Rhydian? That's a recent development."

"Maybe for you, but I remember everything. He healed me, but he did it for you, not out of the goodness of his heart. You just threw us away and took my choices away. Talk about a passive aggressive breakup."

"Dan—

"Seriously? You took away my choices and what we were together. God, Willow! Did I mean that little to you? How fucked up is it that you pushed me toward Lucy, your best friend. You've mourned our breakup, but for me, this is fresh." He stands, the chair moving with force as he turns back to pace in front of the window. His shoulders are square on his lean, muscular frame, his blond hair messy from constantly running his hand through it.

"Daniel. Please look at me." When he turns, my stomach twists. "I'm truly sorry. What I did was horrible. I know how it feels to have your choices taken from you, and I can't believe I did that to you, regardless of my intentions. I don't want you in this crazy magickal world. It's dangerous. My father, Mrs. Scott —" My voice hitches at their names and tears threaten to fall. "Daniel, I can't lose my friends as a result of who I am. It would break me."

"I understand, but I'm pissed about it." His shoulders relax. "It's like all my closest friends are in this secret club, and I'm looking through the window. Lucy has been lying to me for over a week and pushing our relationship. I just don't know anymore, about anything. And Marco—well, he let me in on it a long time ago, actually, but not . . ."

So, Marco confided in Daniel, sharing who and what he is? He trusted Daniel and gave him a choice. Marco is the smart one among us.

I finish his thought out loud. "The same."

"Yeah."

"In my defense, he's had more time to be used to what he is. I learned at the start of the school year."

Daniel laughs almost mocking. "And from what I hear you're the Queen? And have some serious powers."

"Yeah, something like that." I try to grin back. "Listen, this world is only expanding for me and sounds like it will for Lucy too. You'll need to really consider what you want for your life, Daniel. No warnings or opinions from my side." I hold up my hands in surrender.

He pulls me into a hug. It's nice, but different—not like the closeness we had before. Our history connects us. Goddess, I miss him. He was my first love. "I'm going to check on Lucy. Do you want to come?" Daniel declines, saying he needs space.

Lucy is crying when I find her. Quinn is near the refrigerator, staring at the floor with his hands in his pockets.

"Lucy?" I grab a napkin and sit next to her in the breakfast nook.

"Are you going to take Daniel back now?"

"No, no. Why would you even think that? Listen, it isn't like that anymore. I should have been a better friend to you, Lucy. I've been all over the place and I should have been more open about everything."

"Daniel is so angry with me. Hell, I'm angry."

I hug her around her small shoulders. "I'm sorry, Lucy. I really am."

"Tell me then."

Sitting at the table, I tell Lucy about my vast Wiccan heritage, the throne, my grandmother, and how I accepted the crown and am now the Wiccan Queen in Edayri. She doesn't ask any questions, just listens intently. I tell her about how she was abducted with my father and how Emily and I found and rescued her. Her face softens, and one stray tear falls down her cheek.

She doesn't remember any of it. It's as if I'm telling her a story of fiction, except now that Emily has revealed her heritage and she's seen the phantom attack, she has no doubts.

"I haven't been honest with you, Willow. I have a confession too. I've always been jealous of you and Daniel. I've had a crush on him since he and I were in elementary school. When he asked me to prom, I knew it was as friends because he had asked you first and you said no."

Watching her, I realize that she's bottled this up for a long time. Didn't I always realize she had a crush on him? Was I selfish in dating him in front of her? "You never said anything. You even encouraged me to date him, junior year."

"I wanted the best for you both then, and, well, now I just—I don't want you and him together. I'm in love with him, Willow."

I'm not sure how to respond to the torment in my best friend's eyes. "Lucy, it is in the past. Let's just move forward. There is no ill will at all, truthfully."

We hug.

"Well, can I join in?" Emily asks.

Lucy's back straightens. She stands and leaves, silently walking past Emily. Emily and I follow her into the foyer.

Eoin, Cross, and Rhydian are in the foyer with Daniel and Marco.

"Can you give me a ride home?" Lucy asks Marco and Daniel. "Sure."

"Lucy, you can't avoid me, or this." Emily reveals herself in her valkyrie warrior mode, complete with brass armor and eagle headdress. She produces her fighting staff and hits the floor with it. The echo rumbles in the silence.

"You have to accept this, Lucy."

Lucy looks away from Emily, her jaw locked, and walks outside. Daniel follows her.

Marco looks at Eoin. "Being compelled by Wiccan rule takes away a bit of my free will. Can I leave?"

"Do you have any additional intel?" Eoin asks.

Marco tells Eoin that the phantoms have been conjured by very powerful Wiccans. He warns that someone is toying with Lucy and most likely with me, but he doesn't have a clue who it is. Clearly, they are tracking us somehow or they wouldn't have known our location at the party.

"Thank you, Marco," Eoin says. He turns to Rhydian and the other Guardians to give orders about perimeter sweeps and guard schedules.

Marco rolls his eyes behind Eoin's back. I can't stand that my friend is being forced into watching and reporting, or that he's being treated like a second-class citizen because he's not a Wiccan.

Wear the crown.

"Marco," I call out. He stops and I approach him. "I'm done with compulsion. Marco, I release you from the compelling order." I touch his shoulder, instructing my word and magick to undo whatever was cast on him to obey orders. I concentrate, allowing my magick to guide me. A dull light enters my finger-tips, as if pulling the magick off him. It is working.

Eoin's face is stone and unmoving, but his eyes say he isn't happy with me. I don't care; the smile on Marco's is the only one I'm looking for. It gives me satisfaction.

"Thank you, Willow. I would have helped you anyway." He leans to the side to eye Eoin. "Because we are friends." He turns to go, closing the front door behind him as he joins Daniel and Lucy on the front lawn.

Turning back to the foyer, I see that Cross is grinning with Emily. Rhydian is smirking, but Eoin is unmoving.

CHAPTER 14

Emily stays over at my house without asking, which makes me smile. She's already shed her warrior valkyrie armor for the clothing she was wearing before. I wonder if she has something like the wrist cuff the Guardians wear to retract her armor. She looks tired from the long evening.

Emily makes her way upstairs. When I go to follow, Rhydian reaches for my hand.

"Can we talk for just a second?"

Eoin and Tullen are making their way back toward my father's office.

"Sure. Emily, I'll be up in just a few minutes."

"Don't take too long. I will not be responsible for the mess that may ensue." She laughs as she takes the stairs two at a time.

Just when she's out of sight, Rhydian sits down on the stairs. "So, I sort of eavesdropped on your conversation with Daniel."

Okay . . . That's interesting. I don't think I said anything that he wouldn't expect, but now I'm starting to get a little nervous.

He clasps his hands together, almost wringing them. "You had a powerful connection with Daniel—"

I put my hand on his and stare into his eyes. "Rhydian. I didn't go about things the right way with Daniel, and I needed to apologize to him. That doesn't change anything between Daniel and me. We will always have a past and an affection for each other. He was my first love, but you—it doesn't change how I feel about you. I just want to make sure it is a personal choice."

"Why wouldn't this be our choice? I don't want to be the only party who's feeling this way."

I watch his handsome face, the way his eyes are cast down. His confidence seems to have gone.

"It's been a long night," I say. "Maybe we can talk about this more tomorrow? Maybe go on another date?" His lips quirk to the side. I push his arm, trying to lighten the mood.

"Absolutely. Although I anticipate Eoin's going to restrict your travel, so maybe we can have a night in. Watch a movie?"

"That sounds perfect." I kiss him lightly on the lips before I run up the stairs with a pep in my step. Opening my bedroom door, I find Emily sprawled on my bed and Duke lying next to her in full snuggle mode.

"Girl, you cannot have my dog. Duke, what are you doing?"

Duke jumps up, and this has Emily clutching her stomach as she rolls away in laughter. Duke bounds over to me his whole backside wagging in happiness. My mood immediately elevates. I waggle his ears before he darts out my bedroom door.

"So, do tell. I want all the deets on Rhy and you." Emily moves over and I plop next to her.

"I really like him, but this whole blood vow thing . . . He's, like, proud about the vow, and half the time I'm just embarrassed that he can sense my emotions. I'm trying—"

"And you feel guilty. Like you're taking advantage or something?"

I close my eyes because, yeah, if I can do things with my magick just by thinking about it, how do I know?

"Get over yourself a little, Will. If he says he likes you, let it be as simple as that. Don't overcomplicate. My motto: love who loves you back, end of the story."

"Oh, what a motto. Is this an equal opportunity for Cross

and Marco too?" I laugh and throw a small pillow at her. She smiles, her eyes glinting.

Emily stands on the bed and, in dramatic fashion, falls on her back and yells, "I can't help it! They are both so delectable in different ways. What's a girl to do?"

"Ah. According to you, love who loves you back." I smash her with my bigger pillow. She grabs and hugs it.

"Exactly. And see how happy I am?"

We start throwing my stuffed animals and laughing so hard I can't stop. Emily blares the music, and before I know it, we are dancing and jumping on my bed like we are twelve. Maybe she is right to live for the moment and keep things simple. Duke bounces around my room, knocking my cell phone off its charger.

I jump down from the bed. Picking up my phone, I notice that Lucy has texted me.

Please tell Emily to give me some space.

"What is it?" Emily asks.

"Lucy. What is going on? Why is she so angry at you specifically? I mean, it's all crazy town, but one minute she doesn't want exclusion, then when we open up she does?"

"She is not handling this as well as you did. Lucy is headstrong and good at playing victim, not unlike my sister, her mother."

"Wow. Well, it is a little trippy that you're her aunt, Em. Come on. You guys were friends and hanging before I even moved here."

"Yeah." Emily's breath hitches. "I was never quite sure if she would present valkyrie traits. Honestly, I figured if it didn't happen by her sixteenth birthday, it wouldn't. But then your magick was unbound, and magick in this realm was happening, and I thought, heck, she could be a late bloomer."

"So, what happened that landed you in the Terra realm?"

Emily seems far off in thought before she speaks. "My family stayed to get everyone to Edayri safely during the Norse realm collapse. My sister gave Lucy to her father. She would have most likely raised Lucy in Edayri, but my father demanded Freya stay in the Norse realm. I promised to watch over Lucy." She shrugs and smiles.

Her story doesn't make complete sense, but she's too quiet, so I ask, "Inquiring minds want to know—how old are you?"

She smiles extra wide before saying, "A shocking seventeen years old for about seven hundred years—but only the last seventeen here, of course."

I whistle in shock, which has Emily laughing even more. "Impressive, right? I'm so down with the adulting of life but refuse to be one."

When did I fall asleep? Emily and I stayed up talking about everything and nothing all at once, and it was glorious. Emily's snoring, on the other hand, is anything but pleasant. As I blindly pet Duke, my mind wanders.

Happy that I released Marco from the spell that was forced on him, I think about Rhydian. Can I release him from his blood vow? Would he be as happy as Marco? I doubt it; he says it's an honor. I can't help but think about how we'd be without the vow. Would he still have as much interest in me? Is there something that attracts me to him as a result of the vow? I shake my head. The man is well beyond attractive, so no, I'd still be drawn to him. But it's not just his appearance anymore. It's the way he teases and laughs with me; how he touches me and holds me. He knows when to back off so I can think without pressure.

I'm going to go crazy mulling this over. I'm totally over-thinking it all. I slip out of bed and go down the back stairs to the kitchen, following a delicious smell.

Eoin in the kitchen. I look at the clock. It's 5 a.m.

"Wow. Early riser, huh?"

Eoin turns his head from the gas stove and smiles. "That or

insomniac, but let's go with early riser. Want a veggie omelet?" He tosses the folded egg in the pan and grabs the plate next to him. In a single fluid movement, the omelet is on the bar in front of me.

"Thank you. This is amazing," I mumble through the first hot bite in my mouth.

Eoin whisks the egg mixture and starts cooking the next masterpiece on the stove. He does have a skill in the kitchen.

"What's on your mind?" he asks.

It's a simple question, but I don't want to share about Rhydian. It's awkward since Rhydian is under his command. Eoin feels like a parent figure to me, and he's a straight shooter. My parents come to mind, then my connection to Evan and the memories he keeps showing me of his life as a MacKinnon.

"Evan, huh?"

"What, can you read minds now?" I almost choke.

He pats my back. "No, it's what I've been thinking about. Just a good guess. We haven't fully talked about it still—the abduction and Evan." Eoin raises an eyebrow at me and waits for me to talk.

"The kids who abducted me did so because they wanted me to reverse the magick that I cursed Evan with when we fought those months back, when my father died. And I guess I did curse him, although it's not clear to me how . . . But Evan says it's a gift." I shrug my shoulders.

Eoin is calmly finishing the last bites of his omelet, so I continue. "There are so many different sides to every story. I don't know which side I'm on and where I fit into the grander scheme. I thought I wanted my old life—what I've been calling normalcy—but every time I try, I'm thrown into the complete opposite. But being the Wiccan Queen fits. And that scares me. And I think my mother and father felt the same way, and Evan seems to be directing me toward that too. I'm afraid because . . . what I've always wanted will be gone."

I exhale the words sharply. My eyes sting. This is the piece that I've had yet to say to myself—the reality that "normal" is teetering on a high wire. The more I walk, the less likely I can turn around to go back to my life before.

"That's a lot to grapple with. There is certainly a lot of pressure on you, Willow. But I promise you, I am here for you. Not Sabine or the noble covens—just you."

The words mean so much from Eoin. In Eoin's way, I am like a daughter to him. As my parental figure, he lives in this house for all the requirements of the Terra realm. But it doesn't feel like just a legal relationship. I trust him.

"So, can I ask you something?" He nods. "Can you tell me anything regarding my parents and Paris?"

Eoin's shoulders stiffen at my question. "Maybe this is something you should ask Sabine about. She is, after all, your grandmother and understands the story at a different level. My view is purely a military one."

"So does that mean you're not gonna tell me? I don't think I can ask Sabine. I think she will shut down as soon as I ask her. Besides, Evan doesn't trust her, and although she's changed from who she was in the past or is trying to, I'm not sure—"

I cut myself off. I cannot believe I just said that out loud. Eoin doesn't seem shocked by my comments at all though. Does that mean he doesn't trust her either?

Eoin gathers our plates and starts washing them in the sink. Not looking at me, he begins. "The Wiccan King commanded the Guardians to retrieve Nuala and kill whoever interfered. She was on the run with a bounty on the head of your father; the complete order said he forced Nuala against her will. The assumption was that he had bewitched her. They were located near Paris and a large battle ensued. Souls were lost and your father was wounded—by my hand. It was a family squabble turned into a military operation. I do regret that, Willow." He looks at me finally, his eyes sad at his admission. "However, there is no room for discussion or push back with a King's orders."

He looks at me as he dries off the dishes, his eyes a little softer around the edges. "Your mother was very powerful, although not as powerful as you, and she broke through the spell that prevented transportation. It's a spell we do when we are going after Wiccans and other magical creatures so that there's no easy getaway. By breaking that, many were able to escape. It was the start of what we called the Great Hunt. It became clear that Nuala did have free will and was clearly attached to your father, revealing that the King had other intentions against his headstrong daughter."

After seeing Evan's memory of Mr. Boward and my mother, I certainly understand my mother fleeing. My father would have never bewitched her. I'm sure Harkin and Sabine would have known this as well.

"You have to understand, the Guardians are loyal to the crown. There are laws to enforce, but you do not disobey direct orders from the one who wears the crown."

"Do you think that is right? For me to give orders to the Guardians unchallenged? I don't know anything about the military. I don't want that power."

Eoin shrugs but looks directly in my eyes. "I've never had the option of talking about my opinions in twenty-five years as a Guardian. But I think you need to be very careful after last night's encounter with the phantom. The Emissaries are expanding their hate crimes against Wiccans. It seems that it's not a time to be too radical—but then again, maybe it's the perfect time."

I like this Eoin, not dictating orders as he does with Rhydian, Cross, Tullen, and Quinn, but just chatting like we're friends.

"Do you think the Emissaries are bad?" Eoin raises his eyebrow but doesn't respond. "I honestly want your opinion."

He scratches the incoming growth on his chin. "I believe that here, you would call them protestors. I don't think they are bad, but some of their methods are extreme and lead to dangerous outcomes. Maybe a more fitting description is that they rebel against the status quo of royal rule and Wiccan superiority."

"Eoin, I rebel against the status quo myself. Does that make me part of the Emissaries? For that matter, my mother was next in line, and as I understand, she would have taken the crown. I have the feeling both she and my father held similar beliefs—she could have ended Wiccan superiority. Is that why she was killed?"

Eoin's eyes are dark and soft. "The Great Hunt was a cleansing of those who rose against the crown and Wiccan rule in Edayri. It signaled the formal start of the Emissaries, whose beliefs would have ended the power cycle within Wiccan families. Willow, I think your mother was going to take the crown, but it was clear she and Aiden had a different idea of how Edayri should be governed. It caused a rocky family dynamic. Those in the High Coven have motive for ensuring the crown continues in their favor, complete with a magickal power that is bound to and used by royalty. A hierarchy that's no longer needed?" He whistles low. "There are a lot who wouldn't stand for that. They have too much to lose." Eoin's smile is soft and reassuring. "But then again, a seventeen-year-old came into the Hallowed Hall, disbanded the High Coven in one night, and was crowned by the Goddess, so that's already rocked the foundation of tradition."

"I almost didn't accept the crown. Hell, I think about that day a lot—destiny and all that."

"You assume destiny requires your permission to exist. It doesn't. There is always someone who will battle those who are hungry for power and status," Eoin says.

Am I hungry for power?

Yes.

CHAPTER 15

Late Sunday afternoon, I'm called back to MacKinnon Manor. Sabine is adamant I return for training and a meeting with her because of the phantom situation at Coral's party. I'm leery of the intention since she also requested I bring Duke with me. I have a terrible feeling my return to Chepstow will not be in time for school tomorrow.

Mr. Boward enters the office suites just after I arrive. Duke growls when he enters. The tall man eyes him and Duke settles. "The party that you and Rhydian went to yesterday evening—how was it?"

"It was a good party." I shrug and pet Duke from my chair. I don't want to reveal anything about Lucy and the phantom attack. If I do, he may use that information to keep me in Edayri full-time.

Mr. Boward sits across from me and leans forward, interlacing his fingers. "Rhydian did provide a full report to his commanding officer, and since I'm acting as your Scepter, I have access to all reports."

Shit. Rhydian's commanding officer is Eoin. I sit back in my chair and let the curved high back hug my shoulders.

"I'm thankful that you were with Rhydian. It could have been an unmanageable situation. And considering others were attending who could have been injured, it would have been—"

I cut him off, flustered. "I don't know what details you have access to, but everything has been taken care of and is fine."

"Willow, it is important that we have trust and transparency. I'm just learning that you are close to valkyries and shapeshifters? Who would have thought such powerful beings would be in the Terra realm and make themselves known to you." Mr. Boward's tone is smug.

Is this a challenge of knowledge? Does he want me to share those details? My blood starts to boil as he looks down his nose at me for what happened at the party.

"Is this a test? Interesting. You're not so forthcoming yourself. You were betrothed to my mother, and you fell to a lower coven status once she left you for my father. Why didn't you reveal that to me?" I pause, watching his eyes change from soft edges to a hard determination. "Are we working on trust and transparency?" I stand and walk to the big bay window that overlooks the grounds. The window's reflection shows me that my magick is flowing on my skin, which satisfies me.

Yes—show him who you are.

"That's fair. I was friends with your father, and I loved your mother most of my life. It wasn't a returned affection, but I didn't do anything to upset my friendship with your parents. They were both dear to me. I did marry and have my own children, Willow. I have my own life story."

"Why didn't you say anything to me before?"

"To be frank, I told you we grew up together. Your mother— what was I to say? She married your father, and I married Vanessa. It was a lifetime ago."

Esmund stands next to me and gestures back to the chair. "I suppose we are working on trust and transparency, but I think current events are relevant when your safety is in jeopardy. Based on the report, it was." I say nothing. After a moment, he says, "Are you ready for your lessons today?" He looks every bit the uptight college professor I'd imagined I would have next year in his dark pants, white oxford shirt, and brown jacket.

Will I even get to go to college?

"We have a fun-filled afternoon of royal history and a few papers for you to sign . . ."

I don't listen to him drone on. All I can seem to focus on is what next year might be like and how I will possibly manage. Mr. Boward's mouth is moving, but I'm not registering anything he's saying, it's as if the sound has been sucked out of the room. I will have to be in Edayri full-time next year; I'm expected to be here. Will I ever see my school friends? I will see Emily. Maybe Marco? The change is so hard to wrap my mind around.

He clears his throat before I hear, "Willow? What did I just say?"

Busted.

Mr. Boward is frowning, forehead crinkled as he waits. His eyes are similar to Rhydian's, but not the same—the luster of a hazel storm mixed with blue, green, and gold is flat and dull.

"Um, sorry."

"I thought so. I know the legions of the lunar fields are not exciting stuff, but this is important Wiccan history."

I nod and open my eyes wide to focus. He's right, it's not exciting stuff at all—the takeover and domination of the moon fairies. Or rather, as he puts it, the "organization and peace-keeping mission for the benefit of the once-mischievous fairies who were ill-equipped and unfocused."

"Yes, it is important. I'm sorry, Mr. Boward."

"Please, if you insist I call you Willow, will you please call me Esmund? After all, you are dating my son, and I am your Scepter."

He smiles, but his eyes seem indifferent to me, like it's all an act or performance he's grown accustomed to.

"I'll try."

By the time I leave the office suite, I'm wound tight. A smiling Rhydian approaches me. "Hey." His eyes change from joy to concern when he reaches for my hand.

I pull back; I don't want him to sense my feelings. I try to block him searching me, my magick already flowing, but it doesn't matter because his father opens the door.

"Hello, son." He nods to me and smiles. "Willow." He adjusts the leather satchel over his shoulder and walks down the hall.

I weakly return Rhydian's smile.

"Everything okay?"

Truthfully, I can't wait to hit something—hard. Gah! Mr. Boward—Esmund—is so frustrating. It gives me the creeps to think of him by his first name. How can he be Rhydian's father? Talk about polar opposites—or maybe not? That thought is scrubbed from my mind as soon as it comes.

"I'm running late. I'm meeting Cross for combat training." I try to leave but Rhydian grabs my hand.

"Want me to take you?"

"No, no, that's fine. I know where I'm going." I gently pull my hand from his. "I'll catch you later." I quickly walk down the hall out of sight, then transport into the gym locker room.

Cross wastes no time. We shuffle on the mat. I land punches and kick as directed. I revel in it—there's no thinking required, and I get to hit something.

"High, low, right, left, high knee . . ."

I'm more confident and landing every hit and kick.

Cross counters in offensive moves. I'm prepared and block. His big body directs me toward a wall. I duck and slide under him, and his eyes grow wide and appreciative.

"Oh no, I'm not being directed today." I huff and jump side to side, knocking my gloved hands together.

"Excellent," Cross says with a smirk. He continues to attack, and we go back and forth.

Three rounds later, both Cross and I drip in sweat.

"Yer confidence and abilities are improving in just weeks. It's impressive."

I agree. I don't feel helpless. If I don't have magick, I can fight. I will fight, because, damn it, I'm a fighter.

I help Cross clear the equipment in the room.

"So, what's going on with you and Emily? Any interest there?"

His eyes light up at her name. "Yeah, for sure. She's amazing, not to mention not bad on the eyes."

"Really, you're that superficial?" I laugh and push him.

Holding his hands up, he steps back with a laugh. "Nah, not at all. She's a warrior like me and, well, I love me." He winks.

"Apparently. No overinflated ego here."

"What! No ego, just truth." He flexes his arm and nods in appreciation.

We put the last of the extra mats in the wall locker and he closes the door.

"What about what Marco said yesterday?" I'm surprised to hear Marco's name from Cross. "Do you think someone is conjuring phantom's?"

"I would guess it's possible. Emily isn't happy about it."

"Ya think it's a schoolmate of yours?"

My thoughts go to Coral. She wasn't frozen, but it still seems crazy to think of her. Maybe someone else? Cross can't be too off; just look at Marco and Emily. There is no telling who else might be magickal.

I shrug. "I guess it could be? I don't know. How would I be able to tell?"

"There would be a magical signature, but to follow it would be hard, especially when you're battling the phantom."

"A magickal signature?"

"Yeah. I imagine with yer power, ya could tap into seeing the threads of magick that they're using. The phantom's like a puppet. Trace it back to a source." He shrugs. "If it's conjured, that is. Someone's gotta be commanding it. Rhy and I thought it could be possible."

My heart softens a bit at the mention of Rhydian.

"I hope not to see another one, but if I do, maybe I could look for the signature."

Cross claps me on the back, and we go in different directions toward the locker rooms.

I change and look for Sabine in her office. It's empty. I spy books stacked on the bureau and pick them up. The one that catches my eye and stops me cold is titled *Apparitions and Phantoms*. Sabine walks in with her assistant.

"Training is done for the day?" she asks, walking to her desk and sitting in a high-back chair.

"Yes, I suppose so, unless you have something else on my schedule."

She doesn't catch my sarcasm, or if she does, she ignores it.

"No, actually. I just want to ensure you and Esmund met today."

"Okay." I roll my eyes.

She finally looks at me and dismisses her assistant.

"What happened?"

"He wants more trust and transparency." I study her face, but it's indifferent.

"Well, it's suitable for his role."

"So I'm told." I sit in front of her. "How did he become Scepter?"

"I appointed him. I can't be everywhere, and I need someone who knows the crown's formality and will help you."

"That would be Eoin, not Mr. Boward."

Sabine huffs at me. "Eoin is the commander of the Guardians." She waves her hand in the air dismissively. "He has a huge responsibility outside of acting as your Terra realm parental Guardian."

"You're right. In my world, I would have a family member as a parental Guardian. Plus, I'm dating Rhydian, and this is just weird!"

For once, Sabine doesn't have an immediate response. A good thirty seconds go by before she asks, slyly, "So, you're dating?"

I nod and can't help mirroring the small grin on her face.

"Stop," I laugh. "Yes, we are dating, and I like Rhydian. A lot." Her grin spreads and so does mine. "Okay. Stop it."

She shakes her head and brings us out of our grinning showdown. "Esmund has arranged a big meeting tomorrow with the former high council and noble coven families without our invitation. I suspect they will try to reinstate the high council. There is a movement to move the crown out of the family. It's a rumor, but I believe that Esmund is seeding it. He can be quite persuasive."

"You don't trust him and you want to keep him close?" As I say it, relief floods me. Talk about keeping enemies close. Is he a real enemy?

"I trust him to protect himself, but you're not off-base."

"I don't want to be directed by him anymore. I can't be some royal dictator to everyone in this realm. I'm not Harkin, and it's not right. This tears apart everything. If this place is to survive in harmony with everyone, there has to be a change."

I'm prepared for a verbal battle with her, but she smiles gently at me and says, "Yes, I know."

"Then why are you letting Mr. Boward in so close?"

"Willow, not all storms come to disrupt your life. Some come to clear your path. Have some patience, but with open eyes. Esmund is someone to keep an eye on."

I sure hope the storm that's coming isn't a category six hurricane, because there may be nothing left.

PART III

By knot of six, this spell I fix
By knot of seven, events I'll leaven

CHAPTER 16

On Monday, Sabine and I leave MacKinnon Manor together for the first time and transport to the Hallowed Hall. The Hallowed Hall is the center point of Edayri, like a capital building. The white marble, columns, and Goddess fountain are a shining symbol of Wiccan rule. The Guardian headquarters are attached to the west.

We have a plan and are not going to be blindsided. Sabine agrees the royal rule of solidarity needs to change; she is entirely supportive. I want to heed Evan's warnings, but I can't. Sabine says the magical ties that bind us to Edayri should be honored; otherwise, someone will chance a claim.

The only part I'm not overly confident about is staying ahead of Mr. Boward and the former High Coven members. This quorum is for hearing proposals for the reworking of the royal governances. Still, Sabine feels the noble covens will make a move for the high council because of the draw of magickal position and influence.

Political games.

"Good afternoon." Eoin is waiting when we arrive. We have transported to a back entrance near the Guardian training grounds, so our arrival isn't noticed by the quorum. "Are you ready?"

"Yes." My voice sounds more confident than I feel. Eoin smiles and nods, utterly aware of our plan.

"Let's go through the back passages so that we can be announced ahead of the quorum opening," Sabine directs.

"It will be more inconspicuous if I'm not leading you. I have ordered Quinn and Tullen to meet us halfway."

Sabine and I follow Eoin, making quick work of the twisting tunnels beneath the Hallowed Hall. When we reach Quinn and Tullen, Eoin touches my shoulder and looks directly into my eyes. "Good luck. Remember who you are. Don't let them get the sense they can control you." Nodding to everyone else, he walks back in the direction we came from.

No one says anything as we continue down the passageway. Tullen is in front of us, Quinn behind. We start on an upward walk that drives us closer to the audience room where the meeting is being held. Instead of coming into the hallway from the front doors, we enter from behind the throne and raised stage.

Mr. Boward turns to watch us enter just as he is calling the opening of the quorum. His lips purse close. The doors shut, and Eoin follows procedure and enters from the side. Mr. Boward's eyes follow Eoin, who comes to stand next to Sabine.

Instead of calling the quorum, he takes a moment to come to the throne. "I see we still need to work on transparency."

"Yes, I believe we do," I reply.

"Sabine? Should I call an end to the quorum? The one, I might add, that you once assembled as a former high council member?" Mr. Boward's smirk hovers on manipulation. Still, I stay steady, staring ahead at the large audience of noble coven attendees in front of us.

"Oh Esmund, I think you can continue, but as you know, the high council was abolished by Willow when she accepted the crown. The Guardians are here just in case there is any trouble.

This quorum of noble coven members is important to the crown. It is such a good thing we learned of it just in time to attend."

He looks like a fish for a second, as if he'd been about to reply with a witty retort but thought better of it. Mr. Boward turns on his heel and speaks into a microphone at the end of the raised floor.

"As above and below, I call this official quorum into order as Scepter to the crown." There is the sound of a bell in the back of the room. Everyone in attendance sits, robes of various colors fluttering. The looks on the faces nearest to me are almost entertaining—the wide eyes, parted lips, and nervous wringing of hands.

Mr. Boward stands still for a moment before Sabine interrupts the silence. "Shall we proceed, Scepter?"

"Yes, thank you." He clears his throat. "The call to quorum is to hear the reinstatement of the high council. Please bring forth your declarations for the crown."

A previous High Coven member, Renata, stands. I remember her by her distinct white hair, striking in its spiky fashion.

Her eyes move from me to Sabine. "The high council would request a vote of abdication of Willow Warrington from the throne so that Sabine may continue in the royal rule."

The gasps throughout the room are audible. My focus is on Renata. She steps back, and it's clear her bravery is only on the surface of her words.

I wonder if Sabine anticipated this. Would she stay on the path we agreed or take a new direction to become Queen? Pansy, another previous High Coven member, vocalizes her agreement in a high pitched, nervous voice. When I look at her, she shrinks in her seat. I can't help the smile that creeps into the corners of my mouth.

They should be scared of me.

There is a rumbling of voices and Mr. Boward says, "We have

a motion which makes to reinstitute our esteemed high council. Based on recent events—"

Eoin interrupts. "As Scepter, your role is not directive but only informative to the crown. As she is present, the quorum will now be informed." The satisfaction in Eoin's eyes is rewarding to watch Mr. Boward retreat from.

"Of course, of course."

"It seems I have crashed the party today," I say. I stand up, and, with my magick flowing to show my crown clearly, I steady my nerves. I push my shoulders back so that I stand tall. "The proposal to vote for the reinstatement of the high council is no longer applicable. This council was abolished with my acceptance of the crown. The fact that it has continued to be pressed in quorums behind my back could be considered treason."

Gasps echo throughout the audience room. Guardians have been placed at the entrances and the room is under a spell to prevent transportation. The faces are priceless, mostly of fear—a few look on more curiously. The noise level rises to a dull roar.

Mr. Boward speaks up. "If it pleases the crown, may we have a private word? This was a peaceful meeting of declaration and discussion."

I ignore him, and Sabine stares ahead without acknowledgment.

"Do I have your attention?" I wait until the noise subsides. "I am instituting an equalized representation for a self-governing society. The royal rule will remain in the background, used only for tie breaks and oversight as majority rules. The Guardians will serve society, and a small contingency will continue to serve the Royal family—the Royal Guardians, as already named."

I have practiced this, and I was focused and unrushed. I am more empowered than I ever have been.

You are power.

"A bold move, and one that would bring old traditions and new ones together. It is time to come out of the past and grow to the future," Sabine says.

The eyes that look back at me are wide. Mr. Boward is lifting his chin and staying quiet as if he is in on this arrangement. Everyone is stunned into silence.

"Who among you would be willing to support the crown in building this new governing body? Understand that others within Edayri will be in this governing body—fairies, demons, and the like. This will be a body not overrun by one group, but a balanced mix of all."

"I would." The voice comes from the back. I recognize Aren, another former high council member. She was the one I met who seemed misplaced in the high council of older women and who looked so bored the last time I saw her. She walks forward, shoving away from an older female who reaches for her. "This has been a long time coming," Aren says as she approaches us.

"Thank you, Aren." A rumble begins to spread throughout the room as others are pulled from their stunned silence.

"As Scepter, I will support you in whatever way you see fit," Mr. Boward says, then bows to me.

Sabine puts her hand on his shoulder and says quietly, "We should talk privately."

The quorum ends peacefully without more attempts to abdicate me or establish some grand overthrowing of power. Instead, we leave with two Wiccan representatives, one a former High Coven member and one a younger noble coven member. Next, Ax will reach out to the demons and others to find representatives for the new governing body of Edayri.

CHAPTER 17

I'm back at Trinity Cross High School on Tuesday. Mrs. Gunther, the civics teacher, is droning on about the Depression era in the United States, noting a direct correlation between the economy and the culture of warfare, as well as its effect on future days. Typically, I would be listening to Mrs. Gunther because she always has interesting parallels in class, and you don't want to be caught off guard when she calls on you. But the way Coral keeps side-eyeing me from her desk has my attention elsewhere. Usually, she's looking over at Rhydian or one of her friends, but Rhydian isn't in school today. Mr. Boward requested him for some important task today that Eoin begrudgingly allowed. Why do I have her full attention?

"Willow, if the crash of the 1940s were to happen today, what would be the first to fall in our current economy?"

Darn it. I knew she would target me. "I would anticipate the downfall of the free market. I would also expect that societal prejudices might be reintroduced." Edayri would be the same.

"Ah, so you are listening." She pauses, looking out the window. "Interesting thought that prejudices would be reintroduced to society. The scale of those prejudices would be based on what? Coral?"

"Fear. Most prejudice is based on fear, but then, of course, the power of influence and money ensures it."

I'm unsurprised by Coral's response, but she isn't wrong. Here, despite the regulation school uniforms, family wealth and names dictate your status in the social hierarchy. I rebel against the school uniforms with my purple Converse, but Coral's rebellion is made up of high-end backpacks, expensive jewelry, and expensive makeup. There's an expectation to flaunt your wealth, which is just ridiculous. Still, Coral and her cronies live and die by the social popularity of success of the school.

Coral is staring at me again, her eyes a bit wider. She seems to be tilting her head, trying to communicate with me, but I don't understand. I mouth the word "what?"

She circles her face with her finger. Her eyes look worried and not condescending. Something is on my face?

Before I can do anything, I hear the hum. As soon as I'm alerted to it, I notice my magick growing. The designs on my hands glow faintly under the skin. Coral can see it, but she doesn't seem to be disturbed by it. I realize that she is watching my forehead, where my crown would be starting to show.

I need to leave.

Not wanting to call attention to myself, I pull my hair from its ponytail and pull the strands forward. Coral rolls her eyes. I can't believe she's halfway trying to help me.

No one else notices me; everyone is focused on Mrs. Gunther. Maybe I can put a spell on the room so that no one will see?

Before I can think much further, the entire school shakes. It feels like an earthquake, like nothing I've ever felt living in Massachusetts. The hair on my neck is rising at the sense of something magickal.

Mrs. Gunther shouts, "Everyone stay calm. We need to move out of this room and down the hall in an orderly fashion—"

The window along the outside wall cracks and a girl next to it yelps. Everyone scrambles from their seats. The fire alarms go off at a second shake of the room. It's hard to stay upright; a few students fall to their knees. Mrs. Gunther raises her voice above the piercing alarm. "Leave everything. Meet me in parking lot B, now!" She grabs a clipboard by the classroom door just as the windows break with a great burst of air.

I instinctively throw my hands out to stop the momentum of the glass. The wind is a funnel of pressure that pushes Mrs. Gunther out of the room with half the class and slams the door, leaving myself, Coral, and a few of my classmates inside. I drop my hands, and the remaining glass falls. Steve tries the door and yells that is locked, then begins beating on it with another student.

The lights flicker off. A dark, gauze-like material hovers like fog around a corpse form. The phantom enters the class through the window and shrieks, "Thhee Wicccannn Queeeen."

Another phantom sweeps in with a long, high-pitched shriek that drowns the screams of my fellow classmates.

One phantom rushes at the door and grabs Steve, who is blocking it.

My chest is pounding in my ears. My hands are shaking.

Show them.

Coral reaches for my arm. "Be careful," she stammers, kneeling behind an overturned desk.

I gather my magick and move between the overturned desks toward the front of the classroom. I push my hands toward the floor with a scream; everything touching the floor except my classmates is thrown into the air in a quick snap, then falls again.

I grab the air that I've gathered and throw it out the window along with the phantoms. The classroom shakes again. Everyone seems to be unconscious on the floor except Coral, who is barely holding on.

"Who are you?" Coral asks weakly.

I consider her. Why is she being helpful? I can't take the risk. I can remove this memory like I did with Daniel. I begin to move my magick, designs flowing on my arms. Coral pushes herself up and yells, "No! You tell me how it happened at my party. I have proof on my phone."

"Coral, we don't have time for this—"

Someone is yelling in the hallway. I flip my hand, and the door is thrown off the hinges, slamming into the whiteboard behind where Mrs. Gunter's desk used to be. Cross runs in dressed as a fireman and motions for us to move. I help Coral up and she leans into me. Cross easily hefts Steve over his shoulder as the others wake.

We follow Cross. The hallways are full of papers, books, glass, and rubble. Dust is everywhere, like an eerie fog. Doors are flung open, the floor is uneven and broken, and the lights flicker on and off.

I've pulled back my magick so that I'm no longer lit up like a Christmas tree, but I have to concentrate. Most of my class-mates are well ahead of us. To my relief, most of the school is already outside when we reach the parking lot.

I help Coral to a curb. "Tell me and I'll forget what I saw, but never use your witchy powers on me," Coral says, smirking.

Cross laughs, then bends his towering, muscled frame over her and whispers, "Willow can do whatever she feels like, so best be careful when tryin' to blackmail her. Maybe ya should just say 'thank ya.' "

Coral's face is pale, and her mouth opens, clearly in disbelief that Cross knows my name.

"Coral, don't—ugh—Cross?" I can't believe he just said that.

Coral's eyes are wide, but the audible gulp makes Cross laugh louder. "Thank you," she says.

He shrugs and touches his earpiece. "Copy that." He turns to me. "You stay here. I've got to go back to the east wing." He runs off. The lights of fire trucks, police cars, and ambulances are all around us, along with television crews.

"Listen, Coral, I do need you to keep quiet about me." I plead with my eyes.

"Willow—I will. Thank you again."

"I bet that tasted awful to say to me." I smile weakly.

"Yep." She nods as Mrs. Gunter yells our names, and we respond together. "Here."

CHAPTER 18

My mind is filled with the echo of the last several hours. Sitting alone in the receiving room at MacKinnon Manor, I see the dirt and dust, smell the smoke, hear the fire alarm and the screams, watch the terror on my classmates' faces. I keep replaying the phantoms busting through the glass. They were there for me, not Lucy. But Lucy was at school. Is she okay? What about Daniel, Marco, and Emily? I didn't find them in the school parking lot. Everyone is a blur of faces in my memory— classmates, teachers, parents, first responders—until the moment Eoin signed me out and I transported here.

I jump when Rhydian and Eoin enter.

Rhydian reaches me in two giant steps. "Oh Goddess, Willow."

He's wet and covered in dirt; he must have come from the school. He pulls me to his body in a hug, and I cling to him. "The school's foundation on the east side has crumbled completely. Several students were injured. Your friends are okay —Lucy, Marco, and Daniel."

I only realize I'm shaking when I pull away, then collapse back into him. I've almost forgotten Eoin is in the room when he speaks.

"Willow."

My eyes follow his voice to find him not far from where Rhydian and I stand.

"I'm sorry, but the student from your class, Steve, is in the hospital. He's not conscious; it's not clear if he will wake up."

Steve. An image flashes in my mind of Cross carrying him over his shoulder out of the school.

"How? Why did this happen?" Tears are streaming down my face. I wipe them away as quickly as they fall. Stepping away from the comfort of Rhydian, I hug myself. "I should have acted faster. I tried to protect my identity, but my magick was warning me, and I didn't pick up on it. It's my—"

"It's the phantoms' fault," Eoin interrupts. "Along with whoever is controlling them."

I can't go back to Chepstow. I would be putting everyone at risk. At least here in Edayri, there are Guardians, and I can use my magick freely. I drop onto the french sateen bench, my mind spiraling.

"Willow, I have several people looking into this. For now, you will only be in Chepstow if multiple backups are always present. It was a mistake not to have Rhydian on campus today. Ax, Cross, Tullen, and Quinn will work backup rotations with other Guardians for support." Eoin continues to update me on the status of the school. It's been heavily damaged by fire and smoke. The blame is being placed on a fault line and an overrun electrical power grid—the perfect storm for Trinity Cross High. The story has already been casting at local and national levels.

I only catch bits and pieces of his words. My thoughts go back to the classroom. My magick tried to warn me before it all went to hell. What else am I not paying attention to that I should be noticing?

"How about you come to my home for dinner? Get out of your head and here?" Rhydian asks.

Still hugging myself, I take a deep breath. "Yes, okay. Let me change and talk with Sabine."

I'm dreading talking with Sabine. She was right; I need to be here. I put everyone in danger with my selfish need to keep my old life.

Eoin speaks up. "Sabine is meeting with Thaxam about representation in the newly established government. By the way, they've adopted the name 'Legion Council.' She won't be back till late. I'll advise her further before you leave with Rhydian."

Rhydian touches his earpiece. "Come through again. Okay, I'll grab it from you in ten. Yeah, Cross got it."

"What?" My heart is pounding. Please don't let it be—

"Cross has your cell. I'll pick it up for you. That way you can connect with your friends tonight too. Emily is staying with Lucy." Rhydian grins. "Oh, by the way, school is closed for the rest of the week."

My mind is stuck on the comment about my phone. The ability to contact my friends is a blessing. Tears well in my eyes again. "Thank Cross for my phone and the update."

Later, in the shower, I crumble on the tiled floor and hug my knees. The water slowly takes the dirt and mud to the drain. Death is following me. I can only hope Steve isn't another causality. I was too slow, just like with Mrs. Scott and my father. This is my new norm, and it is crippling. I shake and sob beneath the shield of cold water, letting it all wash down the drain.

Rhydian and I transport to his home in the Guardian housing near the Hallowed Hall. The housing reminds me of row housing in the suburbs. Inside, it is warm and cozy without an ounce of pretension. Overstuffed couches and chairs in dark grays and neutral colors are complemented by splashes of vibrant color in the pillows and abstract art on the walls. I'm not sure how I envisioned Rhydian's space, but this seems to match him.

Mr. Boward welcomes us at the doorway where I imagine his

idea of casual clothes—dark slacks, a sweater vest, and a collared shirt. I hear a female voice call out, and I realize that Rhydian's sister is here too.

"Abigail?"

Before Rhydian can answer me, the voice calls, "Yes, and I've been looking forward to meeting you too."

When she comes into view, I recognize her immediately. She was at the campsite where the Emissaries were. She was talking to and taking care of Evan in the memory he showed me! I'm stunned to the spot as she extends her hand to me.

"I'm pleased to meet you. I'm Abigail, but I hope you'll call me Abby."

She doesn't seem much older than Rhydian. Shaking her soft hand, I try to act as normal as possible. Do Mr. Boward and Rhydian know she is in the Emissaries? Would it matter now that things are changing for Edayri rule? Evan trusts her.

"Nice to meet you, Abby. Hello Mr.—ah, Esmund."

We all sit down in an alcove near the kitchen for dinner. Rhydian and Abigail set out a roasted chicken with vegetables and bread. Rhydian cuts the meat and places some on my plate.

"Abigail here works in the Hallowed Hall as a coordinator in the finance department."

"Actually, dad, I'm doing something a bit new now. The department is evolving, and I volunteered to be part of the coordination group to integrate the new council."

The look on Mr. Boward's face is one of shock and a trace of disappointment. Abby continues to eat and shrugs her shoulders, dismissively at her father.

"I thought you had advancement opportunities already within your department? Why make this move? It is not what I would call stable. It adds no real value. Well, what I mean is—"

"I think you may have just insulted the crown for which you work," Abby teases, looking at me.

Rhydian chuckles and squeezes my hand under the table.

"Father, times are changing. I commend Abby. It's good to see everyone coming together, embracing change."

"Look! Even the exalted son, with all his advancements in traditional rank, agrees." Abby smirks and continues to eat.

I want to stay invisible during this conversation, but Mr. Boward's eyes are on me.

"No, you're right, absolutely right," he says. "This is a wonderful opportunity for the family."

Abby smiles again in a mocking way. "Yes, a wonderful opportunity for me."

"Isn't that what I said?" Mr. Boward stands and clears his plate. He asks Rhydian to help with the table.

The tension is palpable. Rhydian's right—Abby knows how to push her father's buttons. She's an adult and clearly living her own life; I envy her that independence. Although I want to continue to eat the food on my plate, I push it off to the side.

"Sorry about that. The old man is full of old traditions, and it will take a little bit of time for him to come around. Stubborn as a mule, that one."

I drop my voice. "Does he know that you're part of the Emissaries? Or, for that matter, does Rhydian?"

Abigail leans forward and, in a hushed voice, says, "This is still illegal, so no, they do not. If you can keep that between us, that would be great. I would hate to be taken in by both of them tonight. It would certainly put a damper on the evening."

Illegal? How is it illegal? I don't have time to ask because Mr. Boward and Rhydian return with dessert.

"Do you like cheesecake?" Rhydian asks, setting a large piece in front of me with syrupy purple fruit drizzled on top.

"Oh, Abigail is famous for it." Mr. Boward says.

I take a bite, and the cheesecake melts in my mouth. "Oh Goddess. This is incredible!" I look at Abigail in wonder. "How do you get it to be so fluffy and dense all at the same time?"

They all laugh at me, and the tension in the room seems to lift. We make jokes and lighthearted comments throughout the rest of dessert, Rhydian and I teasing each other more than the others.

"I'm so happy at how well you both get along. Aiden would've loved to have seen this."

"Father," Rhydian says in a warning tone. Abby absentmindedly stirs her coffee.

"I'm sure he would've loved to have had dinner here tonight with his old friend. I do miss him a great deal." For a moment, he looks regretful and sincere.

Mr. Boward and Rhydian get up to clear the dessert dishes. I start to follow them with my own when Abby stops me.

"Be careful of my father. His motives are never for the greater good; they're always for the betterment of himself. I love my father, but I'm certain of this, and you should second-guess everything he does and says."

I'm stunned. In thirty seconds, Abby is telling me to be wary of her father. I already am, of course, but is this a trick? I don't think so. I could reveal her as part of the Emissaries right now to her father and brother. She's got nothing to gain by warning me.

Rhydian appears from around the corner. "What's taking you guys so long?" He grabs the two plates from our hands and disappears back into the kitchen.

"Abby—"

"Forgive me. I wasn't sure when I'd have the opportunity, and the night's almost over. Just one last thing—Evan sends his good wishes. And I'm delighted you're in Rhydian's life." She smiles and encompasses me in a hug that I am entirely unprepared for.

When he joins us again, Rhydian is all smiles and completely relaxed. I say farewell to Mr. Boward and Abby as they settle down in the sitting area near the fireplace.

Outside, Rhydian takes my hands in his. "So, back to MacKinnon Manor?"

My magick flows on my skin. I meet his eyes with mine. The way he looks at me and all he does provides a feeling of protection and respect that I want to soak up and never let go of. I hesitate to go back to MacKinnon Manor and revisit the day's events, but there is no escaping them.

"Yes, I guess so."

We transport to the front steps of the manor. The gas lamps illuminate the entryway.

"Thanks for coming to dinner tonight at my home. You're welcome anytime." His eyes move from my eyes to my lips.

"You have a lovely home. Thank—"

Rhydian's lips are on mine, cutting off my words. His kiss is claiming and my return just as urgent. I can drown in his affection. His kiss creates a sensation that reaches all the way to my toes. My mind is quiet, full only of wonder.

"Willow—"

Hearing my name, feeling the absence of his lips on mine, my brain fills with all the doubts that were drowned just moments before.

"Willow, I need to go back home, but damn. I would stay here on your steps all night with you if I could."

Looking in his eyes, I tamper down my emotions. "Okay. I should probably go inside then."

"Yeah." His hands still steady on my waist, and I don't move. After a beat, his hands fall, and I back toward the door.

"Thank you, Rhydian, for dinner." I smile, and he waves awkwardly. I laugh.

"Anytime," he smiles, then transports away.

CHAPTER 19

It's been over two weeks since the incident at the school. This is my first time out of Edayri. Quinn looks out of place following Emily and me to various dress stores in the mall, an outing prompted by Emily. Despite the school's initial cancelation of prom, Coral's family put up the money for a swanky hotel and additional security. So, prom is happening, and dress shopping is on. For me, though, it's more about hanging with Emily the way we did before all the magickal craziness of our lives—well, my life. I wish Lucy had joined us, but she is continuing to keep a distance from Emily.

"I'm starting to feel bad for him," Emily says, interrupting my thoughts. "He's gotta be extremely bored."

Quinn pokes his head between Emily and me. "If I may, I suggest we go to another location. These dresses are not what I would call fashionable or suited for you, lovely ladies." I look at him, eyes wide. "There are three shops in Town Center that you should consider. You will find a unique and lovely dress at any one of them."

"Okay. And how exactly do you know this?" Emily asks with her hand on her hip.

"I've had to escort noble covens before. Let's just say this isn't my first dress shopping assignment, and Town Center is definitely better than here."

I can't help but chuckle at Quinn's dress shopping expertise. We all agreed to go.

Quinn drives us in a large SUV like political dignitaries who require high-security vehicles. Since it means I'm allowed back in the Terra realm, I won't complain.

"If you had to choose between the Terra realm or Edayri, which would you choose?" Emily asks Quinn.

He ponders her question for a moment. "They each offer something different. Because I grew up in Edayri, you think I'd want to stay. But it seems like there are so many more freedoms here in the Terra realm. So, if I had to choose one and never see the other . . . It would break my heart, but I would probably choose here."

I'm surprised at Quinn's response. "What types of freedoms are you speaking about?"

He shrugs, keeping his eyes on the road. "Where do I begin? So many political, sexual, religious, and creative freedoms. Because you guys have always had them here, you take them for granted. I understand this isn't the way in all regions of the Terra realm, but still. To be told who you are and how to live and what to believe . . . It makes my skin crawl."

"So, who is he? Or am I reading too much into what you're saying?" Emily asks, smiling.

This seems too invasive of her, but at the same time, I am curious. I would like to know Quinn on a deeper level.

"He's someone of an important position and, although not new, it isn't something I can flaunt openly." Quinn's voice is soft, but he sounds hurt.

"Wow. That sounds heartbreaking, Quinn," I say.

"It is, and it isn't. It depends on how much I overthink it. But if I accept the moments that I have, it's wonderful."

Am I doing the same thing? Am I overthinking myself and Rhydian with the blood vow? Emily certainly thinks so. Maybe I should appreciate our moments for what they are. They are wonderful too.

I settle into thoughts about Rhydian. Quinn isn't talking much either. I assume he's thinking about the guy we were just asking about.

After a while, Quinn takes an exit that I'm unfamiliar with. Several turns later, we arrive in the parking lot for Town Center, an outdoor shopping center with unique boutiques and high-dollar shopping.

The first boutique where Quinn introduces us to the shop-keeper, who, according to him, is the best, has amazing dresses. I'm in a dressing room with two dresses that Quinn helped me pick out. The first one is blue with an empire waist and a lovely, flowing skirt. The second is a light peach with a sweetheart neckline and bolts that drape around the dress. Both are stun-ning. I don't have the green light to even attend prom, but I hope I can go if just for an hour.

When I walk out in the first dress, Quinn smiles. I must admit when I see my reflection in the mirror that he has excel-lent taste.

"You look stunning. I can't wait to see the sunset dress on you though. I think it will be super flattering with your coloring."

When I slip into the peach-colored dress, I feel myself falling in love with it.

"Get out here! I want to see the dress. I found mine." Emily sings.

"Okay, okay." I fasten the hook on the side and turn, watching the skirt twist with the folds. I can't help but spin again, grinning, mesmerized at the mirror's sight. Yep, this is the one.

When I exit the dressing room, I find Quinn smiling and laughing with Emily. Emily is in a short, black, lacy dress with red ribbon accents. I come up between them, and we all smile.

"So, Quinn saves the day, and we are all ready for our last prom," I say.

"Wow, our last prom. I can't believe the school year is almost over. Wills, do you think you'll be going to college like Lucy?"

I shrug. I am barely managing high school attendance and look at what just happened on our closed campus. How could I possibly achieve this on a larger scale—attending college while setting up a new governing body and reviewing laws in Edayri? I want to be selfish, but how many lives would I disrupt for a college experience I wouldn't be able to use in Edayri anyway?

"I think I will defer and decide later."

"Nothing wrong with that, Wills. I'm so done with school. I'd love to check out California if Lucy's okay with me going. I think she's starting to come around anyhow."

I'm happy for them, glad Lucy and Emily are mending their relationship, but deep down, I mourn the loss of both of them already. I try to shake this thought out of my head, but it lingers as we change out of our dresses and go to pay.

Quinn and I return to the MacKinnon Manor and are met by Esmund and Sabine. I'm holding my dress in a garment bag from the store, and Sabine smiles weakly when she sees it.

"How was dress shopping?"

"It is beautiful. I can't wait to wear it, whether at prom or not." I'm hoping she'll come around and let me find a way to go, but I don't want to push my luck.

Mr. Boward grins. "How about you go? I spoke with Eoin, and he's drafting plans to work out security. You could attend for an hour or so."

I can't help smiling even if Sabine is tight-lipped. "Willow, I'm not going to allow this if Eoin cannot execute a solid protection plan for this dance."

I have a real shot getting to go to my senior prom! I keep

myself from screaming with excitement. I don't care that it's only for a short time; this is more than I anticipated. Even better, I would get another chance to dance with Rhydian.

"Rhydian is looking forward to taking you to this formal event. Wasn't it originally canceled because of the death at your school?" Mr. Boward asks.

And there it is. That's more like the Mr. Boward, I know. "No one died. Fortunately, Steve Carlin is doing well and is out of the hospital. One of the student's parents contributed a hefty amount to have a prom for the seniors. The money that would have funded the prom is going toward the reconstruction of the campus."

Sabine's eyebrows raise, and she touches a finger to her chin. Mr. Boward says, "Interesting. So, you do plan to go despite the danger that could follow. You'd risk your fellow students and friends to do this?"

Sabine steps in quickly before I can respond. She deters him in a masterful, political way with a conversation about how the replacement of existing governmental structures will work. I lay my dress over a couch and sit next to Sabine.

"I understood this was well underway. What's come up?"

"Because you are split in your availability, we are having discussions about providing executive royal powers to both Esmund and myself to help you govern swiftly while you're at school. We have people in holding cells awaiting judgment for various types of hate crimes."

I hear precisely what Sabine is telling me, but I'm having a hard time believing it. Executive royal powers? Why are these needed? I was putting in place a new structure that would govern over everything. Why do they need this royal piece?

"What types of crimes? Are they considered capital offenses?" I ask.

Sabine says that most are property crimes and other minor offenses.

Mr. Boward scoffs. "Small crimes lead to larger ones, and

your rule over these situations will be on symbolic display for all of Edayri. That prom really shouldn't get in the way of anyone's future. If you allow Sabine and me to help you, you can maintain your education in Chepstow and Edayri. While you're away as Scepter, I can manage these small little facets." He waves his hand as if this is a small issue.

I'm being scolded like a child, and his passive-aggressive comments irritate me. Still, he knows he needs my approval for the power he is seeking. After meeting Abigail, I have no question that his request has nothing to do with helping me. Sabine, on the other hand, would help me under the circumstances. It could serve to keep her closer to Mr. Boward if he is doing something suspicious.

"Sabine, can we review after dinner this evening?" I ask, directing away from Mr. Boward's request. The ease with which he puts his fists into his pockets suggests he's irritated. The smirk on my face is one I can't hide.

"Really, Esmund, it will be fine. I can meet you after, and we can do the various processes required for these individuals with Commander Eoin and the Guardians," Sabine says.

A sly smile creeps across his face, giving me the chills. "Willow, it is helpful to use me in all capacities as Scepter, but something is off between us. I hope it has nothing to do with my son?"

"Why would you suggest that? It could have everything to do with the High Coven coup."

Sabine's eyes grow large, and her pursed lips give warning. Mr. Boward seems unaffected by my statement.

He moves to sit across from me and leans in. "I know you've gotten close to each other, and Rhydian is very fond of you. I don't want that to come in the way of our roles and the change of structure that you are trying to implement. He worries that you worry about the blood vow and the future betrothal."

"Esmund," Sabine huffs in warning.

Betrothal? Good grief, I'm seventeen! I can't even fathom the idea of marriage. He's trying to bait me. Abigail was right—he would hurt his own family for power and position. How does Rhydian not see this? Or maybe he's like Abigail and just accepts it?

"No, my relationship with Rhydian doesn't change anything. You and I are still working on transparency, I think. The important part is that Sabine understands the complete structure as well as Aren, Thaxam, and others starting to form the legion council. I understand that Abigail is doing a wonderful job in her new position." It's a little stab of my own because he has no part in any of these discussions and has very little knowledge in this area.

His raised eyebrow slowly drifts down. It feels like a chess match between us. I don't trust him.

CHAPTER 20

Sitting at the white vanity in my room in Chepstow, I brush my long wet hair. I contemplate prom. The royal Guardians are going with me just to make sure everything happens safely. Eoin has had Guardians busy ahead of prom too, placing enchantments that will shield me in the hotel. Is Sabine right? Am I bringing danger by going? Is it selfish for me to go? I accepted the crown so it would no longer be up for a challenge, but it hasn't done anything to keep others—or even me—safe. Staring at my face, I see the eyes of someone who is naive, still a teenager. I have no life experience beyond a privileged, catered life. That isn't going to change as Queen, but I can't live in a cave. Emily thinks the phantoms are controlled by a powerful Wiccan, which would have to be someone from a noble coven. I wonder if the goal was to come after me, Emily, or to trigger Lucy's valkyrie side. Emily is happy with that outcome, but I'm not sure Lucy is so delighted about it.

"Would you like a virtual chocolate shake? I recall how you love chocolate mint; they might have that." Evan interrupts my thoughts, and my stare fest with my mirror. Instead, I'm at a white, silver-trimmed counter staring at the milkshake machines lined up against the white-and-red tiled wall. The red stool swivels, and I face my uncle in a paper hat, red-and-white striped shirt, and white pants. His name tag reads, Fun-cle. I'm underdressed in my terry cloth bathrobe.

"I'm actually getting ready to go to my senior prom. And I really want to go, but . . ."

"You wonder if danger will follow you and if it's selfish to go?" I nod. "It is." He says this without any amble of sensitivity, merely as a matter of fact. He's right, and so is Sabine. Having them on the same side is not something I even want to think about.

He turns on his red and silver stool. "Willow, you need to understand who you are. It will always bring a sense of danger. You are a Queen. You are powerful, magickal, and not many would challenge you. But here's the thing; do you live atop your throne and do nothing? Or do you live your life?"

Without thought, I say, "I want to live my life, but not at the detriment of harming others around me just because we are in the same location."

Evan smiles, and it reaches his eyes. "I remember Nuala saying something similar before she ran. Don't run. Live, flourish, change."

"I'm not running." I haven't run from any of this! I've dived in the best way I can.

"I've been running, and it's like I'm having an asthma attack, and I don't even have asthma."

I giggle at his comment. Until recently, I never felt that strong or capable, but now, thanks to Cross's training, I do. It isn't that fear has left me, but now I have fighting skills and control. It strikes me that Evan running from something sounds absurd. He's a leader in the Emissaries; what could he possibly be running from?

"What have you been running from?"

Evan holds his chin and closes his eyes. I watch him and wait. When an entire minute has passed, he finally speaks. "The

Horned God. Do you know who he is?" I nod and sip my shake.
"You may be aware that the Horned God has returned. This was
right before the Goddess crowned you, not long after I was
crowned by the Horned God. We—you and I, my niece—are
intertwined on the path that the Goddess and the Horned God
could not travel." He stops and slurps some of his vanilla shake.

"What are we going to do that they couldn't?"

"Come together in forgiveness."

I touch his arm, and my hand goes right through it. We are
not in this place, only in the confines of our minds.

"I'm ghosting out, Will." He's laughing like a child. I smile at
him weakly as we both fade, and I'm staring at my reflection in
the mirror again.

"Thanks, Evan, for the time and advice," I say in my mind.

"Anytime, jellybean. Live and run toward it; don't look back,"
Evan replies. Before our mind connection fades, I hear other
voices talking to him.

Knock knock.

"Come in."

Emily enters holding dress bags, tote bags, and caddies. "So,
like, I thought we could get ready together since Cross, and I are
your secret security tonight." Her face beams with excitement as
she hangs her dress on my door with mine.

"So, Cross? Not Marco?"

She makes like she is swooning. "That man—those eyes and
those muscles! A girls got to have some options, so don't you be
all judgy."

"Never," I laugh. "I'm happy you came over because me and
makeup have a bare-bones relationship," I say, eyeing the
makeup caddy that she sets down on my vanity.

"Exactly! Not tonight though. We are glamming it up. Dry
that hair, and let's move. We only have a little over an hour."

Emily does her makeup first as I twist my hair in an updo and
curl the ends on top of my head with my flat iron.

"So tell me, how's it going with Rhydian? He's such a hottie! I mean, really. Though that Boy Scout honor is a little downer for me anyway."

I push her playfully. "Stop. You're not dating him."

Emily applies her makeup setting spray, whatever the heck that is, and smiles. "Yes, true. Well, it seems like he makes you happy. Do tell me more. I love hearing about it all." She moves me so that I'm no longer facing the mirror and begins to apply primer to my eyelids. "Seriously, spill."

"I really like him a lot. It's just . . . that whole blood vow and Guardian thing. Like, I'd like him to just be a guy at school."

"Will, may I remind you that he is a guy at school."

"No, that's not what I mean," I laugh. "It's this veil that hangs over my mind. Because of this blood vow he made to my father, I'm not completely certain his intentions are his decision rather than something he's compelled to do."

Emily moves quickly over my eyebrows, then she's back at my lids with small brushes. "Just because a vow uniquely connects you doesn't mean his brain is mush and under some ultimate control. His decisions are his own, Will."

But are they?

"Another thing. Stop trying to find a reason that he can't like you as much as you like him. Don't sabotage it by pushing people away. You don't have to be some martyr of a Queen either."

She really knows me and how to nail what I'm thinking, and we don't even have a vow, just our friendship. She's totally right. I pout for Emily as she applies lip gloss to my lips.

"You are my masterpiece!" Emily announces at last.

I'm stunned when I see myself. Highlights and delicate glitter showcase my cheekbones, and there are yellow and burnt orange shadows on my eyes. I never do much besides a colored face lotion, mascara, and lip gloss.

"Speak, Will, speak!"

I pull pearl drop dangle earrings through my ears. "Wow, Emily. Thank you. I could be a model at a photo shoot."

Emily puts on her black lacy dress and finishes tying on her bright red high tops. She looks glamorous in her own spunky, styled way.

Eoin knocks and opens the door. "Are you ladies ready?"

CHAPTER 21

I stop at the end of the hall and look down the stairs. Rhydian is waiting for me in the foyer, gorgeous in a formal black and white tuxedo, his dark wavy locks styled. I spot the leather wrist cuff, and the glinting silver of the earpiece clipped on the ridge of his ear. He's forever a Guardian, and right now, he's all mine. My heart beats loudly in my chest. Emily is right; I'm head over heels for him, and he didn't even have to do any of the small things like the fairies at the lake, the dinners, the hugs, the kissing, the moments of pure comfort.

Eoin clears his throat and, finally, Rhydian looks from Emily and Cross up the staircase to me. His immediate smile reveals his dimple.

At the bottom of the stairs, I turn, and the skirt spins out from my waist in a beautiful canopy of folds that stretch in a tulip shape around me. "So, Quinn and Emily did well?"

"I'd say they had a beautiful subject for whom they only accentuated what was already there."

I hope I'm not turning beet red.

Rhydian slowly reaches for my wrist and places a beautiful silver and white rose corsage on me. "This is customary, right?"

I smile in response and touch the roses. "Yes. This is beautiful. Thank you." My skin tingles at the touch of his hand on mine. The silver elastic band of the corsage has small knots tied in it. I smile at him and rub one of the tiny balled knots. "So, more knot magick. What do you wish for?"

He whispers in my ear, "A few slow dances with you." I close my eyes, feeling his body so close to mine, and I wish for the same thing.

I faintly hear Cross ask, "Are ya both ready?"

They're talking, but I don't hear them. I'm caught up in Rhydian's presence. He holds my hand and leads me to the front door, where Eoin stops us.

"Wait, let me get a few pictures before you leave." He snaps a few pictures of us at the door with my phone, and I put it back in my clutch. Rhydian kisses my forehead lightly. When we walk outside, I see what was supposed to be a limo but looks more like a HUMV with an extended back end.

Cross laughs out loud and claps his hands together. "Excellent!"

Tullen waves to us and opens the passenger side door. "Shall we?"

Emily smiles. "Yes, we shall!"

Cross helps Emily into the vehicle. He looks younger when he smiles. Emily mirrors him, and they look good together.

"May I?" Tullen asks, his hand outstretched to assist me into the HUMV. I gather my skirt in my other hand and use a hidden step to enter.

Inside, I slide over and find Cross and Emily on opposite sides of bench seats laughing and opening a bottle. Emily plays with the ceiling lights overhead and the volume of music coming through the speakers.

Rhydian slides in next to me.

"This is quite the tank," I say.

"Oh, you have no idea," he says. "I think Eoin would have preferred a tank. I'm surprised Tullen and Quinn were not able to secure one." I giggle and snuggling into his warm shoulder.

The ride to prom is nice. The car is warm, and I like how Rhydian's eyes keep gravitating to mine. I want to kiss him, and I can sense that he wants the same thing. The only thing keeping us apart is Emily and Cross laughing and joking in the car, though they didn't seem to pay us much attention.

When we get to the hotel, Rhydian and Cross exit first, then help Emily and me out of the car. A red carpet leads us into the fancy hotel as if we are arriving at some big awards ceremony. We are late as planned, and I can only stay for a short time, but I'll take it.

Interlinking my arm with Rhydian's, I lean against him and walk into the lobby. The hotel is resplendent with marble floors and crystal chandeliers that lead toward the check-in desk. Some signs and balloons direct us to the Trinity Cross Senior Prom.

Cross and Emily's matching Converse squeak against the clean floor.

"It's like we're following ducks with all that noise they're making."

I grin. "I'm surprised there's not a fountain full of swans with this hotel's high caliber."

The pathway pivots around the lobby's back wall, and a four-tier fountain comes into view. A gentle flow of water cascades from the fountain's peak into the larger body of water that is illuminated in jewel-colored tones.

"Wow, you called it. The swans must be in their beds asleep at this hour."

The archway we approach leads to two sets of double doors decorated by a white and black balloon arch. The music and noise coming from the room is loud. Now that we're here, I can hardly believe we've made it to the dance.

There are two security guards stationed outside the doors—Guardians with clipboards.

"Name?"

Cross laughs as Emily gives her name. When the younger

Guardian waits for Cross to respond, Cross reaches behind his head and smacks it. "I'm her guest, ya dim wit."

Rhydian and I approach the other Guardian, who seems nervous. He says in a low whisper, "A pleasure, your grace." The veil of being a typical teen at prom was never going to be a solid one anyway. Even here I reign the Wiccan Queen at her senior prom.

I nod to him. "Thank you." Rhydian leads us through the balloon arch to the dance.

The ballroom is high class. Coral's family spared no expense on the decorations, flowers, or buffet with finger foods and drinks. The front is a staging area with two huge screens that flash pictures and videos while the DJ operates the music. Round tables are scattered to the left and right sides of a large dance floor.

"Let's go to the left."

We follow Emily and Cross, passing a photo op wall for students to take pictures at. Everyone is smiling and dancing. I spy Marco laughing across the room with several of his friends from the football team.

"Are you hungry or thirsty? Would you like anything?"

"Maybe a drink?"

Rhydian pulls out a chair for me, and Emily and I sit at the empty table with little tea lights glowing around a flower centerpiece of white, black, and gold.

"Wow, can you believe it? Prom, Will."

"It's more than I imagined it would be. It's surreal. I didn't go to prom last year. I wasn't sure what to expect."

Emily's smile is prominent as she watches Cross.

"So, did you work out the stuff in your head about Rhy?"

"I'm the girl in the moment."

"That's my girl." She touches my shoulder and looks in my eyes before standing as Cross and Rhydian return to the table.

"These are foo-foo alcohol-free drinks." Cross hands Emily a pink cocktail. "But they are pretty tasty."

My drink looks almost holographic with opulent colors in the clear liquid.

"What is this?" I ask

"They call it lovers lane, so I took a chance."

His eyes are on my lips. I take a sip, watching him watch me. I don't feel nervous, just at ease.

The drink is refreshing. It has a slight taste of coconut and smells of vanilla and rose. It's like spa water, but the color and ice give it the effect of something more.

"And?"

"Quite refreshing. Would you like to try?"

The music changes from a slower tempo to a thumping beat.

"Yes! Let's goooooo." Emily and Cross make their way to the dance floor, and we follow.

The music is thundering. I gather my long skirt up in one hand and swing my hips as Emily jumps up and down. Cross and Rhydian move with us. Cross's jumping with his thick brown arms over his head pulls his shirt out of his slacks. A second song continues with the same pumping beat, and the sheen on everyone starts to show.

Rhydian says something, but all I can recognize is my name on his lips.

"What?" I yell back, and as I move closer to find out what he said, a kiss lands on my lips and stops everything. His hands are at my waist, pulling me closer to him. The crowd of bodies on the dance floor fades away. I only know him, his breath, his lips, and tongue. I breathe his name and smile when he pulls back from me. He grins.

"Wow. You're so happy and beautiful, I couldn't resist any longer."

My heart is beating fast in time with the music. We stand still as everyone around us moves. I lean up to Rhydian and kiss him gently as the beat changes, and we are holding each other to the slower tempo.

Those around us move, and space opens for couples. My face

almost hurts from smiling. I put my head on his shoulder with our bodies pressed together, dancing. This feels so good. His hand is on my lower back, the other holding my hand tucked to his chest.

"Willow?"

"Yeah?"

"This is good, Willow. It really is."

He says what I'm feeling, and the confirmation doesn't make me nervous or flush. It seals worry away with an agreement. This is his choice. I'm his choice.

The song ends, and the lights change. I spy Daniel dancing with Lucy. They are not far away, but the idea of them is. The normal that I want fades into the light.

There is a disruption in the music with a mic tap from head-master Ms. Chin.

"Seniors, please come together with me in thanking our benefactors for this event, Mr. and Mrs. Yang."

A light shines on Coral's parents. Her father is distinguished in his custom-fitted suit. There is some gray in the hairline near his temples. Her mother looks not much older than Coral herself. She is not of Asian heritage, which surprises me. Coral stands near her father with a wide but not authentic smile.

"I also have the honor of announcing your prom court. The votes are in and tallied to represent the prom court tonight. Your prom king is . . ." Ms. Chin opens a large white envelope. "Steve Carlin!"

Several girls wipe at their eyes, and few guys near us clap as Steve approaches the stage with a cane.

"Thank you for this honor. I'm glad to be out of the hospital and, of course, looking forward to the afterparty." Everyone cheers. Rhydian squeezes my hand, and I squeeze back. I will be back in Edayri; no afterparties for me.

As the noise drops, Ms. Chin continues. "And now for your prom queen . . ." She opens a second white envelope and announces, "Coral Yang!"

"No way any of that is a coincidence," Emily whispers to me.

"Who cares, really." I smile and clap with everyone.

"Come on, Will, where is your sense of justice? Rebecca or Shelly would have been better choices."

"Because wearing a plastic crown is the pentacle of achievement? Let her have it. Who cares." Emily wiggles her eyebrows and laughs mockingly. All I can do is shake my head and grin. I doubt Ms. Chin was surprised by these white envelopes. It's appropriate for Steve and for Coral, as much as it would have pained me to think kindly of Coral in a friendly way before. The weight of old grudges has no place in my thoughts tonight.

The dance floor parts and Steve leads Coral to the center, where they sway to the Post Malone song "Circles." Coral's parents watching with smiles while talking and shaking hands with Ms. Chin. My attention is taken by hands on my waist turning me, and I look into Rhydian's hazel, green-blue eyes. I lay my head on his shoulder, and we sway through the songs. I lose track of time, and the changing music blends into one blissful moment.

"Are you having a good time?"

"I am. Are you? Having a good time?"

"Anytime with you is good." He glances behind me. "Let's go sit for a bit."

We walk to the table where Emily and Cross are chatting with Marco and his date, and I realize the ballroom is bare for the first time. Less than twenty students remain.

The lights flicker, signaling the end of the night. It's been a full hour since we arrived.

Lucy taps me on the shoulder and gives me a hug. "Hey, you look beautiful!"

"Thanks! So do you," I say in return. Daniel and Rhydian stand next to each other awkwardly.

"You've been dancing all night. Are you going to the after-party? There are two different options, which is kinda awesome." Lucy says.

"No, I think we have to go. I was pushing it for the time I was here, I don't want to tempt fate further." I look over my shoulder at Rhydian. He turns with his hand to his earpiece, speaking low. Cross's face is all business when he approaches Rhydian and the air in the room shifts. The night is over—my stomach sinks.

"There is an issue outside. Cross, check-in with Tullen. I need to check in with Eoin at the house." Rhydian looks at me. "You and Emily stay here." There is no worry in his voice with the simple request.

CHAPTER 22

The lights flicker overhead, and the hotel staff come in and begin to break down tables. The ambiance of the ballroom changes from a swanky room filled with formally dressed teenagers to just a place. The balloons and decor are removed from view. Rhydian transports to Eoin, and I hug my stomach, awaiting the news.

"So, which party should we all go to?" Emily asks.

Daniel pulls me into their conversation, "Willow, will you be coming too?"

"Sure. Maybe." I shrug my shoulders. It's not on the agenda, and I don't want to push my luck. I don't want this night to end, but maybe it wouldn't have to end with Rhydian. Am I hoping for a more intimate situation with him?

"Coral invited us to Steve's parents' lake house. It is farther away, but it could be fun," Lucy says with a lilt to her voice. Emily's face scrunches up at Coral's name.

"How about the party right here, in the hotel rooms on the eighth floor? There is a whole suite of rooms on that floor. We could just hang here. Let's at least check it out." Emily says.

We agree and move toward the double doors. They slam shut, and the lights flicker again. The screech that reaches my ears is unbearable. The sound vibrates and shakes the entire room, bringing us all to our knees. A dark mist shapes itself into corporal forms draped in tattered robes, and they swarm the ballroom. Phantoms.

Emily pushes Lucy and me behind the catering table to obscure us from view. Daniel runs toward the closest door and tries to open it, but the door doesn't move. He rushes back to us.

The screams of the staff all but drown out the high screeching sound. There is a light behind the DJ stage—a door. I watch the hotel staff escape. "Em, look over there. An escape, but it's on the other side."

Lucy's eyes are wide, and tears threaten to fall. Her shoulders are shaking. Daniel's eyes are full of fear too, but he takes off his coat and pulls it around her.

"That's too far—"

"We feel you. You belong to us. You will free us." The phantom voices are clear and many.

Lucy's eyes beg Emily in a plea for help. I kick off my high heel shoes. There is only one way out; we will need to fight. They are after Lucy, and I will not let that happen. My magick hums and swirls on my skin at my command. I know my crown is showing because my vision has a hazy glowing sheen right above it.

I pull Emily's attention to me. "Only one way out." She nods in agreement. Daniel stares at me, mouth slack, while loosely pulling Lucy into the crook of his arm.

"See if you can reach Rhydian through the blood vow thing," Emily says.

I close my eyes, focus, and reach out to him, but there is nothing.

"Rhydian, we're under attack. The phantoms—"

Bang!

The double doors crack loudly, and I hear yelling outside. Emily smiles and says, "It's Cross."

The door busts at its hinges and flies over tables and chairs.

Cross is in full Guardian armor, bulked and ready to fight. We all move toward the opening he's made.

A mist forms around me when I stand and instant pain elicits my scream. There are screams all around me, too. Then I'm thrown. I'm flying away from the door, still screaming. I tuck my head before hitting hard into tables and chairs. I'm a tangle of dress, chair legs, and limbs when I finally stop moving.

"Em! Willow!" Cross's voice booms.

I see him fighting figures in the mist around him, ducking and turning, his massive sword connecting with a semi-corporal form. There is the blur of another phantom behind him with more fog. I tug at my dress. I'm pinned. I pull and feel my magick fading. There is blood from cuts on my arms and legs. Pain shoots up my right leg as I come free.

Fuck!

"Willow, use your magick!"

Emily is in her full valkyrie battle gear on the opposite side of the ballroom, swinging her staff and surrounded by mist.

I try to stand but fall to my knees when my ankle collapses under me. The throbbing sensation of fire makes me shudder. I call to my magick and place my hands on it.

"Mend the broken and torn—"

The mist is around me suddenly. It yanks me high in the air, but I push my own magick at the fog and drop, landing on my toes and not falling flat on my face. My ankle screams in pain, and I roll. My skirt is torn. Cursing, I magick it away and replace it with leggings.

Emily pounds her staff on the floor. The shock wave clears the mist from the ground up to the roof, and Cross is at my side.

"Heal it, now!"

I reach for my ankle, but Cross yanks my hand to his bloody side.

The roar of a tiger echoes through more screams.

I mutter the spell to myself. I feel his lungs fill with air, his muscles repair themselves in knitting fashion as his skin molds back. My hands are slick with Cross's dark blood.

The humming grows dull. My magick is fading on me.

I push through a veil in myself to hold onto the hum, the magick, the unwanted part of myself that is now who I am, who I'm meant to be.

Cross pats my hand. "Thank ya."

He's healed.

Emily is shaking; the bubble she formed is only around the three of us. Marco is in his tiger form chasing a phantom away from the few classmates and hotel staff in the ballroom.

"Where is—"

"Tullen, Rhydian, Quinn—all unreachable. Something is wrong." Frustrated, Cross holds his broken ear cuff.

"My magick isn't—"

"Fight anyway." Cross hands me a dagger. "The mist is a diversion from their bodies. Find the soft spots, don't let them connect with you, then do some fuckin' damage. They bleed and can be killed."

I stand, favoring my weight to the side opposite my injured ankle. My back to Cross, I take my defensive stance.

My body shakes. This isn't training anymore.

"I can't . . . hold . . ." Emily's stance is wavering, the mist pushing at the bubble, the screams and shrieks piercing.

"Don't. Let 'em come!" Cross yells.

The rush is immediate. The mist surrounds us, and the pain cuts all over me. I thrash out with the dagger and move. The mist follows the movement. It can't stay on me; I can't handle the pain. I duck and roll to the ground, calling my magick to surround me and protect my skin. Popping up, I stand and thrust the dagger forward. It connects with something substantial, and I push forward to sink then twist the blade. Something howls and hits my face, knocking me back, and the dagger is lost from my grip. The dagger looks suspended until the phantom appears, corpse-like hands pulling at the hilt.

I run toward it, jump, and connect my elbow to its head. Grabbing the hilt, I yank the dagger out and slice hard where my elbow hit—the shrieking stops. The phantom falls to the floor and dissolves away in its mist.

The agonized screaming continues around me. My friends.

Cross runs toward me, the mist behind him growing. He's yelling, one hand up to his wrist cuff. His face is stone and determined. He cups his hand in front of him, and I know what he wants me to do. I run toward him, dagger in hand, swinging my arms hard. He leans down, and when I put my foot in his hand, I soar high above him, swinging the dagger down from above my head and connecting with another phantom.

Landing hard, my ankle buckles. Cross is next to me.

"One left. They got this. I need to transport you out—"

Emily and Lucy get thrown. Daniel grabs her staff and swings it, but the phantom's arm goes right through his stomach.

Time turns to slow motion. The sounds are gone from my head. I watch Daniel fall to the floor. I yank my arm from Cross and transport to Daniel. The mist surrounds me, pushing. I swing the dagger, connecting and slicing, moving in a dance of rolling, ducking, swinging. Pain is all around me, all through my body and mind. I hear myself screaming.

Kill. Save him.

I'm glowing. My magick finds the phantom and twists it. The shrieks and howls match my yells until it dissolves in front of Daniel and me.

"Willow?"

I turn to Cross, blade raised. His hands are up in surrender.

Not a threat.

"Willow! Oh my God, help him!" Lucy screams behind me.

"The phantoms are gone, for now," Cross says, his arms slowly dropping to his side.

Turning, I survey the damage. Dark blood pools around Daniel. His stomach is dark and gaping, a hole right through him. His arm is at an unnatural angle, his face pale, his eyes staring off in the distance.

He is gone.

My mind, my body, goes numb.

Death follows me.

Lucy and Emily are yelling at each other, Emily holding Lucy back. I'm a spectator. Cross's lips are moving, but I can't understand him.

My magick leaves me.

Lucy and Emily's voices fade.

I couldn't save him. He is gone.

Lucy pulls Daniel to her.

"You can't do this!" Emily yells. "You don't know what you're doing!"

My voice breaks free of my mind, and I hear myself say, "He wouldn't choose this."

"He'd choose to be alive!"

"No, Lucy. Not like that," Marco says.

"AAAAH!" Her scream rebounds around us, chilling my blood.

Lucy is glowing and encasing herself with Daniel. I can't help the streaming tears and anguish that push me to the floor in a heap of emotion.

A tiger's roar echoes through the ballroom.

PART IV

By knot of eight, it will be fate
By knot of nine, what's done is mine

CHAPTER 23

I'm watching the same events unfold. First Mrs. Scott, then my father, and now Daniel. It's as if I'm watching television without the sound. I see it all unfolding, but I can't completely comprehend. Daniel is no longer here. His body is present, his eyes unmoving, his face stone. There is nothing left to do.

Death the one constant you can count on in the end. I tried to protect my friends and failed. I wanted to attend prom. Was I the impetus that brought the phantoms here? Was it Lucy? Does it even matter?

She's mumbling and chanting, her hands moving over Daniel in weird patterns and waves. I call to my magick, but the familiar hum is gone. I'm an empty shell on autopilot. Looking around, I find Cross surveying the room. We need to move. It's not safe here.

"What are you doing? You dismiss who you are, then draw from a force you don't respect or understand. You've heard everyone! He wouldn't want this. Stop what you are doing!" Emily yells at Lucy.

Marco paces in tiger form on the other side of me, his pads soft on the ground. He's keeping watch as well.

Emily holds her hands up in surrender when Lucy continues

her chant, then carefully slides next to Lucy. Em stares at Daniel, expressionless. They chant together and emanate a glow all around Daniel's body. When Emily moves her hand over his stomach, Daniel's chest rises awkwardly, and something cracks loudly. A bone-breaking or mending? Lucy gasps at the sound, but Emily shoves her shoulder into her, still concentrating, and they continue. His body starts to respond by contracting inward like a pulse.

They are making him an einherjar warrior.

This is part of Norse culture that Emily told me about— bringing dead warriors back in service to the valkyrie. Not all dead warriors take to the magical calling from the valkyric, so this may do nothing.

As if I'm speaking to Daniel, I contemplate the questions in my head. Did you want to be a soldier in service to the valkyrie and Lucy?

I shake my head hard. What am I thinking! If he could come back, he should, right? What wouldn't I give to have my father and Mrs. Scott back? Is it selfish to want them all back, to want Daniel again, to feel like I didn't fail?

Cross approaches. I pull myself up and stand next to him.

"My magick is gone."

"How do ya know? Ya may have just used all that ye had. Maybe ya need time to recover."

"That's never been the issue before." Maybe I've done something wrong by the Goddess?

Cross points to Emily and Lucy, who continue to chant around Daniel. "No kidding." He shakes his head. "Tullen wasn't near the car, and I can't reach any of the Guardians. We are on our own. Feels like a setup."

The pallor of Daniel's skin is coming back to life. He turns his head and looks directly at me. His eyes are cloudy; this isn't quite Daniel. Lucy stops chanting. Emily moves quickly as Daniel jumps to his feet and crouches in a fighter stance at a speed I can barely track with my eyes. Cross throws his arms in front of me and yanks me behind him. Lucy, on the floor closest to Daniel, gasps when he snarls at her. Marco crawls between Daniel and us.

Daniel scans the room. His eyes stop on me. His head tilts like a bird's; he recognizes me. Lucy reaches her hand toward him, but he doesn't seem to understand. His mouth opens without a sound, but his face says it all—agony and rage. Tears well in my eyes and my shoulders quake.

"Daniel," I whisper, and his face turns to look at me through Cross and Marco.

In one quick movement, Cross turns to me and transports me to the door of the ballroom. I waiver on my feet. Daniel is running and leaping toward us with Marco trailing.

I've lost sight of Emily and Lucy. Cross puts me behind him. Daniel halts his speed just before Cross and swings his hips in a roundhouse kick that connects with Cross's face, pushing him to the floor. The power and strength to move Cross like that is more than what Daniel had before.

Marco transforms back to his human form and holds his hand out in surrender. "Daniel, buddy, what are you doing? Do you need to protect her?"

Daniel nods in a small, quick, awkward movement.

My voice shakes. "I'm safe. Cross is my Guardian. We are all safe, okay?"

He straightens and moves toward me, tentatively as if he doesn't want to spook me. I'm totally spooked. This is Daniel, but not.

"Can you talk?"

He opens his mouth as if testing the function. "Yes." His voice is low and deep, but it's still Daniel's voice.

"Daniel!"

Lucy and Emily come up behind him too fast. He turns toward them and snarls in warning, protecting me again. I'm close to him, and I reach my hand forward. Marco and Cross protest behind me, but I ignore them and touch Daniel's shoulder.

He relaxes.

"It's okay. Those are our friends, Lucy and Emily."

Lucy repeats his name, but he continues to stare at me, his eyes searching for an answer from me.

"What is wrong with him? Daniel, it's me, Lucy. Your girlfriend."

Daniel watches her but makes no response, then looks back at me. He steps closer to me, reaches up, and touches my face. His hand is cold and stiff.

He's here.

I reach my hand out to Lucy, and she puts her hand in mine. I bring her closer to Daniel. His eyes shift between Lucy and me. "Lucy. Daniel, do you remember Lucy?"

Her eyes are wide and searching his face, almost pleading. This is heartbreaking. She is crumbling in front of everyone.

"Daniel." Emily's commanding voice orders him. "Fall in line."

He moves swiftly behind Emily, who looks like a supernatural general in her filigree eagle headdress and brass armor that has replaced her ruined dress.

"What are you doing?" Lucy's voice waivers.

"This is what you've made him. He's a solider. He will protect the Queen as that is what I've sworn to do. As a valkyrie, you've made no declaration, Lucy. If you want to be in his life, you'll need to make the declaration."

"No. No." Lucy pulls away from me. It's a rejection that I wasn't expecting to hurt so strongly. I think about Evan and his story about the Horned God and the Goddess, their rejection and anger. Lucy throws her hands in the air. "This? Look around, Willow. This is what you've brought—you and Emily! We almost died."

"If not for the friends yer rejecting, you would have. Ungrateful," Cross spits.

I give him a warning look. She's not entirely wrong.

Emily laughs hysterically. Marco is standing behind her with Daniel. "No, Lucy, this is what *you* brought, what *you* did to Daniel. Play victim though! That's a role you've got down. Make a mess and take no responsibility for it."

"Fuck you!" Lucy is shaking.

Cross pulls my attention away. "This is their family matter. Let's transport—"

Boom!

Crack!

Evan transports a few feet opposite Cross and me with Theon and one other. The vibration pushes me back a step and awakens the pain in my ankle.

"We've got to go," Evan says.

Lucy is staring daggers at me as if I'm responsible for Daniel and Cross, putting themselves between Evan and me.

I want to experience sadness for her, but right now, all I feel is her jealousy.

"Now, Willow! Everyone grabs a hand." Evan yells.

Cross grabs mine, and when Daniel reaches for me, I pull away. "Emily, Marco, take them somewhere else. We need to split up."

The ballroom lights flicker, and the temperature drops. Phantoms are coming.

This is officially the prom from hell.

CHAPTER 24

The push and pull of the transport magick is anything but smooth. My magick usually steadies and helps with transporting. Now my eyes can't track from the motion of being jerked around, and I try to hold down my stomach, knowing if I don't, I will vomit all over Cross and Evan. When we stop, vertigo overtakes me. I bend over and throw up on the ground.

Evan is next to me, patting my back in weird circles, and I stand.

"Where are—" I cut myself off when I see the overturned logs and blazing fire surrounded by tents. We are in the same place the demon teenagers took me. Theon walks away from us giving orders that I can't make out.

"What the hell is going on, Evan?"

We are in the heart of the Emissaries camp. Cross has moved off to the side and is talking to General Thaxam and Abby, leaving me with Evan. Ax smiles his fang tooth grin and shrugs his boxy red shoulders. It's like watching the devil try to put me at ease. Still, the menacing horns and exterior are anything but innocent.

"It's complicated," Evan says.

"Seriously! We are well beyond complicated!" I scream at

him. "Phantoms were at my prom! They killed Daniel! And where is Rhydian, Quinn, and Tullen?" The tones of conversation around me pause, and all eyes are on us.

"Prom," he says as if testing the word on his tongue. "Around and around we go, the dancing does continue."

"What does that mean? Evan, no riddles! I need you to fully pull it together."

"I am always fully together. Are you questioning my sanity?" The looks around us catch my anger in my throat.

"I'm sorry, Evan. Truly, I am," I say in defeat.

"I'm not. It was a catalyst of change for something much more."

I turn to Ax and Abby. "Tell me now."

Ax begins to talk, Abby filling in his pauses. "Phantoms are emerging from the fountain in the center of the Hallowed Hall. The Guardians are supposed to be containing the threat but—"

"But the Guardians have been taken over by some sort of spell and are fighting any who resist."

"It's a genocide, Willow. They are wiping out anyone who fights back. There seems to be some type of gateway in at the manor. It's an all-out clash of Edayri. The phantoms scream for you, Willow. There is something they need to complete the task. We think they are attempting to permanently connect the fallen Norse realm to Edayri. A Convergence."

"Meaning the destabilization of Edayri as well," Abby finishes.

"So, we must keep ya here, away from all of it," Cross says.

"We can't do that. How will we ever win? She has the strongest magick. Everyone in our family is strong, but she's the most," Evan says. The absence of a hum makes me flinch at Evan's words. I have nothing to help. Also, what about everyone else? This is horrible.

"Evan, we need to know what we are walking into," Abby replies.

"The Guardians. Does that mean that—Rhydian is at the manor?" I start to shake. "Abby?"

She shakes her head. "We're working a plan of interception to move out those that are hurt and—"

Evan dramatically closes and opens his eyes, inhaling sharply. "He's there."

"What? Are you sure?" I ask. I'm ready to leave and find him, but I can't transport without magick or a plan. I need others to help me get to him.

"If Evan had a vision, then yes, Rhydian is there," Theon says, surprising me as he comes up from behind Ax.

I stumble back, and the weight makes my ankle smart again.

"Are you hurt?" Abby looks at my ankle. Before I can move, she places her hand on my foot. It warms to her touch.

"Abby, what are you doing?"

"She's a healer," Cross says. "Ya need to be in top form. We've got to go to MacKinnon Manor. Eoin has reached out." Cross taps his Guardian wrist cuff. "He and a small contingency group are trying to contain the phantoms from wreaking havoc all over Edayri. They have closed the Hallowed Hall, and the focus now seems to be at the manor. This could be where the control is— whoever released them."

"Just a minute, Cross. Willow, follow me."

I follow Abby to a tent. Looking around the small space, it feels more like a bedroom than a tent for camping. There is a full bed at the back wall with a nightstand and lamps, a dresser off to the side, and a small table with two chairs in the center. Rugs cover the floor.

Abby hands me a pair of boots. I quickly pull on and lace them. I had forgotten I was barefoot until she healed my ankle. I catch sight of myself in a standing mirror opposite, dressed in leggings and the bodice that my ruined prom dress has been reduced to. I gesture to a dark shirt with a hood lying on the table and, when she nods, I pull it on.

"Do you need anything else?" Abby asks.

"No. Thank you for this." Looking at her, I see Rhydian's resemblance in her dark hair and the shape of her nose and mouth. Their eyes are different, his a dark stormy ocean with blues and greens while Abby's are dark brown. I finger what's left of the corsage on my wrist and touch one of the small knots of the silver band.

"Do you live here? Does your father—"

"I don't live here full time, but I'm here a lot. He knows nothing. Neither does Rhydian, but I'm guessing it will come out soon." She looks at her hands. "I never betrayed your intentions of an Edayri governing body, the legion council."

"I never thought you did," I say quickly.

"I think what the Emissaries stand for is exactly what you're putting in place, so coordinating allows me to weave the two together."

"I see that."

The relief on her face is surprising. Abby gets up to leave, and I tell her I'll be a minute. I call to my magick, but there's nothing—no hum, no tingle, no awareness of anything lingering.

Can I call to Rhydian? I focus on the quiet of the tent and reach out through my mind, thinking of his handsome face when I came down the stairs in my dress just several hours ago before prom.

"Rhydian." I breathe.

Silence answers me.

I open my eyes and take a deep breath before opening Abby's tent's flap to leave.

"Willow, come find me. I'm hurt."

Rhydian. I hear him clearly in my head. He's guiding me to him, the outreach pulling at my mind and my body. This is a tether to me, to my whole being. Where is he?

Evan grabs my arm. "You're not going to him without us. It's a trap, Willow." Evan closes his eyes before he says, "He's at the manor."

"Trap or not, I have to go." My voice is almost pleading.

"Yes, you do, but with us in tow." His hold on my arm is gentle, and everyone—Cross, Abby, Ax, Evan, Theon, and other demons—reaches out and touches someone else in the group.

"I don't want to ask this of you, coming into battle, but I thank you and—be careful," I say

"In your name, Blessed Be," Abby says as a prayer.

Cross guides us in the transport. Evan keeps his hand gentle on mine as Cross leads us onto the grounds of MacKinnon Manor, my new home.

The realization comes to me the moment Evan releases my arm.

This is a bad idea.

CHAPTER 25

We are hidden on the side of the property where the tree line begins. The fighting is chaos, armored Guardians fighting against other Guardians and Wiccans fighting Wiccans. Phantoms screech and charge through a group of demons at the side of the MacKinnon Manor. They all fall flat on the ground, unmoving. I can't tell who is fighting who; it's just a swarm of magick, swords, punches, and blood.

So much blood.

The Emissaries around me are organizing and entering the fight. I can't move. I envision my father flat on the ground, dead, not far from where I stand. His body is bloodied and broken from the torture imposed on him to get his power and lure me in for mine. This is, once again, the goal.

I block out the image and stare at my hands, flexing them and calling to my magick. A faint light shows at the tips of my fingers. I'm limited, but is it coming back?

The longer I watch, the easier I recognize who is being controlled and who isn't. The noble covens are fighting with the rogue Guardians under some type of spell, their movements mechanical. It looks all wrong.

Cross is next to me. "Don't go all hero. Be smart and use yer training, mind, and body. Yer a warrior; ya don't need to rely on magick. Get blasted mad, woman!" he yells.

I smirk at the compliment from Cross. He just called me a warrior, and I can't help but stand a little straighter despite being scared.

"Ya fight best when yer pissed off at me. Do I need to tell ya something offensive?" I shake my head. "Fuckin' tear it up. Don't over complicate this; find Eoin and end this spell. Pocket that other shit. Let's go."

"Eoin's there!" Evan points.

Following his gesture, I can barely make out Eoin on the front entry stairs, but I recognize it's him by his armor with golden shoulders.

"Rhydian!" Abby screams.

I follow her to where she is looking and find him. The armor covering his body has dark blood smeared all over it. His movements are fluid and undeterred as he cuts through those in front of him. He brings his sword down and slices through two magical beings while behind him, a phantom protects his blindside.

They are working together.

Rhydian's face is mechanical, zombie-like with everyone around him. His eyes, dispassionate, focus on Abby and then shift to me, his target.

His mouth is moving, but it's too loud for me to hear him. I step out of the tree line as a demon crosses in front of Rhydian, distracting him.

Evan grabs my hand, and we transport too Eoin. Evan places a protective magickal bubble around the three of us. I gasp. Eoin has burn marks on one side of his face and scorches down the side of his body.

Evan places his hand on Eoin and begins healing him. "Sabine? Is she here?" Evan spits Sabine's name like a sour lemon.

"Yes. I narrowly escaped control." He shows his palm with a specific mark of protection that glows like lava in his skin. "The

Guardians have been taken over by a spell, and only severe pain and fire of high magick is releasing it. I'm not sure how long it will last." Eoin starts to cough. "The phantoms are guarding the manor. Someone is letting them in. They are collapsing the bridge between realms. The only way to do that is to siphon your powers." He reaches for my hand, "Once you are drained—I don't know what's next."

My heart beats faster knowing it's someone else doing this. Why did I think something was wrong with me? The Goddess crown me, but the royal powers are also mine, along with my own and my father's. I had the notion deep down that the Goddess could take away magick as easily as she gave it, perhaps as a punishment for Daniel. But she wouldn't take my powers like this.

"This doesn't seem like an unsolvable puzzle, then," Evan says. "Where is the source of the siphon?"

"From what I can tell, it must be in the house, in the lower basements."

The dungeons. That was where father and Lucy were held before the rescue.

I hear Cross's familiar battle cry muffled behind us. Rhydian must be near.

Evan pulls his hand from Eoin, and we are no longer in a bubble. The sound of the battle is at full volume. I flinch.

"Sabine." Evan takes off running.

Sabine stands ahead of him and to the side of where a Guardian lays motionless. Her purple cloak billows behind her movements, her brilliant red hair like a flame fanned out around her. I can't see who she is fighting; is she fighting with the Guardians or against others? The phantoms are concentrated near the lower end of the manor and are moving her direction.

Sabine conjures a hard blow to a massive demon that knocks him down at Evan's feet.

The distance closes between Sabine and Evan.

My breath is gone. I can't do anything to stop it.

Evan has a light ball in his hands and throws it at Sabine, blasting her with a direct hit. She falls in a heap on the ground. Evan turns and throws a light ball at Quinn, who is running at him fast.

Did he kill her? My feet move of their own accord toward the purple cloak.

"Sabine. Sabine." I shake her, and the grimace is immediate. Her shirt is burned, and the mark on her shoulder is like Eoin's. Evan woke her from the trance of the spell controlling her. He didn't kill her.

"Willow." Sabine is no longer under someone else's control. She pulls at her ear and holds out an earpiece that I've only seen on Guardians. Grabbing a rock, she crushes it.

"It's how they control them, us—"

"Evan!" I yell. He's a good twenty feet away from us. "The earpieces! That is how the Guardians are being controlled."

Evan and Quinn are exchanging blows. Evan grabs his neck, pulls the earpiece off his ear, then drops Quinn. Quinn sees me and stops with his eyebrows raised. He seems to understand quickly and immediately transports to Eoin. They fight in tandem against others at the entrance.

The battle is closing in on us.

Rhydian is closer to me now. His face is unfeeling. I recognize his calculation, his determination. He won't kill me, but he will hurt me, subdue me—it's the order.

Bring her by any means necessary. I hear it in my head like an echo from Rhydian.

"Rhydian, no!" Abby hits his back with a magick light ball. It covers his armor but does nothing. He stalks forward, matching my steps as I step backward. He uses his magick to throw Sabine into Evan.

If I turn and run, I won't be able to track him, and I'll get caught. He'll use magick. I must keep this physical; otherwise, I won't have a chance. Unless . . . Maybe I can overpower the spell by using his loyalty to our bond. Isn't that what he told me before? He couldn't hurt me unless I allowed it, and it would tear our bond.

"Rhydian." I hold out my hand, and he stops advancing. "Your vow. Do you remember what you vowed to my father and pledged to me?"

His eyes wander around me, no longer focused.

Eoin yells from behind me. "Follow your Queen, Rhydian. Protect what you vowed—"

I'm thrown back, and I hit the manor's stone wall hard. I expect pain when I fall, but I'm cushioned with air before I hit the ground. Eoin is stopping my decent, his hand outreached to me.

Rhydian pushes himself up from the ground and throws a dagger at Eoin, who catches it in his hand and throws it back at him. Still, it's too late. Rhydian and Evan both run toward me as I try to stand.

Rhydian slams into me and we are transporting before I have time to think. I reach for Evan, my hand just shy of his fingertips. Everything blurs. Rhydian pulls me into his chest, and we land hard on a dirt floor.

CHAPTER 26

Breath escapes my lungs at the force of impact. I moan through the pain and push myself up. Rhydian is next to me and I crawl away, frantically trying to get out of his grip. I roll on the dirt floor and try to gain traction with my feet as I kick him in the stomach. He grabs my ankle and yanks me back.

"Please, Rhydian, let me go," I plead. Kicking, my free foot lands in his hand, and he twists me onto my back, looming over me.

"You're hurting me!"

His eyes are full and imploring me as if he understands, but his mouth is a thin line.

I hear a whisper in his earpiece. An order. Whoever is giving it must be nearby because the whisper is echoed somewhere ahead of us. Eoin was right—someone is calling the shots, and Rhydian has taken me right to them.

Rhydian pulls me up by my arm, so we are both standing. His grip is tight. I recognize the familiar dirt, the earthy smell, and the fallen ceiling that I caused to rescue my father and Lucy. We are in the dungeon of the manor.

Rhydian isn't close enough for me to get that earpiece off him. A faint voice speaks to him through it, and he pushes me forward. The air around me shifts as someone transports near us. It's Tullen, and he has Abby.

"Abby . . . Tullen?"

Tullen taps his earpiece. "Both are here as requested. Rhydian and I will deliver the packages."

No.

Tullen pushes Abby forward ahead of me. Rhydian is at my back, blocking me from going anywhere but forward. We are guided down the stone stairs into the belly of the beast, the ancient dungeon. The sign announcing MacKinnon Manor looms overhead, swinging from its chains. There's a light source in the middle of the room beyond the doorway. I squint my eyes to see better. A male figure stands on a platform over a black liquid looking hole where the dungeon's floor should be. He waves his hands, and I watch the familiar designs glow on his hands and arms while a crown wavers over his head.

That is my magic, my familiar hum with someone else. It seems to waver toward me. A phantom rises out of the black hole and goes through the male figure. He grunts as if in pain, and the colors around him turn from bright light to a dull gray momentarily before becoming bright again. The phantoms take part of him when they emerge from the collapsed realm.

Is this how he controls them?

"Oh my Goddess, you have lost your mind," Abby sobs. She snatches her arm from Tullen. "What are you doing? Do you want to destroy Edayri?"

The man turns and walks down the stairs of the platform that hangs over the portal. He has a regal demeanor that makes my stomach sink when I see his face.

Mr. Boward.

"Thank you, Tullen. Take your post. Rhydian, guard our two hostile guests."

Rhydian pushes me forward so that I'm beside Abby and he stands behind both of us.

"What is your plan, father?" Abby asks, spitting his name.

A sinister laugh falls from Esmund's lips. "It is a simple mind that believes realms should be separated. I will collide them all. Rule over them. The Wiccan Queen supplies the power. Why should any of us fear the earthly planes? The Convergence is happening; it is no longer just conjecture. I simply found a way of speeding it up. Equality does not balance, but a merger and cleansing does."

"You're insane." My voice is loud. "Just because you have some power does not mean you will ever overcome the many who would oppose you. You won't succeed. All you are is a murderer and a thief."

He walks over to me, smirking, then smacks me hard. My head whips to the side. I taste the iron of blood in my mouth. Rhydian flinches in my peripheral vision.

"I succeeded in so many things leading up to this point, and you were oh-so willing. Duty is damned by the ignorance of youth. Do you want to whine some more about leaving normal behind? Don't worry. Your reign will be insignificant for another few minutes until your blood is spilled and your full magick released to me. The Boward family will become the royal family they were always meant to be."

The air shifts again. Esmund's eyes widen.

"Tsk, tsk," Evan says mockingly. "When Nuala broke your engagement, you were no longer part of the royal family, Esmund. Man, do you take a breakup hard. That was over two decades ago."

I peek behind Rhydian and see Quinn and Sabine with Evan. They use magick to hold back two Guardians around the portal. They move their hands and control light bolts and air.

"You bore me, Evan," Esmund coughs.

Esmund twists his hand, and Evan rises into the air. Evan twist midway like a gymnast, throwing out his arms, and light surrounds him. He gently lowers himself back to the ground before throwing a blast so severe that the platform crumbles into the portal.

"No!" Esmund reaches for it with magick, trying to stop it, but he's too late.

The portal ripples like a storm on water and pulls the structure into itself like a raging ocean, swallowing it whole. The screech of the phantoms outside of the dungeon makes everyone cower except Evan. He strides toward Esmund.

Evan gets the upper hand on Esmund, who recovers quickly. The pull of my magick from me to Esmund looks vaguely like a lightning bolt. Does he notice? The hum of my magick is still light but more present than before. Maybe I can use it to get that earpiece off Rhydian.

Esmund throws a large object that crashes where Evan was standing, but Evan disappears right in time. Tullen surveys the threats from beside Esmund and moves in to attack Sabine and Quinn.

The laugh that comes from Esmund is manic. He turns to Abby and me.

"Subdue them! They are subservient to our objective."

Rhydian pushes us to our knees.

"Son, it is almost time for the sacrifice. It must be her so that I can retain the Goddess gifts she is so unworthy of. Bring her here."

Abby moves in front of me. "No! You can't do this father. The blood vow! It will kill him! Father." Tears stream down her face.

"The blood vow might transfer to me, but even if it doesn't, we all make sacrifices—something you, Abigail, know nothing about! Rhydian has always known his duty. That is what makes him the best captain of the Guardians," Esmund says.

Evan comes up behind Tullen and boxes his ears. The earpiece flies off. Tullen turns in shock. Evan transports to another Guardian and does the same, one after another. They all shake their heads, clearing whatever spell was controlling them.

Esmund is not consistently giving orders; there must be someone else helping him. Rhydian doesn't acknowledge what

Evan is doing behind Esmund. He pulls me up to stand. Abby grabs my hand, and Rhydian yanks me from her. He pushes me forward with his outstretched arm, a knife to my back.

Esmund is laughing. Abby pleads with her father, but when it yields no response, she spits at him. "Monster! You bastard."

Esmund's back is to us as he tries to repair the podium structure over the raging portal. My magick flows over his arms and wavers over his head.

I twist sharply to face Rhydian, putting my hand over his knife. Maybe I can influence him through his blood vow. My cheek still throbs from Esmund smacking my face.

"Rhydian, make your own choice. Pull away from your father's command."

He stares at my hand and the knife that now points at my stomach. Rhydian hears me. He is warring inside with what he's been commanded to do. He wants to protect me but doesn't have the freedom to do so, and it's tearing him apart.

"I can't." His worried eyes are at odds with his stoic warrior nature.

"But I can," I say. His fingers soften on the hilt and I hold him steady. I should be terrified, shaking, but I'm not. I'm resigned to what I need to do. I know how to break this control, how to get close enough to reach his ear.

The dungeon shakes and parts of the ceiling fall. Sabine is yelling, and the air moves with people transporting out of the dungeon.

I yank the knife forward into my stomach. The pain is instant and radiates all over my body. Rhydian catches me as I fall, unable to hold my own weight, and guides me to the ground. His eyes close; his lip trembles.

Our souls intermingle and rip. I reach my hand to his face and he leans into it, our faces not an inch from each other. Despite the roaring, burning pain in my body, the fact remains that Rhydian's hand went against his oath. The blood vow is broken.

I shock him with my lips on his and grab the earpiece, crushing and throwing it.

My hum rises faintly on my skin. "I love you."

"I failed you," he whispers, his forehead to mine.

I don't expect the welling tears in his storming eyes. He's back.

Tullen pulls Rhydian back from me, and it's as if limbs are being removed; both Rhydian and I scream in agony. Evan lays his hands on me before yanking the knife from my body, a pressure I barely register.

"Rhydian!" I yell.

"We're transporting," Evan says, and he gently picks me up. I grab his neck with my bloody hand.

Evan lays me on the ground beside Eoin at the front of the manor.

Eoin gasps. "Willow."

Evan's hand glows, and warmth eases my wound, so much so that I'm able to sit up. His demon horns shine in the twilight. He is quite powerful in his own right. My uncle just saved me. We've been here before, but this time we are not fighting each other. This time we are on the same side, fighting together. My mother would be so proud of him.

"I'd rather have your admiration than my dead sister's," Evan says.

"You read minds now?"

"No, but it's written all over your face. I'm just highly intuitive." He taps his temple. "Better?"

"Yes and no." My wound is healed, but—

The manor and the earth crumble around us. I hang on to both Evan and Eoin as we move away from the manor. The west side collapses into the dungeons with a massive groan. Smoke rises from the structure as stone and mortar fill the space below.

Silence.

I spot Cross with Rhydian near the collapsed part of the manor.

Several phantoms float around and dodge into the rubble. The portal is buried while the phantoms remain here.

A light ball hits Eoin square in the back, and he stumbles forward, carrying me with him. Evan rolls gracefully to the side and throws air toward the aggressor.

Quinn appears in front of us and drags Eoin to the side to heal him. Eoin holds Quinn's hand. I survey my surroundings quickly before I jump and roll to dodge a weak light ball from Esmund. Sabine attacks Esmund, her red hair wild behind her and her purple cloak rippling like a storm. She is fierce and powerful.

Esmund screeches in a tone that makes the phantoms rush toward him, but when they do, they go through him, and he crumples. They are no longer under his command.

The air moves and Emily transports in a lightning flash with Daniel. They are both in brass armor, Emily familiar with her eagle headdress.

Evan grabs me and we transport on top of the unsuspecting Esmund. Evan's hand is at his throat as he lifts him into the air. Esmund grasps at Evan's hand. He doesn't look so powerful anymore; he seems pale, fragile, and frightened.

"It's your bracelet, Willow! Remove it!" Evan commands.

I yank the silver elastic band from my wrist and call my magick. It flows freely. The warmth of the flow centers me. I'm home in myself again.

Esmund chokes and pulls on Evan's hands. "Call them," Evan sneers. He throws Esmund to the ground. It's like a beacon for the phantoms. They go through him over and over again. They are lost. Their portal is closed, and they are stuck here with no purpose. Their guide has tricked them, and they are angry.

Esmund screams with each pass as black blood wells and pours over his skin.

"Do you trust me?" Evan asks.

I nod. He grabs my hand, and I watch our magick connect. My crown is glowing, my body whole and powerful, covered in my magick. Evan is covered in light too, his horns more prevalent and gleaming atop his head.

"Gather them. Push them into the vessel."

Somehow, Esmund finds the strength to crawl toward a sword lying near a fallen Guardian. Emily jumps on top of Esmund with her staff and sinks it into his stomach. Evan guides our magick to the staff, and the phantoms funnel through it into Esmund. When they've all gone, Emily raises her hands and lightning hits it. What was once Esmund is now a black hole. The staff is gone too, leaving only ash.

I'm being lifted in the air with Evan, our hands still together. His voice echoes in my mind. "Speak to them. Fulfill a new destiny."

"We stand together as a family and as Edayrians united— Goddess and Horned God."

Cheering erupts from most of the crowd below. Others are stunned in place.

"The fighting is over," Evan says in a booming voice.

Sabine is smiling at us as we come to the ground. Emily hugs me while Daniel watches everyone uneasily. I see Eoin and Quinn with their heads together. Tullen, Abby, and Cross are surrounding Rhydian, his head hung low and his shoulders shaking.

I make my way to Rhydian with Emily and Daniel in my wake. Cross taps Rhydian on his shoulder. He turns to me, and everyone moves off to give us some space. The beating of my heart feels off. My voice is paralyzed. We stare at one another, saying everything we can't say. It feels strange to no longer be in each other's mind.

"I—"

"Willow—"

I smile weakly. "I am sorry, Rhydian. I didn't know how else to release you from control—"

He won't look at me. He kicks the ground with his boot. "Willow, I knew he was doing something, I just didn't' know—I was complicit in duty to him. I broke the vow long before you forced me to. He helped me with the corsage." He shakes his head. "I never would have—"

He's taking the blame, but that is Rhydian for you. He wouldn't want me to blame myself. Another form of protection. I step forward, wanting to comfort him and wanting him to comfort me, but he steps back and holds his hands up. "Wait. I—"

"Rhydian. Please," I plead.

"I loved you, but I can't be here. I can't be what you need—"

I want to stop my tears from falling, but I can't. He loved me. Past tense. My heart crumbles; my feelings haven't changed. I want him. I want us. Not us duty-bound by a vow, but by love.

"I've got to go. You won't see me for—a time. I'll send in my resignation to Eoin."

"Please, don't go—alone." Take me with you, I plead with my eyes.

Rhydian looks over his shoulder at Tullen before turning back to me. "I won't."

"Can you do me one favor, and not as an order or command?" Rhydian flinches at my words. "Can you hold off on resigning? Take time, and please check in with Cross or Quinn when you can."

The weight of this moment, his eyes the color of the troubled ocean, and a picture of grief and torment are things I will never forget.

Rhydian closes the space between us and his lips crush mine. His hands are on my face pulling me closer, reaching beyond ourselves. I give in to him and cling to the hope that this isn't goodbye. In the most selfish way, I will it not to be, but not through my magick, just through the panic of my heart.

Rhydian pulls from me and puts his forehead to mine—a last connection before we step apart. There isn't one path, the right path; there is only our path. I know in my heart things between us aren't over permanently, but then again, my heart is hopeful even when it shouldn't be.

"Goodbye, Willow."

I let him go, and it kills me. I hug myself as I watch through my tears him walk to Tullen.

Abby squeezes my shoulder. "Willow?" She watches her brother, then jogs after him. "Wait! Wait, Rhydian!" He stops short, his back to her. "No! This isn't what you want, Rhydian. I know you love her. Father wasn't innocent. This is his own outcome. He would have sacrificed you and anyone to get power, and you know it!" she yells.

He walks away, never turning to face her. Abby's shoulders fall.

The fog on the ground seems to rise to the trees. Rhydian transports away with Tullen.

Eoin starts giving orders behind me to the Guardians with Cross and Thaxam. Bodies are transported to the Hallowed Hall. Death and blood are all around us, all for the normalcy I wanted so badly.

My vision is too blurry to recognize Emily in front of me, but I hear her voice as she holds my shoulders and says, "You are not alone, and you have not lost everything. You are not to blame, Willow."

"Why would you say that?"

"We may not have a blood vow, but I am your best friend. I know you, Willow."

I hug her and let my tears fall.

CHAPTER 27

Fourteen days later . . .

The sun provides welcoming warmth. I soak it up in my black robe, sitting tall in the white plastic chair with my ankles crossed. The grass tickles my feet through my wedge sandals.

The sounds from the stage and podium have become a blur over the last thirty minutes. My mind keeps wandering, replaying all that occurred in the days leading up to now, thinking about the mass funerals and honoring of heroes in a time of change in Edayri. The hum of my magick comforts me, along with the sense of freedom that came when Evan and I released Wiccan royal rule over Edayri from our family all together. The new legion council, the governing body in Edayri, was appointed for its inaugural year. After a full term of three years, an election will be held for the replacement of its members.

The establishment of a militarized police body has been appointed by the legion council and guided by General Ax and Commander Eoin. A charter has been drafted for equalized laws of no harm toward others. Evan and I are no more than figureheads of a royal family and more commonly seen as directed decedents of the Horned God and the Goddess. The idea of a different future here in the Terra realm isn't something I dwell on anymore. This is my life. I turn and see Sabine, Eoin, Quinn, Cross, Thaxam (substantially disguised), and Evan sitting in the riser seats.

I let my mind wander to Rhydian. I haven't spoken to or heard from him since we said goodbye at the manor's ruins. The text message I got from Tullen was brief, but they are okay. They are traveling, not staying put in one place for very long. Tullen revealed that Rhydian is beginning a search for his mother.

My mental fog dissipates when Ms. Chin introduces Lucy, our class valedictorian. Lucy joins her on the stage. Her smile is pasted, her handshake formal. I don't recognize Lucy as my best friend anymore. We haven't spoken much, and when we have, it's not meaningful. She is pulling away from me, but maybe I am doing the same. She approaches the podium and pulls index cards from a pocket in her robe.

Lucy is rejecting the part of herself that I once rebelled against. She and Emily barely speak anymore. I imagine she'll head to the west coast and begin college life we always talked about. I'm happy for her.

"Seniors, today is the day that begins your future. Your hard work, planning, and partying—" a few jocks holler in support, garnering laughs from everyone "—have provided you with a skill set that will grow and expand as you carry it with you on your next adventure. You have choices and know that you can change your mind. Change it frequently, for that matter. Now is the time to stumble and find your way. Find the person you were meant to be without the labels of who you are expected to be. Define who you are by living and trying—"

I'm proud of Lucy. I miss her and cherish our past friendship. Daniel isn't here, and Emily hasn't shared much about his whereabouts. I haven't pressed it. Marco and Emily sit next to each other a few rows ahead.

Ms. Chin begins the procession of students to receive their

diplomas. It's the start of an independent life for so many, and all I recognize is the absence of what was—of my mother, Mrs. Scott, my father, and Rhydian.

I'm toward the end of the procession, and when I walk back to my seat, I can't help but be grateful. Despite it all, I'm here, and my family is expanding. The unwanted is my new normal, and it's growing on me.

Ms. Chin approaches the podium and clears her throat. "Ladies and gentlemen, I now present to you the graduating class of Trinity Cross!"

In celebration with my fellow classmates, I throw my graduation cap high into the sky. Everyone is smiling and laughing.

The sky ripples unnaturally with purple and blue. A loud clap of thunder makes me jump before lightning streaks across the sky followed by another significant boom. The sound echoes over the crowd. To everyone around me it's the start of a storm. To me and everyone from Edayri, it's a warning.

The Convergence has begun.

BONUS: THE KNOT SPELL

WICCAN ROYAL SCEPTER

By knot of one, the spell's begun
By knot of two, it cometh true
By knot of three, so mote it be
By knot of four, this power I store
By knot of five, the spell's alive
By knot of six, this spell I fix
By knot of seven, events I'll leaven
By knot of eight, it will be fate
By knot of nine, what's done is mine

SACRED

THE UNWANTED SERIES, BOOK III

PART I

The cycle of the moon begins where it's desired; for it's the call and forward actions of a waxing moon.

~The Goddess

CHAPTER 1

F iddling with my hands, dressed in my academic black robe, I feel like I'm dressed for a funeral, not graduation. My mind is wandering in the past. The absence of those gone and the changes for those who remain, me included.

I've made it somewhat unscathed through my last year of high school in Chepstow, Massachusetts, all while becoming the Wiccan Queen of Edayri. Two parts of my life collided, and I came out scarred but stronger.

Headmaster Chin approaches the podium and clears her throat.

"Ladies and gentlemen, I now present to you the graduating class of Trinity Cross."

The breath I hold releases.

I try to mirror the joy on my classmates' faces. In celebration, I throw my graduation cap high into the sky. There is a ripple overhead before the bellow of thunder. Lightning streaks across the sky within seconds of another loud crack and boom. Light rain becomes a downpour with a third crack of thunder. So much for the lovely outdoor ceremony and the weather forecast of sunny skies.

The graduation caps and paper programs litter Trinity Cross

High School grounds. I turn from my row and follow my class-mates to meet our friends and family in the stands placed in a square around the campus greenway. I wave to Sabine, Eoin, Quinn, Cross, Thaxam (under substantial glamor), and my Uncle Evan in the metal riser seats on the opposite side of the quad. They are looking up and around, faces full of concern. Except for Evan, whose eyes are closed, and head tilted. Not paying atten-tion, I run into the backside of Coral.

"Sorry," I mumble, but she doesn't acknowledge me because she is looking straight up. A purplish-blue hue moves and swirls fast in the now clouded sky.

Loud voices are incoherent near me, no longer echoing with the cheers and well wishes of graduated classmates and their families. The sky crackles and reveals a kaleidoscopic pattern of symbols. They appear and disappear in the clouds.

Magick is humming like a vibration in my arms and legs. A supercharge of power. I suspect, without looking down, my magick is revealing itself on my skin to everyone around me, the glowing patterns on my skin, and the crown that floats above my head. I panic before scoffing at myself as if anyone is paying attention to me with everything else happening around us. Regardless, I mentally pull it back in with a concentrated inhale. The storm is its beacon—a calling. I stand still, trying again to regain control of the power within my veins.

I'm losing my mind. This is only a storm. We're not in Edayri, where magick is standard. The weather in Chepstow, Massachusetts, at the end of May, is unpredictable. I remember the one time it snowed. I shake out my hands, grateful I can hide my magick from outsiders.

Rain isn't anything to get worked up about, right?

I walk to the side of Coral and pass her to find Sabine running toward us. Her red hair is no longer pinned back, but wild in the wind. Lightning strikes and smacks the ground, throwing me and scattering those nearby. I shake my head hard to rid the clouded vision, along with the muffled sound of ringing in my ears. But the burning smell invades my nose and makes me choke.

I kick my feet at the grass that is smoldering closest to me. Black burned patches of grass surround the quad. Black smoke surrounds me. Vertigo strikes hard, and I roll onto my hands and knees. I push down my overwhelming need to heave as I stumble to stand.

People are running, and the first thing I hear is Sabine's muffled scream of my name. Then a roar of an enormous wild cat? Everything is off balance. My hands are numb and shaking. I pop my jaw with an exaggerated drop of my chin, and sounds become clearer. I shield my eyes from the now pelting rain and see a dark fissure in the quad.

Phantoms.

I remember the Phantoms rising from the earth near McKinnon Manor. Are they back?

No. They can't be.

The gate closed with the death of Mr. Boward. This rationale doesn't stop my mind from running wild, staring into the open wound in the ground of dark mud. My heart is thundering in my chest. Again, the roar of a cat echoes, followed by more screams. I buckle over to a sharp pain in my stomach. An additional pulse and pull with a new crack of lightning.

"Help! Help me!"

The shrill scream is nearest to me. It's Coral. I barely find her with the black graduation robe and her dark hair. Dark smoke concealing her only. It's her pale hands that I see first clutching into the side of the muddy ground, struggling to climb out. I focus on the bright blue sash of our school colors. On my knees I slide forward, and I stretch out.

"Grab my hand!"

A cramp tugs on my insides, but I keep my arm outstretched.

"I can't! Willow, please . . . Help me!" Coral cries.

My shoulder pops when I thrust my magick down my arm, into my hand. It pushes back, pain twisting and radiating throughout my body, a rejection. Black smoke rushes at me like a magickal whip, stinging me.

Yelling in my head, I command my magick to obey my intentions. We get tossed in the air together, limbs smacking and flying in a heap of mud; my back slams into the ridge of the sidewalk near the front office of the school.

"Ah!"

Stunned, I curl into myself. The pain is spreading through me, the sting the smoke. I can't breathe. I reach for my magick, finding its weak tether. I must pull it—force it.

Tick . . . tock.

"Willow? Hold on," Sabine says. The warmth of her magick flows into me and eases the sharp pain.

Sirens sound in the distance, and a few people are running toward us with umbrellas. I turn to Coral, who is lying prone with her hands over her face.

"Can you move?" I ask her as a muscle in my back tightens.

She nods, and we move from our knees and scoot under the closest awning. Coral's parents rush to her the black smoke vanishes into the ground. Sabine is wet from head to toe, whereas Coral's parents are untouched by the rain with their umbrellas.

"We need to go. It isn't safe here. Cross and Quinn should have the SUV waiting for us."

"Thank you for your help," Coral's father says with a weak smile, watching me before he hugs Coral tight again. Her stepmother pats Coral on her back in a stiff, forced way.

With half-lidded eyes, she says, "I'm so glad you are both fine."

Despite her wrinkled forehead, I doubt her sincerity. Her voice is more penetrating than I expected and almost accusatory.

"I'm Vanessa, Coral's stepmother. I learned about Willow's father, your son's passing? Sorry for your loss."

She reaches for Sabine's hand, but Sabine keeps both her hands on my shoulders.

"Thank you. He was my son-in-law."

Sabine plasters on her political smile, and in one minute, we have said goodbye and passed under the arched front gates of Trinity Cross High School. This isn't how I thought I would exit high school for the last time, but then again, why would this day be typical?

My stomach twists with a new roar of thunder that claps in the distance. Sabine's face contorts. She senses it, too. The surrounding air is electric, and the hair on my arms rises and prickles. Both my and Sabine's magick flickers to the surface of our skin and it fades just as fast. Sabine steadies herself on a nearby car.

"You feel that?"

"Yes."

Quinn pulls up in the SUV. I shrug off the muddy graduation robe and get into the vehicle.

"Let's go!" Cross yells.

Quinn maneuvers through the parking lot. We're on the main road in less than a minute, passing the firetrucks and police who are arriving at the high school.

"That's one hell of a graduation, Willow," Cross laughs.

Despite the good nature of his comment, Sabine scowls. "Those patterns in the sky are Druid symbols."

Again, my stomach twists, and I lean over in my seat. Quinn's eyebrows furrow as he stares straight ahead.

"We all sense it. What is this?" I ask.

"I'm afraid this is the beginning of the Convergence. Esmund has hastened what we feared. I expected we'd have more time, years even. The legion council and Evan began preparing for—"

At the mention of Mr. Boward's name, my thought is of Rhydian. Is he okay? Does he realize what's going on? I hang onto the last moment we shared a kiss that made my toes curl and my stomach drop.

He left us—me; he left me.

I sigh before I swallow hard and focus on her mentioning Mr.

Boward. He planned to kill me and so many others. In the end, I turned it on him, which resulted in his death instead. Rhydian's father's death . . . Rhydian must hate me. My heart squeezes in my chest, the familiar pain radiates through me, and my hands ball up into fists. Every time he enters my mind, I regret my actions in breaking the blood vow. His absence, another type of constant suffering.

My thoughts go wild in the vehicle despite Sabine talking about the next steps and her assumptions about what is happening. The Convergence is here, and again, my worlds are colliding. This is inevitable, right?

Quinn pulls into the drive of my father's house—my house. The protection enchantments surround the house. The lawn wavers as if surrounded by a bubble, a type of iridescent glow from the sun's rays escaping the clouds. I could never visibly distinguish them before. Does that mean anyone can see them? Is this magick visible to everyone?

We drive through them. My stomach releases, but the knot replaces with a pounding pulse in my head. I exhale and shake my hands from their tight grip. I look up to find Theon and Ax standing in the garage.

My immediate thought is: Where are Evan and Commander Eoin?

CHAPTER 2

W hen Theon and Ax enter the house from the garage, they hardly acknowledge us pulling in. Ax ducks so his horns don't catch on the door frame while entering the house. A blood demon is a sight you don't easily forget, considering how enormous he is.

Quinn touches the button on the roof of the SUV that closes the garage door.

"Well, this was fun."

Sabine gets out of the car and slams the door. The sound echoes. I gnash my teeth as I jump, still cold, wet, and muddy. I brush past her when we enter the house into the laundry room. Grabbing a towel, I wipe my face and wring my hair. Everything appears excessive, not only the rain and mud, but the surrounding air. I feel heavy. I take off my shoes with my toe.

Can't I have just one regular event in my life? I know the answer, watching Cross and Quinn toss each other towels.

Absolutely not.

Sabine waves her hand, and she dries her clothes as magick moves up her body. As magick reaches her hair, Cross whistles low. Her hair is turning white.

"Goddess, stop!" I shriek.

Sabine looks over her shoulder, the widening eyes as we watch her red hair turn white. She clutches her hands into fists, to stop the magick. But it doesn't completely stop what's already in motion. She now has stark white strands at her temple and crown. The once vibrant red is dull, mixed with white hair throughout. She resembles the part of my grandmother, now more than ever.

I'm not sure of the sound escaping my open mouth. Shock or amusement, but either way, both Quinn and Cross echo me.

Sabine squints her eyes at us before; she gives a grim smile because now we are all in a full-on belly laugh between me, Quinn, and Cross. Are we laughing or crying?

"You're laughing at me?"

"So, do you typically magick your hair color?" I ask.

The rumbles of laugher slowly die away.

Sabine replies, "An afterthought, but I've always had red hair. I'm going to have to concentrate on not using magick. Magick is not working correctly with these rifts." She throws her hands up. "I'm sure it's not safe to transport. We are not testing that out!"

"So, you know what this is? What did you call them, rifts? At graduation? The storm broke the earth apart . . . I had déjà vu from the Phantoms."

"Me too," Quinn replies. His eyes soften. He knows the part I relive. A shiver trails up my spine along with a squeeze and ache—Rhydian.

I depart for my room to shower and change out of the wet and muddy clothes.

Getting dressed, I bend forward, and my muscles strain and pinch. I twist side to side to surrender the weight and pressure of the events, but nothing pops or releases. There is no relief as I stretch. My magick is under the surface of my skin. Usually, my magick is bright and vibrant, but now my eyes strain to see the flow of patterns from my magick. The connected hum isn't strong, but it's there.

I look at myself in the mirror before leaving my room. I'm

not noticeably changed on the outside, but on the inside, I grasp the boldness and courage I need to face the unknown. Downstairs, I overhear voices in the formal living room and gravitate toward them versus standing at the top of the stairs.

"Quinn, comms are still down," Cross says. He taps his wrist cuff, but nothing happens.

"Commander and Evan transported to Edayri, at the beginning of the rifts. I don't suggest we try. The ability to control magick is . . . Well, is clearly off," Quinn replies with a small smile toward Sabine and her now white streaks of hair.

"The Guardian wrist cuff is not working?" Sabine huffs. "This is unfortunate."

That doesn't mean all communication is absent. Holding my ruined phone, I hold up my finger and rush into father's office. Ax and Theon sit in the wing-backed chairs in front of the gas fireplace.

"What do you need?" Ax asks, joining me at the desk.

"Dad always had a backup cell phone," I say. Rumbling in the first drawer of his desk, which is full of pens and minor items. I find the cell phone, plug it in, and the boot-up begins.

"What are you doing?" Theon asks. When Sabine, Quinn and Cross join us in the office, I smirk.

"The twenty-first-century magick of all teenagers. Let's text and get some information."

At least I hope this works. It beats sitting and doing nothing.

Theon rolls his eyes. "It's just a cell phone."

"Not just any cell phone. One magicked for non-regional and realm communication."

Quinn explains how Rhydian had magicked my phone number. It enabled me to talk and text my friends from either realm, no matter where I am physically.

"If I import my information onto this phone, it could work," I say to no one in particular. At least I can reach Emily and Marco and find out what's going on with these storms and rifts. The hair on the back of my neck rises and the sensation of electricity runs down my back. Possibly these are aftershocks of what happened in Edayri with the Phantoms.

"How long is it going to take?" Cross asks.

"I need to charge up this backup phone, and then I can transfer . . . It will take a bit of time."

Sabine is pacing back and forth in the office's doorway. I've never known Sabine to be impatient. But I don't blame her. I'm impatient too, but at least I have something keeping me less idle —a task, a plan.

Goddess, I hope this works.

Maybe.

Cross and Quinn sit in front of the long windows for a game of chess at the small table. Whereas Ax and Theon have taken their residence in the wing-backed chairs. Theon has a book in his hands, reading. Ax has leaned his head back and closed his eyes. He appears peaceful, the huge red demon with horns on top of his head. He seems out of place, and yet Duke is at his feet sleeping.

Time is slow sitting in my father's chair for a half-hour, watching the old phone blink while accepting all the data from my phone.

"How can you all just sit?" Sabine says.

Ax, with shut eyes, responds, "Do you have a better idea?"

Quinn responds, "We suspect the Commander and Evan are in Edayri coordinating efforts. You sense it, right? The rifts of magick moving like tectonic plates shifting here in the Terra realm, like a magickal earthquake?"

Theon's half-closed eyes reveal his exhaustion before he continues. "Evan told us to come here. So, we did. Brought back the Ford Escalade we drove."

Sabine stops pacing. "Willow, try to move something. Your magick is the strongest here, blessed by the Goddess, the Wiccan Queen. Do nothing to yourself or others directly, we learned that lesson." She twists her white hair around her finger, and Cross smirks.

"Why? This changes nothing."

Does it? I could help others if I could use my magick reliably with nothing strange happening.

My eyes gravitate to a small porcelain flower vase on the side table next to the wingback chairs.

Tick-tock.

The hum rises when I call to my magick. But it's off, not the soothing liquid flow that I usually receive in my veins. It's a staccato movement. The echo that only I hear isn't a hum, but like the static, you sometimes hear on the radio. I focus on the flow to calm it, and it gets a little smoother. Sabine and all of them are watching me. I slowly twist my steady hand and pick up the flower vase with the air surrounding it, to move it to the matching side table of the opposite wingback chair. The vase moves, hovers, and then floats between the two chairs. I sense the pulse, the interruption. I force the air before—

Boom.

"Dammit!"

"Well, one thing is for certain: we have magick, but it's unpredictable. Or . . ." Sabine says.

"Or what?" Cross asks.

"Magick is disappearing?"

Sabine's face drops, and her eyes shut as she looks away from me. Her shoulders shake a little, only I notice the bend in my stoic grandmother's back. My desire for an everyday life seems so long ago now. The idea of magick leaving isn't one I'm ready to take as truth. I'm used to who I am with magick and how it makes me feel strong, empowered, confident. Part of it ties me to my father and my mother. If it somehow disappears . . .

"It's possible, Willow," Sabine says, wholly composed now. Her emotions are in check. How can she do that? I want to yell and cry, but what would it solve?

A phone signal radiates in the room. Charging is complete, and notification beeps sound one after another. Sabine hovers over my shoulder.

"Who are ya going to text?" Cross asks.

Why is it my first instinct to check on Rhydian? He's made it clear he will not reach out to me, but it doesn't mean I stop caring. The twist and ache in my stomach, the pounding at my temples, is something I'm used to. There is a part of my brain that wars over respecting his decision and being angry at him because of the rejection that I feel from him needing space. Is it wrong to worry about him in this crazy storm?

I stare at the smartphone in my hands, and it makes a choice for me when a text message appears.

Eoin: *Do not use magick, do not transport. This is a broad public message.*

I read it out loud and text back.

Willow: *What is going on? Do you need Sabine and me in Edayri? Ax, Theon, Cross and Quinn are here too.*

Cross is now pacing back and forth in front of me. It is like we are awaiting news in the lobby of a hospital. The notification ping brings everyone's attention back to the phone.

Eoin: *No! Stay put. People are being lost in the magickal rifts. I cannot do my job if I worry about you. Stay put until it's safer.*

I repeat the response.

Theon throws his hands in the air. Ax grunts before sitting.

"What are you thinking?" I ask Sabine and Quinn, standing in front of me.

She hugs her waist. "Guess we wait for now. You like the idea as much as I do. I don't know what we could walk into. We need to stay here."

Nodding in agreement, but even staying put doesn't mean I can't reach out or know what's going on. "I'm going to text my friends."

Sabine leaves with Ax and Theon to show them where the guest rooms are. Cross and Quinn stay and play more chess. I curl up in a chair that faces the window and stare at the phone in my hand.

I want to text Rhydian. Instead, I reach out to Emily.

Willow: *Em, are you okay? Daniel? Marco? Any news?*

Em: *We are at my house right now. Marco can't control his shifting, which, at least at my home, isn't problematic—for the moment.*

Willow: *That can't be good.*

Em: *No, it isn't, but at least we are shielding him from—*

A minute passes with no response.

Willow: *Em?*

Em: *Gotta go. Be safe. Check-in later.*

Willow: *Okay, you too.*

Duke is curled up at my feet, and I stroke his fur with my hanging foot as I stare at the empty screen. My fingers are working faster than my brain. I type a message to Rhydian.

Willow: *Are you okay? In Chepstow, at the house. Would you mind letting me know if you're okay?*

The message is delivered, and within only a few seconds it shows as read. I wait, chewing my fingernail. The read receipt stays static, no motion, or blinking cursor to show an active response is coming. Does he care about how I'm doing? Gah, I'm so selfish. I wonder if he's hurt or something? Before my mind takes the swan dive into the dark abyss of worse possibilities, the phone pings, alerting me to a new text message.

I wave off Cross's grunt.

Rhydian: *Yes. Crazy storms. Are you okay?*

He's asking about me. Me. I type back quickly.

Willow: *I'm okay. Magick isn't working right. The storm created chaos at graduation, including a massive hole in the school's quad.*

I wait for what seems like a few minutes, but it's only been thirty seconds. There isn't a response.

I type, *I miss you.* And it blinks back at me, mocking me. I delete it; I can't send it.

The phone buzzes in my hand. It's Rhydian. He's calling me! Quinn and Cross turn toward the sound. I look away. I should have called, but I'm a coward. My heart pounds, and I wait for the second buzz before I answer it.

"Hey," I say, but the voice that reaches my ears is not the one I am expecting.

It's Tullen. He's been with Rhydian since he left Edayri.

Before I hear what he is saying, I ask him to hold on for a minute. Hitting mute, I stand and walk out of the office, away from Quinn and Cross. I needed the voice to be Rhydian. Taking two calming breaths, holding in the tears that threaten to fall, I sit on the stairs.

"Hi, Tullen. Are you okay?" Hopefully, he doesn't hear the disappointment in my voice.

"Well, it's relative, but yes, we are fine. I'm waiting for orders from the Commander and right now it is to stay put. We haven't heard yet from anyone else."

I'm the first.

"Where are you? Are you in Edayri or still—"

"Actually, we are in Tulsa, Oklahoma. We were making our way out of town when the storms began here too, so we're at a restaurant waiting it out," Tullen says.

"Tullen, is Rhydian? I just, yeah, I—"

"He's better, but it's a process. Be patient with him and me," Tullen says.

"With you?"

"I have this notion that I deserted you. I know I didn't, but the global storms have me second guessing everything at the moment."

"Sabine suspects it's the Convergence, too. Do you think so?"

Tullen is reticent and then he continues. "I think so, yes. Mr. Boward accelerated it, and I think it's started. The realms are unstable, so magick is volatile, transporting isn't an option right now."

I swallow, and my throat is dry.

"Tullen, you didn't desert me," I say. After all, I asked him to take care of Rhydian and go with him.

"Thank you for that. If you hear from Quinn or Cross, can you tell them we'll be in touch as soon as we can?"

My heart beats faster. "Does that mean you're heading toward Chepstow? Quinn and Cross are here with me."

"No, Rhydian has another destination first. I can't tell you more, but we'll be there before you know it."

My mouth is braver than my brain. "Can I speak with Rhydian? Is he there?" My heart is loud in my ears. I hear a muffled sound of a hand over the phone. "Tullen? Are you there?" The instant sinking sensation in my stomach tells me that Rhydian is next to him.

"Willow, I need to let you go. Rhydian will call you when he can, okay? Be well."

The call ends too soon.

I stare at the phone, willing it to ring again, but it doesn't. I toss it on the foyer table before I walk back into the office.

"How is he? Or more to the point, are you okay?" Quinn asks.

I don't know if they heard much of the conversation. I try my best to smile and pull off the outer appearance of being fine, even though I'm anything but. It's nice that they are here. I don't like to be alone in this big house.

"I'm the same—no better, no worse. And they are okay. Supposedly, he'll call me when he can, but I suspect that won't be for a while. It was Tullen that I was talking with."

"I figured as much." Quinn walks to me and holds my shoulders. "I'm sorry that he left."

Cross is studying the sky from the windows. "Right now, we need to keep our heads about ourselves."

Can I do that? Keep my head when it comes to magick and to Rhydian?

Tick-tock.

CHAPTER 3

The doorbell echoes through the house. I rush from my bedroom to the top of the stairs, where I find Daniel holding a box with a red ribbon. He's smiling and politely talking with Sabine. His face lights up when he sees me, and despite his polite smile, the corners of his mouth pull as if he can smile more. I laugh and run down the stairs. Happy for the freedom from my insane boredom of this crazy day.

"What are you doing here?" I ask.

Sabine scolds me playfully, "Is that any way to greet a friend who's come to see you?"

Daniel stands a little straighter before he says, "Actually, I was asking your grandmother to get you out of the house."

I look from Sabine to Daniel and back to Sabine. "Really? You're okay with me going out with the storms?"

I say storms, but the weather has receded around Chepstow. Storms now are code for the Convergence. I assumed we were under house arrest until we got further news from Eoin.

"Why not? Our plans following graduation were disrupted, so you might as well enjoy some time with your friends. Just be careful and stay close to town." Sabine walks away.

I point to the box in Daniel's hands. "What do you have there?"

He hands me the box. It has some weight to it.

"Just a little something I thought you would enjoy. Not every day we graduate from high school." His face, although happy, is a mask. He wasn't at graduation. I know why, but it still pulls at my heart when I think about it.

"May I open it now?"

"Ah, absolutely." He stands back and watches as I pull the ribbon and lift the delicate top of the box. Moving the tissue paper, I find a journal with my name engraved.

"Daniel, this is beautiful."

My fingers touch the smooth leather and trace the indentations that spell my name. I set the box on the foyer table. I open the journal. The spine cracks and moans as I turn the pages to the thick, blank paper.

"Drawing pencils are at the bottom of the box."

I want to say more, but I don't. I touch the smooth pages.

"It's a sketchpad and a journal. I figure it might be a good idea for you to get your thoughts down and out of your head. I remember when you used to draw during Junior year. You loved it."

It's the most thoughtful gift I've received. He's right. To get these rumbling thoughts out of my head. I lay the sketchbook next to the box. Stepping into Daniel, I hug him.

"Thank you."

Two brief words say so much and so little, for the boy who I once loved.

"Willow, let's get out of the house. Go to A Cup of Joe's? Anything is better than seeing you mope."

"I'm not moping. Well, not a lot anyway."

His eyes are assessing. And I can't help but laugh. He taps me playfully on the shoulder.

"Okay, fine. Let's go to A Cup of Joe's and catchup."

"How about you drive."

I nod my head to the back of the house. Daniel, being the car guy he is, can't resist breaking into a big grin. I could have sworn I overheard him say, "Hells yeah!" In the garage, he carefully assesses the six bays with various cars, including mine, that my father gave me. Daniel walks over to the dark gray Audi R8 and claps his hands together and rubs them vigorously.

"Okay, fine."

I grab the keys off the key hook by the front door and toss them over to him.

Getting in the car, it still has the new car smell. His grin is so wide it's hard not to laugh as I lean back into the curve of the seat. He's being careful as we slip out of the neighborhood. On the main road, he puts the pedal to the metal, and we accelerate with the easy speed of the car.

I roll down the window part way and the weight of the day lifts despite all the unknowns. The fresh air of new blooms in Massachusetts fills the car. Summer is almost here.

"So, what do you think of the car?"

"I think I need to take it further than A Cup of Joe's, like we need to drive all around. And maybe even find some nice straightaways."

It's easy hanging out with Daniel. He's how I remember him when we were dating, more like his old self, more comfortable in his own skin. My heart warms at his smile and his bright eyes. Not that long ago that he died right in front of me. Then Lucy brought him back as an einherjar soldier. It was Lucy's first time using her magick as a half valkyrie, but she did it with Emily's help as a full and trained valkyrie. However, it didn't turn out the way Lucy wanted for her boyfriend. This only drove them further apart. He's now under Emily's tutelage, since Lucy still doesn't want any part of her magickal heritage.

As he drives, I stare out the window. We enter the town center and see people shopping and continuing on as normal in the twilight of evening. I'm not sure what I expected, but business as usual was not it. It was as if nothing out of the normal occurred earlier today, despite the global news reporting it all.

"Strange, huh?"

I turn to Daniel. "What's strange?"

"How the world carries on, unaware of the changes."

"I'm not sure it's unaware, according to the news. But yeah, I get your meaning."

Daniel's face drops as he slows down to turn into the square ahead. "Do you? I guess you do, in hiding who you are. I'm doing the same. My parents think I'm depressed and are ready to put me in therapy. Emily keeps saying I need to regain my humanity, but I need to pull away from them."

"Where do they think you are?"

"The only lie I've told them is that I've joined up with the Army. Cross helped Emily out with that. And I have credentials until the next lie happens. It's brilliant, but . . ." His face loses all emotion. The wheel turning in his hands, he looks away. He's always been close with his family. It makes my heart twist for him to leave them in such a way and plan his fake death in order to cut ties.

"But it's a lie."

"Yeah. I don't enjoy doing this to my family. The fact is, I will not age. Did you know that? My aging has slowed exponentially that I will be here when everyone has died." He shakes his head. "It's a lot to come to terms with this rebirth; it's wild and well, I guess it is what it is."

I thoroughly understand Daniel and feel connected. We both are on different paths from where we started last school year; a lifetime ago.

We pull up into a parking space near A Cup of Joe's. It's a small coffee shop that sits next to an old, independent bookshop. It's been here for decades. The couches remind me of a swank old gentlemen's club. Everything is dark wood and forest green, remarkably different from coffee chains. It's unique in its own quirky way.

"So, what are you going to get?" Daniel asks me.

"I think I'm venturing out with a caramel macchiato."

"Oh, that sounds so good. I think I will do the same. Do they have those little scones too?"

I forgot how much he loves blueberry scones. We're teasing each other as we walk into the door and the little bell jingles at the top hinge, wiping away the heavy air of the day.

I hear her voice before I see her. It's Lucy. Daniel's shoulders square and his back straightens. We walk over to the counter and put in our orders for scones and caramel macchiatos. As we turn down the counter, there sits the group: Lucy, Emily, Coral, and Marco.

Emily waves at us. And I look at Daniel, who shrugs, and we walk over to where they are.

"Hey, guys, out for a coffee run?" Coral asks.

"Is it that obvious?" Daniel teases Coral, who immediately smirks.

Lucy shifts in her seat. Her hands touch Marco, who she's sitting next to. He nods at us and leans into Lucy. That's odd. The brief smile she puts on is strained, not authentic. I falter in returning the gesture.

"It's good to see you, Daniel. How are you doing? All good?" Coral asks.

"Yeah, everything is fine. Just thought I'd hang with Willow and grab a drink."

"Obviously," Coral replies. She smirks, and Daniel grins back. Daniel turns his attention to Lucy, who seems to wait with wide eyes before he turns to me and says he's going to check on the order.

Standing there, I'm an outsider. I'm between an invisible wall of tension, one side is Daniel, and the other is Lucy. It's at odds with how it used to be around our friend group.

"So—graduation was crazy," I say to no one directly.

"Yeah, you could say that again," Coral replies. She shrugs nonchalantly, drinking from a mug.

Emily nods, but keeps looking at her cell phone.

"Um. Lucy, your address at graduation was great, by the way."

"Thanks. I was nervous at the beginning but got into the swing."

We flow into simple conversation. Coral and Marco leave for the bathroom when Daniel returns. His stone face, stare and shoulder snub all directed at Marco are surprising.

Lucy says, "Strange huh, how friendships change?"

"What?"

"Ours, there's . . . it's like time has fast forwarded and made things complicated. Sometimes I wish we could go back to prom or before. What about for you, the Senior Camp trip?"

I don't think I would change it. That's when I met Rhydian. I cringe, thinking of Tertium, the blood demon who hunted me in the woods. The first attempt on my life. I nod at Lucy when Daniel stands next to me.

"Yeah, too bad we can't live in the past."

Although his voice quips, it's not accusing or mean.

"Change sometimes can be enlightening. Take graduation, for example. On the news, the conspiracy theories are all over," Lucy says. "Magick is not something that will be hidden for long."

"Yeah, the storm was crazy, magickal or not."

Lucy's stare makes me squirm. I sit on the edge of a large wingback chair. I look over at Emily, and she shrugs. Her demeanor is at ease, but her eyes wander and assess everything around us.

The girl behind the counter calls mine and Daniel's names for our order. Relieved to be saved from the awkwardness, I turn toward the coffee counter, but I trip on the corner of the claw foot wingback chair. Daniel turns and reaches for me, but it's Marco who is lightning fast. I fall onto my knee and bounce up into Marco's arms, his hands clutching around my waistline.

"Whoa."

Marco tries to spin me away from Daniel as he spills our

drinks, but the hot coffee hits my back before going down my leg.

"Get your hands off her!" Daniel shoves his way in between me and Marco.

Lucy is up on her feet. "Oh, good grief, Daniel. Get a grip, it was an accident!"

They argue, and my back is burning. I pull my wet shirt away from my back.

It's Coral who gives me a hand towel. "They're remaking the drinks. Are you okay?"

"Shit, Will. Give me that. I'm sorry." Daniel is behind me with the towel touching my lower back.

"It'll be . . . Oh, damn," I gasp. The burning sensation increases to fire like with the pressure of the towel in Daniel's hand. Did I just see smoke?

"Willow, are you burned?" I hear Marco's tenor voice over Daniel's blockade.

Pulling my shirt away from my skin, it remains hot and wet.

"It's fine," I say to Marco, and repeat myself to Daniel.

I summon my magick into the area of my back and command for my skin to cool. Remembering that I can't use magick, I wince, trying not to show the pain. Marco has an extra hand towel and hands it to me to blot the liquid from my ruined shirt.

"You've done enough," Daniel says to him and grabs the towel. Marco lifts his hands in surrender.

"Whatever, man. What is wrong with you?" Marco turns to Lucy before he walks toward the counter with his mug.

"It was an accident," Lucy says.

"Don't go there, Lucy," Daniel warns.

The tension between Lucy and Daniel surmounts, and the surrounding air thickens. I didn't know they still had so much anger between them.

Putting my hand on Daniel's shoulder. I say as reassuringly as I can, "I'm fine. It's not a big deal. It's just a shirt."

"See, she said no big deal. Why are you so butt-hurt over it, anyway?" Lucy lowers her voice. "Not like Willow can't heal herself."

Emily is the only one still seated. She hasn't said two words or even moved from her relaxed state in the chair. It's like she's watching a movie as her head turns from side to side, watching the four of us. It is very unlike Emily to observe from a distance, especially a scene like this. Everyone else who was watching us seem to be back in their own conversations now.

"It's one storm after another," Coral says, when she sits down. "Willow, how are you always in the middle of it?"

"Good question. I don't intend to be."

Lucy's mocking huff pierces my heart a little. It's not as if I seek this stuff . . . or do I?

The barista calls our names again, and Daniel and I go to gather our order with no accidents, ready to leave the awkwardness.

As we leave, I say, "Nice to see you all. Emily, call me."

Emily stays focused on her smartphone. Maybe already texting me?

We close the car doors and set our drinks in the cup holders.

"What was that?" Daniel gestures to the storefront of A Cup of Joe's. "Lucy, Marco? She has changed so much, and I wish I didn't hate her. Hate's a strong word, but I don't like who's she's become."

"You know they aren't together, right?"

Lucy is putting on a show. Marco didn't return any of it, but maybe I misread it? That would be so weird if they were something. I shake my head to rid my mind of the little conspiracy theory. I don't disagree with Daniel, picturing Lucy picking me up to go to school. Us laughing, me making fun of her musical choices. We rarely speak now. Our friendship is changing and has evolved to only acquaintances. She's changed so much I don't recognize her actions anymore. Is it the same for Daniel and Marco? Is that the way of things? The gradual evolution of our friend group upon leaving high school.

"Yeah, I know, but Marco knows better. They both can push my buttons."

Daniel drives us back to my house and we hang out for another hour before he leaves. We avoid discussing our changing friend group.

CHAPTER 4

My head sinks into my pillow, which cradles my weary thoughts like a shield. I stare at the text message from Rhydian and wonder if it was him, or was it Tullen who replied from earlier in the day? I torture myself by scanning through pictures of Rhydian and myself on my phone. The picture Eoin took of us before we left for prom, and the few quick pics during it I took of us. If I had only made him stay, events would have unfolded differently, instead of it becoming the worst prom in history.

Tick-tock.

I shake my head at the image that led to Rhydian leaving. The pressure at my temples is building. I exhale to combat the tension in my neck and shoulders. The thrumming pain in my head, the internal pain, and the squeezing of my chest are all consequences of the broken vow. It didn't just cause Rhydian's suffering; its residual pain is mine too. It pulls and taunts me.

It isn't only a broken heart.

I've had a breakup before, but the physical reaction differs from anything I've experienced before. The only thought I can summon to comfort myself with is that it must serve a purpose. It has to, right? Is it possible we will move beyond what's happened? Will he forgive me? Do I want his forgiveness? His father's intention was to sacrifice me, but he was gambling on the life of his son, too.

I hate that man. The conquest of power poisoned Esmund. He didn't care who he hurt.

Touching a picture of Rhydian on my phone, my finger slides along the smooth surface, aching for a genuine connection, a physical touch, or even the timbre of his voice. I set my phone on my night table and turn on my side and pull my blankets up under my chin.

"Rhydian . . . I'm sorry," I whisper into the dark of my room. Calling to my magick, I try to force myself to sleep within its comfort. My breath is measured and relaxed with each inhale and exhale.

I drift.

The grass is dense and colorful beneath my bare feet. The moonlight is bright, and I hear the fairies and their music off in the distance. He's here. I see the outline of the blanket ahead. Joy is a liquid elixir that floods through me. The tall reeds are further away from where I stand; I'm near the Lunar Falls. Taking large steps toward the blanket, I turn to see where he is.

"Rhydian? Where are you?" I call out.

"What? I'm right here," he responds.

Behind me, he grabs my waist, pulls me into him, and kisses my neck. His hands on my stomach are warm. I put my hands on his. I turn in his arms and revel in this moment. His face is unmoving, eyes dark, and his forehead touches mine.

The tear that escapes is one I don't wipe away. Blood and dirt cover us both. We are at McKinnon manor on the grounds. The surrounding has changed.

This is our goodbye. My heartbreak is instantaneous. The kiss I desperately want to remember, but can't. I relive this memory night after night. His hands on my face, the tilt of my chin.

The picture changes, as it has before in my dream. It's the

back of him walking away from me; his head hangs from his shoulders. Tullen walking at his hip. I could have called his name, reached for him, but his image waivers in my tear-filled eyes.

The wound is deeper than I want to admit, even to myself. So many nights my dreams vary, but they always end with Rhydian leaving and me doing nothing.

"Willow. You must stop."

Startled. I turn toward the familiar voice.

It's my uncle Evan. His disheveled appearance familiar except for the plaid pajamas and fluffy unicorn slippers on his feet.

"Goddess, I want to," I reply.

"No, you don't."

He's right, I don't.

The surroundings change, and I'm in a fluffy pink cloud chair across from Evan, who lays back with his arms behind his head in a bright white room.

"Edayri is collapsing into itself. Ol' Esmund was successful in his attempt. Alas, what he didn't know was how unstable he made the entire realm."

"So, you know what is happening?"

"Are you listening at all? Is it your generation, or do I need to do this in a 30-second video, so you'll pay attention?"

"Funny."

I wait, but it's my huff that finally has Evan talking again.

"Edayri is collapsing, Willow. Everyone is being displaced. It's a merger of sorts. Edayrian's are plopping into Terra like the outsiders we are. People here are confused, the Edayrian's dazed —wait, is that a movie?" He looks ridiculous crossing his unicorn feet, then, shrugging his shoulders, he continues. "The point is Edayrian's are refugees now, and they have no option to return, because what's left is dying."

"Edayri is dying?"

Evan's playfulness turns serious.

"Can't you feel it? Beyond your pain of the vow and your

broken heart? The countdown, the inevitability of it all? I feel it. I assumed as the embodiment of the Goddess, you would too."

"The countdown? I'm not the embodiment of the Goddess—blessed only, Evan," I say, ignoring his comment about my broken heart. I can't deny it, so why bother? Coward. Is the pulse, the beat, the flutter I feel what he's speaking of? I haven't paid it much attention, thinking it was part of the rift. It's erratic. It is a countdown?

Tick-tock.

Evan's finger swings back and forth to the clock feeling. His eyes wide and waiting.

"Yes, I felt it. I wasn't sure if it had to do with the other—you know, the vow. Him leaving." My uncle's eyes are staring through me, and I glance away from him.

I shake my head trying to push my emotions to the back. "It's stupid. Can I help? I can't sit in this house waiting."

Evan doesn't move. The stare down is creepy, his eyes moving as if something is playing out in his mind. His half grin plastered on his face.

"Evan?"

He breaks his trance with a quick shake of his head. "Go about a normal day. See your friends, be in town. Take Theon with you wherever you go tomorrow."

"Where were you? Like, just now?"

"Seriously, I'm right in front of you," Evan replies. "Your ability to stay focused is almost as bad as mine."

We both laugh, his booming over mine. Am I losing my mind?

"Can't I help you in Edayri? Surely I'm more useful there."

"You're useful wherever you are. Have patience, my sweet niece."

Evan smiles, we stand, and I hug him. For a flash, it's like my father hugging me. "Willow, you are anything but a coward. Flex your badass side. You're stronger than you're allowing yourself to be. Don't be what another wants or demands. Be you. That's more than enough," he says.

Light is coming through my curtains, and I wake up. I stretch and the tension in my neck and shoulders are gone. It may be the first night I've slept completely through the night. Duke isn't in my room. My phone shines back to me the time—it's 9:30; I slept in.

Rubbing my eyes, I recall everything so clearly. I remember speaking with Evan. Throwing my covers back, I get ready for the day and to go into town with Theon.

CHAPTER 5

Downstairs, Sabine is opening and closing cabinets in the kitchen. She has a bowl, flour, and milk on the counter.

"What do you need?" I ask.

She turns with her hand on her hip. "Caffeine, for starters. I've got this part. Oh, of course. By chance, how do you operate that intricate-looking machine?" she asks.

A look in her weary eyes says caffeine stat. It's great to know she is like the rest of us and needs a jumpstart in the morning. I open the cabinet next to the cappuccino machine on the counter.

"We call her Fancy, and yes, I steam milk and make coffee and teas. Father used to say I would be the best-trained barista who's never worked in a coffee shop. She's my baby from two Christmases ago."

Sabine laughs, and I smile at the memory of my father presenting Fancy with a big red bow. There are coffee houses that have this exact model. It's extravagant and sturdy. Of course, I love it and use it all the time. I power her up and begin making a cafe latte for us. Sabine is making some kind of pastry that resembles round drop biscuits when both Ax and Theon wander into the kitchen.

"Smells wonderful," Ax says in his deep baritone voice.

"Thank you," Sabine says.

Ax, with wide eyes focused on Fancy, asks, "Where do I find the cups?"

I get a cup that is large but looks like a teacup in his large hands. "As your barista, this morning, would you like lattes or flavors?" I ask.

To my surprise, Ax and Theon both requested mocha lattes, and from the looks on their faces, they surprised each other with the same request. I serve them their requested caffeine.

Ax sits at the table, and I sit at the island and turn toward Theon. I say, "Evan said it's important that we proceed like a normal day, whatever that means. So, how about you come with me for a drive today. See what has happened with this storm?"

Theon nods while drinking his mocha. The storms seem to roll in and out with no warning or pattern. It has stumped meteorologists around the globe. So many conspiracy theories. Most think it's global warming.

"I don't think that's wise. Commander Eoin said to stay put. It's one thing to go out with Daniel, but it's completely another if you're looking for—" Sabine says, bringing a plate piled high of the circle pastry she has made.

"It's not like we're transporting. It's a car ride, like yesterday," I respond.

"It could be helpful to examine what has been affected from yesterday's events. We are isolated in this house; and to what is on the news. Maybe, drive by the school?" Ax adds.

Looking out of the bay window, it looks like it's going to be a beautiful, sunny day. It's quiet as we finish eating. Ax helps Sabine clean the kitchen. The image of a large, blood-demon warrior wiping down and cleaning the table is something I will never unsee. His dark red skin and his horns are intimidating. His six-foot eight-inch frame of muscles, that makes Dwayne Johnson, aka The Rock, look like a skinny kid. Despite all that, here Ax is with a tea towel in hand, talking with Sabine about plans for lunch and dinner.

Theon and I leave and decide we will grab lunch out and take a tour around town. He hides his smaller demon horns by tucking his longer hair back over them in a plait. His style is grungy and relaxed. He has a type of assurance that is comparable to Evan's. I pull out of the drive of the house and turn toward the school.

"Theon, why do you stay around, Evan? Are you good friends?" I ask.

I really know little about Theon, only that Meghan was his sister. Evan's wife. Harkin, the Wiccan King, had Meghan killed because of Evan's defection and rejection of any royal duty on the crown. If I were Theon, I'm not sure I'd want anything to do with Evan or this family.

"We're family. He's my brother," he answers. "Meghan was my sister, but I knew Evan well before they met. Plus, I feel like although Meghan isn't here anymore, that doesn't change who we are to each other."

I nod my head, thinking about how Lucy dated Daniel. Although he's my ex-boyfriend, it doesn't change who she is to me now. She's still one of my best friends, right?

"Why do you ask?"

I turn into the town center. "Well, you risk a lot to support Evan, and even me. The first time I met you, I threw you against a wall to escape." I laugh, remembering when Evan and Theon took me, thinking Rhydian was going to hurt me. My dramatic escape.

He rubs the back of his neck. "That seems so long ago. I don't hold grudges. Plus, you are important to him, so . . ."

"Do I get to call you uncle too, then?" I laugh, parking the car near the courthouse in the middle of the town square.

He has a kind, calm smile. I think it's the first time I've seen it.

"Absolutely not. My name is fine."

Exiting the car, he pulls on a ball cap and cups the sides of the bill in to shield his eyes. We walk toward the end, past A Cup of Joe's, toward the small Italian eatery. I feel the pulse quickening in my veins and stop walking. Holding my arms at my side, I turn and lean on the storefront nearest to me.

Tick-tock.

"Give me a minute," I say.

"I sense a change in the air too, but it physically affects you?"

Theon watches me with inspecting eyes, nodding toward the bench on the small greenway on the west side of the courthouse. We sit, and I lean forward, prepared for the pain that follows, but it doesn't. It's a small wave and the lights and air shift around us. I spy Lucy with Coral and Coral's stepmother, Vanessa. They are exiting the eatery together. It's strange to see Lucy with Coral's stepmother. Coral is walking ahead of them with her head down, while Lucy and Vanessa are smiling and talking like friends.

I turn and face Theon.

"Did they see us?"

"I don't think so." Theon leans back and is watching them. "They are behind the building, just toward the parking area. She can't see you now—ah, wait. What the—" His face turns serious.

I turn, but Theon is already at a jog, and I follow him, the soft pain subsiding as I move. The pulse, however, remains like a clock in the background of my mind.

The voices are intense and angry, coming from the alleyway between two buildings.

"What the freak are you?" says a deep voice, mocking.

A groan answers and we see something cowered into a lump with two guys standing over it.

"You're one of those that don't belong."

One of them kicks it.

"Stop it!" I yell, scrambling over to the lump.

Theon is squaring off with the men, guiding them away as I get closer to what I expect is a shapeshifter. It's a boy who is half naked, his back cut and bruised. The rift transformed them back into their human form.

Oh, my Goddess, it's Marco!

Barely registering what the guys and Theon are saying to each other. I kneel next to Marco, but before I even touch him, he recoils from me. What did that group do to you? Concealed by the shadows of buildings, I can hardly see him. The unforgiving pavement eats into my covered knee with my full weight on it as I assist Marco. He leans on me.

"I can help," I say, seeking to comfort him. Does he even recognize me?

The yelling increases when I hear Theon.

"You fucking heard wrong."

He inserts himself in front of the jerk, who's outspoken.

"What's it to you?" The taller guy squares himself and pushes Theon.

The smirk on Theon's face is one that says he's ready. Theon is an experienced fighter, and it takes no time for him to hit, kick, and chase them out of the alley.

I call to my magick and feel the hum. My hands light up with the designs I've grown so familiar with. I reach out to touch Marco.

"Don't, Willow, they will see, don't use magick," Marco says through strained breaths.

One of his eyes is swelling. A busted nose. Blood and bruises are all over him. Scraps of a shirt hang on him. He's even lost a shoe. What have those jerks done to him?

"I can't leave you like this. And I dare them to come back." When I say it, my magick flares even brighter. I reach my hand over his shoulder.

"Wait. The rifts, magick isn't reliable, it's—"

"It's reliable with my direct touch, Marco. Trust me?" I ask. My heart squeezes because there is no way I'm leaving him like this.

He nods, and I put my hand on his shoulder. The healing magick I've conjured flows from me to him. His back bends at ease, his neck is no longer straining, and his face is clearing of all cuts and bruises. Gently, he touches my hand. Bloodied gashed knuckles have faded to brown mocha skin that turns soft and taut. I guide my magick as it repairs and knits; the scrapes and the blood disappear. I stand as he moves to sit upright, then stands with me. Healed, he reaches for my hand and his lips lift to the corner of one side.

"Thank you. And we should probably go somewhere else," Marco says, worry creasing his forehead and his eyes looking behind me.

Theon is walking toward us with a hoodie and Marco's missing shoe.

Marco puts on the hoodie and slips on his shoe. I look back at the town square. "Do you want to go to the diner?"

He leads the way. Theon and I follow him in silence. The door chimes to alert the waitress, and she gestures to the booth along the window.

After she takes our order and walks away, I ask, "Marco, what happened? Who was that?"

"It wasn't those hunters, just some assholes. I had a shifting phase that happens because of the rift, and I tried to get into the alleyway unnoticed, but those guys saw me."

"Hunters? Wait, what?"

"I'm not sure of their true name, but they are organized and seeking those with magick. Word is spreading about them. They are hurting and killing."

I can't believe it, hunters. Or even in this case that someone saw something unexpected, and their initial thought would be to harm someone?

They should try it with me.

My magick is at the ready in the background. I feel the steady hum rise on the surface of my skin. I take a deep inhale of air to calm myself. The shimmer and glow fades, but it's there.

I'm concealing my magick from everyone in the diner, including Theon and Marco.

"I can't believe they even approached you," I say.

He falls back in his seat and rolls his eyes. "Willow, look at me. Just my skin color already has me at a disadvantage for prejudice. If I add shifting to it—I'll be enemy number one. I'd rather fade into the background right now." Marco's eyes wander around us, before he continues as a group of girls walk into the diner, "This is your standard, good ol' hate crime."

"It's happening everywhere, isn't it?" Theon asks.

I stir my soda with my straw. Gah, I hate the way some people lash out at differences.

"Yeah, can you imagine if you couldn't glamour to be us even? You better hide or find a new home elsewhere, 'cause you're going to be at the top of that list. I guess I'm lucky that at least I have my human form, which is my stable side." Marco pauses. "My little brother, on the other hand, he has trouble not being stable. It's the case for most youth right now."

The waitress brings us our lunch orders.

"I'm so sorry, Marco."

"It's my fault for leaving the house, I suppose. My folks left for my aunt's farm in Idaho with my younger brother. I'm supposed to tie up loose ends here and meet them there. But thankfully, mail is all forwarded now, and I should be able to leave in the next day or so." He shrugs it off and takes a big bite of his apple pie. I'm saddened to think the hate for his skin color is not unexpected for him, regardless of the magickal rifts.

I'm so naïve.

"Marco, this is going to sound stupid, but how are you getting to Idaho?" I ask.

"Driving, why?"

"Well, as you mentioned with the rifts and shifting, maybe it isn't wise to drive."

He turns and opens his mouth before he says, "Ah, I don't—"

"Hear me out. How about you stay at my house. You can

keep an eye on your house, and I have plenty of room. Shifting there is no problem, because, well, my closest neighbor is nearly a mile away in a private estate."

Theon makes this face that I can't quite read. He squints his eyes and almost smirks.

"I don't want to put you out or anything," Marco says.

"Seriously, you've seen the mausoleum of my home. We have plenty of room. You can have any of the remaining bedrooms."

Marco looks from me to Theon. "That's really cool of you. Are you sure? 'Cause, hell, I'm not sure I can keep it together in here, to be honest. Everything is unpredictable right now."

It's late afternoon when we drive back to the house. Marco is going to his house first to gather a few things before he comes over to my house.

The rift noise seems to have stopped for a moment. I expect that Sabine and Ax will have a ton of questions, so Theon and I decide we will call them in the car and explain instead of having them bombard us right at the door.

"Willow, you need to be careful out in the open, because you attract magick," Theon says.

"I can't sit on my hands, Theon. You saw what happened to Marco."

His face is unreadable.

"I'm saying we can't roam the streets looking. We need a coordinated plan. I wholeheartedly agree, what happened isn't right."

"Well, what does a coordinated plan look like? Do you think Evan expected we'd find Marco? And he knew we'd be able to help him?"

His grumble is preceded by, "No telling with Evan, but most likely."

If that is true, thank Goddess.

CHAPTER 6

Outside, everything from the front window of the sitting room is green and lush, full of life. I watch as Emily's car pulls in at the front of the house. Marco and I are at the door when we see Daniel opening the car door. I smile and wave at the sight of both of them, but Marco's shoulders square off.

"What's up with you and Daniel?" I ask in a quiet voice.

"He's different. The ego won't fit in your foyer right now."

His lips curve into a mocking smile as Daniel walks up the stairs.

We all walk into the house, and I barely register the large duffle bag that Daniel swings off his back onto the floor.

"What's this? Do you need somewhere to stay?"

Marco clinches his jaw at my question.

Daniel looks from Emily to me before Emily speaks up.

"Yeah. Daniel needs a better permanent stop, and I thought since you had all this room, it would be okay?"

She lifts her hands in a slight gesture, and her eyes open wide, awaiting my response. As if I would say no. This must be the favor she didn't elaborate on when I called her about what happened to Marco.

"Of course, absolutely. It won't be a problem. You can take

the guest room across from mine. Cross and Quinn are here too."

I watch Emily as she shifts her weight at the mention of Cross's name.

"Maybe this isn't a good idea," Daniel replies.

"Well, it's up to you. I'm okay either way."

"Marco, what say you?" Daniel asks.

Marco's shoulders relax. "Yeah, man, it's fine. But I'm not taking any more crap. I've got my own shit right now with this ongoing magickal chaos. Feel me?"

Emily and I watch the two of them like a tennis match.

"Deal. It's off the table then."

"Good, because for the last time, it never should have been on the table."

Men, direct and to the point; once something airs, then it's dealt with. I wonder if Emily, Lucy, and I will ever be like we were before. I miss our trio.

Daniel's half-grin is easy, and he leans in and kisses me on the cheek. Then he hugs Marco in a macho half-hug kind of way.

"Man, I'm glad you're okay," Daniel says to Marco.

Marco laughs and says, "Yeah, me too, thanks to Willow and Theon."

Daniel picks up his duffle, and they make their way to the stairs.

Emily points toward the kitchen. "I'd die for your famous latte."

In the kitchen, I start up the cappuccino machine and ask, "What was that with Daniel and Marco, anyway? Where does Daniel's family think he's gone to?"

"Just a misunderstanding with Lucy. She's been starting a little trouble with Daniel."

That doesn't sound like Lucy at all. She always avoided crazy antics, unlike Emily. For her to be playing games with Daniel, someone she loves is off from her personality.

"Daniel's family thinks he's off to Army boot camp. Little do they know it's an immortal military type of boot camp. Plus, my place is just as nutty with me moving out and finding other living arrangements away from the foster parents."

"Emily, they aren't foster parents," I reply.

Although Emily's mannerism says carefree, it's a facade. Her hair is dull, and her skin is pale. "But they aren't my real parents, either. I need to break the magickal ties as quickly as possible to keep them out of all this. Hell, it's awkward as it is because the rifts are playing with magick all over the place. I almost got hit with a bat during one attempt because they thought I was robbing the place."

She pretends she doesn't care, but I know she has loved living with her parents and Brody, her big brother, for the last several years. She magicked them with a spell so that they think they've always known her as their daughter. I wonder how she will break the magickal tie. Will they remember her at all? I know Emily. She has a hard exterior, but inside she is mourning the loss of yet another family. I hug her before I hand her the latte. We have a lot in common.

Cross sweeps in, turning on his foot, and laughing with Duke on his heels in some kind of chase. "Easy, yes, I'll get you a treat—"

"Hey," Emily says and smiles weakly at him.

He nods up but says nothing back. Instead, he returns his attention to Duke and, before grabbing Duke's treat, he turns. "Willow, Evan is coming by shortly."

Cross turns to leave, but stops when I say, "Hey, we have a new resident."

Cross's jaw sets.

"Daniel is going to be here for a while," I say.

I barley register the audible sigh from Emily.

He nods and walks out of the kitchen with Duke on his heels. Although eager to hear from Evan and get the details on what's going on, I turn my attention to Emily, who is staring out the window. Her downcast eyes and the sniffle of her nose say it all.

"Em, what's going on with you and Cross? Is there something I can do?" I ask.

Her face falls. What little light there was but a moment ago in her face it's vanished. No pretense at all. She looks how I feel. "No, there is nothing to be done. It's gotten complicated, but it'll work out . . . or not," she replies.

"You know I'm a superb listener. I totally get complicated. Have you seen my life? Oh right, you've witnessed most of it." We both laugh as a tear escapes her eye. "When you're ready, know I'm here." Before I can say anymore, I'm being hugged, and I gently return it. I could have sworn I heard her say, I wish I could.

Evan slides into the entryway of the kitchen dramatically with no shoes, only socks.

"I've always wanted to do that."

I laugh as he balances himself.

"Thank Goddess. He's not in his underwear," Emily laughs.

"What?"

I'm shaken to the core. I do not need to see my uncle in his underwear. Thankfully, Evan is fully dressed in jeans and a collared shirt that is open with a white tee-shirt. Definitely an improvement from pajamas and unicorn slippers.

"Eighties movie." Em shakes her head at me.

Evan smiles and points at Emily. "Yes, but they don't have this." He holds a hand up, and a light orb forms. I'm excited to see the fully formed magick in his hand is solid and nothing crazy is happening.

"Damn it!" Cross yells from the office before we hear a loud crash.

We all get to Cross in my father's office quickly. He is soaking wet as if he was in a dunk tank. Duke is shaking his body, and water is going everywhere.

"What happened?"

"I was communicating with Tullen before we got separated, and then the magick broke and literally washed away." He shakes his enormous arms, and the water falls to the floor in a puddle. "Any chance that yer magick or Evan's is a little more reliable that ya can dry me off quickly without setting me on fire?"

"Because that has happened?" I ask as I roll my eyes, shaking my head, knowing that most likely it has.

Before Evan can say something strange, I step in front of Cross and place my hands on his shoulder and call to my magick and command the air to dry him and clear the water from the room. It comes up like cool steam before it disappears in front of our eyes.

"Showoff." Evan smiles and winks.

"I'm glad it worked. Feels good to use it in any capacity."

Evan laughs, but Cross's lips are in a thin line. I follow his eyes to Emily.

"Still here?" Cross snaps more than asks. The tension in the air is thick. Emily squares her shoulders.

"Really? Is this your house or Willow's?" Emily bites back. She turns to Evan and me. "There is another reason I'm here, Willow, besides the great latte and Daniel. I need to talk with you, and it works out that Evan's here."

"I do know the importance of timing, like no other," Evan replies, then nods his head toward the sitting arrangement in front of the window. Daniel and Marco come into the office. Cross extends his fist, and Marco pounds it like they are old pals.

What have I missed in the last twenty-four hours?

"Let's let them chat, fellas." Cross ushers them out the door. But not be before Daniel eyes us warily.

Emily sits down in front of Evan.

"It feels like it was before, in the Norse realm. I'm not sure how to describe it, but this is going to be permanent, Willow. The chaos and displacement. Maybe even the control of magick? I'm not sure."

"This is our Ragnarök," Evan says, not asking. Emily nods, her eyes cast down before she shrugs her shoulders.

"Could it be the same?" I ask. As soon as I say it, I recall how Emily told me about how her realm collapsed.

"It's what you call the Convergence—semantics," Emily replies.

"Toma-toe, Tam-ah-to. Still the same gross veggie," Evan says. His facial features pinch tight, despite the off-handed comment.

Quinn enters from the hidden library where my father's coven space is. His face has ash streaks at the temples and his fingertips. "Oh, hello." He sits next to me on the small couch. "What's up?"

"Did you find anything helpful?" I ask Quinn.

"I believe we've found a way to transport reliably. The legion council has found patterns in the rift of Convergence, an open timing that is uninhibited." I must have looked like a deer in headlights because Quinn shakes his head as if to clear his mind. "Basically, transporting safely with a magickal pass that over-writes the rifts as they do now. They are working out the kinks."

"That is good news," Em says to Quinn.

"It is and isn't," Evan says, but no one gives him notice except me. Although he's full of riddles, Evan's insight and power are essential. He continues, "tell us about the Norse realm. How did you come to Edayri? What led you there?"

"When we found Edayri, a series of events set off Ragnarök: battles, the death of Odin, elemental disasters. Willow, this feels the same, and I'm worried that the only realm to inhabit is here, in Terra."

"But that's okay, right?"

No one is looking at me. They all seem to study the room. I feel stupid staring at Evan. Yes, I'm that naïve.

Quinn turns to me. "Willow, the collapse of any realm, especially one of magick, is not okay. Who knows what effect it will have here, on Terra, which is quite populated. Also, our popula-

427

tion is full of different species that rarely pass as humans. You have already seen what happens. Look at Marco."

Emily stands and thrusts her hands through her hair. "Exactly. Edayri was built by gods and is fueled by magick itself. Do you think all creatures would be welcomed here? Willow, it's not safe for anyone with any abilities. If you wanted magick to be hidden for you here—it's just not . . ." The silence drags before Emily speaks again, but she looks directly at Evan. "There are magick hunters here on Terra. That's what happened to Marco," Emily says, and all eyes focus on her.

Evan silently walks to the tall window and looks out as if searching for something. "Because we've seen it before, haven't we, Quinn?"

Emily is the first to respond. "We noticed that those with higher powers were targets that attract attention. Several of my family members were hunted and killed here just for blatant displays of power. They did not welcome us in Edayri, but it was safer than here." Her eyes are wary and distant. Emily focuses on her hands and intertwines her fingers in a pattern, back and forth. "The fact Willow, you have Goddess powers, and Evan, you have Horned God powers. What Marco experienced? It's not any different. There will be more hunters. It's a lot like my past. Your combined power and nearness to each other is going to be a calling of magick."

"A calling of magick?" I ask.

"Yes. Calling like to like, kindred spirits will gather."

Evan laughs as if he just told himself a private joke.

"What?" Cross's voice booms in the room when he enters. "Ya should have said something before now! What is wrong with you?"

Quinn stands and puts his hand on Cross's shoulder.

"So, what do we do?" I ask.

I'm energized at the thought of a task. It's got to be better than staying out of the way as others handle what's going on in

Edayri. I'm not letting anyone hurt anyone with magick because they are different.

Emily answers, "You need to be in a different place than Evan. You can't be together for any length of time—"

"Do you know who these hunters are?" Cross is in front of Emily, his shoulders tense, and his face is stone. "Is Willow safe here?"

Shit. Cross is hurdling over the line and being too aggressive, almost accusing her of something. Emily doesn't retreat from him. She stands firm and looks like she may hit him with lightning if he isn't careful.

"There are magickal wards on this house. But all of us being here right now is a risk? Is that what you're saying? That it is because of the individual powers we possess?" I ask.

Emily nods in confirmation of my question. Evan is looking at everyone. He turns before he speaks. "You'll be safe here. I'm needed elsewhere, somewhere over the rainbow." His head tilts like he is listening to someone no one else can hear. He nods, as if satisfied with himself.

The magick shows on my skin and pulses with liquid-like light patterns. I'm sure the crown is floating above my head. I'm sick of being sidelined. What, am I supposed to sit here on my hands? Eoin and the Guardians have tasks for helping those who are displaced. All while I'm sitting on my ass. This is such utter bullshit, especially if there are hunters here in Terra.

"Why?" I ask no one.

Evan answers me after a pause. "Oh, if I had a dime, for every time that simple question has been asked."

Cross claps him on his back and says, "What, you'd have a dollar and fifty cents?" The tension cuts with chuckles and laughter.

Emily leans into me. "I've got to get back. Anyway, Willow, be careful and be mindful of what's happening."

I walk Emily to the front door and hug her goodbye. When

the front door shuts, a loud sound echoes from the heavy door. The jolting sound vibrates from my hand up my arm. I stand alone in the house's foyer.

PART II

An inward reflection and surrender of the full moon; weighs on decisions and acceptance.

-The Horned God

CHAPTER 7

I t's been a couple of days since Daniel came to stay at my house. Sabine is making fresh pasta for dinner. I'm tucked away in the private coven room behind the bookcase in my father's office.

I'm learning more about my family in the Book of Shadows. Who, unfortunately, isn't answering my questions directly. I keep reading it repeatedly. The eight-ball type answers given are not direct answers.

Typical.

Tick-tock.

I hate the radio silence from the outside world and not fully knowing what is happening in Edayri. It was only yesterday the news reported on television: the storms globally are part of the environmental changes. The unfortunate part is it's also bringing up discussions about refugees and the increase in other strange phenomenon. I cringe at a spokesperson who said that we need to police our community and alert the authorities of suspicious, otherworldly behavior. I can imagine the looks on people's faces when they come across a demon or someone who is a shifter, mid-reveal or transformation as a result of the rift. A Wiccan is easy to hide, unless they transport in front of a crowd.

Knock. Knock.

"Hello?" I ask, secretly hoping I don't see Sabine's bright red hair coming around the corner.

Instead, the tall shadow reveals my uncle, Evan, who enters the coven room.

"Evan! I'm surprised to see you. What are you doing here? Does—"

He shakes his head and smiles. I greet him with a hug and can't help the small tear that escapes my eye. The rush of movement ignites a throbbing pain in my head.

He touches my temple and says, "Worry not."

An immediate liquid feeling of relief floods my mind. The beat that is always thrumming in my head is quickly a quiet whisper. He's used magick on me to ease my pain. That makes me want to cry more, but in relief, because popping medicine has done nothing. Drinking gallons of water per Sabine's constant orders has done nothing but make me pee every hour. I pull back from him while he holds my shoulders and studies my face.

"What's wrong?" I ask. Trying to contain the quiver in my voice.

"Not unless you call this Convergence wrong? But then again, what's wrong is putting things right, but either way it's painful; change always is."

Evan and his riddles. His wandering mind is something I now cherish.

"Not what I meant. You're here. I thought that transporting and magick were only to be used in dire need, or for the Guardians and Council."

I touch my temple where he used magick to ease my constant pain.

He shrugs.

"We're figuring it out. Come, I'm not alone and have the 411."

He turns and walks through the short, concealed hallway, the lanterns extinguishing as we leave. My heartbeat is present in my ears, with a pulling sensation at my ribs. I close the open book-case door and find Abigail, Rhydian's sister.

"Willow!" Abigail launches herself at me and hugs me tight, and I reciprocate.

Sabine enters, wiping her hands on an apron.

"Abby, I'm happy to see you."

It isn't completely true. I do like Abby but seeing her only reminds me that Rhydian is absent. I think of the broken blood vow, which causes the constant pain that Evan just relieved me of.

"What report do you bring?" Sabine asks. She sets down a platter as if this is some grand social visit and she expected company.

Abigail and Evan look at each other. She exhales before explaining, "McKinnon Manor is sinking into the land because Edayri is breaking apart with the collapse. Your house staff are working to save what they can in terms of cherished house items. They've requested your assistance in the move to Terra."

Abby continues, "The Royal Guardian's will protect the Queen at this residence for the foreseeable future, per the Commander's orders. However, I'm here to retrieve you."

"I can help you, Sabine." The opportunity to leave the house and see Edayri is a lure.

Evan is the first to respond. "No, Willow, you're to stay here. There is more need for you here."

Before I can respond, Sabine and Abby are repeating Evan.

"What? Why should I stay here? I'm sure I can do more in Edayri," I almost yell, like a child.

Sabine places her hand on my shoulder.

"We don't know what they are facing in the collapse of Edayri and that is dangerous, Willow. The fact that it isn't imme-diate and seems in stages . . . we have to be careful. Who knows when this could change? We must follow Eoin's instructions,"

Sabine says. The voice of reason. But then again, she won't be stuck in Chepstow under guard.

"But McKinnon Manor . . . is really sinking?"

Evan is dramatic when he crosses over toward the windows. "Like a yellow submarine."

"When do we leave?" Sabine asks Abby.

"In just under an hour." Abby looks at her watch. "Only pack necessary items, if any."

Sabine nods. "Okay. We have enough time to eat. How about a quick bite?"

How can they eat and act as if this is a normal day? I smile awkwardly, watching Sabine and Evan leave with his lazy steps in a delay. Leaving me alone with Abigail. My stomach knots, knowing she will ask about her brother.

"Have you heard from Tullen and Rhydian?" She moves closer to me on the couch.

I adjust by turning my knee on the couch to put distance between us. I want to say yes, I've heard from them. But the disappointing part is I haven't since graduation, when the Convergence started, and now I'll have to admit that to her. It makes it more real verses continuing to be ghosted. "No, I haven't." Pursing my lips, I try to look anywhere except at her large pitying eyes that are similar in color to Rhydian's.

"Have you?" I ask, my voice feeling small.

"Only briefly."

Why does my chest feel heavy? The squeeze of air that escapes my lungs as if I'm being hit without expecting it. Of course, he would reach out to her. She's his sister. What am I in his world? Am I his girlfriend anymore? The crack widens; the fissure that seems impossible to close. I'd rather have the headache Evan magicked away.

"I'm sure he'll reach out soon to you. He's looking for our mother and he's torn and struggling too, Willow."

He's looking for his mother. My heart aches and I should be supportive, but all I can think about is my selfish ass.

SACRED

"I feel inconsequential—Abby, the blood vow is broken. It's like something is missing from me and I can't repair it without— Hell, I don't know if it can be fixed. I've tried a few things but—"

Evan's voice is there before I see him. He must have stayed nearby. He says, "An ache of a broken blood vow is not partner-less. It takes two to tango."

"What?"

Abby turns in shock, as if what I said was the ramblings of a broken-hearted babbling girl. Aren't I though?

Duke follows Evan into the living room, his tail wagging in greeting. Evan pets his head when he sits in a chair across from us.

"Willow, tell me I'm wrong?" he asks me.

"It's true but, I've got used to it. I can sleep fitfully at night. There is something else like a—"

"Clock," he fills in. "Since graduation when it began?" Evan is speaking about the Convergence as if it's different from the broke blood vow pain.

"Oh, my Goddess, Willow, if he knew—" Abby says.

Right if Rhydian knew? I tighten my jaw because I want to yell at her. If he knew what? That the broken vow causes me pain? That would bring him back, but nothing else? His duty and loyalty over his personal feelings?

I take a quick breath to steady myself. I don't want to put my frustrations on Abby.

"Doesn't matter, he's not reaching out and talking to me," I say.

Abby shakes her head, as if clearing off too many thoughts. "I just don't understand, the blood vow. Rhydian took the vow seri-ously. If he knew he was causing you direct pain, he would be beside himself."

"I wish that he never gave me that damn blood vow. I've doubted so much, and I'll never know what was real or just influ-enced by the vow. Now it's all gone except for this hollowing

437

ache and pain."

"He didn't give you the blood vow directly. He gave it to Aiden," Evan says as Duke rolls on his back for the scratches to continue on his tummy by Evan.

He's right! I didn't accept the blood vow directly. My father did this on my behalf.

"Oh!" I suck in my breath so fast I cough. "You're right!" Why didn't I figure this out?

Abby looks from Evan to me and asks, "You didn't accept the blood vow directly?"

She is smiling, and I can't help but laugh mockingly.

"No, I didn't. I didn't even know what it was. But—what does this mean? Can it be reversed? My father is no longer—"

The vow didn't die with him. Remembering my father, my hero, my magick hums to life on my skin. My father asked me to trust Rhydian.

I think about Rhydian and see his face clearer than I have in my mind for the last week. His stormy ocean eyes when he's troubled or serious versus the clear blue in happiness. His dimpled cheeks that only show in a full smile. My heart pulls in my chest and my ribs constrict. The familiar hurt of the broken blood vow.

I didn't want this. Maybe I can reverse it or better yet, absolve it? I have royal powers, why not?

Evan interrupts my thoughts. "Rhydian will not agree to any reversal or spell. He feels responsible and likes the pain, the reminder."

Did Evan read my mind? Rhydian likes the pain. Typical. He would punish himself.

"I will talk to him and—" Abby says.

I interrupt, "No, I need to talk to him."

More like he needs to talk to me. I forced his betrayal by helping him hurt me, which broke the tenants of the vow. "Right now, the connection is our pain. He needs to talk to me, Abby. You can't solve this for him or for me."

Will there be us? The pain in my ribs makes it hard to breathe. I feel heavy but stand against the emotion that's holding me in place. I walk out of the living room and go to my room with Duke on my heels. His head nudges my hand where I lay on my bed. I hug him, petting and rubbing his sweet face, and cry silently.

I overhear Quinn ask where Evan and Theon are when I enter the living room.

"They are discussing something in the kitchen. The time for transporting is coming up in the next several minutes."

Now transporting occurs only by specific points of departure and entry. I'm not really sure how they figure this out, along with the beating pulse like thumps of the rifts and the changes in the air. It's not a consistent thing. And it's not necessarily something that is regulated, but Evan says it has a pattern.

Cross and I follow Quinn into the kitchen.

Theon claps Cross on the back. "How goes it?" Theon asks. I never realized they knew each other, but it makes sense.

"Good enough."

Evan is in front of me. His eyes are piercing.

"Are you okay, Evan?" I get a brief hug before he lets me go. "Why do I feel you're not telling me something?"

He winks, then pats my head like a child.

"Seriously," I push at him. "What is going on besides the fact that I feel like I won't see you again? I don't like being kept in the dark."

"Don't fear the dark—"

"I don't! You're hiding something important from me. I'm not a child!"

He says nothing. It feels like a confirmation before he says, "It's unclear how events will play out, so I'd rather not play at something that I could influence wrongly. That's something Doc Brown warned Marty about in that movie. It's good advice."

What can I say to that? This scrambled view of the future Evan sees is because of magick I cast when we were fighting each other. Although often confusing, he now considers it a gift, and I'm not sure he's wrong. I'm connected to him not only by family but by a destiny I'm still unclear about. It has to do with Goddess and the Horned God. It's a family legacy for the ages, or so Sabine and Tullen have told me.

Quinn comes over and says, "I think it's time for you and Theon to transport. You have a five-minute window in which to transport to the Hallowed Hall. Eoin will meet you. Ax will be there, Theon, and he will provide you with details for lodging within the Guardian grounds. Abigail and Sabine, it's the same entry point."

Evan smiles and moves to the foyer of the house. Cross opens the front door. "Actually, it's better if you are outside, for transporting."

Quinn gives me a look, and I follow him outside to the front yard. The advantage of living on private estate grounds is that my neighbors are far enough away that they won't see or notice anything.

Evan and Theon stand together, and Theon touches Evan's shoulder. They look like old pals and friends. The wind swirls around them and I notice a flock of birds coming overhead as Evan and Theon disappear. A bird lands in the yard. Sabine gives me a quick hug before she and Abigail do the same. They disappear in an instant.

The bird on the ground is squawking loudly. Duke launches himself from the porch and the bird takes flight just in time.

CHAPTER 8

I t's late afternoon. I'm on the couch with one foot lazily
rubbing Duke's side when Cross and Quinn find us.

"Hey, Willow. We need to talk with you," Quinn says, sitting
across from me.

Cross enters a code on his Guardian wrist cuff, and a light
bounces around the room.

"To ensure we're having a private conversation."

"About the patrols? You know what happened when Theon
and I found Marco. Is it more hate crimes?"

Quinn only nods. Cross's jaw juts out.

"Listen, don't you dare shield me like I'm a dainty flower. Tell
me what is going on! I've been through hell this past year, so it's
not like I can't take it. Plus, I should fucking know." I steady my
voice as much as I can.

Quinn looks at me straight in the eyes. "No one, and I mean,
no one, knows better than we do what you've been through in
the last year. We know you are more than capable. As our
Queen, we are here as your royal Guardians to report. That
being said, it's for your ears only."

I sit a little straighter, and Cross grabs my attention when he
huffs, "Will, I'll give it to ya straight. It's a shit show. Sometimes

we patrol and find corpses. Other times, we transport the lost to where we have the refugee camps and try to reunite families. Other times, it's nothing but fear. It varies day to day."

"I'm not useless." I flex my hand, and my magick dances over my skin with a white flame as I move it finger to finger before clutching it in my hand. "I don't understand why the legion council, and everyone wants me to stay here. I could be helping."

"Magick doesn't solve everything. Willow, these hunters follow the path of magick. If you use your magick, you could do more damage than you intend to. Innocents could get caught in the middle. You're a magick beacon with your power."

Quinn's right, and I wouldn't say I like it.

"So, pretend it's a normal day?"

"Well, when have you had a normal day?" Cross laughs.

True. Every time I leave this house, something happens: graduation, A Cup of Joe's, and Marco?

"Having the two of you as my babysitters is not normal, Quinn."

Cross covers his heart as if he's hurt. "Right, so we pull together a schedule. Training, study, the whole thing. I'm not the babysitting type. I'm a Royal Guardian and, hopefully, a friend. So, let's get it straight in yer head."

He's right. Sitting on my ass isn't helping me, anyway. I might as well train and prepare, because I'm not useless and can't play that part. I need to be ready for anything.

"Okay," I say in agreement.

"So, here's the deal. We don't want Daniel and Marco involved in Guardian business and updates that we give to you." My inhale stops Quinn, but only for a moment. "You may trust them, and we get it; they are great. However, now everything is sensitive and confidential information per Commander orders."

I shrug. "All right, then we meet every day. This is just a precaution, right?"

They both nod.

"So, it's okay for my friends to come over here then?" I ask.

"Certainly, that's something we can contain better here at the house."

"Sure. Who's coming over?" Quinn asks.

"Emily," I reply.

Cross's exhale is something I don't press since he won't look me in the eye. I'm not sure what's occurred between him and Emily, but I will ask her tomorrow.

"Is that a problem?"

"Nah. Not a problem. This house is enormous enough that I won't be seen," Cross says before tapping his wrist cuff, and he turns out of the room.

I look at Quinn for an explanation. He shrugs before he says, "Cross isn't keeping secrets, but he's hurt. He won't admit that. It comes out as hostility and anger, but he'll simmer down."

I want to press for more information, but who am I to get involved? My relationship status is non-communicative at this point. Maybe he reads it on my face.

"She said she didn't have time for him, and they've been fighting about Lucy. Emily feels she has an obligation to Lucy, her niece, and Cross feels that Lucy uses Emily. It's been radio silent for about a week, so the wound is oozing."

"Why would he think Lucy is using Emily?" I ask.

Quinn is hesitating.

"You will not hurt my feelings. Tell me."

"All right." He steals a glance toward the open doorway. "We don't trust her. She seems to have conflicting motives about magick and who she is. According to Marco, she guilts Emily all the time. She also manipulates Daniel, and they still speak a lot, but they are constantly arguing."

That is so strange. Daniel acted like they had nothing in common anymore and rarely speak. She was acting weird at A Cup of Joe's, almost taunting Daniel with Marco sitting next to her as if they were on a date. Daniel was upset with Marco, but clearly Marco wasn't giving Lucy the same attention.

"It's odd. Should I talk to Daniel about it?"

"No. Let's keep this as a confidential discussion. We have watchers out on the situation. They are magickal, and there is concern right now for the safety of all misplaced Edayrians. Let them go about their business. We honestly don't have the manpower, anyway."

"Okay, but I can't act like I know nothing."

"Yes, you can. You don't want to bring any attention to this. Let it all play out."

I nod in agreement, but not sure I can do that. Daniel is staying here. What if someone is in danger? A shiver climbs down my spine and I stand up, taking a deep breath. Duke is at my heels.

Tick-tock.

CHAPTER 9

The last few days passed quickly because of the routine I agreed to with Cross. Every morning I train with Cross in our basement gym. I like physical training because I can't think about anything but the present, what is in front of me. My arms and legs are stronger. I'm getting better, faster, and more daring where it pays off.

Cross, Quinn, Marco, and Daniel are my norm. We all eat together and chill in front of the television together. Marco and Daniel seem to have worked out their tension and are back to being their typical selves. The days seem to go by, until the stillness of the dark in my room, when I think about Rhydian. I don't stay in my room much anymore. I wander around this massive house with Duke at my heels.

Tap, tap, and pow.

I hit Cross's padded hands and dodge his overhead swings, one and two.

"Combo," Cross says.

I kick and hit Cross's padded body. I smile when he uses his back foot to anchor himself. Daniel pops up and taps me out when he lunges away from Cross, who takes the offense.

"Nice, Danny," Cross says, and he smiles.

I stretch my calves sitting next to Quinn.

"You're quite good at fighting, Willow." He hands me a water bottle.

"Thanks, I am improving for sure."

I watch Cross direct Daniel. "Cross is a talented trainer. I'm careful not to say that too loud." I chuckle.

"Oh, trust me, he knows it. That's okay"—Quinn raises his voice— "he still can't play Black Ops for shit against me!"

Wrinkles form on Cross's forehead, his lips a thin line. He focuses on Daniel, who is attacking him with various punching combos and a roundhouse kick. Daniel has gotten great at fighting.

I nudge Quinn. "Hey, are you taking another shift tonight?"

Quinn and Cross have been taking various Guardian shifts for patrols, helping with refugees nearby. My goal is to go with them. Daniel and Marco are eager to help, too. They have urged me to talk to Quinn. We all have cabin fever and need help. I know I need a function besides being guarded behind glass windows.

"Most likely. The work is increasing, and we don't have as many Guardians covering the whole of the Edayrian population."

"So, I have an idea. How about me, Daniel, and Marco accompany you."

Quinn shakes his head. "The commander gave strict instructions because it's too volatile. Plus, the enchantments put on this property will warn everyone and anyone at the Hallowed Hall."

"Oh, how I love being under lock and key like this." I slink back onto the concrete wall and slide to where I can place my arms on my knees straight out. "I want to see what you're seeing. I've been practicing, and I can control my magick through direct touch. It could be useful. Besides, you guys have a harder time controlling magick."

"It won't be like this forever."

"Don't put me on some pedestal like I'm breakable. I haven't broken yet, despite everything."

Quinn nods with confirmation.

That's an unsettling notion, forever a future. What is mine? Deferrals for college? I'm not even sure if that is what I want to do anymore. Being left out of the loop with Edayri, I'm just a figurehead to be protected. I am the Wiccan Queen and have powers that most only dream of, but they don't want me involved. I am a spectator, and it sucks.

Duke barks, and I startle when I hear him.

Bam.

I turn to see another bird hit the small window high on the basement wall. Then a third, almost as if it was flying into the house, but didn't notice it. I run out to the front yard, and there are about twenty birds. I squat down to one and call to my familiar hum.

Marco, in his tiger form, is running from the back of the yard.

"No! Don't heal it!" Quinn yells behind Cross.

"Why? It shouldn't harm them if I touch them—"

"That's not the point." Cross frowns and looks around the yard and runs off to the left, yelling, "Marco, shift back if you can or get in the house!"

Daniel moves to the side as Marco runs through the back door.

I point at the birds. "This is cruel. What is this?"

Quinn shakes his head. "We aren't sure, but every time I go to investigate a magickal death, there are small dead animals like this around. Not everyone has controllable magick like you do, since the rifts, and we expect these animals are used to identify those who have magick. Could Marco have triggered it? The wards around the house don't go too far."

Cross comes from the right, having run around the house, and his hands are up, and there is a force barely visible to my own eyes that is shrouding the house in a protective spell.

Quinn flexes his hands, and the Guardian wrist band expands his armor over his lean body. Cross does the same. They pick up the dead birds and place them in a magicked bag of some sort that disposes of the poor little birds.

Is this an omen of things to come, more death? I'm not ready for more death, but then again, is anyone?

In the house, I find Daniel. Marco is pacing in his tiger form in the sitting room.

"Marco isn't able to shift back at the moment, so we're just waiting it out," Daniel says.

"Cross and Quinn are cleaning up the yard. The birds are cursed or something, so when Marco shifted it may have alerted them here?" Shrugging at Marco when his big bulky body stops at my words mid-stride. "It's insane, right?"

"Insane? Kind of brilliant."

My head snaps at Daniel. Did he say that it was brilliant?

"I mean . . . if you want to ferret out something inconspicuously, this is an interesting way to do it."

"I guess, but the poor birds are dead, Daniel. They are dead."

Daniel shrugs, monitoring Marco. I don't like how dismissive he is to the birds. I'm not used to his indifferent response.

"Daniel?"

"Yeah?"

"Are you okay? I know it's a lot to be cooped up in this house. I asked Quinn about joining him and Cross tonight."

His eyes light up. "He said yes?"

"Not yet." I smile.

"You can be convincing when you put your mind to it, Willow."

What an odd thing to say. I wonder if it's a jibe at how I magicked our breakup back in Junior year, forcing him to go along with it unknowingly. Before I can say anything, Daniel sits down and points at Marco.

"He'll turn back to human, here shortly. I'm guessing it's almost time," Daniel says.

Marco's tiger form is daunting and beautiful all at the same time. His muscles move in sleek patterns along his form. He

SACRED

shivers when he crouches, and the shifting is instantaneous. I stand up and turn around to give Marco privacy because he is entirely naked.

"Um . . . I'll go pull together some lunch or something."

Marco laughs. "Sounds good, Willow. See you when I'm dressed."

I hear both of them laughing as I leave. I try to shake my thoughts of Daniel and his stone reaction to the birds.

At the top of the stairs, my back pocket buzzes. I pull out my cell phone and see Sabine on a video call. Closing my bedroom door, I sigh and sit on my bed.

"I was calling to give you an update, but by the look on your face, something is going on there. Tell me?"

I unload everything from Cross and Quinn about confidential information, the birds in the yard, along with Daniel's strange reaction.

Sabine doesn't say a word, and I wonder if we lost our connection because her face looks frozen on the screen.

"Sabine?"

"I'm digesting. I called to tell you, I purchased a new home in Terra and have moved all the worthwhile items from McKinnon Manor. Seems so inconsequential now."

"Not true. You bought a home?"

Am I surprised by her news? Did I think she would live here in my father's house? Do I see myself living here long term?

Sabine's face lights up, her eyes widen, and her hands move as she talks.

"I did! I found a large enough estate to house all of McKinnon Manor staff. We didn't discuss it but, it's not in Massachusetts. It's on the side of a mountain in Arizona, of all places."

"Arizona?"

"I know, but there is something about this place. The view is new for me, the desert landscape. I also feel a pull that magick is strong here."

449

"I can't wait to see it."

"How about now?"

Sabine smiles and flips the camera around and walks around the house. It's light and bright. So many windows and light walls. Sabine is right. I see the pull because the view is overlooking a valley. The pep in her voice as she describes the various rooms and where everything will go makes any weight of the day seem lighter.

At the end of the tour, Sabine sits down.

"So, what do you think? Would you want to stay here?"

Yes, I want to scream, but I hold back my ten-year-old-self enthusiasm.

"Is this going to be a hub for Terra?"

"Maybe, but it's not my intention. I have on the second floor an entire suite area, if you'd like it. You could split your time there and—"

"I'd love to move there," I spit out before I think too much. I need a change of scenery. I don't want to be in this house alone. There is nothing keeping me here in Chepstow.

Sabine's voice hitches with excitement. The more we talk about it, the more excited I'm getting. Its forward movement. She will arrange a few staff members to help me pack. We don't talk about the inevitability of selling this house, but it's on my mind, along with those staying here.

"Sabine, before we get off the call. Do you have any ideas about these birds? Do you think Daniel or one of my friends are involved?"

A chill runs up my spine thinking about it. It's like I've betrayed my friendships thinking this way.

"I don't know Daniel the way you do, but people change. Motivations and circumstances change. Be mindful and take everything at face value. There is no reason to take risks with yourself or those around you."

She's right. I need to see things as they are now, not as how they once were.

Sabine continues, "With all that is going on, the collapse of a magical realm. It's frightening for everyone. We are fortunate that our displacement is one of privilege."

I can't get Sabine's last statement out of my head.

I know it may not be much, but maybe I can use the money left to me by my father's will or even this house to help those who have no home. I make a voice memo to myself to call the estate attorney on Monday.

CHAPTER 10

I dress nicer today in anticipation of Emily coming over. Daniel is sitting on my bed reading one of my books when I come out of my bathroom.

"Whatcha got there?"

Daniel laughs. "Actually, I'm not sure, but it's fairly entertaining." He waves the paperback in my direction before setting it back on my nightstand. It's one of my sci-fi books.

Duke's ears perk up, and I pet his head on my way to my closet to grab my hoodie.

"Want to go outside before Emily gets here?" Daniel asks.

"Nah, I'm just a little cold today in the house, and besides, this is my comfy hoodie," I laugh.

"Oh, right, I forgot you had classifications for hoodies," Daniel teases and follows me down the hall toward the back stairs. "What is it, comfy, outdoor, workout, and what am I forgetting?"

"Duh, it's the formal hoodie."

His smile reaches his eyes. "Right, right . . . formal. Now, let me ask this, when is a hoodie considered formal?"

I laugh before I can answer. The alert from the enchantments around the house notifies us that Emily is here. It's like

SACRED

vibration to the wrist that tingles. But it signals more than once, which is odd. We both pass by the kitchen toward the foyer.

Knock-knock.

I open the door to find not only Emily, but Lucy and Coral.

"Hey." Did my voice just lift two octaves? This is unexpected, seeing Lucy and Coral.

Cross will not be happy about this, and what's more surprising is Emily said nothing about bringing others.

"I know it's been a while. We were all together and thought we'd join Emily coming over. Is that okay?" Lucy smiles easily and walks in as if nothing has changed over the last six months.

"Um . . . sure." I open the door wider and notice that Daniel is no longer behind me. So, I'm going through this alone, I guess.

Coral's eyes and head turning each way, surveying the foyer as she enters the house. I guess she hasn't ever been inside my house before.

"I'm thinking of a movie in the entertainment room to just hang. Soda and popcorn?" I ask.

"Okay, but I have dibs because we still have not watched Pretty in Pink yet," Emily says, and Lucy groans.

"I was thinking something a little more from this decade? What is it with you and the eighties lately?" Lucy jabs at Emily as they walk up the stairs, familiar with the location of the entertainment room.

Coral slowly walks to the bottom of the stairs. "You've got a beautiful home, Willow. Thanks for letting me crash."

We've been through a lot together, with phantoms attacking our class and graduation, so I no longer look at us as opposing teams. I'm not sure we are on the same team, but since we have the same friend group, it seems like I should let it go.

"So, you've been hanging out with Lucy more," I say as we walk up the stairs.

Coral shrugs. "We've been friends for a long time. Although, of course, her parents and mine have been hanging out more, yeah, I guess."

We walk into the entertainment room, and Emily and Lucy laugh and look at the touchpad that we use as a remote control.

"Yes, let's watch it!" Emily smiles.

"Absolutely not. I say we watch this." She points to some romantic comedy.

I come up behind them and see Emily has chosen the newest hero flick. They both look at me with wide eyes. I respond, "I don't really care either way."

Coral gives the final vote, and the romantic comedy plays. The popcorn machine begins to turn and heat to cook the popcorn. I grab water and sodas out of the small fridge behind the reclining couches with Emily.

"Glad to see you and Lucy are getting along," I say to Emily under my breath.

"Yeah, it's definitely gotten better. How's Daniel? I recognize he's staying out of the way. It's a double whammy with Lucy and Coral both being here."

I shrug, but she's right. Could he have more ex-girlfriends under one roof?

"By the way, thanks for the heads up on that one."

"Sorry, lately I've been caving to Lucy's whims and trying to be more supportive. And Daniel?"

"He's doing well, training with Cross and staying busy. He might as well be a Guardian."

Emily's eyes light up, and she smiles. "Cross is here, still?"

"I'm sure he'll see you before you all leave. Is it better? Have you guys talked?"

"We have had little opportunity." She shrugs. "He's probably still standing his ground like a testosterone idiot."

"Does he have a good reason?"

She shrugs and shakes her head. "It's just the way it is. I can't give up on my family and what she needs right now." She reveals nothing further. It sure seems like Emily is giving up a lot for Lucy, including her own happiness.

When the popcorn stops, I gather two large bowls and fill

them up, and Emily carries the drinks and napkins. By the time we sit, the movie is already kicking off with the two central characters meeting.

I stare at the screen but don't really pay attention to the movie because Rhydian comes to my mind. Was a romantic movie really the best idea? I wonder if he's been talking with Quinn and Cross. I'm sure they would tell me if anything was wrong.

Before I know it, the movie is about halfway over. I excuse myself and go to the bathroom. Out in the hall, Marco pulls me into his room, and Cross and Quinn are sitting on the bed, making it look like a twin. Daniel is missing from the room.

"What the heck?" I stammer. They stare at me with their arms folded over their chests.

"They need to leave. There were more birds at the perimeter, and we've taken care of them, but it was more this time," Cross says.

"It could be the increase of magick users with Emily? Also, Lucy is part valkyrie, so who knows," Quinn says.

"Okay, the movie is almost over, then I'll say I have to do something or whatever."

"I can help with that excuse." Cross smiles.

"Where is Daniel?"

"He's hiding out in his room," Marco replies.

This is strange, and I wonder if Emily is aware someone might track her and Lucy. But if she is knowledgeable, would she have come here? Surely, she would have said something to me. I sit down and nudge her when she eats the last popcorn in our bowl and smiles at me like a Cheshire cat.

"You didn't want anymore, right?" Emily says lightheartedly and drags her finger on the bottom of the bowl to get the last of the white cheddar powder topping that had settled to the bottom of the bowl.

"Something is going on. Be careful when you're in public, okay?" I say under my breath.

Her eyebrows pinch together, and she nods and turns back to the big screen.

When the movie ends, the lights, which are on an automated timer, brighten, and I stand. Lucy is stretching and yawning.

"Another movie?" Coral asks.

"Actually, I'm tired suddenly. I hate to be a buzzkill, but I have plans later. I'll need to get back home," Lucy responds.

I don't need an excuse after all.

"Yeah, me too. I need to do a few things tonight," Emily says.

Coral fidgets with her hands. "Hey, Willow, where is your bathroom?" I point her down the hall, hoping that the guys have dispersed.

We are cleaning up and turning everything off when Coral pops in the doorway. "Okay, ready to leave."

Down the stairs, Coral is lingering as Emily, Lucy, and I say our goodbyes. Emily and Lucy have odd looks on their faces when Coral approaches me. She grabs my hand and clasps it in her own. Then I feel something: a piece of paper.

"I know we didn't always see eye to eye in high school, but thank you for allowing me to crash with you all this afternoon," Coral says to me. Her eyes are intense and staring directly at me as she pushes for me to palm the paper from her hand to my hand.

"No worries, all in the past," I respond. Following her lead, I cup the paper in my hand and press my thumb over it, so it's secure when I bring her into a hug. "No worries, Coral, I'm glad we're putting things behind us."

I went too far. She is stiff as she steps back from me. I laugh. "Sorry, too soon?" I quickly slide it into my back pocket.

She laughs and says, "Yeah, maybe. See ya."

Lucy follows her out the door, but not before giving me a quick hug and reaching for my empty hands.

"I'm glad we had today," Lucy says.

When I shut the door, I look out the side window and watch

them leave in Lucy's car. Coral is in the back seat with her arms folded and her lips pursed. Lucy is red-faced and talking loudly.

"What was that?" Daniel says, and I jump at his voice.

"Dang, sorry, I didn't mean to scare you."

Cross, Quinn, and Marco are behind Daniel.

"That was a little too easy, and what was with Lucy?" Quinn asks.

It's a good question. She seemed unhappy to have Coral and me not be at odds with one another. But, also, what's this crap about, glad we had today? Something is off, very off.

"Did Coral give you something?" Daniel asks.

Keeping my composure together, I shrug with my hand in my back pocket over the paper. "No." I shake my head.

He makes light of it but keeps his eyes stay on me before he and Marco walk away.

I usher Cross and Quinn into the formal living room. Touching Cross's wristband, I say, "Do that cone of silence thingy."

"Liar. She gave you something," Cross whispers in a sly grin as he secures the room.

I pull the note from my back pocket and hold the small, folded paper in my hand.

"Coral passed me this and didn't want Lucy or Emily to see it. She was even shielding it from Daniel since he was right next to us."

Quinn cradles my hand. "I'm not sure you . . . it could be cursed or something?"

"It's not cursed. It is Coral, and she owes me twice for saving her life. Besides, she must have just written it when she was in the bathroom."

Cross points. "Well, yer just gonna stare at it?"

He's right. I'm staring at it. I am careful to open it, the ink is smearing, it's dark and wet. Part of it gets on my fingertips.

"This is blood," Quinn says.

I open the last fold and read it in a quiet voice. "Don't trust them. Lucy, Daniel, or Emily."

Cross's voice gets louder. "What the hell? Tis the girl serious or playing with ya?"

Coral isn't the type to play games like this. It must be serious because she wouldn't go through all this trouble to hand me a note in secret and no less in the blood that is probably hers.

I stare at them and say, "No, this is serious."

"Do you trust what she wrote?" Quinn asks.

I don't want to. They are my friends, my good friends. Although Coral and I haven't been friends in the past, we have an understanding now. Whereas my friends are acting odd. Emily has never given me any doubt of her loyalty to my friendship or the crown. She's always been by my side, and I by hers. Lucy is a wild card since her outrage at prom when she turned Daniel into an einherjar warrior.

"I don't want to, but we need to be careful."

"This is bullshit! Daniel!" Cross yells.

I grab Cross's arm and say under my breath, "Don't out Coral."

The room is still secure. Daniel didn't hear Cross, and he realizes it when he taps his wrist cuff.

"Listen, don't go all hot-headed on Daniel yet," I say.

Cross's jaw is clenched.

Quinn holds the note. "Coral could be in danger. We need to be very careful."

"Daniel! Marco! Where you guys at?"

Marco is the one who responds. "Kicking my ass gaming."

"Seriously, can you be stealth at all?" I ask.

Cross turns, with Quinn on his heels, back to me. "Yeah, it's a 101 course at academy training." Cross's eye roll makes me want to smack him.

"That's it! You don't say two words about any of this." I put the paper back into my pocket.

"We won't. I promise." Quinn nudges Cross. "We will need to

report in later to the commander. Who, I expect, will say Daniel needs to move out immediately. He can't be here."

How will I explain that to Daniel or Emily?

"Right, but keeping a watch on him here gives us a tactical advantage, possibly. I say we put some tracers and coms in his room," Cross adds.

It's come to this already. Spying on Daniel in the house? Shit.

I agree with Cross and Quinn.

In my room, I pull out my phone and find a text from an unknown number.

It's true.

I text back.

Who is this?

I wait and there is no response, but there is this feeling in my gut: it's Coral. I try one more text.

I can help you.

I wait for several minutes, but there is no response.

CHAPTER 11

Cross looks satisfied as he takes a second bite of the greasy pan-fried burgers, he's made for us. Wide-eyed, I pick up mine and compress it to take a healthy bite.

"Am I right?" he asks, waiting as he swallows his mouth full.

He's so right. It melts right into my mouth. The gooey cheese he pushed into the middle of the beef is absolute heaven. Cross got into a Food TV marathon over the past day, and it's really paid off.

"I'm sure glad I made two for everyone because there is no way I'm not eating another one."

I laugh and realize that there won't be any leftovers.

Quinn walks in and gets a burger and fries for himself. "So, what burger did you go with, Cross?"

"Rachel Ray's cheese in the middle combo."

"Excellent," Marco and Daniel say in unison, joining us in the kitchen.

I'm sitting at a table with all of them and realizing Cross and Quinn are not only Guardians or my friends. They are my family. Living here in the house and us doing so much together has been a much-needed distraction. Between the silence of Rhydian and the second-guessing of Coral's note about Lucy, Daniel, and

Emily, my brain is on its last circuit, and it's all I can do to hold it together. Who knows, except that Cross is one helluva cook.

"So, are we playing *Call of Duty* tonight?" Quinn nods to Daniel.

Daniel easily fits into Cross and Quinn's groove. It's like he's a guardian himself, over and above being an einherjar warrior.

Cross has learned nothing on Daniel, which I hope stays that way. Of course, we're probably overreacting. I hate this need to be secretive, but that note is a like question that hangs in the air.

They continue chatting about video games and various online professional players I know nothing about.

"Willow, do you want to hang and check it out?" Marco asks me.

I smile, fully knowing it's a pity question, because video games are out of my league, at least at the level they are chatting about.

"Nah, I think I'll hang about reading and maybe catch up on some other stuff."

After dinner, they all head to the spot they've carved out in the entertainment room. I make my way to my father's office. In this house, I will always see this as his office. I walk past the desk and run my hand across the slick wood and open the hidden doorway from the bookcase to reveal the solitary coven room. The lamps light the way in the short, dark hallway to an oval room with an overstuffed chair and footstool. I flip my fingers, and the floor lamp illuminates with the fireplace that is shared with the office. There is a table with a mortar and pestle. Dried herbs and other liquids in glasses line the shelf above the table.

My father showed me this room when I learned about my heritage. Being here is like a warm hug from my parents. It no longer brings tears to my eyes. I breathe in the air and the lingering scent of sage that I burned yesterday.

Plopping my butt into the overstuffed paisley chair, I hook my legs over the armrest. On the ottoman is our family book of shadows. I lay it in my lap and trace my fingers on the raised covered crest design engrained beneath a triquetra. It wasn't long ago that I was learning what a triquetra was from my uncle. I've learned so much since then.

My phone buzzes and shakes my hip with a notification. Pulling it from my pocket, I see it's Cross.

Got to check in with Eoin. Will be back soon.

Willow: *Why, what's going on?*

Cross: *Check-in on a family nearby.*

Willow: *Is Quinn going too?*

Cross: *Yeah.*

Willow: *Want some company? When are you leaving?*

Cross: *Just me & Quinn. We'll leave in about 15 min.*

Staring at my family's book of shadows, I open the front page and flip through it casually. So many of the pages appear to be empty. It's deceiving though, because as I scan through the pages, they fill in. I stop midway and stare at the pages with newly formed ink. The ownership of the crown and family lineage. I've seen it before, but I watch it unfold. My picture is under my grandfather, Harkin McKinnon, the Wiccan King. He followed my great grandfather, Thurmond McKinnon, and prior to that was my great-great-grand-mother, Gabrielle Baudelaire. They based the lineage on power and arranged marriages, and they held it for hundreds of years in my family. My mother should be here, but she isn't on this page, only those who have held the Wiccan Crown in Edayri. The script of my name appears, *Willow Sola Warrington.*

With something so powerful, why do I feel so useless? I feel like a schoolgirl under house arrest, a punishment to keep me safe, even though I am one of the most powerful Wiccans. I resent that I have to follow the decisions of the legion council. Yet, I'm the one who made it and gave it power. I didn't want Edayri to be ruled as a monarchy. So, why is there a voice in my head that taunts and pushes me?

The words morph on the page, the ink dissolving in the page's cotton fibers, then reappearing.

Concentrate and ask again.

I touch the words. I should be involved, right?

Without a doubt.

Then why aren't I?

Reply hazy; try again.

I sit up and let out a huff in frustration. The book is correct. I haven't been involved and can't sit by the sidelines anymore. Same with Rhydian. He can't ignore me forever. I need more, even if it's over. Enough is enough.

Yes.

I laugh.

"Oh, I agree," I say to no one, just the empty room and the book of shadows. But, with Rhydian on my mind, do I dare ask the question? Despite knowing some answers from Evan . . . can the broken blood vow be forgiven of its commitment? I doubt an eight-ball type response will help me, but maybe—just maybe the book can point me in the . . .

Without a doubt.

The book's pages turn, and I stare in amazement when the words scroll across the page. A blood vow to the crown. I can't read the words fast enough, and the sentences soak into my mind like an already wet sponge. I'm not comprehending what I'm reading. I stop and breathe and re-read the second paragraph for the third time.

If the giver breaks a vow, the recipient may absolve the giver of the vow, should the connection not be in treason to the Goddess herself. No blood vow should be taken lightly; the giver's death is imminent upon the recipient's death. The Goddess may have cause to strip a vow if haste is made for the crown or in sabotage to the crown of the Goddess herself.

Can I forgive the blood vow myself? Am I the embodiment of the Goddess? Evan said I am, but is he right? Am I?

Concentrate and ask again.

Fuck! I'm tired of this ache, this pain because of Rhydian and me being apart. Is he punishing me because I helped him break the vow to free him? Is it a pride and loyalty thing? Is the Goddess punishing me? This is uber fucked up!

It is certain.

Geez, thanks for the support. My eyes are heavy thinking about Rhydian. I miss him, and my heart hurts. Maybe I should forget it like he has. I don't want to hate him, but my resentment builds like a disease with every passing day. It's been almost three weeks.

I think about kissing him, laughing, and his smirk. His hand is holding mine. The warmth that comforts me. Him seeing me for the first time, his all-business warrior face. Us grappling on the training mat. His face when I came down the stairs in my prom dress.

"Willow! Willow! Where are you?"

"Hum?" I rub my eyes, and Daniel is coming into the coven room. His face is pale. I stand and go to him, and the book falls to the floor with a loud thump.

Outlook is not so good.

"What happened?"

"We got a text from Cross. We got to go help them."

I follow Daniel out of the coven room, and Marco is pacing back and forth.

"Do you know where they are?" I ask.

Daniel hands me his phone with an address that's three towns over. We can't drive there and get there quickly. I will need to transport all three of us there.

"Are we sure they need us? Daniel, they were clear before they left—to stay here." Marco stops pacing. "I mean, you were talking with Lucy a minute ago."

"Really? You've seen the text . . ." Holding his phone, Daniel reads it aloud. " 'Could use some backup, put that training to work.' Then the address. You're overthinking it."

Usually Cross sends simple text messages. Maybe I'm overthinking it.

"I don't feel a shift or a rift in the air. We could pop over. I know generally where this is."

"Yes, we can't wait."

Daniel stands next to me, and I hold out my hand. There is a sensation, a connection when our skin touches. He is excited. An opportunity to be out of the house. Marco is slower, reaches for my free hand. I concentrate on the address, and the push of air surrounds us. It's risky transporting.

Holding both Marco and Daniel's hands, we land with little effect under cover of the dark trees in the backyard of a massive house. The dense cloud cover makes it hard to see the house. It doesn't look like anyone is inside. There is no light anywhere.

"Are you sure we are in the right place?" Marco asks.

Daniel nods before speaking. "Oh yeah, this is the house."

How would he know? Before I can ask, there is a loud crack and a blinding light that shatters all the windows. Marco and I duck and cover our ears. Daniel is running toward the house.

"I guess this is the right place then."

I follow Marco, and we make our way into the house but lose sight of Daniel. It's too quiet. We are in a mud room that leads to a longer hallway. The hallway leads to an open floor plan that is completely wrecked. Furniture tossed, items on the floor all over, and pictures barely hanging on.

"Cross. Quinn. Where are you?" I yell. My magick surfaces quickly, the hum radiating all over me.

This is wrong. Something is wrong here.

"Willow."

It's Cross's voice. It's faint, and he's coughing somewhere to the left of me. There is a staircase in the middle of the space, and I see a woman laying head toward the bottom of the stairs, eyes open, but there is no life there. Marco goes to the woman and shakes his head after checking for a pulse.

There are holes in the ceiling with burn marks everywhere. Water is dribbling down a wall in the center.

"Cross?" I call out.

I barely make out his hulking body near an overturned soft. As I get closer to him, I hesitate because he looks like a wounded animal that may strike. He has burn marks all over him. He takes a few seconds to recognize me.

"Willow, over here now!" Cross commands. He's leaning over something small. I see others in my periphery unmoving on the ground, but the one Cross is over and protecting is a little girl.

Her slight frame is still, and she has blood all around her. I reach to her and my magick flows instantly. Her skin brightens, and she gives a weak cough.

"Shit, Quinn!" Daniel says. He's on the opposite side.

As I stand, Cross grabs my hand to stop me. His shaking courses through me.

"Cross. What happened?"

"It was an ambush," Cross replies.

He won't look at me. Then his shoulders heave and his eyes snap to mine. "She was the only one who stood a chance."

The little girl sits up and starts crying.

Marco runs into the room and slides to a stop surveying the damage.

"He's gone, Willow. Gone."

"What does that mean, Cross?" I look back at Daniel, who is only staring at the familiar shoes and pants that were in my house a few minutes ago.

Quinn.

I listen to Cross explain that he and Quinn came to this house on the routine check-in with this Wiccan family. When they transported in, the hunters were already there.

His voice breaks, but he continues, "Quinn was calling it in when lightning came and—I was a target in the room and . . ." His voice hitches. "But Quinn. He pushed me out of the way, and he was—"

I can't process this right now. Quinn. Oh Goddess, Quinn. I can't comprehend what Cross is saying. It's Marco's voice that takes me out of my head.

"Murdered."

"It should have been me," he says.

Cross's heavy-set shoulders bob with his head down. I reach out to him. He flinches.

"Are we safe here?" Marco asks.

"We have to get out of here, if they come back . . ." Daniel stops short, still staring at Quinn on the ground.

"I've called in. The legion council representatives for refugees and other Guardians are coming because of the mass casualties. Let them come back, I will—" Cross turns from us.

I reach for the little girl, picking her up to hold her. She clutches my neck and buries her face in my shoulder. Her tears and mine mix. I rock her in the swing of my hips to help comfort her, but maybe I was doing it more for me. I can't go to Quinn and see him there, lying on the floor.

Am I sure I'm not still sleeping, and this is a nightmare? I don't know how the time passes, but I track the movements of everyone. Including Guardians' and council members' arrival.

My heart squeezes when the legion council representative takes the little girl from my arms.

"It'll be okay," I whisper to her when her little hand reaches for mine.

Do I believe that?

All I can think about is the burn marks all over the house. Lightning, a signature of a valkyrie. I know others must think the same thing. Although a Wiccan can do the same damage, why would they turn on their own in this way? Why would any magickal being?

I try everything I can to think of what could have done this horrible crime to this family, because I don't want my mind to wander to the note from Coral. The accusations of Lucy, Emily, and Daniel. Daniel led us here. Marco said Daniel was just speaking with Lucy.

The grief is heavy in this house, from everyone I see. Guardians surveying the house and removing four bodies, including Quinn's. But it doesn't look right on Daniel. It seems rehearsed and disingenuous. I want to grab him by the collar.

"Cross, when did you text Daniel?" I ask.

Daniel is a good fifteen feet away, but he hears me and turns. His stare is holding mine. He lied.

"What?" Cross shakes his head.

Eoin stomps into the house. Daniel's eyes move to him.

"Yeah, maybe, Willow, I might have," Cross says.

Daniel turns away and goes with Marco outside. They are being driven back to my house.

I barely recall Eoin talking with me and Cross. Cross gave a blow by blow on the hit. He didn't know exactly how many hunters were involved, but he suspected ten surrounded the house. It was firepower they hadn't seen yet on at this magnitude. Eoin was all business, but his voice was louder and more authoritative. He knew Quinn died tonight, but he doesn't show it.

The focus comes back the moment Eoin shakes me. Before I'm enveloped in a hug that is stiff from Eoin. I speak, but he cuts me off.

"Sabine is outside in a vehicle with a Guardian to drive you home. Cross will need to go back with me."

"No."

"Willow . . ."

"Cross needs to stay with me. This is too close to my home. He's a Royal Guardian—"

"Fine. Cross leaves with you."

Eoin turns toward a young Guardian, barking an order. I walk out the front door and find Cross in an SUV with Sabine in the passenger seat.

In the car, it is quiet. Sabine didn't talk, and neither did Cross. We were together but silent in our sadness. The ride felt short as we pull into the tree covered entryway of the driveway toward my father's house.

The Guardian who was driving us parked and turned off the engine.

"I will stay outside tonight, with another Guardian soon. Please get some rest."

"Thank you," Sabine says before leading me in the front door.

Cross closes the heavy front door, and I jump at the sound.

"Oh, sweetheart. I can't believe this happened." Sabine hugs me by her side.

Marco is at the top of the stairs.

"Where is Daniel?" I ask.

"He left as soon as we got here. Said he had to see Emily and would be back later."

I want to say something to Cross, but I don't know what I think I know. He said he texted Daniel, right? I can talk with Daniel later. Daniel wasn't there when this happened, anyway. He was with me and Marco.

Cross passes Marco, making his way up the stairs slowly.

"I'm staying here tonight. Do you need anything? How about tea?" Sabine asks.

"Maybe? But I can't move. I don't want to think about Quinn —and how—he . . ." The burst of my lung's pulses with each heaving cry because I can't form a sentence.

Sabine and I sit on the formal stiff couch because it's closest to the foyer. She holds me and we both cry until I am taken upstairs to my bed and covered with a blanket.

CHAPTER 12

Thanks no way, absolutely no way, I'm staying in this house. I'm going to Quinn's funeral. Over the last three days, the hunters have killed over twenty Wiccans alone. This group of people, these hunters, who are slaughtering anyone with magickal abilities, is a priority threat. The legion council is holding funerals in mass in the realm of New Haven. New Haven is a refugee holding post outside of Edayri that seems unaffected by the rifts, or at least that is what Sabine and Eoin have said. It should be safe, where the funerals are, plus if anything happens, my magick and training are an asset. I keep rehearsing this in my head, walking down the stairs dressed in black with my long overcoat.

"Ya think yer gonna get by me? I know what ya think. Hell, I want to go too, but we can't. Willow, and the last thing I need to do"—his voice a whisper when he looks away—"is failing, again."

Cross doesn't look at me. He's staring at the floor.

"I believe the instructions were to stick with me. And guess what, I'm leaving. So, if you want to continue your assigned duty, you will need to follow me."

Marco is in black slacks, a gray shirt, and a dark jacket. He shrugs his shoulders at Cross. "I've known her a lot longer than you have. When she sets her mind to do something, especially tied to a friend, it's gonna happen."

I can't help but weakly smile at Marco. I hate we are here in this situation.

"This is nice and all, but you don't have a pass or transporting ordinance for the funeral. If we transport, we're shooting in the dark."

I pull out of my pocket a glowing paper with the coordinates flashing in a sequence of alphanumeric code. It wasn't hard to get from Sabine without her knowledge.

"Well, aren't you the little thief," Cross says. His smirk is approval enough we are going to the funeral.

"No, just resourceful."

And then Marco adds, "In a stubborn-headed, beyond-belief way."

We wait while Cross changes his clothes in happy defeat.

We each hold on to the card with our thumbs and forefingers. Marco hooks his arm into mine on one side and Cross to the other. I'm a magickal battery. This was the only way we can get there without coordinates in the Guardian wristband together. Calling to my magick, the familiar hum rises to the surface, and I attach it to the code in the card that guides us in transport. It isn't smooth transport; we get jolted, and my shoulder knocks into Cross's muscled arm. It feels like a running stop as we land in New Haven. The greenway strip is holding the mass funeral. Others are transporting around us, and it conceals us in the crowd.

Cross like me has a hood on his coat, and we pull them up to obscure ourselves to those around us. No one would recognize Marco unless we run into Sabine or Eoin.

My heart aches for Eoin. Quinn was so happy being more public in his relationship with Eoin. My mind replays the memory of Quinn feeling comfortable enough to tell me about it after prom dress shopping. I didn't realize, at that time, it was

Eoin until we were fighting at McKinnon Manor. I can't think about it, or my eyes will pool with tears.

Cross pulls me out of my reverie. "Everyone's walking this way, go."

Marco and I follow Cross through the crowd.

The dull ache of my heart twists, Rhydian. He still hasn't responded to me, and most likely he's here for his best friend. Will we see each other? I clench my fists and release them while steadying my breath. I'm not here for Rhydian. I'm here for Quinn and Cross, and all of us who are grieving. Isn't that what a funeral is, anyway? It's not for those gone, it's for those left behind.

The legion council has a stage set up in front of the new Hallowed Hall on the outskirts of a refugee camp. There is a podium and several chairs on the stage. I see her bright hair flowing behind her as she walks up onto the stage. It's Sabine. I glance to the side to avoid her spotting me in the crowd. Abigail is on stage, and sitting next to her is Evan. He's looking straight out like a statue. I wedge between Marco and myself behind a large man, so he obscures us. Knowing Evan, he probably knows I'm here with his gift of knowing future events, but maybe not.

A member of the legion council at the podium taps on a microphone that booms their voice over the crowd. The noise of those gathered quiets when Aren approaches the podium.

"It is with great sadness that we gather today to mourn the loss of several in our community. We are fortunate to have found temporary homes in New Haven and Terra. We grieve for our lost lands and homes, but most of all, we feel the loss of our fellow Edayrians. May we honor our ancestors in our final resting place and carry those we've lost to the homeland." The surrounding people are watching movements on the stage and podium. At the sound of the horn, all the Wiccans say together, "As above and as below, blessed be."

A new member of the legion council reads the names of those who have died. Cross moves to the side, away from my eyesight, giving us space, but I know he's here. This is horrible, a mass funeral. I try to be as inconspicuous as possible, watching those around me, some staring ahead, seeing the names magickally carved into a pillar behind those on the stage. Others lean on their loved ones with tear-stained faces, and their eyes cast down to the ground. The cyclical rumination about Quinn and the fact he's no longer with us is a pain I know all too well. I've cried, hit things, blamed myself, and let the sorrow wash over me only a few days ago. Right now, I feel numb.

The ache I want to feel—is missing.

Marco steps in front of me before a person in the gray hooded coat turns and lowers his hood.

"You've got some nerve . . ." Marco says.

I barely touch Marco's shoulder, and he moves.

His name, it's on the tip of my tongue, but I can't speak. I look into his stormy ocean eyes. He's doing the same, assessing my face. His eyebrows pinch together, and his lips part. I'd almost forgot how his lip quirks to the left before he speaks. My heart isn't twisting in pain, but my pulse is rushing through me. He's calm, as if we just saw each other. Rhydian doesn't seem like a broken shell of a man. He looks like himself.

"I thought you weren't coming," Rhydian says.

"I'm sorry to ruin that for you," I reply, trying to keep my tone even.

He shakes his head and turns around, away from me. I can't believe him. One sentence that punches me in the gut. That's it? That is all he's going to say?

He was hoping not to see me. I swallow the bitter medicine that he is, in fact, avoiding me. I've had enough. He will not ignore me! I grab his arm before he's entirely lost to me in a crowd of people.

"Are you fucking kidding me? That is all you're going to say to me? Well, I've got a lot to say to you, Rhydian."

His mouth opens as if he's about to say something, but he doesn't. He looks like a puppet, his jaw opening and closing.

"Am I that intimidating? You can't say whatever it is you're going to say? I know Quinn means more to you than me, and I'm sure he's happy you are here, but you're late! You're very fucking late."

His exhale was audible. And he reaches for my elbow and leads me off to the side of the crowd. No one is taking notice as we slip by quietly, despite the rage in my head. He turns to me when we are far enough away from the greenbelt of the crowd and near a gravel pathway that enters through dense woods.

"I don't know what to say to you. Everything I needed to say, I said at McKinnon Manor that day. I just am not ready."

Ready? What the hell is he talking about?

He continues and looks around me before meeting my eyes.

"I feel if I say it, it's more real, and I'm drowning in disappointments and failures. I found my mother. She passed away only three years ago. So, I had a lovely conversation at her gravesite. Another failure, one I can't even press my father about or yell at him for. And I have to come to terms with the fact that the man who raised me was also willing to kill me. Last, one of my very best friends died. I wasn't there—"

He pushes his hand through his hair, and he's looking everywhere except at me.

I want to yell, but I can't. Aware of what his father did and was prepared to do. I did not know about his mother. We both have so much loss in our lives, both of our parents have died. My fist releases, and my pulse steadies.

"So, when do you leave? Are you only here for the funeral?"

He takes a step back from me.

"I've been back with the Guardians for the last month. They kept it confidential. It was an agreement I had with Eoin. I needed to be a soldier again, with purpose. I needed the routine, the missions, the direction."

I can't hear the rest of what he is saying, just the fact that he's been here for a month. That wasn't long after graduation. He must've found out about his mother earlier. He was nearby to me, and he actively avoided me. Abby said it's not like him to run away. Did he hide it from his sister too? My breathing is getting harder. I can't hear what he says. I'm shaking my head, trying to clear the preaching thoughts in my mind.

It was the blood vow; that's what tied him to me.

None of it was real.

Why do I continue to hurt? Why am I still mourning us?

"Why are you running from me?" I didn't realize I asked until he answered.

"What? I'm not running, I'm—"

"Are you? What about the damage and the hurt you've left in your wake?" I raise my voice, and he flinches in his shoulders. "Tell me I'm right."

Tullen is coming toward us and allows Rhydian to avoid my question.

"Hey, Eoin is looking for you, Rhydian." Tullen looks at me before saying, "He knows you're here. He spotted Cross and Marco. It's okay, although I wouldn't make it a habit to not tell Sabine what you're doing."

Rhydian walks away from us, and I want to follow. I need to follow, but I resign myself to throwing my hands in the air.

"Tullen, this is so messed up! He won't—he doesn't even care."

"Willow, that's not true."

I spy Rhydian and Cross in a quick hug and talking. "I just don't understand why he won't even talk to me. Am I that awful? Did it all just evaporate? Were all those feelings just part of the unwanted blood vow?"

Tullen blocks my view so that he's in front of me. "Absolutely not. Rhydian is punishing himself in his own private atonement. You feel that ache when he's not near, right? His is 100-fold, and it's a pain, an ache that he wants because he's so—for lack of a better word, ashamed. For a man like Rhydian, loyalty is every-thing, and he broke his—"

"But not of his own awareness. It was his father who manipulated everyone and—"

"Yes, his father. A man he loved. He's reconciling a lot about who he is. You've got to understand that the blood vow you helped him break pulled at everything he believes is at the core of who he is."

My arms shake and I clench my hands. "I didn't have a choice. There was no other way."

"Willow, you know what it's like to lose loving parents. Can you imagine his scenario, and he lost someone he was falling in love with?"

I want to cry and hit something, listening to Tullen. But he's right. I'm grieving over it and have been for months. But for me, avoiding each other is worse. There is no closure, and it's a sitting ache that haunts me. I can't live like this.

Rhydian is moving from Cross, and Marco is walking away from me. Sabine and Evan are walking toward me at the back of the field.

I'm not done talking to Rhydian. Not done yelling and—my vision waivers as I take my steps toward him in the opposite way of Sabine and Evan. I push through the crowd that is trying to swallow him from my reach.

"Rhydian!" I yell.

He stops, and his head drops, only for a moment before he walks again through groups of people. He is walking away from me again, but this time no goodbye. My steps get faster, and before I know it, I'm running toward him, yelling his name again. That is almost a curse. I grab onto his arm, and when he turns around, it is instantaneous. We need to talk, and I'm transporting us. His lips push together in a line. His eyebrows pinch together. I don't care because it's a mirror of how I feel. The transport pulls and pushes us. My death grip on his arm isn't allowing him to leave, not this time.

The transport pulls us; my magick flares. He pulls my hand from his arm, and when we land, we break apart in darkness. The air leaves from my chest as my ass hits the hard surface. The atmosphere is musty, and my hands feel like I'm touching a chalk-like substance. Clapping my hands, I stand in the darkness. I can't see anything in front of me.

"Willow! Shit. Where did you transport us?"

His voice is close to me. Holding my hand in front of my face, I barely see it. The smell of the stale air is unfamiliar.

"I don't know, obviously this isn't my home in Chepstow, that's for sure."

I call to my magick and it hums to life in the various patterns and designs on my skin, along with the hovering crown above my head. Rhydian is close behind me. I turn to face him. He hits his wrist cuff, and light surrounds us when he tosses an illuminating stone to a red dirt floor.

"Goddess, Willow, where the hell are we?"

Is it a hole? The sides look like the red dirt ground but are carved, arching overhead and far above.

"It must be a cave? I'm not sure."

He paces. "What were you thinking? Have you lost your mind? We didn't have a pathway, a time point—we could be anywhere!" His voice is rising, and so is the pressure in my chest.

His yelling fuels me—finally, communication.

"If you would have turned and faced me, talked to me. I wouldn't have resorted to this." I stomp.

"I had nothing left to say!" His lips are tight, and his face is stone. The ridge of his brow bone gives a shadow over his face that is intimidating.

"Well, I do!"

He mockingly gestures to me. "Well, did you ever think I don't want to hear it?"

"You're a fucking coward then, because I'm not done. Ignoring me does not make me disappear." My voice carries, but it doesn't stop me. "You left, and your pain is mine! Did you know that? You left and that pain you feel, the one you enjoy punishing yourself with, that it also punishes me?"

He's not surprised by this, his face still stone. I can't stand this. All I wanted was closure, and now all I want to do is smack him.

"You knew! Your silence is deafening!" I yell.

With a thrust of my hands, I push the air with my magick and hit him. Did he expect it? He touches his wrist cuff, and his guardian armor extends to cover his body. I don't let it finish before I'm in front of him, and my arm is moving of its own volition with conjured light and air. He jumps to the side, and my magick misses him.

My legs are being swept out from under me, and I quickly rotate to my side. The jolt goes to my mind. If he won't talk to me, at least this is real. I fall into my training. I'm on offense and attacking with my body, arms, and legs, falling into a rhythm that Rhydian easily blocks and deflects. My eyes water in this dance, and I'm blind, but my movements are steady and connecting.

I scream and scream.

Ah!

The echo around me fuels me, and my magick hums, connecting and compounding. I'm bursting with the absence of the ache. His continued rejection.

Rhydian is not striking back. He's only protecting himself. His arms deflect.

I just can't anymore.

My arms fall to my side, and I stop. Heaving, I bend over to catch my breath and wipe my eyes. My magick flows all around my skin. I'm controlling it. My magick is not misfiring. It's working as I intend for it too.

"Willow."

My name is a whisper, and as much as my heart lifts to my name on his lips, I sink.

CHAPTER 13

My wrath, my anger, and my sadness are rolled into one. All I can think about is the comment from Evan; that the blood vow was not something I accepted. The blood vow made was to my father, not directly to me, but for me.

"I can't continue like this. You're dwelling on your own self-pity and suffering, but it is also causing mine! Do you have any idea that our separation causes constant pain to me? You're making me suffer."

His eyes relax, and his lips part.

"Oh, you didn't know that? I figured you wanted me to suffer because I helped to break the blood vow against your commitment, your loyalty to the Guardians, the crown." My voice breaks. "To me!"

He reaches for me, and I step back. "And FYI, the blood vow you made was to my father, not directly with me!" I give a mocking laugh, a moment of courage, and I step forward into his space. "Do you want to hurt me? You've done a magnificent job making me suffer with you. What my pain was of some silly heartbroken girl? What is your goal, Rhydian? Avoidance? Do you think it will all go away if you avoid it? Avoid me?"

He looks everywhere except at me. I move to block him so

he has nowhere else to look but at me. This is it, my only chance for him to face me. My heart is thundering in my chest.

"Say it. Spit it out. I do not know what you're feeling, but I can tell you that if you don't speak now, I—"

It comes rushing out of him and feels like a smack in the face.

"I should've never made the blood vow. I would take it back if I could. Is that what you want to hear? Tell me what you want to hear!" he says.

He regrets it all.

He regrets me.

At that moment, it was all I could do not to look away. I pushed him to hear it, and—his kiss is crushing and unexpected. I grasp on to the threads of pain in our lips, the desperation and pull of it, the past that haunts us both. He doesn't push me back. The urgency of his kiss is welcome because it's his, mine, ours. It's a cursed hell we've both been living, and it has to end.

I pull the tether—the ache—the loss. It's tangible, the light and shadow pull. Lifting my hands from him, I direct the magick, the vow, our hurt into a magickal bubble above us.

"We can we be rid of it. A blank slate, a new—"

Rhydian pushes me.

"No!"

Before I can release my magick, I'm pushed off my feet. I stumble to catch my balance before pushing off the wall, and I direct my blast to Rhydian, who easily ducks and rolls to the side.

"Why! Why?" Tears. Pitiful, exhaustible tears threaten to fall. I hate them.

He's in front of me, trying to pull me into him. I don't want to be comforted. The opportunity to be rid of this connection of pain, and he doesn't want that? I can't. I don't want to love him anymore. My tears fall. They are the catalyst. My arms are moving and throwing punches.

He's deflecting my offensive moves, and we are moving in a

circle as we used to train in the Guardian gym with Eoin. Yes! It's familiar, and his eyes light up, and my frustration rises at the friendly taunt.

Rhydian is holding back when I kick, and he grabs my leg and hooks me to him. My side is open to him. I take the advantage and hit him with my elbow and come down onto his shoulder. We break apart. He's fighting back.

Isn't that what I've wanted? A reaction. How much will he fight for it? I won't stop. Screw him and his noble, silent suffering.

I conjure my defensive magick in my hand; it lights up, and I toss it toward the contained magick above us. I pulled, but he pushes me, and I miss it. I use the combo Cross taught me, and I hit him, one, two, then spin and sweep his legs—but he grabs my leg and twists me, and I fall on him.

I try to push, but he rolls us, and he's on top of me, breathing hard.

"Get off of me," I say with little conviction.

"No." His eyes are searching. "Willow, I—stop."

The bubble above us dissolves, and the magick settles over each of us. The hurt of the blood vow, because we are near each other, doesn't ache. Goddess, I want to hate him. I cover my face, and the tears stream down my cheeks. My entire body shakes in heaves. It only takes a few seconds. He sits up and helps me do the same. My effort to wipe away my anger with my tears fails.

"I'm sorry, Willow. For how my father manipulated me for my connection with the crown—with you . . . for being so blind. I needed time to sort out my place in all of this. I didn't know that the broken blood vow caused you pain when we're apart, too. I thought it was one-sided. I—"

"It's not the same."

His kiss, the connection we share, is still there with or without a vow that connects us. My finger traces my lips in the rough absence of his.

"Rhydian, I'm a mess of feelings. Are you settled? Are we d
—" I can't bring myself to say it. Are we done? It still hurts, but
the pain is becoming a familiar friend. I hate this.

"Do you hear that?" he interrupts and turns away from me.
His brow furrows.

I slow my breathing to listen and turn toward the faint
sound. He's right. We are not alone, maybe a voice? The magick
on my skin ripples in patterns.

"It sounds like water. We must be deep in a cavern. It must
direct out toward—"

"I think we should go toward the water." I point to my hand.
"Look, my magick is moving with it, on my skin."

Rhydian nods, and he picks up the light stone and shines it in
front of us. We walk toward the source of the sound. It takes
time before it gets louder.

"It sounds almost like there is rushing water? Maybe it's a
way out," Rhydian states more than asks.

There is a light string of melodic melodies that float to our
ears.

It's fairies.

Rhydian holds the light stone for the glow ahead of us, its
soft white light beckoning us forward. The walls give way to an
opening that leads to a vast cavern with soaring ceilings and
surrounds us like a stadium. The light above is over a cliff-side,
where water is cascading down, filling a spring. There are reeds
around the edge and grass fans out around the edges with tall
redwood-type trees scattered out of place.

"What is this?" I ask.

"I don't know, but it reminds me of the Lunar falls. Fairies
are inhabiting the shores and the trees. Do you see the lights?"
He points.

"They've found refuge here. Are we in Terra or New Haven?"

"Good question," Rhydian says, looking around.

A squeak alerts our presence to the fairies, and one flies
toward us. The wings move so quickly, like a giant dragonfly, but

she is no dragonfly when you properly adjust your vision to her. She hovers in the air at my eye level.

"Is this your new home?" I ask.

She smiles and waves. The pitch of her voice is high and small. I don't completely understand her, but Rhydian says, "We are in Terra, somewhere in the desert. She says this is part of the Lunar Falls, and it's supporting magick here in Terra."

"Is there a way to leave here?" I ask.

Rhydian puts his hand out, and the fairy settles on his hand. Her wings fold behind her back, and her dress shimmers in the light. Her high-pitched voice, without the fluttering of her wings, is easier for me to understand.

"It is but a half day's walk, in the direction you came. However, it is nightfall, and there's no reason to go in that direction. The next town is very far away, and it gets extremely cold at night. It would not be safe to leave the cavern until morning."

My heart skips a beat as Rhydian nods, and I realize we have the entire night together.

"May we stay here?" I ask.

"Of course, my Queen, it would be our honor."

She leads Rhydian and me toward an enormous tree on the other side from where we came from. It's closer to the falls and away from a majority of the fairy lights. When she touches the side of it, a door appears, and Rhydian walks in. The magick is incredible for something so simple. I'm stunned as I walk up the stairs that circle up into the treetop. It's as if I'm in a hotel room from an amusement park. The wood of the tree is smooth. The floors have rugs laid throughout, with the open balcony, and lights strung on the rails that come inside along the ceiling where the walls meet. That takes my breath away. A large bed is in the middle with a small stove-like fireplace off in the corner. This must be for someone who stays here often. I turn to the fairy to ask, but she's gone.

"Are you hungry or thirsty?" Rhydian asks me.

On the balcony, I take off my red dirt covered jacket and

hang it on the back of a chair. The falls are impressive and mesmerizing.

"No, I'm not hungry. Can you believe this?" I point to the falls and sit in the chair. The water is so blue, suggesting an illumination of light just under it. The open space above, although dark, gives the illusion of stars overhead.

Rhydian sits next to me, his hand close to mine. I'm reminded of when I transported to the beach, having just learned about my father's abduction, and I would need the high council's help. He listened to me and said little. He always supported me.

"Are you thinking about the beach?" He asks.

"I was. How did you know that?"

Rhydian's fingers skim mine on the arm of the chair.

"Just a guess. I don't have access to your thoughts or feelings anymore, but that doesn't mean I don't know you."

The patterns on my arms light up brighter. Is it my magick or emotion?

I stammer, "What do you think we should do next?"

His face turns toward mine. He's so close. "I think we should get some rest, then make our way out of this cavern and try our best to transport back to your home in Chepstow. It's the safest place, and I'm sure the others are looking for you there."

I agree. I stare up at the darkness, getting denser, as if the sun has completely set somewhere above.

Rhydian lays his head back and turns to me. I miss him, and yet he's right in front of me. Why was I so rash in pulling us here and forcing this? I don't regret it because here we are. His eyes are brighter. His lips tilt, making a face that I see in my dreams.

"I'm sorry." We both say at the same time and smile at each other.

He laughs. "For which part? The abduction or almost kicking my ass back there?" His dimple appears first before he continues, "Cross has been training you? I'm guessing from the combo."

I laugh. "Yeah, the drills have become second nature. And I'm only sorry for pulling at the magick of the vow. I'm not sorry we are here and talking. You can't shut me out. It's . . . torture."

His demeanor doesn't change. He leans into me. "Yes, it is, and I'm sorry, Willow. I never meant to cause you pain, ever. Being near you eases my pain, but I needed to feel it; own it. But damn, I missed you."

My breath catches in my throat. "I missed you too."

"Will you forgive me?" His wide, waiting eyes make him look youthful and vulnerable.

"Yes. But I have a condition."

"Really, what's that?"

"Never do that again. You can't just cut me out of your life, Rhydian, and ghost me. That isn't what you do in a relationship unless you want this to be over." I can't bear the thought, and I look away from him toward the ground. "Unless that is what we should do? Is this just too much? That's fine, but you have to tell me."

"Do you want that?"

I shake my head no, and his lips quirk at the side.

"Me neither."

His fingers skim my face, his thumb gliding over my lip. "I miss the connection that the blood vow gave me—the insight of your feelings and thoughts. But my need to know you, protect you, and be with you isn't gone. It wasn't only the blood vow that drew me to you."

The space between us is shrinking.

His lips hover over mine before I connect us. The feather touch ignites a fire in my stomach. One of his hands cradles my neck, the other moving in my hair. Our lips part, and his tongue tangles with mine. I can't get him close enough and what started as gentle feels starved. Somehow, we are off the balcony and on the enormous bed in the room. My hands are pulling at his shirt, his at mine. I need him close to me, and we roll together in an uncoordinated mess of limbs. Both of our shirts are off, and only my bra remains. My magick hums and pulses in patterns all over my skin.

He kisses designs that appear on my collarbone. I can't help but laugh at the tickle, but before I know it, his lips are back at mine, and he's settled between my legs.

"Willow."

My name a plea on his lips.

His powerful arms are holding him over me.

Be bold is what my brain and body tell me. I don't object when I reach for the waistband of his pants, and he does the same to mine. We don't stop, and it's a blissful connection between our hearts, pain, and experiences. I've never felt passion like this driving me, as if I know exactly what I'm doing versus the bumbling fingers and thoughts before. I'm guided by one purpose: the connection and the intimacy between us together in every way possible.

His hands are skimming over my arms, and he's tasting my shoulder. I kiss his neck—the warmth of his skin transfers to my heat. Blankets are tossed to the floor, and somehow, we are on the floor. I laugh in the tumbled roll, tangled in Rhydian's arms. My hair is a cocoon around us. My naked back tingles when his finger slides up my spine. His other hand tucks hair behind my ear. His face is unreadable with the slight quirk of his lips and his half-mast eyes.

"What are you thinking?" I ask.

"That I'm an idiot, and I wish I didn't walk away as I did. That I don't deserve you."

I don't feel like I deserve him, either. Is that the way of relationships? Each is in awe of the other, not feeling worthy.

"Rhydian, what is deserving anyway?" I hover over his lips. "I know I want you. That's not changed. Is that enough?" I whisper before he leans up to connect our lips.

The kiss is not as urgent as before, but a slow burn that melts my arms and legs into a puddle of wants and demands. I lose track of where we are until Rhydian breaks our kiss. Now my back is on the firm bed.

"Yes. That's a yes, by the way." His breath is fast, his arms strain above me and surround me. "I have to ask, do we?"

I nod and say yes at the same time. We both smile. I've never felt so wanted and beautiful until now. His desire mirrors my own. His eyes never waver from mine. "Are you sure?"

Any uncertain fear is nowhere to be found. I pull him forward so that his body is over mine.

"Absolutely sure."

There is a joy in my half-sleep when I turn and feel Rhydian get out of bed.

"Where are you going?" I mumble, sleep trying its best to overtake me.

"Just adding more wood to the fire and grabbing the blanket for—"

Rhydian sets the blanket on my feet, and a finger skims my lower back. "Wait, Willow, that mark."

Looking over my shoulder, I can't see exactly where he's touching me, but I have all kinds of patterns and marks that are lightly flowing over my body. Laying my head back down on the mattress, I ask, "Is it new? What does it look like?"

"A hex mark."

"A what?" I say into the pillow I'm cradling.

"I've seen it on the dead Wiccans, Demons, other Edayrians. Willow, someone has marked you."

How would I not know I have a hex mark? My shirt is close by, and I pull it on. "What does that mean?"

Rhydian's forehead wrinkles. "I don't know exactly, but we need to get you back to Chepstow under guard, and we need to tell Eoin and the legion council . . ."

His commanding captain side sends tingles low in my stomach. I reach for him and guide him to lie down next to me. The hard lines of his face relax with his shoulders. "Guard? Have you met me?"

"I have, but someone got close enough to mark you, Willow."

He's not wrong. I shiver before Rhydian pulls me in closer to him and pulls the blanket over us. I lay in the crook of his arm and drape my leg over his. The blanket covers us, and my eyes shut.

"I haven't been around anyone that could have marked me. But, Coral, she gave me a note not to trust Emily, Lucy, or Daniel. I know what you're going to say, but they couldn't have—"

He says it anyway. "A valkyrie killed Quinn, Willow. You must know this."

"It's not them. There has to be an explanation." My chest tightens at the thought that either of them would be responsible for Quinn's death, especially Emily.

Rhydian is drawing circles and shapes on my arm.

"It will be fine," he says, but it doesn't sound reassuring when he says it.

I feel my body settle and my mind quiet long enough that I drift into a dreamless, contented slumber with Rhydian's body around mine.

CHAPTER 14

Rhydian is brushing my shoulder with his fingertips. I don't want to open my eyes because when I do, our night together is over. I feel the light on my eyelids and turn my head toward him.

"Willow?"

I nod. "Just a few more minutes—"

His touch is steady and familiar on my shoulder. There is singing coming from outside. Singing that isn't from the fairies because it's loud and clear. Rhydian is rolling out of bed and tugging on a shirt. I try unsuccessfully to be as fluid as he is, but I stumble to the floor, reaching for the rest of my clothes.

Rhydian's half-smirk has me chuckling at myself from embarrassment until I hear the singing more clearly.

"Her name da dada . . . yellow feather in her hair, da da dada dada . . . Cha Cha."

The singing is getting louder. I walk to Rhydian, who is looking out of the knot in the tree on the balcony.

"Is he singing Copacabana?" I ask.

"Um . . . I've never heard that song, but that is definitely Evan."

Evan is turning and smiling, singing, and then he laughs when a few fairies land on him. He begins a new song and goes to the edge of the water.

"Let's talk to him, obviously he knows a way back."

Rhydian nods and follows me. "He's been here before. How does he know of this place? He's speaking to the fairies as if it's something he usually does."

When we exit the tree and walk toward Evan, he doesn't seem shocked at all by our presence. Instead, he waves and sets down a fairy that is in his hand.

"So, you found it! Nice, right?"

Evan smiles, and his eyes sparkle. I wonder if I have a fully lucid Evan. I shake my head because, lucid or not, this is Evan. This is who he is.

"Stumbled upon, actually," Rhydian says.

"Well—I'm not sure about that. Didn't you transport here, Willow? From New Haven's funerals, right?"

I did transport here, but it wasn't something I had aimed for. "Um . . . not purposefully. I didn't know of this place. Maybe you could clear the air on where we are?"

"We are here, of course."

I say nothing but stare at him, and before I ask, he adds, "The Lunar Falls supports the flow of magick. Magick is attracted to magick. Like magnets. It can attract or repel."

I pull my hairband from my wrist and pull my hair into a quick ponytail. "Are you saying it pulled us here? When I transported, I did not have this destination in mind."

Evan touches his nose and winks.

"So how is the Lunar Falls here? Isn't it supporting New Haven?"

"Good, good questions. Yes, and yes. I helped the fairies with the building of this and New Haven. It needed to be split to stabilize the new realm, needed a support structure beyond a pure magickal one. It would help if you had a foundation when you built a house. You need support beams and—"

Evan is droning on about the building of a house and neighborhoods. I'm watching the fairies around him work and do various things at the edge of the water. They are in trees on the other side of the ridge. This massive cave is their home.

"Yes, but where are we?" Rhydian cuts off Evan.

Evan shakes his head and gestures around. "A cavern. Really? Where did you think we were, at a beach or something? I'm doubting his intelligence."

I tug Rhydian back, who is losing his patience with Evan.

"Sorry, but where is this cavern located? Which realm are we in New Haven or Terra?" I ask.

"Did you not hear a word I said? Foundations?" He throws his hands up and puts them on his hips, clearly exasperated with my question, and all I can do is smile because it looks comedic. "Really? Don't you know? Okay, fine. Obviously, wonder boy doesn't, but, Willow, you don't?"

I shrug and reach to hold Rhydian's hand.

"We are in Arizona."

"Arizona? Why would I . . . ?" Oh my gosh, Sabine's house is here in Arizona. "Is this why she's in Arizona?"

Evan smiles. "Do you listen? Again, magick calls to magick. You were pulled here."

"But you did this?" Rhydian gestures around us, and the fairies near us light up. Evan shrugs with a knowing smile.

"Any more questions? Because I'm eager for breakfast with my friends here," Evan says.

I notice the circles under his eyes.

"Yes, I do," Rhydian replies. He gently turns me around and lifts my shirt to reveal the mark on my back. "Do you know what this means?"

I feel Evan hover near me, inspecting my lower back. His inhale is sharp. "It's a death mark," Evan says flatly. "A hex, the hunters will know you if called."

"How?"

"Detection spells, magick calls to magick. They will use other living things, animals or—"

"Birds," I say before I swallow and look at Rhydian.

"Like a homing beacon," Rhydian replies.

"I'm marked, and the hunters are working to lure me out and do what? Kill me?"

Evan, still behind me, says, "May I?"

I nod before he touches the mark on my back. Looking over my shoulder, his eyes close and the flat of his hand is cool on my back. It's a fast connection before the sweep of my shirt hangs back down. Before I can turn, Evan is in front of me.

"Whoever marked you wants to know where you are and who you are with. I suspect if they wanted you dead, you would have already encountered an assault."

"Do you know what they want?" I ask.

"Eradication of magick, which isn't possible. Therefore, they want to control it or bury it."

Rhydian steps in closer to me, as if protecting me from Evan.

"Why do you say that?" I ask.

Evan continues, "Because not all marks are for death, but they know you, and you know them. Theon and I have seen these marks. I suspect you have too." Rhydian pushes his hand in his hair. "If you use magick, it alerts them. This allows the hunters to find and police you."

"We've got to get to New Haven and tell the Commander. This needs to be reported to the Guardians and Edayrians," Rhydian says.

Evan sits down on the grassy knoll and leans back on his elbows. "He already knows. Several Guardians have this mark, information causes mass chaos, and so the legion council agreed not to share."

"Quinn?" I whisper.

"Actually, no," Evan replies.

Rhydian looks up and says, "Cross."

Evan doesn't deny this, but how would he know? Does Cross know?

"No, this isn't right. Edayrians need to learn what to look out for. We need to talk to the legion council," I say.

Evan checks his watch that doesn't exist on his wrist, and he suddenly stands. We follow him out into the cavern, which is a longer walk than I would have thought. On our way, I ask why we can't transport out, and Evan rambles something about how you don't shake a foundation because that makes a house weak. When we reach a bend that leads to an opening, the sunlight beckons us toward it.

The sun is bright, and the air is crisp, as if it's still morning. The view outside of the cavern is a desert valley with marbled red and orange in the sunlight. It waves like a river and winds down the mountain we are in. Other mountains are in every direction, and dark green trees and cactus dot the landscape.

"Do you see that ridge, the swirl? That is the closest town. You will need to transport there." Evan says, pointing.

"Wait, we need to see Eoin, the legion council. Remember, you're taking us to New Haven," I reply.

Evan shakes his head and looks at Rhydian. "I have other obligations today."

Rhydian spins on the spot. "How are we getting there? Evan, this is serious. Lives are at stake."

"Lives?" Evan repeats.

"Willow's life, this mark. You must realize it's someone close to her, and those around her are in danger. Guardian lives, magickal lives." Rhydian's tone is even.

"What is it with listening lately?" Evan pauses and looks out at the beautiful landscape in front of us. "They are aware of these marks. This isn't new information. What is new information is your renewed union with my niece?"

My neck and face feel hot. Evan never turns to us but continues, "Some journeys are starting while others are midway to their destination. It won't take you long to get to Chepstow. The journey is everything, isn't it?"

"Evan—" Before I can protest, he disappears before our eyes.

Rhydian stomps his foot, and the dirt shuffles around his booted foot.

"You may not like it, but there is always a reason. Be patient with him," I say.

"It's dangerous. It's thoughtless. You're his niece, his family, and he seems undisturbed by this mark." Rhydian pushes his hand back through his hair before turning to me. "Don't say it."

"And what is that?"

This should be interesting since he no longer can feel my emotions or the obvious sign that I trust Evan, as crazy as that is. Evan's purpose is always to a larger scale. He embodies the Horned God. Look at what he's accomplished in the cavern behind us. My magick is more controllable, but to accomplish what he has with the fairies, that is something to be in awe of, transporting part of the Lunar Falls to Terra to support magick. Am I doing enough with who I am?

My stomach rumbles loud enough to betray me.

Rhydian's face changes from hard lines to soft ones, with his dimple showing. "Clearly that you're hungry."

I laugh. "Clearly."

He turns me toward the town, reaches for my hands, and interlaces our fingers as he hugs me from behind. The warmth of the sun is nothing compared to the hug and holding of Rhydian. Transporting back to civilization makes our evening and all that's occurred in the last twenty-four hours a part of our past. Does it set the tone for the future? I tamp down the irrational thought.

"Transporting with intention time," I say.

I feel Rhydian hold me closer. When his lips near my ear, he whispers, "You got this."

Facing the small town we will transport to, I focus off to the side of it and take us there in less than a breath.

CHAPTER 15

There is one car that passes us as we walk into the small desert town. Rhydian points to a restaurant in a small strip mall with a large parking lot and grocery store.

"Maybe we should get a quick bite to eat before we go back to Chepstow?" I ask.

"No, we need a plan before we set foot in your home, a neutral ground—the cabin," he says.

"The cabin?"

A few more cars enter the parking lot, and Rhydian pulls me toward him. His face is open, and his eyes wide. "Remember, I took you there from the woods when we first met. Tullen and I went there after . . ." He shakes his head. "Well, after my father died. There isn't food there. Let's grab a few items, and if we can time it right, we can transport there. It's a shorter distance than Chepstow."

It shouldn't matter the distance for us to transport. It's more time alone with Rhydian, so I agree. In the store, we check out our items, and I'm thankful they have electronic pay, so I pay with my cell phone. Rhydian watches a man and woman who are standing and arguing by the automatic doors. When we leave the store, they exit at the same time. Rhydian tugs my hand and leads me to the side of the building. He pulls me behind him around the corner. His finger touches his lips, and I pull my body flush with the side of the building—the brick snags on my shirt.

A full minute passes, and no one rounds the corner. Rhydian turns to me. "Can you tell if there is an opening in the shifting rifts, so we can transport?"

My heart is beating loudly in my ears. I can't hear the pulse. I attempt to slow my breathing and calm myself. The vibration is a low beat, and it's distinguishable, with long and short bursts becoming more frequent. The pause is brief. It's an opening.

Tick-tock.

"Now, we go now." I reach for his hand, but he pulls me into his arms and hugs me.

"Let me guide you," He whispers and lays a kiss on my temple, and his lips stay there right at my hairline. The connection is brief when his magick mingles with mine; I give up the control. We are pushed closer together in the transporting's movement, push and pull, but it's gentle and easy.

Colors of red and brown give way to deep green in the surrounding blur, and our feet settle in our new location. Floorboards groan under our weight. We are on the porch of the cabin. I had only seen the inside of the cabin before.

Lush trees and green surround us. A gravel drive forks around the house and up to the front porch where we are. The air is cool and crisp. Rhydian releases me and opens the front door. Walking over the threshold is a blast to my not-so-recent past. I take in the lazy boy chair Cross sat in, and I can see Tullen and Quinn greeting me in shock. Then Quinn assessing my injury.

Quinn.

How can someone be here then not? This feels different from both Mrs. Scott and my father. I witnessed their deaths. With Quinn, I couldn't bring myself to look at the aftermath of his death.

My thoughts move quickly when I stand in the small space of the living room. I was nervous the first time I was in this cabin

—large men all around me, the first time I met Cross, Tullen, and Quinn. Rhydian walks through the small hallway to the kitchen with the grocery bag. I follow him, and he grabs two glasses from the cupboard and fills them with water from the sink, and hands me one.

"Is this your cabin?"

Pulling the glass from his lips, "Yes, it was my grandfather's and has been passed down. My father never particularly liked it, but I would come here in the summers, mostly."

"It's beautiful," I say.

His dimple appears briefly before he says, "It's beautiful and peaceful. No one besides Tullen and Cross would come here. We'll be alone."

My mind wanders, drinking water eases my dry throat.

Why does the word alone have my eyes gravitating down his strong shoulders, back, and the well-rounded butt that his dark jeans curve to? Our night together was . . . He turns, interrupting my thoughts, and hands me a small mixed granola bag and a peeled orange that we bought from the grocery store.

I take them and pop an orange slice into my mouth.

"It's strange to be here, in a unique situation," I say when I swallow most of the orange slice.

"Is it a unique situation? Funny how long ago that seems, but yet, it's not. Everything is so different." His brows draw together, and he's fiddling with the granola bag. "Willow, I—I'm sorry for how I treated you. I don't deserve your forgiveness. You've lost more than I have. Your grief is as fresh as mine, and I punished you for saving us because I didn't know how to—"

I step forward into him, and his hand halts me from hugging him or touching him in any comforting way.

"Wait. I didn't know how to handle my father's betrayal. And not just his betrayal of me, but of everything I stand for and for everything I am. The disappointment in his eyes, his death, they haunt me. I'm still scared of what I could have become had it not been for Abby, my mother leaving, my brothers in arms, for all the small events in my life that pushed me in another way, for your father, and for you even."

"My father?" I ask.

"Yes, Aiden knew my father well enough not to involve my father beyond our introduction. His own words said as much. I don't know why he chose me. He saw my dedication to the Guardians as something that would benefit you. I would have enjoyed knowing him more."

"Rhydian." His name was a whisper of my lips. His eyes finally meet mine.

"Since being near you, the pain that was a consistent reminder of the broken vow has subsided. My head is clear, and I am truly sorry that I didn't realize I was punishing you by being away."

I move again, and this time he meets me, and we hug. The comforting and encompassing kind, with his powerful arms wrapped around my upper back and his head down on my shoulder. He's breathing me in, and I feel a shudder move through him.

"I'm glad we're talking," I say.

"Me too."

"I'm not numb to your pain. I'm sorry for all that you've lost: Quinn, your mother, and your father. Maybe we can comfort each other in the face of it all," I say.

He kisses the side of my face.

"Of all the events that lead us here, I wish what my father orchestrated wasn't one of them, but I would never have traded the blood vow or us willingly. I hope you know that," Rhydian replies.

Placing a hand on his chest, I feel his steady heart. "I do."

His face is a mixture of awe and rawness that I'm not used to seeing. Rhydian is typically self-assured and confident. Right now, in front of me, it's as if he's waiting for a terrible response. Part of me was so hurt and angry when he ghosted me for weeks. That was my selfishness and my need to be comforted after all that happened. He said he needed time, and there was no end date. My timetable was not his. The pain of the broken blood vow a consistent reminder that felt like a rejection, but it wasn't.

"Why, Willow, why me?" His eyes are searching mine before the quirk of his lips. "Surely it's not all physical, but I can't say I object to that."

I smile and chuckle. "Yeah, I like the physical."

What? Did I say that out loud?

Shaking my head, I continue, "Rhydian, I can't say why, but it wasn't an overnight thing for me. Certainly, there's an attraction, but I respect who you are as a Guardian warrior, your loyalty, your protectiveness, that you treat me as an equal in training and don't mock me for not knowing Edayri but show me and explain it to me . . . I—I fell."

His lips hover over mine. "I fell too."

Our lips connect and test each other before we are open, and tongues tangled. His pull on my waist has our bodies fitted together in such a way that I don't want it to end. Ragged in my breath, I barely register a knock at the door. Rhydian moves so quickly that the sudden coolness of the surrounding air sends me into a moment of vertigo.

"Fuck!" Rhydian says when I hear the door open.

"Now, how's that fer a greeting?" Cross's voice bellows down the hallway.

I wipe my mouth and tidy my clothes, trying to look more put together than I am. In the hallway, I am surprised to see Tullen.

"Hey," I say. I wave awkwardly before putting my hands in my pants pockets.

The squinted eye, assessing me, makes me shake my head at Tullen. His grin says it all.

"The whole, he will talk to me, happened I see," Tullen says. Turning to Rhydian, he continues, "I'm happy to see the reunion, but it's going to be short-lived. We've got a timeline.

We have approximately four days before the full collapse. It's expected before the new moon."

"The Commander has requested we escort ya to New Haven. The legion council are meeting in the next day."

I'm still focused on the fact that Edayri is collapsing in four days. If Eoin needs me in New Haven, there must be a reason.

"Why am I needed at the legion council meeting? Did Eoin or Evan say?" I ask.

Cross shakes his head.

"Is everyone out of Edayri?" Rhydian asks.

"Yeah, most who are resettling and grabbing key things. We're ahead of the timeline." Cross pauses before continuing. "It's okay, Willow, I promise. The big issue is these hunters. We don't have a beat on them. They are wide and funded. The hate crimes are not subsiding, so most of Edayri is split between here in Terra and New Haven."

Rubbing the back of my neck, I think about being marked.

"I don't get it. Why mark us and not just kill or attack us on the spot?"

"The theory is that if you're marked, and they have a large group, they look to get the most casualties. It's a follow and scout for a bigger payoff strategy. It isn't well organized. They are clumsy. It's a bonus we found you both here. They ordered Cross and me to scout this area as several High Coven members have property in this area," Tullen says.

Rhydian is leaning on the hall wall. "So, this going to be your home base?"

"Cross thought maybe we could catch you both here."

"A regular Sherlock." Rhydian smiles and pats Cross on the back.

"When do we leave?" Rhydian asks.

After several minutes, we agreed we would leave closer to the evening hours after Tullen and Cross's scouting of the area. Rhydian and I go upstairs to clean up. The upstairs landing has a small hallway with three doors leading to three separate bedrooms. The one at the end of the hall is where Rhydian leaves me.

Out of the shower, looking around the room, I'm comforted being somewhere familiar. The patchwork quilt on the bed in dark maroon and navy colors. The oak chest of drawers. I pull the top draw to find clothes as before—Rhydian's shirts. I run my fingers over them and select a dark one that looks more fitted.

A soft knock at the door before Rhydian peeks his head in.

"Hey, Abby had some clothes here. They have got to be better than my shirts." Rhydian laughs. He's wearing jeans that hang on his hips and no shirt. His wet hair is a ruffled mess. He lays the clothes on the corner of the bed.

Still wrapped in the towel, I hug it a little tighter.

"Thanks."

His eyes are watching me and pinched together. "Are you okay?" He stands in front of me and holds my shoulders. "What are you thinking about?"

"Last time I was in this room. I felt insecure and uneasy."

"Why?"

His open eyes are searching mine, and I have a hard time looking at him directly. Are we back to leaving each other? We've both said so much in the last twenty-four hours. I have no idea what it means for the future. Is it stupid that I want to hear the words?

"I guess it's just old memories."

Coward.

"You're not telling me something. After all, we've been through. I thought you were the one who said we needed to talk and not close up."

Great, throwing my own words back at me. The slight sensation in my chest is the squeeze of my insecurities.

"I—I want to know where we stand. We are both going to be pulled into our duties, our jobs, and we've said a lot to each other to mend, but what exactly does that mean?" I ask.

"Willow, is it a label you're looking for? I'm not sure what label I can give us, but I want to be with you. Is that enough for now?"

Gah, I'm silly. I shuffle my feet when his hand gently lifts my face.

"Willow?"

Instead of answering, I kiss him, and he pulls back.

"I want to continue, but with Tullen and Cross waiting . . ."

"Thank you for the clothes. I'll see you downstairs."

Rhydian turns to leave and eases the door shut. I put on the clothes and feel tired. Sitting on Rhydian's bed, I lay down and watch the sun hide behind the blinds one by one by one.

I roll onto my side as he lays a blanket over me.

"It's okay, rest."

I open my eyes, and Rhydian is over me.

"Wait, what time is it?"

"Almost five. You've been asleep for a little over two hours."

Rubbing my eyes, I sit up. "When do you guys want to leave?"

"Tullen came back about twenty-five minutes ago, and we expect Cross in the next half hour."

"What? Have they already looked around? You stayed here?"

He nods before elaborating that he stayed while I slept. They'd report in if they needed backup, but so far, everything is quiet. I follow Rhydian downstairs, and we find Tullen with a book in his lap, head leaned back, and eyes closed.

I'm not the only one who needs rest.

PART III

Enters intention and wishes of the waning moon, brings about the circle of trials.

~The Horned God

CHAPTER 16

Cross's arms are full of fast-food bags and drinks. I open the back door, taking the drinks from him.

"Scouting paid off?" Chuckling, I lead the way into the cabin.

"Actually, it did." He uses his back, bracing the door, so it doesn't slam. However, the thud that sounds makes both of us jump.

"Wha-the?"

Smack.

Two small birds are on the back porch. Rhydian and Tullen come from the front of the house and stand in the yard.

Shit.

"Do they carry the hex identification spell?" Tullen asks.

I reach down over the small dead finch. A light glow lifts from the bird and touches my fingertip. It stings briefly before it evaporates.

"Yes. But the spell is not strong. Someone spelled them a while ago." Shrugging my shoulders, the other small bird struggles to move. "Oh, look, he's okay." I place my hand on the small bird, and the spell evaporates. The bird's head turns in slight movements. It's too tired to fly away. "It's okay. I won't hurt you." I hold out my hand, and it hops in and squats as if it's going to nest.

"You've found a new friend," Tullen says.

"Hmph. Duke, will not stand for it."

Cross's consideration for Duke makes me laugh; it is as if Duke is his dog.

Focused on the woods around the cabin, Rhydian starts toward the porch steps. "We need to secure the area. I don't want to be the next beacon on the—wait a minute."

The guys talk, but my attention is on the tiny bird resting his head on my thumb. I allow magick to warm my hand to keep the bird comfortable. I see the guys are nodding at each other.

"What? What's going on?" I ask.

"Can you redo the magick on the bird? Have it guide us back to where it originated from?"

I look down at the bird. Maybe, but this sweet little bird trusts me. Heck, he's in my hands. Could I do that? Its eyes are closed.

"I'm not sure I could—What if I hurt the bird? It looks like they both were so tired." I try to keep my voice even. "I mean seriously, look at it in my hands, sleeping! He's traumatized."

Rhydian sits next to me. "Maybe we could go about it differently. You pull the magick back when we reach the destination. Willow, we need to find information about these hunters. It's not safe for any Edayrian here. What happened to Quinn. You are being chased. The magick drew these birds to your mark."

The air is thin at the mention of Quinn's name. With this bird, we could figure out how this originates and possibly stop location spells that help them do these heinous crimes of physical abuse and murder. Maybe there could be a way for us to know who they are. He's right. We should try this.

"How do I do what you're suggesting?" I ask.

Tullen answers, "Call upon your magick to replicate the magickal signature that you touched and place it on this bird.

Can you command the bird? Have it show us back to where the magick marked it?"

"You expect me to be Dr. Doolittle here?"

"No, but these hunters are using these birds like carrier pigeons, and we're betting it knows the way home. Otherwise, the signal they give is useless—unless they are close by and hunting. These spells last longer than a few hours or a day. Why do it any other way? It's strategic. Otherwise, it's a shot in the dark to magick these birds," Rhydian says.

Cross nods. "Makes sense."

"You've seen this before? I don't want to hurt this bird," I ask no one directly, but Tullen responds.

"Something similar to the war games in Guardian training. Willow, it's worth a shot."

I nod. He's right. We have to try. Cross runs into the house and grabs a bag. Rhydian and Tullen are placing spells around the cabin. Me, I'm the babysitter to the little bird in my hands, and I'm thinking about how I'm going to get this little bird to show us where to go so that he can stay right in my hands and continue to rest.

I spy a small bird flying from the west before it falls near Rhydian. Tullen yells from the front of the cabin. Another bird is down.

"I have an idea. Bring them to me," I yell. "Cross, do you have a map?"

"Why?"

"I will pull the magick from the birds, then plot it back into a map. This way, we won't need the bird to guide us. Besides, if someone sees me holding the very birds they are using? The wrong person sees that, and . . ."

Both birds are exhausted but still alive. I pull the magick spell from both of them and hold it in my hand. The birds' chests rise with what seems like a relief. Cross taps his wrist cuff and displays a map of the United States. He zooms in on the map to where we are.

"Don't zoom in too much. You can do that after," Rhydian says.

The remanent of the hex spells from both birds are in my hands. It's a familiar pattern. This must be the signature. It's the same. It's like a recipe, and the flavors are the same: sugar and vanilla. I push them together, and they easily mix and get stronger. The magick expands and pulses in my hand. It's faint, but I feel its invisible weight. Flexing my fingers, I'm able to move it. I direct my magick to hold the surrounding air, to contain it. Guiding it to the map, the hex magick stays suspended, waiting.

"Here goes nothing."

With my mind, I command the suspended hex and direct it toward its beginning, origin, and home base. It lights up before the hex breaks into threads. The threads fall and dissolve before touching the map, but others land and begin moving into the map.

"It's working," Rhydian says. His eyes are searching the map as the lines settle in. "Zoom out, look." He points toward the east coast. The line goes straight to Massachusetts. Home. "Cross, is this recording?"

"Yes, not my first day."

All the lines settle. It's a beacon where hunters are.

"What did you command exactly?" Tullen asks. His hand under his chin, he isn't looking at the map but at the bird in my hand and me.

"I directed it to its hunter origin."

"Clever. These wonderful little birds just scouted out the hunter's primary operations." Tullen says, "This is amazing. It looks like these hex spells are not original to one location. This reveals everything. Well done."

The guys are all smiles. I can't help but smile as well, along with the satisfaction that these little birds are going to be okay. I've seen too many of them die in my yard in Chepstow.

"Damn, this organization is large: Louisiana, Illinois, Massachusetts, and look at Northern California?" Cross nods to where the lines are the brightest. They are leading into cities.

"Focus, let's see what we can learn here. Then we've got to get this to Commander Eoin. We can ensure the placement is outside of these hotbeds—but see there are locations everywhere. And this is only in the US, whereas this is global, true?"

Tullen nods.

Since I've removed the lingering spells from all three birds, we set them into a gathered towel to hold them while I heal them from fatigue with my touch. They seem to take their time before flying off. The guys are eating while studying the map in the kitchen. Looking at the twilight sky, I wonder if any more birds are flying this way. Rhydian pulls me from my spiraling thoughts.

"Willow. Come in. It's getting chilly out there."

I sit at the kitchen table next to the untouched wrapped sandwich and drink. One chair is open at the table. Quinn is not here. The guys are all business, speaking about strategies that I don't track while I eat. I reminisce about Quinn at this table.

"Look." Tullen points to the map, and near our location in the cabin, a line is pulsing. There are dots on it joining from various directions, like travelers.

"Let's follow it," Cross says.

He grabs the keys, and we all get in the car. I sit in the back with Tullen.

"What do you think it is?" I ask, watching the large pine trees pass as we hit the main road. "Do you think it's a meetup of sorts?"

Tullen nods, but it's Rhydian who says, "I hope so, then maybe we can get more intel to bring to Commander Eoin and the legion council."

"Right, but we're gonna stand out. If they know who the members are—"

"I can magick myself and one of you if I'm able to touch you safely without the rift, causing chaos in my abilities," I respond.

"Nice." Cross smiles in the rearview mirror. The map projects on the windshield in front of him like a high-tech GPS.

"I don't think we need magick. If we use it, they may have protection or other animals around to warn them. I think we walk in cold," Rhydian says.

"That would put a damper on things." Tullen chuckles under his breath.

Cross takes several turns, and we are coming off the main road and following an old green Ford truck. Another vehicle comes behind us, and it's clear we are in a line of vehicles and are now one dot on the line of the projected map. The back of my neck feels tight. I stretch it from side to side. I want to go with the flow, to go with what this group has planned. But can we only gather intel? After all that has happened? They are killing Edayrian's—anyone with magick.

Show them who you are.

The designs on my hand flare brightly as I close my fist to extinguish my magick.

"I guess we get to join the club," Cross says. He claps his hands and rubs them together when we're halted on the road. "What do you think this big meeting is about?"

Rhydian's eyes were surveying everything. "If I didn't know better, I think you are ready to knock some heads to find out. Reign that in Cross."

Everyone is sitting upright, muscles tight and ready. We don't know what we're walking into, and regardless of us having magick, it's clear as we pull into an open field and park. They outnumber us. There are over a hundred vehicles here.

"We don't need to start a fight. I thought this was an information-gathering assignment."

Tullen is nodding his head, and Rhydian says in a low voice, "Absolutely, you're right."

The vehicles on both sides of us are empty of people, so we park unnoticed.

"Let's make our big entrance." Cross opens his door, and we all get out of the car and follow.

People gather at the head of the field, where there is an enormous bonfire. Lots of guys are laughing and joking, and I only see a few women. I don't get the impression that this group of people is any different from who I see every day in Chepstow, Massachusetts. Dressed in jeans and coats, nothing reveals they are murderers.

We stay together at the back of the crowd. A speaker comes to life with a tap as someone turns it on.

"Welcome."

A voice booms across the field, and the noise of the crowd quiet.

"As you know, phase three is almost complete."

An eruption of applause begins, and we begrudgingly smile at our neighbors and clap along with them. Except for Cross, he keeps his hands tucked under each armpit. He smirks enough that the biggest guy near him nods, and he bounces back—the hairs on the back of my neck rise. I shift foot to foot, and Rhydian's hand reaches across my shoulder and pulls me into him, and steadies me.

"Willow, it's okay. We are here only to listen," he whispers in my ear.

The booming voice continues over the gathered crowd, "We are lucky tonight that our leader is here. Phase four is underway and will secure our world from being breached by new races who threaten our very existence and way of life." More applause continues. The voice introduces someone, but I don't catch the name.

It's a female voice that takes the mic, "Thank you, thank you all for coming."

I stand on my tippy toes, but I cannot see who is at the front of this crowd. The voice comes across the speaker and apologizes for not being here in person. The voice is commanding and confident. I settle back into Rhydian.

I whisper, "This voice sounds familiar. Are they here or streaming in?"

Rhydian squints his eyes. He taps on Cross and leans in, and whispers to him. Cross's mouth drops just a little, and he nods his head.

"What? Who is it?"

"I've seen her before. But I'm not sure who she is. She's on a mirrored portal, like a projected screen upfront. Wherever she is, it isn't here. Cross says he's seen her before, too. Thinking maybe someone from Chepstow."

I pull Rhydian's hand and try to guide us through the crowd to see if I can see the speaking woman. Rhydian is right behind me with his hands on my shoulders, nodding to those we are passing. About midway, a behemoth of a guy stands in front of me.

"Where are you going?"

I feel the timbre of his voice in my bones. I shrug my shoulders, trying to maintain my composure.

Rhydian replies, "Sorry, we thought maybe there was some Johnny on the Spot upfront. Girl's gotta pee."

"No one goes upfront without . . ."

"Without what?" I summon the sound of a high-class spoiled brat.

He nods to another guy, and we are being surrounded by men in tight black tee-shirts, which are the security.

"What do I intimidate you?" I shrug and laugh, trying to make light of a daunting situation. I look back at Rhydian, and he nonchalantly shrugs.

The man in front of us smiles. Rhydian turns us, but we are surrounded by large men in dark glasses.

Tick-tock.

This is not good. They probably should intimate me, but they ignited the fire in my blood.

"You don't belong," he says to Rhydian. "You need to leave with her before I get out of hand, brother. And no little girl, you don't intimidate me." His baritone voice is just loud enough that those near us take notice.

We'll see.

"Seriously? Do you enjoy talking down to women? Is it because I'm short, have breasts? Prettier than you are."

Rhydian laughs. Keeping hold of my shoulders, he applies a little pressure. "Dude, we're just pumped and high-spirited. How about you let us pass? She is quite the jungle cat when provoked."

He leans toward us. "I don't think so. I know what you are, and you're not welcome here."

"What exactly are we?" I ask innocently, although inside, my hum is beating under the surface, one taunt, and I'm ready to lay them all out.

"Wiccan."

Okay, we're outed. I'm ready to lay waste to—

"So, doesn't mean we had a choice. You're one too," Rhydian says. I try my hardest to keep my expression even. The guy shows his wrist to Rhydian, and it glows blue with a broken triquetra with thorns on it. My hand is on Rhydian's wrist. I command my magick to imprint the same symbol, and Rhydian shows his wrist and gives the guy a fuck-off look.

"Right. Well, next time, show first, talk shit after." He moves. As we pass, a few of the crowd push their shoulders into us. We get closer to the car. Tullen and Cross are in the car as we open our doors.

"We need to get out of here. Did we get anything useful?" Rhydian asks.

Tullen weekly points toward the front and says, "If you were listening, the plan is complete genocide or subjugation to the Human Principality."

Covering my mouth, I try not to look shocked, and fake a cough.

"The leader's name is Vanessa."

Cross eases the car onto the main road and says, "Did you see when you went upfront?"

"No," Rhydian replies. He explains what happened.

"Did you notice other Wiccans there? What was that Rhydian? How did you know he was, and how did he know we—"

A large truck slams into the car, and we spin.

My head hits the window, and I see blood opposite of me from Tullen.

Rhydian is checking and doing something with Cross.

We are being pushed by another vehicle!

"Grab on to me!" I scream.

Thrusting my hands in the middle of the car, Cross, Rhydian, and Tullen grab my hands. I transport us right out of the car, back to the porch of the cabin, and we land in a jumbled mess of body parts in one pile. Cross groans under me, with Tullen and Rhydian laying over both of us.

"What the fuck?" Cross says.

"Shit, that was brilliant. Thank Goddess," Tullen says as he and Rhydian roll off of me, and I slide off of Cross.

Cross stands quickly.

"They will follow that signature. We have to go," Rhydian says. He touches my temple. My blood is on his finger.

"Okay, one more time, fellas? I'm on a roll." I hold out my hands, and they each hold on to me. I transport us smoothly between the pulse and a shift of the rifts, straight to New Haven. Because there is no way I'm leading those assholes back to Chepstow.

CHAPTER 17

T he stairs to the Hallowed Hall are the same in New Haven as they are in Edayri. I do a double-take because this is New Haven, right? I'm familiar with all the surrounding structures. At the mass funeral gathering, I didn't see this many structures and buildings. It's the same, but feels different. Edayri has a particular flow about it, a peace that I felt. When I first came to Edayri, it was the connection; it could've been from my magick or my family's heritage, but here, it's like a sterile surgical room, practical but not somewhere you live.

Evan is standing near us, looking at his fingernails as if he's bored and we are late. Did he realize what would occur from that cave to here for me and Rhydian?

"We need to speak to the Commander and Sabine," Rhydian says.

Evan points behind him. The flowing cape of Sabine is heading in our direction, and Commander Eoin is fast on her heels.

"Willow! Oh, my Goddess. Are you okay? What are you doing here?"

Her questions continue as she looks me over.

Evan interrupts, "Willow has a situation, and it was important for me to get her to safety along with the captain of the Guardians."

"Evan—"

He taps his temple. Did he see that we'd end up here? If he's so omniscient, why doesn't he stop all of this?

Commander Eoin moves in front of Sabine and invades Evan's space. His stubble is almost a full beard, which is at odds with a usual clean face. The dark shadows under his eyes. His stoic nature heightened by the deaths of so many, including Quinn . . . someone he loved.

"What do you mean? And you thought it was safer to bring her here? Cross and Tullen are in Chepstow. Didn't you think it might be wiser to take her to her home?"

Cross and Tullen step to the side, and Eoin sees them and clamps his mouth down.

"Commander. Sabine. The hunters—we infiltrated a meeting, gained a mapping of their locations. They call themselves the Human Principality. Their goal is genocide of magickal peoples or to subjugate them for their use," Tullen reports to Eoin.

"How so?" Sabine asks.

"Magickal beings are helping them. Wiccans even," Rhydian says.

"Possibly valkyries as yer aware." Cross's voice isn't the booming sound it usually is. Eoin's face is stone. Cross looks away before he continues, "We recorded what we could on my wrist band for you, sir. We spread out so we could gather as much intel as we could."

Eoin nods. "That's good. Debrief now. Let's catch up with the rest of the teams."

I watch the four of them jog up the stairs and disappear between buildings.

The tension is steady in my neck from the scrutinizing stare down by Sabine. I breathe deeply because people are watching us. If she's taught me nothing else, it's maintaining my composure in front of a crowd.

"Should we talk here or in private? Because I realize you are hiding things from me. Let me tell you what I'm aware of now. This Human Principality group is marking us, using us, and ending us. And how do I know this?"

Sabine is looking at Evan because she knows.

He gestures to my back as I pull up my shirt at my waist to reveal the mark to Sabine.

"I'm marked. I don't know by whom, and the intention isn't clear. But you learned about hex marks, and I find out by happenstance this is . . . how would you say? Unacceptable." I grit the last word between my teeth.

Her face drops with a slight shake of her head.

"Somewhere private, now. Follow me," she says.

I follow behind her bellowing purple cloak as she leads the way from the grand entrance of the New Hallowed Hall. We pass by the pillars that stand high as if they have been here for centuries, but they have only recently transferred them here per Sabine talking as we walk. It is amazing what the legion council has accomplished.

Sabine turns a corner behind a large building that is being used as a judicial forum and crosses to a smaller one. She opens the door with a flick of her wrist, and we enter a smaller room that leads into a larger hall. The marble floor clicks under her shoes as we move into a room and find several people at tables with laptop computers and headsets on.

"We need the room," Sabine announces. Those sitting stand up quickly, as if eager to leave for a break. Abigail, Rhydian's sister, comes from the back of the room. I wonder if she knows I was with her brother this whole time. Thaxam comes in from a side door. We sit at a small table, except for Evan, who seems halfway between sitting and standing. He leans on the table.

"What is going on?" Abigail asks no one in particular when Sabine responds.

"Hunters have hex marked Willow. They are larger and more

coordinated than we've guessed at. They call themselves—what did you say, the Human Principality?"

Evan adds, "But it's clear this group has magickal beings helping them, Wiccans and valkyrie that we are aware of."

"Your friends may not be your friends. They killed Quinn in a way a valkyrie would, with a lightning strike," Ax says. His voice leaves no emotion. He's laying down the facts. I hate Sabine, nodding her head in agreement.

"This isn't Emily or Daniel."

Evan looks away as if listening to someone. "But . . . you're not sure."

He's right. I understand how it looks. I would point to them if I didn't know them. Heck, Daniel has had all the opportunities living in the same house as me.

Do you know who they are?

"Cross is marked as well," Evan says, his eyes unmoving.

"He is?" Abby responds.

Ax answers, "He doesn't realize he's marked? I suspect you didn't either, Willow. That is until it revealed itself and someone saw it."

I look at Ax and Sabine. My voice changes, more profound and dripping with disappointment. "Are you telling me you won't tell Cross, but you suspected he is marked? Please tell me that isn't true."

"He knows," Evan says. "Quinn pushed Cross out of the way. Quinn wasn't a target, only a bystander."

If my mouth drop doesn't show my frustration, then it would be my wide eyes. "Evan, if you see all of this, why aren't you stopping it? Could you have—"

"No. Some events I don't see until they decide. Pieces of a puzzle. The complexity of the whole."

I stand and turn on him.

"You should have done something! Said something!" I yell.

He doesn't respond. Evan only stares with eyes that are knowing and sad. I want to scream more, but I can't because I understand what it's like when you can't do anything but watch something happen. He couldn't have done anything. It would have been too late. I imagine what he has interfered with to have a better outcome.

Yes, Willow. I'm regretful for your continued grief.

The sting of his words in my head allows a tear to fall before I wipe it away.

Willow, accept completely who you are. This is not one-sided.

"I don't understand," I reply aloud.

It's Ax who answers. "Soldiers die. It doesn't matter, mark or no mark. These hunters, or whatever they call themselves—The Human Principality. We are at war, there and here."

Talking to Evan about his comment privately to me will have to wait.

"So, those marked are not limited to Terra?" I ask.

"No. I've seen several in New Haven. It's not safe anywhere," Ax responds. "We suspected, but our kind is joining their cause. We could have spies here."

"Why would anyone do that?"

Abby responds, "Easy. Anyone who thinks that their life is better without rule and a caste system. Someone could easily sway them. This world is collapsing. If they think they can save themselves or their family in Terra by giving up magick, an option to blend in equally? Willow, it is not so far-fetched. We've only just begun with the legion council. I'm sure many doubt it's staying power."

"This is true. They designed the crown for fear and order. You've changed that. But you, Evan, our family is powerful, and that is a threat to anyone if the old ways return," Sabine says.

Why is this so complicated? I gave up the royal power. I'm just a figurehead in disagreements. I form the legion council of all beings, not just Wiccans or High Covens. Clutching my hands, my nails dig into my palms.

"Why do you need Evan and me? If we go in guns a blazing, doesn't that push us backward? The old ways?"

Evan is pacing on his side of the table. Is it so much to ask him to sit? Goddess, he is always on the move.

"They need us to use our magick, our combined power," he says.

I want to help, I do, but I feel like a toy forced to play a part.

No, you're the embodiment of a goddess whose people are asking for your help. You are the Crown, the Queen of Wiccans. Covens are not coming of their own free will to the aid of Edayrians.

Evan, I pissed off the covens. I made the hierarchy useless.

True.

"Care to share with the class?" Abby asks.

I shake my head and see they are all watching me and Evan, waiting.

"Let's go have a chat with the legion council. I presume they are waiting for us?" Evan asks.

Abby leads the way. They are in the same main building that's part of the Hallowed Hall. Evan holds the door open to the grand circular room. I remember meeting the high council in this room. That seems so long ago. Me asking for help and later learning one of the high council members was one who tortured my father—all a plan to get to me, to manage and control the Wiccan crown.

It's the same large circular table that sits in the middle of the massive room. The difference now is that there are many chairs around it instead of five key chairs at various points. Aren is the first to welcome us. She's closer to my age and seems out of place within the high council. She's a powerful Wiccan, and someone I think I could be friends with. We share similar ideals. Little did she know that when she joined the legion council in its inaugural year, they would elect her the chairperson. I remember the day she stood up to join against her mother's will, pulling at her arm to stay seated.

Aren sighs. "I suppose we should get right to it. But I'd like to wait for—"

A man with long hair and pointed ears walks in, waves, and sits down at the only empty seat.

"Well, we are all here then."

Aren's come a long way from looking at her nails in boredom, as she was the first time I met her.

It feels as if Evan and I are tourists. Everyone is looking at each other in greeting, except Evan. When I look at him, he's staring straight up at the ceiling.

"Pst. Evan, what are you doing?" I whisper to him from the side of my mouth. I mean, Evan does strange things that I should be used to, but I can't help wondering.

Not moving his head or his eyes, he responds to me with the side of his mouth, "Getting the feeling of the room. Everyone's quite nervous. This should be interesting." He closes his eyes before looking straight ahead at Aren. Although she's on the other side of the table, the acoustics must've carried Evan's comment.

"You're quite right. Let's get on with it," she replies. She looks at the other members, and everyone nods in agreement. "As you're aware, we want to reinstate temporary royal intervention in our transition and refuge efforts. We have tried democratic methods, but the most powerful among us in the noble covens won't help because the hunters are targeting them, so they refuse to use magick for others."

Evan smiles, and his fangs are prominent when he leans into the table and puts his hands on the edge. "So, what are you thinking? Prayers to the Goddess and Horned God have delivered us here as saviors? Or—do you want penance because you blame us?"

I suck in the air too sharply.

"We didn't start the Convergence. Mr. Boward started all of this for power and control," I reply. My voice is gruffer and louder than I had intended.

Ax is the first to respond, "You haven't seen the numbers, Evan. Hundreds have lost their lives, and every day the murder tally rises. The Guardians are not enough, and without help, we will dwindle. But you already understand this, or else you wouldn't have helped the fairies and others."

Evan sits back, looking relaxed. I sit stiffly and clench my hands together. Ax said hundreds have died. All I see is my loss, and then everyone else passing with them. The people that anchor me to a home are gone, and those that are helping me rebuild a family are in jeopardy. The little girl that lost her family the night Quinn lost his life. Her future is forever changed, not unlike mine when my mother lost her life saving me. No more children should lose their parents like this.

"I'll help. What do you need?" I say.

Aren and Ax both smile weakly at me. Maybe it's not me they want, but damn it, it's me they will get. Their eyes shift to Evan.

"That was not the response I thought I would get."

Evan puts his hand on my shoulder. "Actually, they need us both. One will not complete the needs required, so if I say no . . ."

"Sorry, so how do we help?"

"Communications on a wide scale. We need to move Edayrians to the refugee camps, both in New Haven and in Terra realms. We need reinforcements of check-ins and reports, so that we can mobilize Guardians effectively."

I nod to Ax. "Okay, how do we do this?"

"We have a system set up for communications, and we have talking points for you both," Abby replies.

Evan and I agree. We complete our recorded messages into what looks like an older phone.

Ax explains that it's an old magick that connected Edayrians and all inhabitants to the Wiccan crown when new laws were decreed, or announcements were made. It feels wrong to me. I can't imagine receiving a communication in my head this way from someone. I hope this really helps. The legion council members leave the grand room.

"Well done." Sabine hugs me.

"I hope that Wiccans and Edayrians heed the call to help where needed and stop hiding in the shadows. But with these rifts from the Convergence, it isn't safe, regardless. I can't blame anyone for wanting to protect themselves and their family."

His deep voice startles me more than his red skin, enormous body, and massive horns. "And this makes you different from your predecessors. This crown and power do not consume you to rule and subjugate. You understand this and your actions show this."

I hug him and catch him off guard. "Thank you. I hope all see it this way. I don't want to repeat the past."

The man with pointed ears stops before leaving the room, giving an odd smirk to Ax.

Sabine's smile reassures me while Evan is still pacing. Abby has left us to talk with the legion council members.

"It's a new era, there is no repeating the past at this point." Ax responds as I let go. I see his fangs in an awkward grin. "Usually Wiccans are intimated by me, not hugging me like a teddy bear."

Laughing, I respond, "Sorry, they don't appreciate what they're missing then."

"Right—I think I prefer intimidation; otherwise, my fellow demons will think I've gone soft." His laugh shakes the seriousness out of the room, along with the weight of all that is coming.

CHAPTER 18

E van and I marvel at how nothing looks different here in New Haven. He's walking toward the Goddess Fountain down the steps toward the garden. How they have moved everything from one realm to this new one is beyond my comprehension. We near the edge of the fountain. I see a ripple in the air like you do on a hot summer day, but here it's like a crisp fall day. Rubbing my eyes doesn't help because I see it again, over the water of the fountain.

"I feel it, but you see it?"

"What exactly am I seeing, Evan?"

"Something is off here, in New Haven. Besides the fact it parallels Edayri, it's . . ."

"It's like a haunted shell," I say.

"Exactly. Where is the grounding magick of this realm?"

Looking around, I realize no one is around us. The next ripple in my vision is over the water again, and I point it out to Evan. My magick hums to life and rises to my skin. I'm pulled forward and stumble over the edge of the fountain into the water. Evan doesn't hesitate. He steps into the water with me. Shoes and all, it submerges us up to our calves.

I'm not sure why I feel so bold, but I reach out before it goes away, and my fingertips look like they have disappeared. Then, of course, I sense them, but it's as if my fingers are in a different place than my body.

"Evan, this is—" I watch him walk right into the ripple in front of me and disappear.

My hand in midair, I follow him and run right into his back in the same spot we just were, but not. It's the Goddess Fountain, but different. I turn, and the ripple moves elsewhere. The steps of the Hallowed Hall are empty, and the buildings missing.

"What is this?" I ask. I follow Evan over the edge of the fountain ledge. Sloshing with my wet shoes and pants.

He spins in a circle.

"This is New Haven—where we were, is not."

"How do you know that?"

"Magick attracts magick." He nods toward gardens. Although it's empty here, it's lush and colorful.

The sun is warm on my face. I breathe in the fresh air. It fills my lungs and radiates down to my toes, filling me and grounding me. Magick flows on my arms and hands. Evan is correct. This is where magick has taken hold. Being quiet and truly listening, it's ringing in my body. The hum is a soft tone in my ear, a beautiful melody. Magick.

"Why are we the only ones—"

Evan turns, and his horns catch the rays of sun and gleam, his eyes bright and large. "Because we are tied to the creation. They are not."

"How are we tied to creation?"

"The OGs are moving on, Willow. When the Goddess crowned you, she chose. You only need to tap in and truly accept it."

Some of the crazy that comes out of Evan's mouth. That can't be right. I've accepted who I am. I've been through hell and back, and I'm the freaking Wiccan Queen. I've dived in with both feet!

His eyebrow arches.

"What! Spit it out." I raise my voice.

"No."

"Is this for real?"

"How can there be a Horned God without a Goddess?" he asks me, as if I know the answer.

"I don't know, shouldn't you know? Aren't you what the embodiment of the Horned God?"

That same arched eyebrow pops up again.

Do I deny myself? Wait a minute. "Aren't the Goddess and Horned God-like lovers? Come on, that is—" I can't finish my sentence and regress to pointing between us.

But Evan laughs so hard he bends from the waist.

I can't help but laugh at him. "Gross, right?"

"Besides the fact we are family, and I'm like too old for you, yes. Absolutely yes!" His laugher dies down as he wipes a tear away. "How can you call me the embodiment without stating that of yourself?"

"Well, I don't feel any different. My magick is the same —but, oh."

There are differences. Magick, it's always been strong since being unbound, but when the Goddess crowned me directly. When she did that, I was tested in trials. It comes back to me, all the versions of her placed on me. The clothes, the hair, all in rapid succession. I only thought she was testing me as the Wiccan Queen, not a test as her successor—I clearly don't pay attention. I'm an idiot.

"Clearly," Evan replies. "Do you really think the power of how easily controlling magick comes from the crown and your family legacy?"

My mouth feels dry. I swallow, wanting to respond, but don't.

He is observing the gardens and walks away from me. I do the opposite and follow the hum internally. The flow of the grounding nature I feel. I am strong and connected, as I was with the fairies in the cavern.

The Lunar Falls is here like it is in Terra. This is confusing.

SACRED

Because if magick is here, and this is New Haven, then we were in Edayri . . . but everyone believes it's New Haven.

"Oh, my Goddess. Evan, this is a set-up," I stammer.

"It's genocide, Willow. It's an efficient way of killing, and the Human Principality is responsible."

This confirms the fear from Ax. It would mean they have someone on the inside in Edayri. Someone with magick who is doing this here.

"Yes." Evan breathes as if listening to my thoughts. "We must course-correct, otherwise . . ."

"Can we trust it isn't someone on the legion council?"

"We won't know until we see opposition. Those who deceive are crafty."

"So, you believe it's someone on the legion council, now?"

Evan smiles. "Don't put words in my mouth. I didn't say that. You did. Maybe your intuition is something you should listen to more often. The Goddess side of who you are—your empathic, listen to yourself more."

I see the ripple over the water again. The mirror of what New Haven should be is mocking us. It's Edayri, a doomed place with people walking and moving throughout it. They are unknowing, and the thought of everyone on that side dying is too much to comprehend.

"Can we reverse this?"

"Edayri is a mirror. This is a brilliant madman, actually. A fake that you're building—a safe realm in one spot—only to realize it's the same quicksand you were trying to escape. Lastly, you pick off those on Terra. Everyone is fearful. You achieve all that you want."

"I think it's a madwoman."

"You're right; we have to reverse this."

"Wha—How, Evan?"

"We roll up our sleeves and get to work."

Tick-tock. Tick-tock.

527

Okay, now I feel the frustration Rhydian usually feels around Evan.

"Everything precious to me, beside you, is on the other side of that mirror is a collapsing realm! I need more than we roll up our fucking sleeves, Evan! Tell me specifics. Do you know a spell?"

His face is one of amusement, and the heat of my face only becomes more intense.

"I swear to the Goddess! If you—"

"Yourself, Willow. You swear on yourself?"

"What?" I say, exasperated. "What do you mean by that? She is still very present. I don't understand your riddles and comments on the embodiment." My frustration is mounting out of my mouth. The words spill without thought. "Just tell me what to do. How to do it. If you're all-powerful and embody the Horned God, why wouldn't you want me to do the same? Save everyone we can? I don't think I can handle more death and destruction. That's all this stupid crown is, it's death!"

"Willow, stop embodying the Goddess—you have to become her, or better yet, become the full you, isn't that all she asked?"

He's insane. I met the Goddess. She blessed me. Nothing more, just as the Horned God did to Evan. Right?

"What did you do then?" I ask, sarcasm dripping from my lips.

"I became the full me and embraced it, accepted it. You may think a god lives forever, and I suppose they can in some form or another. But, own it and believe it, shed the idea you know nothing because you, in fact, are a creator and a protector of your people. You prove this time and time again, yet never believe it."

"Sometimes it is easier to believe what you know."

"That's crap, and you know it. Don't be lazy." Evan's face is hard now. His stare has me step away from him. "You don't want to see what's in front of you: your power, your potential. The truth about your friends. You're afraid of conflict, but what's worse is you won't join the fight for yourself. Where is that girl?"

"I lost most of my family, Evan! Sorry, I want to keep those around me the same. I hate to think that my friends would . . ."

"Betray you? Use you? You're smarter than this. What you need to learn the hard way every time?"

"Evan." I shake my head. I see Rhydian, Sabine, Cross, and Tullen gathering at the stairs of the Hallowed Hall on the other side of this mirror gate. They look concerned and are calling my and Evan's name. They can't see us.

"They are looking for us," he says before he walks through the gate. I follow him, and as I step through, I'm being pulled back.

"Evan!" I scream, reaching out. It's Rhydian's hand that grabs mine, and then Cross that grabs the other hand. They are pulling.

"Fuck, what's this?" Cross yells.

"The hard way," Evan says before he pushes the three of us back with magick, and the gate closes. We are flying and being pushed and pulled. The wind is strong.

"We're being transported," Rhydian yells, clamping onto my wrist with both hands.

I can barely open my eyes. We are spinning too fast.

"Where?" I yell.

"Don't let go," Cross says as we all land flat on our stomachs on green grass with a hard impact.

CHAPTER 19

Tick-tock, tick-tock.

I roll onto my back and stare up at the dark, clear sky.

"Rhy?" Cross groans.

"Still here."

The lush grass hugs me and evades my nose. I roll over and see them pushing themselves up from the ground.

"The hard way? Damn, your uncle is just—" Rhydian helps me up.

The moon and stars are bright. It's easy to see where we are.

"Well, what do ya know," Cross says. He points at my father's house. We've transported to Chepstow.

I'm staring at the back of the house with three, no, four people on the patio. A car is driving down the driveway.

Pointing at the car. "Stay down."

Crouching down, we tuck into a shadow from the tree line at the edge of the property.

There is someone or something near to us in the tree line. We are not alone. They are arguing. Rhydian points and moves behind a tree trunk further into the grouping. And that's when I realize who it is: it's Lucy. The tenor of a muffled response signifies Daniel is with her. Why are they hiding?

Who is on the patio? I squint and realize it's Marco with others I don't recognize.

He's going back into the house when those he was speaking with transport. Maybe they are Guardians, or is it the Human Principality?

The car is pulling up toward the front of the house is Coral's car. Maybe she's looking for Lucy?

Rhydian is giving Cross directions without speaking using hand signals. He points at the opposite edge of the property. I point to the front of the house, and he nods.

Coral is knocking on the front door. I transport when Marco answers the door. My heart is skipping with the clock in my head, and I transport right into the foyer. Coral's hand is shaking. She hands a note to Marco. He slowly opens the note.

"Ah!" Coral screams.

Marco doesn't miss a beat, despite my sudden appearance.

"What's with this note, Coral?" Marco asks, handing it to me.

She shakes her head fast. "You read it, so you know. I can't—I can't say . . ."

There is a wavering dark iridescent thread with thorns around her. She has magick holding her. I see it now and sense the spell. How is that possible? Instead of doubting, I close my eyes briefly, and it's as if I can still see the threads binding her threatening to hurt her. Someone powerful has placed this on her.

"They bound you," I say.

She nods her head.

"The spell would alert someone."

Coral's eyes are pleading and confirming.

And I realize that she's taking significant steps to avoid something.

"And you can't answer for fear of breaking that spell. So, tell me, what are Daniel and Lucy doing here hiding in the tree line? Do you know about the dead birds in my yard?"

Marco's eyes don't give away any surprise at my statement.

He only responds to seeing Cross walk in from the back of the house.

Cross nods to me, "All clear."

Coral's eyes are welling with tears. When she wipes her cheek, I see the band-aids on her fingers. Examining the note's ink, it's clear that this is not standard ink. It's Coral's blood. Someone has prevented her from speaking and using ink to communicate. Blood to paper was her only way, and she did this. She pained herself to warn me not once, but twice.

"I can protect you. What is going on with Lucy? Is Daniel involved?"

"Shit." Marco says.

"I can't. My father—" She yelps and bends forward. I'm at her side, and Cross is carefully watching while listening to Rhydian over the ear comm.

"She's cursed. It's a signal beacon, Willow." Cross says deadpan. "It's not holding—whatever is keeping her quiet." Addressing Coral, he presses her for information, "You might as well let it go because Rhydian just overheard the interlopers tell someone ya finally broke."

It was enough to push Coral to the floor in a blubbering heap.

"Coral!" Marco drops to her.

"She's gonna kill him. I know she will."

Cross and I are in front of her. Cross asks, "Kill who?"

"Her father," I respond before she can.

Cross pins Marco with a stare. "You don't know any of this? Who was on the patio a few minutes ago?"

"Guardians looking for you all. What's going on?" Marco looks genuinely confused. "Why do you think Daniel would have anything to do with this?"

"She's coming for you and your kind, Willow. You, Marco, anyone with magick and who's different. But, Willow, she knows what and who you are. Because of Lucy and Daniel."

I tense at their names. Inside, my heart wants to know why, but my head doesn't care.

"Fuckin' hell. Who? Who is coming?" Cross says, helping Coral up in one smooth step.

"My father's wife, my stepmother Vanessa." Coral takes a shallow breath.

Vanessa. I feel the tingle up my back. The black smoke, the whip, the broken triquerta with thorns. Graduation. It all clicks.

"She is the leader of the Human Principality," I say.

Coral's hands shake, and I hold them. My hum illuminates across my skin. Then, with little thought or direction, I pull the wavering thread surrounding Coral and snap it. Her exhale is one of relief. The curse that caused her pain is no more, but it will also confirm to her jailor that she is no longer controlled.

"We need to leave to keep you safe."

"But where? I can't leave—"

I turn to Cross.

"Sabine's new place?" Cross offers.

He's right. That would be the best opportunity, and she can help Coral there. Maybe retrieve her father?

The ticking of the clock continues. The metronome beat is present in my chest. This is a countdown, and it's getting too close.

"I've not been to Sabine's. How can I transport there, and what about the rifts? Can you tell if it's good? Otherwise, we could end up anywhere," Cross says.

"Coordinates. Meet us there. I'm taking her."

I swirl my hand, and the numbers flicker in the light's glow. "Scan them, save them so you can meet me there."

Cross taps on his wrist cuff and does exactly as I ask him, and now he can share Sabine's location to Rhydian and transport there.

"I can't leave. Willow—she has powers, she—poisons and controls. She can—" Coral is shaking.

533

"So do I. I'm powerful and I don't think you forgot that small tidbit. You wanted my help, Coral. So let me help."

I grab her wrist and tug her through the front door and transport us.

Daniel is calling out to me, but the sound fades as we do.

CHAPTER 20

We arrive at Sabine's house. Coral pulls her wrist from me and starts yelling. This causes Sabine and several members of the household to come running into the foyer.

"Willow? Who is this?" Sabine asks.

"I'll tell you who I am. I'm the friend you just kidnapped, Willow! You have condemned my father and me. She's going to kill us both. What have you done!"

"She will not kill you or your father. Let me do what I need to and protect you both."

The tears that were streaming down Coral's face take a reprieve. She spins and looks at everyone around her.

"Who are you people?"

"Why can't I trust Lucy and Daniel? Is Emily involved? You trusted Marco. He's not involved?"

Her shoulders are bobbing with her sobs. "They have a different magick, and they are using it to tag and hurt people. Willow, they are helping her. They knew of the curse on me. Lucy is the worst and does it all without control. Emily is compliant, which is just as bad. Marco knows nothing but is getting very suspicious of Daniel and Emily."

Sabine touches Coral on the shoulder and says to her, "It's

okay, sweetheart, you are safe, and I'm going to go get your father and bring him here." Coral seems settled by Sabine's calm words. Sabine touches Coral's forehead, holds her back, and finally her shoulders relax down, and her eyes blink slowly.

"Yara, can you kindly take Coral to one of the guest rooms on the east side?"

As Yara leads Coral away, Sabine turns to me.

"She warned us her stepmother, Vanessa, is the head of the Human Principality, the hunters. She placed a curse on Coral so that she could not speak about any of it. So, apparently, she has powers. I think my friends are being influenced by magick or, if Coral is right, working with Vanessa."

"Well, first thing is first. You're safe here. There are plenty of enchantments around this home on the side of the mountain. Of course, no one knows of this place, but I need Tullen." She calls for him, and he walks into the room.

"We need to go get Coral's father now. You must stay here, Willow. Tullen?"

Tullen mutters into his ear com and then says, "Let's go. I have the coordinates and address."

"Willow, it's going to be important to get Evan involved. Based on what he's told me about the mirror gate, you both need to be together to break or flip the gate from the old Edayri to New Haven. I'll be back as soon as I can."

Everything is going so quickly.

Sabine and Tullen transport before I can think of asking a question. I'm left alone, looking around at this massive house. The tile floors, the stucco walls, it's so very different from Chepstow.

Evan. If you can hear me, I'm in the thick of it now.

I hear the paws of Duke on the tile coming toward me. I squat down, and he comes to me, and I hold on to him as he sits. Thankfully, he's here and Sabine's moved almost everything here.

"Be a good boy. I'll try to come back in one piece."

He licks the side of my face.

Tick-tock, tick-tock.

The wind shifts around me as if air conditioning turned on overhead. As soon as it stops, I look up to find Evan standing over me.

"So, this is the new McKinnon Manor?"

I shrug. "Yeah, I guess so."

Evan walks around, peeking down the hall. "Well, I gotta say I like this better than the gloom and doom of tradition in the highlands of Edayri."

He's not wrong. The wood is lighter, the paint here is pale, nothing is dark, everything is terra cotta and light.

I stand, and Duke runs down the hall as if he heard food.

"So, it's all coming together?" He asks.

Sometimes I just don't understand his comments. I shake my head.

"Coming together? Are you serious? Evan, this is a disaster. My friend's involvement, and there's a mirror gate, and what they planned is horrific. Eradication of innocents, just because they were born different or have magick?"

I feel the air shifting within the house. Cross, Rhydian, and Commander Eoin all appear.

I open my mouth, but Evan is already speaking before I can muster the words to say anything.

"When the Convergence finishes, it will collapse on Edayri and all those who are in it. The HP has put a mirror gate that makes it look like everyone is safe. Little do they know they are in Edayri, not New Haven. That's where she's coming up with the eradication comment."

Boy, does Evan know how to get to the point. Commander Eoin's face doesn't budge. Maybe he was aware of it or had an inkling before now?

"How much time Evan? How much time do we have?" he asks.

"I don't think we have a lot of time. Willow, you hear it and feel it now, the pulsing, it's getting closer together. It's soon, an hour, maybe more?"

"What? An Hour?" Rhydian asks.

"Evan, I know who the leader is of the Human Principality. Her stepdaughter is down the hall. Whatever plans she had, she'll move them up. But, unfortunately, the element of surprise is no longer on her side. When Sabine and Tullen return with her father, maybe they will know more, but I suspect Vanessa will be prepared."

Cross interrupts, "Wait, she doesn't know that ya all know of the mirror gate they have put in place. I don't think Coral knows anything about that."

"Maybe we should talk to Coral and find out? I could talk to her," Rhydian says.

I'm sure Coral would enjoy that. Can't believe that thought of jealousy entered my mind. I'm an idiot. Because it's Rhydian. Maybe that would put her at ease. However, she came to me to warn me.

"I think it's best if I talk to her. However, right now, she's taking a nap—courtesy of Sabine."

Yara comes in from the back hallway with Theon.

"I have another looking after our guest. Sabine will come shortly, and I have several of the house staff who will help you move as many as we can to New Haven or here to Terra."

Evan smiles broadly and opens his arms as if he's going to hug everyone. "Nothing brings people together like a disaster."

Theon winces and shakes his head. Rhydian's waiting face smirks as he rolls his eyes at Evan's response.

"Yes, as Commander, I take the help gratefully. Evan, you and Rhydian stay here with Willow. Cross, Theon, and I, along with Yara and other members, will go to New Haven. Rhydian, reach out to Abby and Ax, let them know we need emergency counsel help." Eoin looks down at his cuff that has timing of the rifts. "Tell them we'll be there in less than five minutes at the center of the Hallowed Hall near the fountain."

"What do you need me to do?" I ask, waiting for some direction.

"Wait for Sabine to return—" At the drop of my face, Eoin continues, "Then go confront your friends in Chepstow. We no longer are going to wait for them to bring chaos to us. Stop it there, then join us in New Haven. We need all the help we can get."

Evan slaps his hands together and rubs them maniacally. Rhydian's face is almost comedic. I can't help but bust a huff of a laugh.

"What, you just want me to show up in front of Lucy and Emily and say: what the fuck?"

"Exactly! Confront your so-called friends. Because if I do, knowing they carry responsibility for the death of Qu—" His voice drifts on Quinn's name. "I won't waver. You shouldn't either. They have no respect for you." Eoin looks away from me and turns.

My heart thumps, and the breath gets stuck in my chest.

"Will do, Commander," Rhydian responds.

I feel the change in the house when Sabine transports in with Mr. Lee. He is passed out, leaning on Tullen's shoulder. Theon and Yara help Tullen, and they add Mr. Lee to the same room with Coral. Sabine explains he was resistant to coming with her, so she had to improvise.

"His wife, Vanessa, has riddled their home with enchantments and spells that are quite difficult to get around. I know she'll be aware, if not already, that both of them are gone. I had to pull some of her magick off of him. She is a powerful Wiccan. It was easy to recognize her magick signature. Why she wants to end magick isn't clear to me at all, especially with how much she is using it."

"Just because one is something, doesn't mean they love it," Evan says, looking through Sabine. She nods and sighs in a way that breaks my heart. Both of them know that so well from their past family ties.

"I'm going back to Chepstow to confront them," I say.

"Who's involved, do you know?" Sabine asks.

"Sounds like everyone."

When I say it, my breath holds in my chest.

"Is Marco involved too?" Sabine asks.

Rhydian answers, "No, he's in the dark about what has been going on. He's waiting in the house for our return." His slight smile gives me some relief that not everyone is part of this.

"Is everything we spoke about here, in this house?" I ask.

Sabine nods. "Yes. Your father's home is all but empty of treasured possessions."

Rhydian and Evan look surprised.

"What? It's time. Everyone in that town is having their fresh starts, and now, so will I. I don't want to be in that huge house all by myself." I shrug.

Evan smiles and winks at me.

Before we leave, Sabine hugs me tight. It's no longer the awkward hug from when I first met her and went with her after my father died. Instead, it's a hug from my grandmother, who I love.

CHAPTER 21

During the transport, Evan holds my shoulders, and we land in a dark shadow in the backyard. Rhydian transports inside the house as planned.

Looking at the back of my father's house, I don't feel sad like I thought I would.

"It feels foreign to be here."

"That's because you're pulled toward magick, and that's near the Lunar Falls. This is only a shell of a structure, Willow, not where your heart is anymore."

"Thank you, Evan. Unfortunately, that's not completely true. The good memories are still . . ."

"They're here. We're out of time," Evan says in a deadpan voice. He quirks his head. "It's a distraction to be here together. It's planned. I'm going to the mirror gate, don't take too long." He transports.

Tick-tock, tick-tock.

Goddess, please give me the strength to confront them.

It's dark, but the landscape lights and the eve lights from the house give shape and shadow to the grounds. There are a few birds littered throughout the yard. Dew is now crusted on the grass, and the air has a snapping chill.

I turn toward the edge of the drive. Two people are standing there. It's Lucy and Daniel.

A lightning strike happens behind me in the yard; it sizzles and charges the air. I don't turn to see it. Lucy has one hand in the air. Rhydian is in his Guardian armor.

"You've accepted your valkyrie side?" I yell.

Lucy mockingly laughs at the question. "Not all of us were born how we see ourselves, so we undergo our own metamorphosis. The Human Principality made me see. Vanessa enlightens us to your distorted goals."

There is screaming above me. When I look up, I see Emily hurdling toward me in a bubble that has her suspended in the middle with lightning crackling all around it. I use my magick and hold her with the wind. Lightning strikes the bubble, and she absorbs it and winces in pain.

"Em!"

She looks at me, and her face is tired and wary. Her eyes are wide when Daniel points off to the side of the property. There are several more people who are entering the grounds. Big guys, all muscle and height.

Lucy is staring at me as if we are strangers.

"What is this? Lucy, come to kill me?"

Lucy purses her lips and throws her arms at me to knock me back with a stiff wind. I drop Emily to the ground, and the bubble surrounding her dissolves, and the lightning returns to Lucy's chest, and she smirks. It's as if she's charged.

"What the hell, Lucy!" I yell.

Emily is not moving easily. She looks so frail. "Em? What is this?"

"For what you are!" Lucy yells back. "For what you both have done! To me!"

My heart stops in a moment. It's not what she says, but the venom of it, who I am.

"What have I done to you, Lucy?"

"Doesn't matter anymore. You are an abomination on this

earth. You can't be who you are. The only way to save you is to end you."

"You're insane. Do you think you're saving me? You're killing people! This is murder, Lucy!"

"A means to an end," she says.

Her shoulders square back as she lifts her chin. She runs at me with her hands holding charges of lightning. I allow her to hit me, and she sends a solid blow across my face that turns me toward Daniel. The look on his face is pure victory. I see the hate from them and take it on as my own.

Rhydian moves so fast that I barely track him when he responds with an uppercut to Daniel's face. Cross and Marco join Rhydian, and they are engaging the five big guys that are close to us. Hits and kicks are being traded.

I turn, and with a flip of my wrist, I toss Lucy with my magick and slam her on the ground.

She throws lightning. I command it back to her, and she absorbs it. Lucy is crawling and grabbing the ground to get closer to Daniel, who is running toward her.

I am the embodiment of the Goddess. Screw her little light show.

My hands flare as I lift Daniel into the air and bind his hands in front of him. "Nice storm tonight."

"Put him down, you freak!" Lucy screams.

Daniel laughs. "It's a storm that's been coming. What since prom?"

His bound hands reach to the sky, and lightning cracks across the sky and looks like it will hit him before he throws his hands forward. It hits the corner of my father's house. A light rain follows.

Another strike of lightning nears the front of the house.

"So, having magick makes you what to these hunters, an asset? The genocide of all magick, so you can have it all?" I ask.

"Don't," Lucy says, but she's looking at Emily.

Emily is holding her hands above her head in surrender. No

threat, no action. Cross and Rhydian join us, with mud and blood down the front of their armor. Cross stands next to Emily, looking pained over her injuries.

"Emily, choose. Lucy is not innocent, and she will need to answer for what she's done. You're responsible for murder, so many have died."

"Sorry, Lucy," Emily says before looking at me. "She's gone too far down a lane that I can no longer travel or protect her from. I choose to be and am an Edayrian, a proud valkyrie, and someone who chooses magick in this world."

"Family thicker than blood? That's what you used to say. You're a fucking traitor!" Lucy screams.

Unfamiliar tears fall down Emily's thin, gaunt face. "No, you are! Aligning yourself with someone you barely know! Vanessa is twisting you and manipulating you. You allowed her to poison me and Daniel. He's controled and hates you for it! Her goal was never you. It was Willow! Your jealously is pathetic that you would choose it over your own happiness. You murdered for it! Hell, you're okay with him torturing me and hurting me? Me— your family! Who the fuck are you?"

"What? Who?" Rhydian is in front of Lucy. He grabs her throat, and she shows her teeth in a grimace.

Quinn. Oh, my Goddess, did she kill Quinn?

"Reveal." Is the magickal command Rhydian uses. Lucy's hands light up as Cross rubs his shoulder, and when Daniel's hands light up, my lower back feels like a beacon. Each of them marked us.

"You?" Cross says.

"Yeah, but I got the prize," Daniel says, dripping with contention. Rhydian tosses Lucy in a heap near Daniel. He's still in the air, where I'm holding him.

"Did you mark Qui—?"

"Who?" Daniel says when he looks at Lucy and winks. "I mean, she's so good at the marking piece. She sure hates this group."

Rhydian looks murderous, and it pulses through me. The anger, the betrayal, the hurt and pain. They are responsible for Quinn. Daniel was with me, so she must have delivered the killing blow, along with countless others.

I thrust my hands forward and lift Lucy, twisting her in the air. Daniel drops to the ground. Emily is covering her face and buries it in Cross's chest. The pain I send to Lucy travels across her skin. She screams, and it echoes, but not over my voice.

"Did you kill Quinn?"

I pull back the pain on Lucy. Tears are streaming down her face, and she clamps her lips shut. I repeat the question, but I see her face contort. It's all hate, and I no longer recognize her as my friend.

Lucy reaches toward him, "Daniel, help."

"How do you want me to help you? All the plans and markings you have done. Plans for Emily and Willow's deaths along with these Guardians?" He spits the words as if it tastes terrible. "I believe Rhydian's first because of Willow's love for him. Isn't it all about revenge and hate? Isn't that what we have in common? Because Lucy, no-one hates you like I do. You wanted me, right? Brought me back to this? You're weak—won't even die for your own cause. Pathetic, really."

Who is this, Daniel?

Lucy is shaking her head as if what Daniel has said is unconscionable: that he has spoken the deepest and darkest words aloud. Or maybe because her intention to kill and be rid of us all is no longer a surprise? Emily is being held by Cross. She barely has her eyes open.

Lucy has crippled her.

"I believe your words to me were whoever can mark Willow the fastest wins because everyone around her is subject to magick and is guilty of changing this world," Daniel says with a sneer. "Aren't you the one responsible for me?"

The innocent look on Lucy's face morphs into something else. She is a stranger, and I no longer have sympathy for her. She is lost with no way home. The only reason that I don't break her neck right at the moment is for Emily. Emily's face is pleading, and agony rolled into one.

Tick-tock, tick-tock.

The clock is becoming more like a secondhand and less like a minute hand. The Convergence is happening.

Rhydian looks at me as the air around us pulses. The rift in the instability of Edayri. "You know she's not worth it. She hates magick so much. Take it from her and him."

He's right. She hates it so much that Lucy shouldn't have any of it to cause harm, hex and mark people to use it with the Human Principality.

"I hate you," Lucy says to me.

"If I ever see you again, I will kill you. So run far away. You never wanted this, and now you'll never have it."

I take her magick with a curl of my fist. It's a violent rip from her body. Her scream echoes. I throw the aura that contains her magick into the sky. It disperses into a void as if it never existed.

Daniel twists himself away from us, breaking his hands apart. He directs lightning to hit my father's house. Fire booms across the roof. It's his escape. He's out of reach. When Lucy yells, he only smiles and waves to her before he touches a pin on his shirt and transports away.

"It's happening—countdown is louder. We need to leave. It was their intention to keep us here. The mirror gate at the fountain, now." I say to Cross and Rhydian. "I'm following," I say before they transport and disappear in front of me.

The fire is raging behind us. The light rain is doing nothing to put it out. My heart squeezes at the sight of it. Nothing in there is important anymore. It's a shell of an old life.

Lucy screams. The pitch of her voice is pure agony. Turning my back on her, I put my hand on Emily's shoulder and push healing magick into her.

Before I hear the scuffle, Emily sends lightning from her hand over my shoulder. I turn just in time to see Marco grab

Lucy's hand, which is holding a knife, forcing her to drop it. Her stomach is charred and bloody.

Emily drops to the ground at my side.

"Goddess, what have I done?" She whimpers.

Marco lays Lucy down, then throws the knife away from them. The house continues to burn, and I hear emergency vehicles in the distance.

Lucy rolls her head away from Emily. Even in her death, she'd rather hate.

"Em. I have to leave. To stop the genocide of thousands."

Emily nods her head and slowly reaches her hand to Lucy. Marco stands at my side and puts his hand on my shoulder.

"I'm with you. Daniel can't get away with this."

I transport us to the mirror gate of Edayri in New Haven.

PART IV

The rhythm of a new moon; is uninhibited by past and future events and only measured by the present.

~The Goddess

CHAPTER 22

S omeone trips over me before I fall to my knees. A crowd whisks Marco away. Too many people, it's panic. So many are rushing around and going through a holographic wave of light. It is wavering and moving. The Convergence and the collapse is underway. And not everyone has moved from the mirrored New Haven. That is really Edayri, being torn apart. Evan is pushing at one end of a holographic sheet. There is fighting all around. Guardians are ushering people from this side to the other.

"Willow, conjure magick to keep open the gate—keep the gate open." Abby is yelling at me as she holds two young toddlers and runs through where Evan is. Theon is protecting Evan and fighting off three large men.

I spy Rhydian and see him battling others in plain clothes. The Human Principality is here to prevent us from saving as many as we can. There are so many people on the ground, unmoving. Blood is everywhere. Swords are clamoring. Cloaks, armored Guardians.

"Willow now!" Evan screams.

"What do I do?" I yell back.

"Tap into the connective magick of the realm!" He yells.

Inhaling the air, I sense the connection and the pull of magick, the coursing of my magick within to all of it outside of me. It's a tether, a source. That's it! A combo of the two, a tether of the source and my power.

"I've got it." I transport to the other side.

Tullen is helping an older person across through the gate. So many Guardians are helping as many as possible, yet so many are not going through as they fight off the Human Principality.

My magick flares. I try to lift the mirror gate through my body with all that I am. I can't seem to grasp it. Evan's hands are alight. So I form a light ball, and I attach it to the wavering sheet of this realm and lift it higher. My side rises; the holographic sheet that was collapsing is now clear. I can see through the mirror gate to New Haven which before was almost empty, is virtually full and teeming with life and color, like a technicolored dream. The magick is calling me on the other side of the mirror. Fighting is happening on that side too, but Guardians run back through to help fight back the Human Principality to get more Edayrian's across.

If we stay on this side, we will be on the side of the collapse.

Ax is near me, and he's carrying several little demon children. He runs through the gate, and several more see that it's open. They run, most of them caring for children and the elderly.

I lock my arms and my legs so that everything stays above me. I shake from pushing the gate as my muscles strain.

Tick-tock, tick-tock, tick-to—

I force my magick into my hands, command it to lift the holographic gate, and push it above my head. Evan is doing the same. It's almost as tall as the pillars of the Hallowed Hall. It's thrumming through my body and shakes me so severely that I bite my tongue and taste the iron.

Become more; you are more.

I hold steady, locking my knees as the gate pushes me to the ground. My arms are shaking. Evan is using one arm while casting with a free hand. He's moving people through the gate by force.

Daniel is near me. Eoin is blocking lightning, trying to provide cover for those running. Daniel is indiscriminately hitting as many as he can. Some stumble and keep going, but there are two who stop and fall into a heap. I pull one hand away from the gate, but it drives me down hard, and I put my hand back to push back.

You are the most powerful among them.

In her purple cloak, Sabine is using defensive magick against another woman in a black cloak who is pushing toward me. The woman in the black cloak turns, and it's Vanessa, Coral's step-mother. A Wiccan with powerful magick. But she is uncontrolled and not as experienced or as powerful as Sabine. The unpredictability of her magick is wreaking havoc. Her magick is like a whip of smoke with barbed wire. She sweeps her hands, and nearby Guardians are being struck with magick and dropping to the ground, unmoving. It must be poisonous.

Daniel kicks over a young Guardian whose face is blank.

"No!" I scream. My muscles strain at seeing his evil smile. His eyes find me, and he wipes his mouth and laughs. Then, his hand fills with lightning, and he throws it right at me. Tullen dives in front of it in one leap and falls at my feet. Ax is back through the gate, and he pulls Tullen through.

The rush of people flowing through at various transporting speeds is overwhelming. I do not move. I barely register the colors of the people all around me, but the one that gets my attention is Rhydian. His speed and grace are moving through so many. Theon, Cross and Marco are nearby, and they've made a pinch point for what seems to be the last of the people to get through. Goddess, I hope it's the last of the Edayrians.

I call to Evan in my head, *"We need to fight. She's killing people in masses. We can't let them through to those who made it. The fight needs to stay here."*

Evan responds, *"New plan, on the count of three, let it go—drop the gate. Those left we can get through."*

One, two, three.

I drop my hold on the gate and fly into the air. My muscles breathe, and the gate snaps into a smaller shape, the size of a single door. Lightning flies past me, narrowly missing me.

Daniel.

Marco jumps on his back and throws his elbow into his neck. They roll, and Rhydian grabs a weapon on the ground and throws it at him but misses. Daniel gets him with lightning on the shoulder. Marco, complete in tiger form, roars. Cross is running, his arms pumping, but I get there first.

No mercy.

There is a thrumming noise, loud and echoing. I barely register Rhydian yelling my name when I feel something slice into my shoulder and someone knocking me out of the way. I roll. I see Eoin. His eyes unmoving, his mouth slack, and a bullet hole neatly round in his forehead. Rhydian falls next to him with blood streaming from his side.

Daniel is holding a sword and a gun. With a sickly smile, he is pointing the gun at me, aiming toward my heart. Then he focuses the aim on Rhydian. He knows where to cause the most damage.

I shake uncontrollably and my scream echoes, pushing and throwing anything near us.

Be the Goddess.

My hands and thoughts are the weapons.

I pull the gun from his hands and disintegrate it with a snap of my fingers. He runs at me in full charge. I lift him over my head and scream as I twist him. He turns, lands hard, and throws lightning at me.

Laughable.

Catching it, I bend it to my will like a snake around my arm. I control it and him.

You control it all.

SACRED

Daniel, for the first time, moves defensively.

"Where do you think you're going?" I twist my hands to contort his body at odd angles. His muffled noise confirms his resistance to my torture. So unrelenting at the pain I'm causing him. I feel it, the snapping of his arm, the pulling of his hip. I can rip him in two.

"I could end you quickly," I say aloud.

"What's stopping you? Do it!" He screams.

"Willow." Rhydian coughs blood from his lips. He's next to Eoin.

I've snapped the neck of the woman responsible for Mrs. Scott and my father's death. Daniel, the manipulator, deserves no less. Is he the reason Lucy changed? Or is she why he changed? They've hurt so many—Quinn. Lucy killed Quinn, but Daniel led Marco and me there for some other reason. An opportunity for mass casualties?

Rhydian is closer.

The ticking in my head is speeding up as seconds become milliseconds.

Sabine and Vanessa are in a full-on battle of magick. Evan is casting some enchantment on the gate and continues to move the few remaining Guardians and warriors to Ax, who is tossing them through, including Eoin's body.

Daniel struggles and screams. I break his leg, send his own lightning to hold him by the neck. I hear Marco roar and sense his change behind me.

Pulling at Daniel's feet, stretching him. I hate him despite my tears and my dry throat. I mourn for Daniel before the einherjar warrior they made him into. My first love who would never hurt, let alone kill, anyone.

"Why Daniel? Is there no saving you? Please . . ." Marco pleads.

"No. I should already be dead! You both know it! So do it, Willow! End my suffering and yours because I won't stop. She won't let me."

555

His eyes move to Vanessa. She's controlling him.

My shoulders shake. I let go of the lightning around Daniel's neck, and it severs his head from his shoulders. I give him what he wants, a death that was his months ago. His body and head fall back to the ground, but I don't look, only the sound confirms it.

"Now, Willow!" Evan screams in my head.

Vanessa yells, watching what's left of Daniel on the ground. She turns to Sabine, all fury and rage.

I'm two steps ahead of her. I use the air to sweep all of us in transport through the closing gate. The gate wavers and closes in a big rush of air. The ground we stand on is the true realm of New Haven. It rumbles and quakes; Edayri has collapsed and is no longer.

Guardians are gathering the remaining Human Principality fighters and tying them up. There are so many faces watching me as they hold on to each other.

"Where do you think you're going?" A loud voice booms over the crowd.

I turn to Vanessa, the leader of the Human Principality. She uses her poisonous black line of smoke in a magickal a whip, but before it touches people, I push them out of reach. Then, using the surrounding air, I vault us above everyone, so that they are out of the reach of her magick.

"Others will take my place. You won't win, not in Terra, not even here." She seethes. Her words like venom from her dark red lips.

"Maybe."

Evan's faint voice is in my ear. His words a plan to end the Human Principality—to track it back.

I guide Vanessa's magick around her like a snake. The smoke constricts her, and she struggles. "But you and the Human Principality will no longer have the magick born of the Goddess to persecute others."

"You're nothing but an over-privileged brat."

I radiate the glow from my skin, and it hovers all around me. The magick crown lifts high over my head. The gasps below me don't deter my attention.

"I'm the Goddess and the Wiccan Queen. And you're nothing more than a narcissistic murder whose time has ended."

I look at Evan. His hands make various patterns and shapes with light and magick, and Sabine is at his side.

"Do you have it?" I ask.

"We do," Sabine replies.

I pull the magick from Vanessa and throw it to Evan and guide us both to the ground.

"What did you do?" Vanessa's face is full of fury.

"Magickal signatures, of course. Now we can disband your work completely. You've led us to all of it. Every cell you've got around the globe," Sabine says.

Evan has the magick signatures of the gate and from Vanessa, all contained in a clear magical box. The contents are a mixture of light and smoke. An organized storm of destruction. Ax and Aren, the chairpersons from the legion council, approach us.

"You are in the custody of the legion council for charges of treason and genocide of its people," Aren says.

Ax slaps binding cuffs on Vanessa and then throws a stone to the ground that opens in bright light and envelopes her before it closes in on itself, muffling out her scream and rage. Ax picks up the stone and tosses it a few times in front of his face.

"So tempting to throw this and forget it," his deep voice says.

"There needs to be justice served for all that she's done to Edayrians," I reply.

Ax's grin reveals his fangs in what some consider a scary smile, but I only know it as his. General Thaxam, who is a noble demon and fierce protector of equality for Edayrians.

"You know, I agree." He winks.

I nod and face Sabine and Evan. Aren has the box and is walking from us. Most of the spectators have dispersed throughout the Hallowed Hall grounds and gardens. The

Guardians are grouped together, and healers are checking each one of them out. Those lying on the ground are being covered in sheets.

I spy Eoin being draped and find myself staring at the sheet. I don't know how, but I sense something lift in my heart. A vision of Eoin and Quinn together. Is this real or my mind playing tricks on me, because I see them in an embrace. The Elysian fields, Heaven or Valhalla. The comfort wraps me like a warm blanket to know Eoin and Quinn are together, just as I picture my father and mother are together.

CHAPTER 23

S abine is grinning, her eyes soft. "Oh, sweetheart, you've saved us. You are truly the embodiment of the Goddess."

"Nah, she is the Goddess," Evan says.

"I should have gotten here faster. Done more."

My heart breaks at my confession. Now I know how Evan feels.

Time heals.

"Time does heal," Evan says.

"Did you hear her in my mind?" I ask.

He nods.

I hear a few gasps and hushed tones. Sabine leans into me and says, "Willow, it's the Goddess and the Horned God. Um . . ."

I turn and see the shimmery silk of her roman-like robe and teal cloak floating about the ground, with her hair swept up on her neck in ringlet curls. She is the Goddess. The Horned God is next to her, holding her hand. His large horns on his head sweep back and twist, similar to his long auburn hair. His chest is bare and muscled; his pants are loose white linen.

Evan and I approach the floating Goddess and Horned God. I am a wreck. Dirt and mud—tear streaks down my face. I smile weakly at the two of them. So many died today. Why couldn't they intervene?

"You know why," the Goddess replies.

Do I? Maybe I do? I'm not too fond of it. To be omnipotent of creation, only to let us succeed or fail on our own. It is our choices after all.

"I don't see failure here. I see a Goddess Wiccan Queen who saved her people. Although the cost was high, it was not without a victory. Here is a new realm not of my making but of—"

"Yours." The Horned God walks over to us.

Evan smiles at me.

Arizona?

Yes.

His voice is barely a whisper in my mind, but I knew the answer before he said it.

Evan claps the Horned God on his back as if they are old friends, and they turn away from us, whispering. The Goddess chuckles, watching Evan and the Horned God. I don't feel like I could do that with the Goddess. It seems inappropriate.

Her smile is gentle, and her head tilts to answer me without saying a word.

"We should speak more. My fault for not preparing you for what all that you will be to them." She waves her hand toward those watching us.

I don't want to question her because she is regal and omnipotent. Edayrians revere and fear her. She is the reason for Wiccan creation. Being chosen by her worries me. I'm not without flaws.

She turns to me and lays her hands on my shoulders.

"Being adored and worshiped is something that can inflate one's ego toward defining perfection. My mistake was of wanting perfection instead of realizing that perfection is a construct of flaws while learning to be better. Let's say it took a lot more time for me to understand and appreciate."

"Okay . . . how do I fit into this?"

"For one, you're allowing me and my love to return to our

celestial place together. You now hold my abilities within your being. So that you may lead and mold the Wiccan rule into a modern, tolerant age."

Can I do that?

"You already have, by bringing cultures and beings together within the legion council that you established. For one so young, you are more experienced than you know."

I feel the heat of my cheeks with her compliment.

Evan and the Horned God turn to where the Goddess and I are standing. Like a couple of old pals, they are very comfortable with each other. I bend my head in somewhat of an awkward bow to the Horned God.

His baritone laugh puts me at ease. "Willow, I think it's I who should bow to you. I need no formality. It's a pleasure to meet you finally."

Looking into his eyes, they are dark and holographic. His eyes move like a star constellation. The wrinkles around his eyes stretch upward as he smiles, and it puts me at ease despite his towering figure.

"It's nice to meet you too," I respond.

"So, this is your niece." The Horned God looks at Evan. "I see the family resemblance. She got all the best parts." Evan laughs in response. "I'm sorry to see that it will separate you both, but it is an honorable duty."

"I'm sorry, it will separate us? I don't think I understand."

The Goddess says nothing aloud.

You won't be alone.

Evan looks at the ground and kicks at the gravel pathway. He doesn't meet my eyes. He motions to the Horned God and says, "Would you mind giving us a few minutes? I haven't explained."

When both the Goddess in the Horned God nod, Evan leads me over to the side of the Hallowed Hall stairs.

"Evan? Just tell me, rip the band-aid off."

Evan smiles. "One of us will need to stay in New Haven, and

the other will need to stay in the Terra realm. Ripped off band-aid."

"Is life all about loss?"

I'm sure my response was not the one he was looking for, holding my arms and tears falling. Evan hugs me, and I hug him back. My mother's brother, my uncle, who meant more to me in the last year than I ever thought he would. He is a connection to the family I've lost, and now I will lose him.

"No. All loss brings new beginnings. Try to relish in those opportunities. Because if you don't, take it from a broken man, living in the past will devour you. I know my sister and your father—they would never want that for you."

I nod my head into his chest, still hugging him. "Does this have to happen now? Or do we have time?"

Evan closes his eyes and inhales the air as if to feel a response. I sense nothing but clean, crisp air on a chilly morning. "We have a few days. We must honor the dead and the living before transportation connections are closed."

"Why would they close?" I ask. I already know the answer, the grounding of magick and the flow of the realms.

"It's safer and more stable this way. You know that the Goddess and Horned God, when together, create instability. As we take up the mantel . . . Therefore, it must be this way."

I recall Tullen teaching me the history of the Goddess. We walk back to the Goddess and the Horned God. I spy Rhydian off to the side, not far with a watchful eye on everything we're doing. He is speaking with Ax, Marco, and Cross.

"So, now that you both have taken to your roles, we shall leave you to all of it. We will no longer be its keeper," the Horned Gods says.

"Wait, like ever?" I look at Evan.

"Okay, I thought that was understood." Evan shrugs his shoulders. "Me casa, es su casa?" Evan smiles.

All I can do is shake my head. Maybe I saw this coming? The things I can do when I only concentrate and think them through, I can make happen with little practice. The Goddess did crown me, but I didn't understand that I would take up in her stead. Does that mean—can I remove them—?

"You have a question?" She asks.

I hesitate to ask, but she may be the only one to address the blood vow. Rhydian, I don't feel the ache because he is near. Instead, it's the weight of removing something that pulled us apart to begin with. To right the wrong that I forced upon him. The blood vow he took to protect me, that I helped him break to remove his father's control.

"If it wouldn't offend, I would like to ask what can be done regarding Rhydian's blood vow to me? The blood vow is broken because I forced his hand. We both ache in pain from the connection when we are apart. Can the blood vow be removed? I want us both to have free will to choose, but this failure of protection in the vow is something we—I'd like to remove."

The Goddess smiles and looks from the Horned God to Rhydian, who is still to far to hear us. "The blood vow was quite vain, but I appreciated its loyalty at the time. Willow Sola Warrington, you are the Goddess and you can absolve it."

"Is there a special spell or—"

"Only the will to do so, with concentrated intention. You can do literally, anything."

I pause before putting my hand in front of my chest and pull the vow's threads. A pale, pink light pulses in front of my eyes and disappears. I watch it do the same in front of Rhydian without his awareness. The blood vow is no more.

The missing ache lifts and is replaced with a pounding heart of free will and uncertainty. The Goddess, smiles knowingly.

Both the Goddess and the Horned God disappear before my eyes.

Be well and Blessed Be.

Evan speaks with the legion council and transporting is cleared for all, the rifts are no more. A mass funeral will take place in two days, a day before the closure between realms. The once crowd of people is now down to a handful.

I meet Rhydian near the fountain.

Guardians and others are transporting to various Terra locations.

Rhydian is holding my hands and looking into my eyes. "Tullen is making a full recovery. He will meet you in Arizona. Cross is going to Chepstow to ensure that is all buttoned up; and he'll be with Emily to tell her what happened to Daniel."

Is Rhydian not coming to Arizona? I shake my thoughts and focus on Emily. It crosses my mind that since Emily helped create Daniel as an einherjar warrior, she may already be aware of what has happened.

"You're no longer tied to me. As the Goddess, the blood vow is absolved. I guess, if you had let me finish what I started in the cave, I could have technically done it then."

His face is unreadable when he replies, "Okay."

I pull back my hands from his. "I know that so much about me is—well, Queen, Goddess. It's a lot. The good news is that we are both free of the pain when we are apart, Rhydian."

He is still, his eyes roaming over my face.

"Is it easier for me to stay or is it easier for me to go?" He asks.

Stay. Stay. Please stay. I hope beyond saying the words.

Instead, I ask, "I know what my answer is, but what is yours?"

"This is not a straightforward decision." he replies, his voice deep and discouraging.

Oh Goddess, my heart is in my throat. It's like we are back at McKinnon manor. The blood vow broken, he's broken, or is it me? I can't tell.

Don't leave.

I close my eyes, waiting for him to say he can't stay. It replays in my mind when he turned away from me and left. Lost in my thoughts, I barely register a hand that gently touches the side of my face. It's his hand and I lean into it. He's saying goodbye. We are back to where we were, but it's his choice. I will not impose my wants on him.

I could. It would be wrong.

My tears threaten to fall.

"Willow, look at me," he whispers.

I want to, but I can't.

His lips gently touch my eyelids and my forehead. I savor the feather touches because they could be our last.

"I'm staying, Willow. I'm staying. You are the most sacred person to me."

My tears fall. He's staying, and it's his choice. There is no influence, nothing is compelling him beyond his own mind, his own heart. Rhydian drops to one knee. "I commit myself to your service, if you'll have my blood vow—"

"No. Stop." I shake my head.

His confusion looks unsteady with the emotions across his face.

With tears flooding my eyes, I continue, "What's sacred is our choices and freewill, if I've learned anything over the last year. I'm beyond honored, but how about we date first?"

His smile is wide, and his chuckle comes in a burst as he stands. "Absolutely."

I lean into him, and our lips connect.

CHAPTER 24

F lanked by Rhydian and Cross, I'm incognito to those around us. I touch the marble square that rises high into the sky with the names of the Edayrians lost. Commander Eoin and Quinn. I also think of the names not on this monument, Daniel and Lucy. I've cried so much that my tears hold, but I wear the sadness in my mind and my body. The only thing that really makes it less horrible is Rhydian's hug around my shoulders.

I step back, and Cross moves forward and touches Quinn and Eoin's names before leaving them. One straight tear falls from the man who shows no fear of anything or anyone.

They held the mass funeral on the New Hallowed Hall grounds, as the first Convergence Remembrance Day. All that has happened with the collapse of Edayri will never be forgotten. The legion council has a refugee fund among the families that were displaced. Democratic ideals are finally coming together to help one another within New Haven. Although I sense some still harbor prejudice against each other, more have an open mind toward working together. Evan made an odd but sweet speech about magick and its home.

"I'm getting an ear comm that Evan would like to speak with

you," Rhydian whispers in my ear. I nod back to him and ask where. He points toward a bench where Evan is sitting. "I won't be far behind," Rhydian says.

"So protective." I grin.

"Well, when I need protection, I want the best." He kisses my temple.

I sit next to Evan on the bench, remembering the time when he transported us to France. When I learned about the Emissaries, and my parents' involvement for equality. I feel as if I have aged five years since then, not physically, but certainly mentally.

"So, what do you know?" Evan asks.

I lean into him and bump his shoulder playfully. "Coral is with her father back in Massachusetts. I can collect on insurance money for the house in Chepstow. And I believe the refugee fund will use it well."

Evan looks up at the sky. "Don't tell me what I already know, tell me what *you* know."

"That time will heal? Although saying it feels trite, and I want to hit someone when I hear it. I know I won't see you, and I'm sad about that."

Evan nods his head and says, "Same, I am sad too. You forget our connection, and that we can speak to each other anytime." Evan lightly touches my temple. "Just like how I would speak to Nuala, your mother. We can do the same."

My excitement turns from mourning this day to small celebration. I can still to talk with him.

"Yeah?"

He nods his head and laughs. It's infectious, and I join him. The sound is almost foreign to my ears, but it feels right.

"So, I guess I should leave now. I heard from a certain celestial there might be an opening between realms. Maybe? Have you seen into the future?"

Evan shakes his head. Only riddles and subtext he'll reveal, which I'll never completely understand. But I hold him tight in one last hug before rejoining Rhydian and Cross to go through the portal, back to Arizona.

"Just one more thing." Evan whispers in my ear, "In four years' time, the portal will open. I will see you in white, hand in hand, walking down an aisle of a church, and it will be my pure honor." He kisses the top of my head and leaves me a little stunned.

Rhydian approaches and holds out his hand.

"What? Another riddle?"

"I get the impression the realms will open every so often."

"Oh yeah? Any idea when?"

"In four years." I answer and can't stop the blush that I feel creep across my cheeks.

"A lot can happen in four years."

"How about just one day at a time?"

"Absolutely." Rhydian is squinting and assessing me, but doesn't press for more.

Cross claps his hand onto Rhydian's back, and Tullen comes over and hugs my side. We walk through the portal and transport to our new home in Sedona, Arizona.

CHAPTER 25

The morning alarm is jolting, and yet again, I roll and slap the snooze button. Holding my hand on the alarm, I then press the off button. It's the final alert that if I don't get up, I will be late. I toss the covers over my head, open my eyes, and breathe in the five minutes before I rise and shine.

The tiled floor is cold on my feet as I shuffle across the large room toward the bathroom. Duke stretches one leg out as I walk by him. He is hitting the snooze button one more time.

I'm jealous of my dog.

The water from the shower is a welcome start to a new day in my new life. I dry off and study myself in the mirror. The familiar hum rises to the surface and the light patterns of magick dance all over my skin like a full-body tattoo. So much has happened in the little over two years since I discovered my Wiccan and Royal heritage. Time doesn't erase the loss and pain, but grieving is a process where the edges wear away.

In the closet, I pick out my clothes and walk into my room. Lastly, I sit on the bed and tie the laces of my purple chucks. It feels a little like déjà vu from high school, but I'm starting my first year in college. Although a little later, it's my start. Duke and I make our way downstairs.

Walking toward the familiar voices, I pause at the wall, hidden just enough to spy.

Emily and Cross are laughing easily. A sound that makes me smile. Despite the losses they've suffered, they have found solace in each other. Emily buried Lucy, and they folded her death into the arson of my house. We attended Daniel's burial as a soldier killed in a rogue training exercise. It was hard to face his parents and sister, knowing his death occurred well before that day. Coral and her father have moved on as well, and purposefully, we don't keep in touch. Although the organization of the Human Principality is gone, the risk is not one either of us will take.

The legion council has members here and in New Haven. Guardians are being reestablished with protection and policing mandates to ensure magickal beings blend into Terra and ensure that we are not taking advantage of Terra with magick. Most are scared of using magick, so for now, it's been peaceful. A new commander was named, and Rhydian seems to like him. So much has changed and yet—

"Can you believe it? I'm a Sun Devil now?" Emily says. She sings a tune as she moves somewhere in the kitchen.

Cross, without skipping a beat, responds, "Oh the devil part, I can believe for ya."

Tullen surprises me when his hand lands on my shoulder.

"Whatca you doing out here? We've got a schedule to keep. First day and all."

"Yes, professor." I reply, grinning, and follow him into the kitchen.

"That's adjunct professor." Tullen smiles and straightens his collar. "I'm excited about this, because I'll get to work toward my PhD in theology and mythology."

"So, how did you get that job again?" Cross asks.

He is chiding Tullen. It's been an ongoing joke that Tullen may have influenced the department head with either magick or flirtation, because Tullen didn't quite fit the job description requirements in education, but he certainly knows his stuff.

Rhydian is at the round kitchen table, his eyes focused on the phone in his palm. But not for long. He gravitates toward me, his eyes, his smile, and I can't help but return the look.

"Good morning, beautiful," Rhydian says. He greets me at the coffee machine, Fancy, before kissing my temple. "Missed you on the run today."

"I wouldn't say I missed it," I reply.

Duke pushes up against my leg, then Rhydian's before Rhydian pets his head. "So a run, huh? You weren't being lazy sleeping in, traitor." I waggle his ears, and it feels like Duke smiles before I hand him his morning treat.

This is my life and my people.

We all live in this house on the mountain in Arizona with Sabine and several others. It's close enough to the cavern where the Lunar Falls is that we can monitor when the New Haven portal might open or if there is a shift. So far, there's been none, which has been a blessing. The only part that is missing from this bliss is that my family is no longer with me, but then again, looking around, I have the family that chooses me, and I choose them. Tullen in his slacks, hair pulled into a messy lower bun with his full red beard. Cross all muscles and strength towering over the slim Emily, who could drag him around by his pinkie literally. Rhydian, his ocean eyes no longer storming but calm, his dimple threatening to show with his smirk.

"What are you thinking?" Rhydian asks. He holds me at my waist. His smile lightens any downtrodden mood that could lurk in.

I wrap my hands around his neck. "That I'm one lucky girl."

"Are you ready to start the rest of your life?" He asks.

"I'm ready."

The End

BONUS: EPILOGUE
FOUR YEARS LATER...

The sunset bathed the desert garden in a warm embrace as Rhydian and I stood at the altar, our hands intertwined. The soft rustling of leaves and the distant chirping of birds created a serene backdrop for our momentous day.

Uncle Evan stood beside me, his proud gaze never leaving us. His presence, though unseen by most, because the gate remained closed between New Haven and Terra.

The surroundings were a symphony of colors, with vibrant flowers and delicate ribbons adorning every surface. The air was thick with the sweet scent of blooming flowers.

As the ceremony began, I could hardly tear my gaze away from Rhydian. His bright ocean-blue eyes held a depth of emotion that mirrored my own. With every word spoken, every vow exchanged, our love seemed to intertwine, creating a bond that felt unbreakable. A life we chose together.

"I promise to stand by your side, to support you in every triumph and console you in every defeat," Rhydian's voice resonated, "although I'm not sure you know how to fail."

A loud laugh burst from Cross. I shook my head, looking at

Cross standing as Rhydian's best man. Rhydian continued. "I promise through this vow, my heart and love are only yours."

My chest filled with emotion looking at the man in front of me. We've grown over the last four years. Earning degrees and establishing advocating services for Edayrians who stayed in Terra.

"And I promise to cherish you in every moment, to hold your hand through every challenge, and to love you fiercely for all the days of my life," I replied, my voice steady despite the overwhelming emotion coursing through me.

As we exchanged rings, I felt a profound sense of unity. The cool touch of the metal against my skin symbolized the unbreakable bond we had formed, a bond that had weathered storms and emerged stronger than ever. A bond that was an equal choice, with autonomy of self.

With the ultimate declaration of "I do," a wave of happiness washed over me. We had done it. We had faced our fears, embraced our destiny, and now, as we stood as husband and wife, a new chapter of our lives was ready to begin, along with a small surprise I couldn't wait to share with Sabine and Emily.

The reception was a whirlwind of laughter, music, and celebration. Our friends and family were gathered to toast in our celebration, their smiles reflecting the happiness that radiated from within us. Rhydian and I shared our first dance as husband and wife under the twinkling stars, our steps perfectly in sync as if we had danced together a thousand times before.

Rhydian grabbed the mic from the DJ to grab everyone's attention, as I stood in the middle of the dance floor surrounded by Sabine, Tullen, Aren, Thaxam.

"Thank you, everyone, for coming to celebrate our wedding. I know we've already enjoyed many toasts this evening, but before we finish out the night, Willow and I have a surprise announcement."

Sabine's grin was suspect, while Emily clasped her hands,

looking back and forth from Rhydian to me. It's been difficult to keep this to ourselves for the last several weeks.

Cross shouted back, "is it what I think yer gonna say?"

Emily jabbed him with her elbows in his ribs.

Rhydian smiled and outreached his hand and I went to him. "Willow and I are lucky that our family is growing starting now. We are expecting."

Sabine's eyes went wide with a big grin with an enveloping hug around us both while everyone cheered. We were rushed by everyone congratulating us, and I wondered if we should have kept the secret a little longer. Abby, Rhydian's sister, was the last to hug me. "I wish Evan was here for this."

"Oh, I'm sure he's aware." I responded knowing full well he was still here with me, in a black suit, hair all mused, with fluffy unicorn slippers on his feet that no-one but me could enjoy.

"I can not wait to meet my little niece or nephew." Abby said.

Evan spoke shaking a silver rattle. "I can't wait to meet our new little guardian warrior."

"Me too, Evan, me too." I responded.

As the night continued, the people who had supported us throughout our journey surrounded us. Emily and Cross, who had found their own happiness, danced beside us, their love story a testament to the transformative power of love. Tullen, now an accomplished scholar, shared stories that made us laugh until our sides ached, reminding us of the moments that had shaped our lives.

"We did it," Rhydian whispered, his voice a gentle caress against my ear as we swayed under the starry night sky.

"Yes, we did," I replied, my heart full to the brim with love.

As I leaned into his embrace, I knew that our love story was far from over. Together, we would continue to face the adventures and challenges that lay ahead, hand in hand, hearts intertwined with our growing family. Our love, built on an unwavering foundation of trust and boundless passion, was a force that could conquer anything.

And as I looked into Rhydian's eyes, I knew our future was going to be filled with friends and family.

A smile tugged at the corners of my lips as I placed his hand gently over my abdomen, over the tiny life that was growing within me.

"Rhydian, we're going to be parents," I whispered, my voice filled with a mixture of emotion that words couldn't capture.

Tears glistened in his eyes as he pulled me into his arms, his embrace strong and filled with a love that seemed to transcend time itself. He pressed his lips against my forehead, his voice a soft murmur against my skin.

"Willow, I don't have the words to express how wonderful I feel right now," he whispered, his voice choked with emotion. "Me, a father."

I nestled into his embrace, feeling the steady rhythm of his heartbeat against mine. "I couldn't imagine a more perfect partner to share this journey with."

He pulled back, his hands framing my face as he gazed into my eyes. "You've given me everything I've ever dreamed of, Willow and more."

"And you, my Royal Guardian, have done the same for me." I responded.

As he leaned in to kiss me, I felt a surge of happiness that seemed to envelop us both. In that moment, surrounded by our love and the promise of new life, I knew our story was far from over.

And as I looked into his eyes, I knew that our future was as bright and boundless as the stars that shimmered above us.

AUTHOR'S NOTE

Book reviews matter. If you enjoyed The Unwanted Series, Limited Edition Collection, please leave a review where you buy and/or review books, so that this book can be discovered by readers just like you. This support helps so that I can continue publishing. Thank you for your support.

The Unwanted Series

ALSO BY C. M. NEWELL

The Unwanted Series

MAGICK

His Blood Vow (Exclusive)

REIGN

SACRED

Coming Soon

The World's Awakening, Tarot Trials Book 1

For more details visit the author website & join the newsletter for behind the scenes and future updates:

https://AuthorCMNewell.com

ABOUT THE AUTHOR

C. M. Newell is an award-winning YA fantasy author, receiving the 2016 New Apple Fantasy Award for her debut novel Magick in The Unwanted Series.

C. M. is a lover of all things fantasy and fairytale, especially the twisted ones. She loves to write strong female characters who don't fall victim to circumstance but instead rise above. She prefers a world where a princess can save herself.

Originally from Tennessee and a nomad from various states and countries, C. M. now calls home to sunny Florida with her family.

Printed in Great Britain
by Amazon

45811440R00334